ANNO DRACULA 1976-1991

JOHNNY ALUCARD

ANNO DRACULA

1976-1991

JOHNNY ALUCARD

KIM NEWMAN

TITAN BOOKS

ANNO DRACULA: JOHNNY ALUCARD

Mass-market edition ISBN: 9781785657627
E-book edition ISBN: 9780857685360

Published by Titan Books
A division of Titan Publishing Group Ltd
144 Southwark Street, London SE1 0UP

Mass-market edition: August 2018
2 4 6 8 10 9 7 5 3 1

A CIP catalogue record for this title is available from the British Library.

Printed and bound in the USA.

What did you think of this book? We love to hear from
our readers. Please email us at: readerfeedback@titanemail.
com, or write to us at the above address.

To receive advance information, news, competitions, and
exclusive Titan offers online, please register as a member by
clicking the 'sign up' button on our website
www.titanbooks.com

For F. Paul Wilson

ANNO DRACULA
1976-1991

JOHNNY ALUCARD

'As the Count saw us, a horrible sort of snarl passed over his face, showing the eye-teeth long and pointed. But the evil smile as quickly passed into a cold stare of lion-like disdain. His expression again changed, as, with a single impulse, we all advanced on him. It was a pity that we had not some better organised plan of attack, for even at the moment I wondered what we were to do. I did not myself know whether our lethal weapons would avail us anything. Harker evidently meant to try the matter, for he had ready his great Kukri knife, and made a fierce and sudden cut at him. The blow was a powerful one; only the diabolical quickness of the Count's leap back saved him. A second less and the trenchant blade had shorn through his heart. As it was, the point just cut the cloth of his coat, making a wide gap whence a bundle of bank-notes and a stream of gold fell out. The expression of the Count's face was so hellish that, for a moment I feared for Harker, though I saw him throw the terrible knife aloft again for another stroke... It would be impossible to describe the expression of hate and baffled malignity – of anger and hellish rage – which came over the Count's face. His waxen hue became greenish-yellow by the contrast of his burning eyes, and the red scar on his forehead showed on the pallid skin like a palpitating wound. The next instant, with a sinuous dive he swept under Harker's arm, ere his blow could fall, and, grasping a handful of the money from the floor, dashed across the room, threw himself at the window. Amid the crash and glitter of falling glass, he tumbled into the flagged area below. Through the sound of shivering glass I could hear the "ting" of the gold, as some of the sovereigns fell on the flagging.

'We ran over and saw him spring unhurt from the ground. He, rushing up the steps, crossed the flagged yard, and pushed open the stable door. There he turned and spoke to us: –

'"You think to baffle me, you – with your pale faces all in a row, like sheep in a butcher's. You shall be sorry yet, each one of you! You think you have left me without a place to rest; but I have more. My revenge is just begun! I spread it over centuries, and time is on my side. Your girls that you love are mine already and through them you and others yet shall be mine – my creatures, to do my bidding and to be my jackals when I want to feed. Bah!"'

Bram Stoker (attributed to Dr John Seward), *Dracula*

'That Count Dracula's no good for anybody, and he never was!'
Mario Belato (Joe Dallesandro), *Blood for Dracula*

PROLOGUE

PROMISES TO KEEP

ANNO DRACULA 1944

Even before the War, Transylvania was the country of the dead. These forests and mountains were homeland to the dead that walked.

The boy had no fear of vampires. Nor of the Germans and the Russians. Nothing more could be done to him.

Once, the boy had known a home. His world included parents, a larger family, church and school, playthings and playmates, food preferences, choices of clothing. Now that was a hazy dream, a story told around the campfire. The Iron Guard – Romania's SS – had come to his village to put an end to 'Red activity', blotting out his former life with flame and blood. The boy couldn't separate his own tattered memories from the images which sprang into his mind from the others' stories.

In the dark, he remembered things which had happened to Brastov, Nicolae or Magda. Sometimes, he even sank into the golden, embroidered past of the Baron Meinster, whose tales of lost elegance and privilege no one believed. Over half the partisan band were Reds, but they let the Baron retain his title and the pretence of command. The boy thought the vampire Brastov, who'd once let slip that he could also claim a title, was the true leader. The sullen living man Nicolae was the brute who made sure the sly, cat-like Brastov got his way most of the time. The fiercely independent Magda Cuza, a Jewish social democrat, always argued her own course, forcing the men to take her into account. The boy never added to the endless debates. They all knew better than to issue him orders. He did what he did and that was the end of it.

Alone on the ill-maintained road to Dinu Pass, the boy leant on his rifle while he made a slow path upwards. Stood on its stock, the Russian gun was fully three-quarters his height. Inherited from a fallen partisan, the rifle was his only true comrade. Well after midnight – the whole band had fallen into the sleeping-waking habits of the undead among them – the air was thickly moist. Either heavy mist or light drizzle. There was no moon. On the plain below, it was summer, hot August made hotter by the still-burning petroleum refineries of Ploieşti. Poisonous black smoke was everywhere. High in the Transylvanian Alps, the ice grasp of winter never fully relaxed and the air was clear and sharp in the lungs.

The boy saw little – the occasional glistening patch of wetness on black granite or blacker fir tree – but heard all the sounds of the night, the tiny, scurrying creatures who were justifiably afraid of him (his staple diet, when they could be had) and the ancient, ever lasting creak-breath of mountain and forest.

No Germans had been to Dinu Pass for three years, since the Wehrmacht abandoned the ancient Keep that perched above the deepest gorge. The Iron Guard was smashed, thrown away by the Nazis in the War against the Russians. Their passing didn't make this a safe country. The forests were infested with bandits, deserters, wolves, rival night-creatures. Often, the partisans didn't know who they were fighting until the skirmish was over and bodies could be examined.

Carefully, solemnly, the boy made his way up the steep road.

He did not know how the message had been received, but they were summoned to Dinu Pass, to the Keep, to meet with the one they all respected and feared, far above circus clowns like Hitler and Stalin.

Dracula.

Even a boy without history, with little sense of what came

before or after any moment, knew the name. It came with many titles, more even than Meinster claimed: Voivode, Prince, Count, Vlad Tepes, Prince Consort, Graf, King of the Cats, Prince of Darkness, Sovereign of the Damned. In these mountains, the peasants and the gypsies knew the titles were a cloak, meaningless and unnecessary. Here, the name was enough.

Dracula.

For months, Baron Meinster had regaled them with yarns of Count Dracula, his father-in-darkness, father and furtherer of almost all the vampires in the world. Transported by his own stories, the Baron seemed little more than an excited boy himself, with his wave of golden hair, natty grey cloak and odd fastidiousness about feeding. He spoke of the old times when the undead were masters of the warm, as fondly as a Red spoke of the coming age when the masters were killed and the workers ruled. Now, at the point of entering the Royal Presence, the Baron was quiet on the subject. Perhaps the father was as inclined to punish as reward, and Meinster too doubted his self-declared status as the favoured get.

Suddenly, the Keep was in front of the boy, radiating cold like a monumental chunk of black ice. He felt no discomfort. Cold was his natural condition, as much as hungry. He no longer shivered, rarely made a sound, never complained. Invisible until its walls were only feet away, the Keep had been built of blocks quarried locally. It seemed grown from the mountain, commanding the pass, moated by a deep gorge crossed by a shored-up causeway.

For generations, Dracula had been away, adventuring in the world, spreading his bloodline across the globe, making and changing history. Now, in his homeland's hour of darkest need, he was returning. Brastov speculated that the Count had been shipped from Cairo to Italy by the Americans or the British, and flown over Transylvania by planes like the bombers that had destroyed the Ploieşti refineries in April. Above the clouds, he would slip out of the aircraft to glide on great leather wings, down towards his native soil. His coming was the blue flame that would spark an uprising, uniting all the partisans, taking Romania out of the Axis. Brastov, looking to Russia, and Meinster, out for himself, welcomed the return of Dracula, but the warm – Magda, the old gypsy Maleva – were wary, fearful that one great evil was to be exchanged for another.

The boy was early. The Keep was empty. If Dracula were here, he'd have sensed it. Such an immense person would disturb the air. He stood on the causeway and made out the arch of the ungated entrance to the courtyard. Nothing was here, not even rats.

He cared little that in Bucharest, General Antonescu was withdrawing from alliance with the Germans and Italians, that the army was on the point of turning against the Nazis they had fought beside in Russia. Even the hotly anticipated uprising didn't excite him, for he had no belief in the future. The others discussed with passion the various factions of Axis and Ally, pitting their imagined saviours, America and the Soviet Union, against each other. The single lesson of the boy's young life was that there were no saviours, no Jesus Christ or St Nicholas, no Hitler or Stalin, no French or Americans. There was only the merciless crush of falling granite, as solid and black as the Keep, as implacable as the night and the cold.

'You are wrong, my son.'

He was not alone, after all. The voice came from inside the Keep, a whisper carried by the stone. It sounded inside his skull, smooth as velvet and harsh as tree-bark.

The boy saw the eyes first.

In the courtyard, eyes shone like a cat's, red around black. The boy approached, passing under the arch.

'I am Dracula,' said the tall vampire.

The boy had no reply. Before Dracula, he was no one.

Dracula did not have leather wings, but a one-piece black jump-suit, autopsy-scarred by silver-white zips, worn over heavy airman's boots and under a woollen cape. His hands were ungloved and very, very white. His face was unlined but ancient, so pale it had a faint moon glow. His hair was night-black, thick and unruly like his eyebrows and moustaches. A leather satchel lay by his feet. He was the only person the boy had seen this past year who was not carrying a gun.

Used to the undead, having lived so closely with Meinster, Brastov and others, he understood how the red thirst that set them apart was as much a weakness as his own hunger, that they were not so different from warm men and women. Dracula *was* different, the creature he had imagined vampires to be before he had met one. Then, all he had known of the undead came from the whispered stories of old women like Maleva, whose memories of Meinster's golden age were of stolen babies and opened throats.

The others were watching from back in the forest, from up in the trees. It had been decided the boy alone should go first to the meeting place. Brastov worried that the Count would see anyone larger as a threat and scent betrayal – every few weeks, he and Nicolae decided someone was a traitor and killed them for food – while Magda claimed they had no proof that Dracula was not secretly on the side of the fascists and would lead them all into a trap and death.

Also, and only now did the boy understand this, the whole band recognised that he alone was truly without fear, truly did not care what happened to him. Once, Maleva had said of him that he was deader than any vampire. When the old woman realised he had overheard her, she was afraid of what he would do but he took a cold pride in her understanding. He was dead as ice or stone, as impossible to hurt.

'It is well we should meet, my son.'

Dracula was not his father. He had no father.

'Again, you are wrong. I shall be your father, and more than a father.'

The boy felt nothing but the absence of feeling.

He had no love, no hate, no fear. He was empty. He noted that Dracula heard his thoughts as if they were words, but did not care.

'Come to me,' said Dracula, extending a ghost-white hand. His nails were blood-black diamonds.

The boy stood before the Count. The red eyes were supposed to overwhelm him, to impose a will upon his own, to draw him close. But there was nothing in his heart to catch, nothing to pull.

Dracula smiled. Pearl-white shark-sharp teeth showed beneath his moustaches.

'It is good you are so hard inside,' he said, not out loud. 'It is fitting.'

Of his own accord, the boy approached the vampire.

Dracula was snake-swift, his fangs so razor-keen their work was done before pain could reach the boy's brain.

He understood the others had known about this, had delivered him to Dracula as an offering. He was not alive, so his death would mean nothing.

At the end, he felt only the cold.

Dracula spoke to him in his mind, all through the sucking and draining. He soothed and demanded, made promises and prophecies, shared secrets and passions.

When the boy was empty, Dracula hugged the almost weightless body to his chest and strode out of the courtyard, onto the causeway. The boy could still smell; his nose filled with the male animal scent of the undead giant, which sparked more memories, hundreds of years of memories, of distant times and lands, of unknown and unknowable things. His own family came back to him – he could remember the name they had called him! – and the whole truth of their deaths. He was swept beyond a cloud of terror into the womb and the pasts of his parents and their parents. Throughout centuries, there was always the black figure with scarlet and silver highlights, the eternal presence of Dracula.

A finger tapped at his temple, fluttering his eyelids open.

Dracula wiped his mouth clean on his sleeve, ensuring that the boy's attention was on him.

'Don't run away yet, my son.'

Dracula poked out his tongue, like a goblin or a cheeky boy. It was long and scarlet, swollen at the end. It looked not like a tongue, but a red adder. The vampire shut and opened his mouth, nipping off the very end of his tongue. A tiny lump of flesh was neatly severed; Dracula spat it out to one side. His mouth filled with his own blood, leaking through the corners of his smile. Even in the night, it was rich and red. He bowed his head and kissed, prising the boy's mouth open with his bleeding tongue. A flow of cold, salt blood came, sliding over the boy's palate and into his throat.

The boy remembered his mother's breast. He suckled.

After seconds that stretched out forever, he was thrown away, off the causeway. The blood in his mouth and stomach burned like ice. The voice in his head was a wordless cry of joy. He thumped against a slope of pebble and leaf-mulch and rolled into the gorge, smacking against bushes and outcrops, shuddering in death and turning and rebirth. His old life – even from moment to moment with the partisans, he'd had a mortal life – was shredded away. His sturdy dead man's clothes ripped on flints.

He lay in a tangle in the dark. Now he could see the stars, even through thick clouds.

Above, he *was* Dracula, arms proudly folded. Meinster's band came out of the forest to kneel before him, to take their orders – the insurrection was set for the twenty-third of this month – to be awed by the Presence.

Below, he was not who he had been, but not yet who he would become.

The boy was, however, thirsty.

PART ONE

COPPOLA'S DRACULA

ANNO DRACULA 1976-77

1

A treeline at dusk. Tall, straight, Carpathian pines. The red of sunset bleeds into the dark of night. Great flapping sounds. Huge, dark shapes flit languidly between the trees, sinister, dangerous. A vast batwing brushes the treetops.

Jim Morrison's voice wails in despair. 'People Are Strange'.

Fire blossoms. Blue flame, pure as candlelight. Black trees are consumed…

Fade to a face, hanging upside-down in the roiling fire.

HARKER's Voice: *Wallachia… shit!*

JONATHAN HARKER, a solicitor's clerk, lies uneasy on his bed, upstairs in the inn at Bistritz, waiting. His eyes are empty.

With great effort, he gets up and goes to the full-length mirror. He avoids his own gaze and takes a swig from a squat bottle of plum brandy. He wears only long drawers. Bite marks, almost healed, scab his shoulders. His arms and chest are sinewy, but his stomach is white and soft. He staggers into a programme of isometric exercises, vigorously Christian, ineptly executed.

HARKER's Voice: *I could only think of the forests, the mountains… the inn was just a waiting room. Whenever I was in the forests, I could only think of home, of Exeter. Whenever I was home, I could only think of getting back to the mountains.*

The crucifix above the mirror, hung with cloves of garlic, gazes down with blind eyes on Harker. He misses his footing and falls on the bed, then gets up, reaches, and takes down the garlic.

He bites into a clove as if it were an apple, and washes the pulp down with more brandy.

HARKER's Voice: *All the time I stayed here in the inn, waiting for a commission, I was growing older, losing precious life. And all the time the Count sat on top of his mountain, leeching off the land, he grew younger, thirstier.*

Harker scoops a locket from a bedside table and opens it to look at a portrait of his wife, MINA. Without malice or curiosity, he dangles the cameo in a candle flame. The face browns, the silver setting blackens.

HARKER's Voice: *I was waiting for the call from Seward. Eventually, it came.*

There is a knock on the door.

2

'It's all right for you, Katharine Reed,' Francis whined as he picked over the unappetising craft services table. 'You're dead, you don't have to eat this shit.'

Kate showed teeth, hissing a little. She knew that despite her granny glasses and freckles, she could look unnervingly feral when she smiled. Francis didn't shrink: deep down, the director thought of her as a special effect, not a real vampire.

In the makeshift canteen, deep in the production bunker, the Americans wittered nostalgia about McDonald's. The Brits – the warm ones, anyway – rhapsodised about Pinewood breakfasts of kippers and fried bread. Romanian location catering was not what they were used to.

Francis finally found an apple less than half brown and took it away. His weight had dropped visibly since their first meeting, months ago in pre-production. Since he had come to Eastern Europe, the insurance doctor diagnosed him as suffering from malnutrition and put him on vitamin shots. *Dracula* was running true to form, sucking him dry.

A production this size was like a swarm of vampire bats – some large, many tiny – battening tenaciously onto the host, making insistent, never-ending demands. Kate had watched Francis – bespectacled, bearded and hyperactive – lose substance under the draining siege, as he made and justified decisions, yielded the visions to be translated to celluloid, rewrote the script to suit locations or new casting. How could one man throw out so many ideas, only a fraction of which would be acted on? In his position, Kate's mind would bleed empty in a week.

A big budget film shot in a backward country was an insane proposition, like taking a touring three-ring circus into a war zone. *Who will survive*, she thought, *and what will be left of them?*

The craft table for vampires was as poorly stocked as the one for the warm. Unhealthy rats in chicken-wire cages. Kate watched one of the floor effects men, a new-born with a padded waistcoat and a tool-belt, select a writhing specimen and bite off its head. He spat it on the concrete floor, face stretched into a mask of disgust.

'Ringworm,' he snarled. 'The commie gits are trying to kill us off with diseased vermin.'

'I could murder a bacon sarnie,' the effects man's mate sighed.

'I could murder a Romanian caterer,' said the new-born.

Kate decided to go thirsty. There were enough Yanks around to make coming by human blood in this traditionally superstitious backwater not a problem. Ninety years after Dracula spread vampirism to the Western world, America was still sparsely populated by the blood-drinking undead. For a lot of Americans, being bled by a genuine olde worlde creature of the night was something of a thrill.

That would wear off.

3

Outside the bunker, in a shrinking patch of natural sunlight between a stand of real pines and the skeletons of fake trees, Francis shouted at Harvey Keitel. The actor, cast as Jonathan Harker, was stoic, inexpressive, grumpy. He refused to be drawn into argument, invariably driving Francis to shrieking hysteria.

'I'm not Martin Fucking Scorsese, man,' he screamed. 'I'm not going to slather on some lousy voice-over to compensate for what you're not giving me. Without Harker, I don't have a picture!'

Keitel made fists but his body language was casual. Francis had been riding his star hard all week. Scuttlebutt was that he had wanted Pacino or McQueen but neither was willing to spend three months behind the Iron Curtain.

Kate could understand that. This featureless World War II bunker, turned over to the production as a command centre, stood in ancient mountains, dwarfed by the tall trees. As an outpost of civilisation in a savage land, it was ugly and ineffective.

When approached to act as a technical advisor to Coppola's *Dracula*, she had thought it might be interesting to see where it all started: the Changes, the Terror, the Transformation. No one seriously believed vampirism began here, but it was where Dracula came from. This land had nurtured him through centuries before he decided to spread his wings and extend his bloodline around the world.

Three months had already been revised to six. This production didn't have a schedule, it had a sentence. A few were already demanding parole.

Some vampires felt Transylvania should be the undead Israel, a new state carved out of the much-redrawn map of Central Europe, a geographical and political homeland. As soon as it grew from an inkling to a notion, Ceauşescu vigorously vetoed the proposition. Holding up in one hand a silver-edged sickle, an iron-headed hammer and a sharpened oak spar, the Premier reminded the world that, 'In Romania, we know how to treat leeches – a stake through the heart and off with their filthy heads.' But the Transylvania Movement ('Back to the forests, back to the mountains') gathered momentum. Some elders, after ninety years of the chaos of the larger world, wished to withdraw to their former legendary status. Many of Kate's generation, turned in the 1880s, Victorians stranded in this mechanistic century, were sympathetic.

'You're the Irish vampire lady,' Harrison Ford, flown in for two days to play Dr Seward as a favour to Francis, had said. 'Where's your castle?'

'I have a flat in the Holloway Road,' she admitted. 'Over an off-licence.'

In the promised Transylvania, all elders would have castles, fiefdoms, slaves, human cattle. Everyone would wear evening dress. All vampires would have treasures of ancient gold, like leprechauns. There would be a silk-lined coffin in every crypt, and every night would be a full moon. Unlife eternal and luxury without end, bottomless wells of blood and Paris label shrouds.

Kate thought the Movement lunatic. Never mind cooked breakfasts and (the other crew complaint) proper toilet paper, this was an intellectual desert, a country without conversation, without (and she recognised the irony) life.

She understood Dracula had left Transylvania in the first place not merely because he – the great dark sponge – had sucked it dry, but because even he was bored with ruling over gypsies, wolves and mountain streams. That did not prevent the elders of the Transylvania Movement from claiming the Count as their inspiration and using his seal as their symbol.

An Arthurian whisper had it that once vampires returned to Transylvania, Dracula would rise again to assume his rightful throne as their ruler.

Dracula, at long long last, was truly dead, had been for more than fifteen years. Kate had seen his head stuck on a pole, heard the confession of his merciful assassin, attended his cremation on a beach outside Rome, seen his ashes scattered into the sea. From that, there was no coming back, not even for a creature who had so many times avoided his appointment in Samarra.

But the Count meant so much to so many. Kate wondered if anything was left of him, anything concrete and inarguable and true. Or was he now just a phantom, a slave to anyone who cared to invoke his name? So many causes and crusades and rebellions and atrocities. One man, one monster, could never have kept track of them all, could never have encompassed so much mutually exclusive argument.

There was the Dracula of the histories, the Dracula of Stoker's book, the Dracula of this film, the Dracula of the Transylvania Movement. Dracula – the vampire and the idea – was vast. But not so vast that he could cast his cloak of protection around all who claimed to be his followers. Out here in the mountains where the Count had passed centuries in petty predation, Kate understood that he must in himself have felt tiny, a lizard crawling down a rock.

Nature was overwhelming. At night, the stars were laser-points in the deep velvet black of the sky. She could hear, taste and smell a thousand flora and fauna. If ever there was a call of the wild, this forest exerted it. But there was nothing she considered intelligent life.

She tied tight under her chin the yellow scarf, shot through with golden traceries, she had bought at Biba in 1969. It was a flimsy, delicate thing, but to her it meant civilisation, a coloured moment of frivolity in a life too often preoccupied with monochrome momentousness.

Francis jumped up and down and threw script pages to the winds. His arms flapped like wings. Clouds of profanity enveloped the uncaring Keitel.

'Don't you realise I've put up my own fucking money for this fucking picture,' he shouted, not just at Keitel but at the whole company. 'I could lose my house, my vineyard, everything. I can't afford a fucking honourable failure. This has abso-goddamn-lutely got to outgross *Jaws* or I'm personally impaled up the ass with a sharpened telegraph pole.'

Effects men sat slumped against the exterior wall of the bunker (there were few chairs on location) and watched their director rail at the heavens, demanding of God answers that were not forthcoming. Script pages swirled upwards in a spiral, spreading out in a cloud, whipping against the upper trunks of the trees, soaring out over the valley.

'He was worse on *Godfather*,' one said.

4

Servants usher Harker into a well-appointed drawing room. A table is set with an informal feast of bread, cheese and meat. DR JACK SEWARD, in a white coat with a stethoscope hung around his neck, warmly shakes Harker's hand and leads him to the table. QUINCEY P MORRIS sits to one side, tossing and catching a spade-sized bowie knife.

LORD GODALMING, well dressed, napkin tucked into his starched collar, sits at the table, forking down a double helping of paprika chicken. Harker's eyes meet Godalming's, the nobleman looks away.

SEWARD: Harker, help yourself to the fare. It's uncommonly decent for foreign muck.

HARKER: Thank you, no. I took repast at the inn.

SEWARD: How is the inn? Natives bothering you? Superstitious babushkas, what?

HARKER: I am well in myself.

SEWARD: Splendid... The vampire, Countess Marya Dolingen of Graz. In 1883, you cut off her head and drove a hawthorn stake through her heart, destroying her utterly.

HARKER: I'm not disposed just now to discuss such affairs.

MORRIS: Come on, Jonny-Boy. You have a commendation from the church, a papal decoration. The frothing she-bitch is dead at last. Take the credit.

HARKER: I have no direct knowledge of the individual you mention. And if I did, I reiterate that I would not be disposed to discuss such affairs.

Seward and Morris exchange a look as Harker stands impassive. They know they have the right man. Godalming, obviously in command, nods.

Seward clears plates of cold meat from a strong-box that stands on the table. Godalming hands the doctor a key, with which he opens the box. He takes out a woodcut and hands it over to Harker.

The picture is of a knife-nosed mediaeval warrior prince.

SEWARD: That's Vlad Tepes, called 'the Impaler'. A good Christian, defender of the faith. Killed a million Turks. Son of the Dragon, they called him. Dracula.

Harker is impressed.

MORRIS: Prince Vlad had Orthodox Church decorations out the ass. Coulda made Metropolitan. But he converted, went over to Rome, turned Candle.

HARKER: Candle?

SEWARD: Roman Catholic.

Harker looks again at the woodcut. In a certain light, it resembles the young Marlon Brando.

Seward walks to a side-table, where an antique dictaphone is set up. He fits a wax cylinder and adjusts the needle-horn.

SEWARD: This is Dracula's voice. It's been authenticated.

Seward cranks the dictaphone.

DRACULA's Voice: *Cheeldren of the naight, leesten to them. What museek they maike!*

There is a strange distortion in the recording.

HARKER: What's that noise in the background?

SEWARD: Wolves, my boy. Dire wolves, to be precise.

DRACULA's Voice: *To die, to be reallllly dead, that must be… glorioussss!*

MORRIS: Vlad's well beyond Rome now. He's up there, in his impenetrable castle, continuing the crusade on his own. He's got this army of Szgany gypsies, fanatically loyal fucks. They follow his orders, no matter how atrocious, no matter how appalling. You know the score, Jon. Dead babies, drained cattle, defenestrated peasants, impaled grandmothers. He's god-damned Un-Dead. A fuckin' monster, boy.

Harker is shocked. He looks again at the woodcut.

SEWARD: The firm would like you to proceed up into the mountains, beyond the Borgo Pass…

HARKER: But that's Transylvania. We're not supposed to be in Transylvania.

Godalming looks to the heavens, but continues eating.

SEWARD: ...beyond the Borgo Pass, to Castle Dracula. There, you are to ingratiate yourself by whatever means come to hand into Dracula's coterie. Then you are to disperse the Count's household.

HARKER: Disperse?

Godalming puts down his knife and fork.

GODALMING: Disperse with ultimate devotion.

5

'What can I say, we made a mistake,' Francis said, shrugging nervously, trying to seem confident. He had shaved off his beard, superstitiously hoping that would attract more attention than his announcement. 'I think this is the courageous thing to do, shut down and recast, rather than continue with a frankly unsatisfactory situation.'

Kate did not usually cover show business, but the specialist press stringers (*Variety, Screen International, Positif*) were dumbstruck enough to convince her it was not standard procedure to fire one's leading man after two weeks' work, scrap the footage and get someone else. When Keitel was sent home, the whole carnival ground to a halt and everyone had to sit around while Francis flew back to the States to find a new star.

Someone asked how far over budget *Dracula* was. Francis smiled and waffled about budgets being provisional.

'No one ever asked how much the Sistine Chapel cost,' he said, waving a chubby hand. Kate would have bet that while Michelangelo was on his back with the brushes, Pope Julius II never stopped asking how much it cost and when would it be finished.

During the break in shooting, money was pouring down a drain. Fred Roos, the co-producer, had explained to her just how expensive it was to keep a whole company standing by. It was almost more costly than having them work.

Next to Francis at the impromptu press conference in the Bucharest Town Hall was Martin Sheen, the new Jonathan Harker. In his mid-thirties, he seemed much younger, like the lost boy in *The Subject Was Roses*. The actor mumbled generously about the opportunity he was grateful for. Francis beamed like a shorn Santa Claus on a forced diet and opened a bottle of his own wine to toast his new star.

The man from *Variety* asked who would be playing Dracula and Francis froze in mid-pour, sloshing red all over Sheen's wrist. Kate knew the title role – actually fairly small, thanks to Bram Stoker and screenwriter John Milius – was still on offer to various possibles – Klaus Kinski, Jack Nicholson, Christopher Lee.

'I can confirm Bobby Duvall will play Van Helsing,' Francis said. 'And we have Dennis Hopper as Renfield. He's the one who eats flies.'

'But who is Dracula?'

Francis swallowed some wine, attempted a cherubic expression, and wagged a finger.

'I think I'll let that be a surprise. Now, ladies and gentlemen, if you'll excuse me, I have motion picture history to make.'

6

As Kate took her room key from the desk, the night manager nagged her in Romanian. When she had first checked in, the door of her room fell off as she opened it. The hotel maintained she did not know her own vampire strength and should pay exorbitantly to have the door replaced. Apparently, the materials were available only at great cost and had to be shipped from Moldavia. She assumed it was a scam they worked on foreigners, especially vampires. The door was made of paper stretched over a straw frame, the hinges were cardboard fixed with drawing pins.

She was pretending not to understand any language in which they tried to ask her for money, but eventually they would hit on English and she'd have to make a scene. Francis, light-hearted as a child at the moment, thought it rather funny and had taken to teasing her about the damn door.

Not tired, but glad to be off the streets after nightfall, she climbed the winding stairs to her room, a cramped triangular attic space. Though barely an inch over five feet tall, she could only stand up straight in the dead centre of the room. A crucifix hung ostentatiously over the bed, a looking glass was propped up on the basin. She thought about taking them down but it was best to let insults pass. In many ways, she preferred the campsite conditions in the mountains. She only needed to sleep every two weeks, and when she was out she was literally dead and didn't care about clean sheets.

They were all in Bucharest for the moment, as Francis supervised script-readings to ease Sheen into the Harker role. His fellow coach-passengers – Fredric Forrest (Westenra), Sam Bottoms (Murray) and Albert Hall (Swales) – had all been on the project for over a year, and had been through all this before in San Francisco as Francis developed John Milius's script through improvisation and happy accident. Kate didn't think she would have liked being a screenwriter. Nothing was ever finished.

She wondered who would end up playing Dracula. Since his brief marriage to Queen Victoria made him officially if embarrassingly a satellite of the British Royal Family, he had rarely been represented in films. However, Lon Chaney had taken the role in the silent *London After Midnight*, which dealt with the court intrigues of the 1880s, and Anton Walbrook played Vlad opposite Anna Neagle in *Victoria the Great* in 1937. Kate, a lifelong theatregoer who had never quite got used to the cinema, remembered Vincent Price and Helen Hayes in *Victoria Regina* in the 1930s.

Aside from a couple of cheap British pictures which didn't count, Bram Stoker's *Dracula* – the singular mix of documentation and wish-fulfilment that inspired a revolution by showing how Dracula could have been defeated in the early days before his rise to power – had never quite been filmed. Orson Welles produced it on the radio in the 1930s and announced it as his first picture, casting himself as Harker *and* the Count, using first-person camera throughout. RKO Pictures thought it too expensive and convinced him to make *Citizen Kane* instead. Nearly ten years ago, Francis had lured John Milius into writing the first pass at the script by telling him nobody, not even Orson Welles, had ever been able to lick the book.

Francis was still writing and rewriting, stitching together scenes from Milius's script with new stuff of his own and pages torn straight from the book. Nobody had seen a complete script, and Kate thought one didn't exist.

How many times did the monster have to die for her to be rid of him? Her whole life had been a dance with Dracula, and he haunted her still. She was not the only one. Geneviève Dieudonné and Penelope Churchward were in the galliard too, drawn in by Dracula and their other persistent ghost, Charles Beauregard. Dracula and Charles had left the floor, but the three vampire women still revolved around their absences, warily friends with each other because of loves and hates they shared.

When Francis killed the Count at the end of the movie – if that was the ending he went with – maybe it would be for the last time. You weren't truly dead until you'd died in a motion picture. Or at the box office.

The latest word was that the role was on offer to Marlon Brando. She couldn't see it: Stanley Kowalski and Vito Corleone as Count Dracula. One of the best actors in the world, he'd been one of the worst Napoleons in the movies. Historical characters brought out the ham in him. He was terrible as Fletcher Christian too.

Officially, Kate was still just a technical advisor. Though she had never actually met Dracula during his time in London, she had lived through the period. She had known Stoker, Jonathan Harker, Godalming and the rest. Once, as a warm girl, she had been terrified by Van Helsing's rages. When Stoker wrote his book and smuggled it out of prison, she had helped with its underground circulation, printing copies on the presses of the *Pall Mall Gazette* and ensuring its distribution despite all attempts at suppression. She wrote the introduction for the 1912 edition that was the first official publication.

Actually, she found herself impressed into a multitude of duties. Francis treated a $20 million (and climbing) movie like a college play and expected everyone to pitch in, despite union rules designed to prevent the crew being treated as slave labour. She found the odd afternoon of sewing costumes or night of set-building welcome distraction.

At first, Francis asked her thousands of questions about points of detail; now he was shooting, he was too wrapped up in his own vision to take advice. If she didn't find something to do, she'd sit idle. As an employee of Francis's studio, American Zoetrope, she couldn't even write articles about the shoot. For once, she was on the inside, knowing but not telling.

She had wanted to write about Romania for the *New Statesman*, but was under orders not to do anything that might jeopardise the co-operation the production needed from the Ceaușescus. So far, she had avoided all the official receptions Nicolae and Elena had hosted for the production. The Premier was known to be an extreme vampire-hater, especially since the stirrings of the Transylvania Movement, and occasionally ordered not-so-discreet purges of the undead.

Kate knew she, like the few other vampires with the *Dracula* crew, was subject to regular checks by the *Securitate*. Men in black leather coats loitered in the corner of her eye.

'For God's sake,' Francis had told her, 'don't *take* anybody local.'

Like most Americans, he didn't understand. Though he could *see* she was a tiny woman with red hair and glasses, the mind of an aged aunt in the body of an awkward cousin, Francis could not rid himself of the impression that vampire women were ravening predators with unnatural powers of bewitchment, lusting after the pounding blood of any warm youth who happened along. She was sure he hung his door with garlic and wolfsbane, but half-hoped for a whispered solicitation.

After a few uncomfortable nights in Communist-approved beer halls, she had learned to stay in her hotel room while in Bucharest. People here had memories as long as her lifetime. They crossed themselves and muttered prayers as she walked by. Children threw stones.

She stood at her window and looked out at the square. A patch of devastation where the ancient quarter of the capital had been, marked the site of the palace Ceauşescu was building for himself. A three-storey poster of the Saviour of Romania stood amid the ruins. Dressed like an orthodox priest, he held up Dracula's severed head as if he had personally killed the Count.

Ceauşescu harped at length about the dark, terrible days of the past when Dracula and his kind preyed on the warm of Romania. In theory, it kept his loyal subjects from considering the dark, terrible days of the present when he and his wife lorded over the country like especially corrupt Roman Emperors. Impersonating the supplicant undertaker in *The Godfather*, Francis had abased himself to the dictator to secure official co-operation.

She turned the wireless on and heard tinny martial music. She turned it off, lay on the narrow, lumpy bed – as a joke, Fred Forrest and Francis had put a coffin in her room one night – and listened to the city at night. Like the forest, Bucharest was alive with noises and smells.

It was ground under, but there was life here. Even in this grim city, someone was laughing, someone was in love. Somebody was allowed to be a happy fool.

She heard winds in telephone wires, bootsteps on cobbles, a drink poured in another room, someone snoring, a violinist sawing scales. And someone outside her door. Someone who didn't breathe, who had no heartbeat, but whose clothes creaked as he moved, whose saliva rattled in his throat.

She sat up, confident she was elder enough to be silent, and looked at the door.

'Come in,' she said, 'it's not locked. But be careful. I can't afford more breakages.'

7

His name was Ion Popescu and he seemed about thirteen, with big, olive-shiny orphan eyes and thick, black, unruly hair. He wore an adult's clothes, much distressed and frayed, stained with long-dried blood and earth. His teeth were too large for his skull, his cheeks stretched tight over his jaws, drawing his whole face to the point of his tiny chin.

Once in her room, he crouched down in a corner, away from the window. He talked only in a whisper, in a mix of English and German she had to strain to follow. His mouth wouldn't open properly. He was alone in the city, without community. Now he was tired and wanted to leave his homeland. He begged her to hear him out and whispered his story.

He claimed to be forty-five, turned in 1944. He didn't know, or didn't care to talk about, his father- or mother-in-darkness. There were blanks burned in his memory, whole years missing. She had come across that before. For all his vampire life, he had lived underground, under the Nazis and then the Communists. He was the sole survivor of several resistance movements. His warm comrades never really trusted him, but his capabilities were useful for a while.

She was reminded of her first days after turning. When she knew nothing, when her condition seemed a disease, a trap. That Ion could be a vampire for over thirty years and never pass beyond the new-born stage was incredible. She truly realised, at last, how backward this country was.

'Then I hear of the American film, and of the sweet vampire lady who is with the company. Many times, I try to get near you, but you are watched. *Securitate*. You, I think, are my saviour, my true mother-in-the-dark.'

Forty-five, she reminded herself.

Ion was exhausted after days trying to get close to the hotel, to 'the sweet vampire lady', and hadn't fed in weeks. His body was icy cold. Though she knew her own strength was low, she nipped her wrist and dribbled a little of her precious blood onto his white lips, enough to put a spark in his dull eyes.

There was a deep gash on his arm, which festered as it tried to heal. She bound it with her scarf, wrapping his thin limb tight.

He hugged her and slept like a baby. She arranged his hair away from his eyes and imagined his life. It was like the old days, when vampires were hunted down and destroyed by the few who believed. Before Dracula.

The Count had changed nothing for Ion Popescu.

8

Bistritz, a bustling township in the foothills of the Carpathian Alps. Harker, carrying a Gladstone bag, weaves through crowds towards a waiting coach and six. Peasants try to sell him crucifixes, garlic and other lucky charms. Women cross themselves and mutter prayers.

A wildly gesticulating photographer tries to stop him, slowing his pace to examine a complicated camera. An infernal burst of flash-powder spills purple smoke across the square. People choke on it.

Corpses hang from a four-man gibbet, dogs leaping up to chew on their naked feet. Children squabble over mismatched boots filched from the executed men. Harker looks up at the twisted, mouldy faces.

He reaches the coach and tosses his bag up. SWALES, the coachman, secures it with the other luggage and growls at the late passenger. Harker pulls open the door and swings himself into the velvet-lined interior of the carriage.

There are two other passengers. WESTENRA, heavily moustached and cradling a basket of food. And MURRAY, a young man who smiles as he looks up from his Bible.

Harker exchanges curt nods of greeting as the coach lurches into motion.

KIM NEWMAN

HARKER's Voice: *I quickly formed opinions of my travelling companions. Swales was at the reins. It was my commission but sure as shooting it was his coach. Westenra, the one they called 'Cook', was from Whitby. He was ratcheted several notches too tight for Wallachia. Probably too tight for Whitby, come to that. Murray, the fresh-faced youth with the Good Book, was a rowing blue from Oxford. To look at him, you'd think the only use he'd have for a sharpened stake would be as a stump in a knock-up match.*

Later, after dark but under a full moon, Harker sits up top with Swales. A wind-up phonograph crackles out a tune through a sizable trumpet.

Mick Jagger sings 'Ta-Ra-Ra-BOOM-De-Ay'.

Westenra and Murray have jumped from the coach and ride the lead horses, whooping it up like a nursery Charge of the Light Brigade.

Harker, a few years past such antics, watches neutrally. Swales is indulgent of his passengers.

The mountain roads are narrow, precipitous. The lead horses, spurred by their riders, gallop faster. Harker looks down and sees a sheer drop of a thousand feet, and is more concerned by the foolhardiness of his companions.

Hooves strike the edge of the road, narrowly missing disaster.

Westenra and Murray chant along with the song, letting go of their mounts' manes and doing hand-gestures to the lyrics. Harker gasps but Swales chuckles. He has the reins and the world is safe.

HARKER's Voice: *I think the dark and the pines of Romania spooked them badly, but they whistled merrily on into the night, infernal cake-walkers with Death as a dancing partner.*

In the rehearsal hall, usually a people's ceramics collective, she introduced Ion to Francis.

The vampire youth was sharper now. In a pair of her jeans (which fitted him perfectly) and a *Godfather II* T-shirt, he looked less the waif, more like a survivor. Her Biba scarf, now his talisman, was tied around his neck.

'I said we could find work for him with the extras. The gypsies.'

'I am no gypsy,' Ion said, vehemently.

'He speaks English, Romanian, German, Magyar and Romany. He can co-ordinate all of them.'

'He's a kid.'

'He's older than you are.'

Francis thought it over. She didn't mention Ion's problems with the authorities. Francis couldn't harbour an avowed dissident. The relationship between the production and the government was already strained. Francis thought (correctly) he was being bled of funds by corrupt officials, but couldn't afford to lodge a complaint. Without the Romanian army, he didn't have a cavalry, didn't have a horde. Without location permits that still hadn't come through, he couldn't shoot the story beyond Borgo Pass.

'I can keep the rabble in line, maestro,' Ion said, smiling.

Somehow, he had learned how to work his jaws and lips into a smile. With her blood in him, he had more control. She noticed him chameleoning. His smile, she thought, might be a little like hers.

Francis chuckled. He liked being called 'maestro'. Ion was good at getting on the right side of people. After all, he had certainly got on the right side of her.

'Okay, but keep out of the way if you see anyone in a suit.'

Ion was effusively grateful. Again, he acted his apparent age, hugging Francis, then her, saluting like a toy soldier.

Martin Sheen, noticing, raised an eyebrow.

Francis took Ion off to meet his own children – Roman, Gio and Sofia – and Sheen's sons – Emilio and Charlie. It had not sunk in that this wiry kid, obviously keen to learn baseball and chew gum, was in warm terms middle-aged.

Then again, Kate never knew whether to be twenty-five, the age at which she turned, or 116. And how was a 116-year-old supposed to behave anyway?

Since she had let him bleed her, she was having flashes of his past: scurrying through back-streets and sewers, like a rat; the stabbing pains of betrayal; eye-searing flashes of firelight; constant cold and red thirst and filth.

Ion had never had the time to grow up. Or even to be a proper child. He was a waif and a stray. She couldn't help but love him a little. She had chosen not to pass on the Dark Kiss, though she had once, during the Great War, come close and regretted it.

Her bloodline, she thought, was not good for a newborn. There was too much Dracula in it, maybe too much Kate Reed.

To Ion, she was a teacher not a mother. Before she insisted on becoming a journalist, her whole family seemed to feel she was predestined to be a governess. Now, at last, she thought she saw what they meant.

Ion was admiring six-year-old Sofia's dress, eyes bright with what Kate hoped was not hunger. The little girl laughed, plainly taken with her new friend. The boys, heads full of the vampires of the film, were less sure about him. He would have to earn their friendship.

Later, Kate would deal with Part Two of the Ion Popescu Problem. After the film was over, which would not be until the 1980s at the current rate of progress, he wanted to leave the country, hidden in among the production crew. He was tired of skulking and dodging the political police, and didn't think he could manage it much longer. In the West, he said, he would be free from persecution.

She knew he would be disappointed. The warm didn't really *like* vampires in London or Rome or Dublin any more than they did in Timişoara or Bucharest or Cluj. It was just more difficult legally to have them destroyed.

10

Back in the mountains, there was the usual chaos. A sudden thunderstorm, whipped up out of nowhere like a djinn, had torn up real and fake trees and scattered them throughout the valley, demolishing the gypsy encampment production designer Dean Tavoularis had been building. About half a million dollars' worth of set was irrevocably lost. The bunker itself had been struck by lightning and split open like a pumpkin. Steady rain poured in and streamed out of the structure, washing away props, documents, equipment and costumes. Crews foraged in the valley for stuff that could be reclaimed and used.

Francis acted as if God were personally out to destroy him.

'Doesn't anybody else notice what a disaster this film is?' he shouted. 'I haven't got a script, I haven't got an actor, I'm running out of money, I'm all out of time. This is the goddamned Unfinished Symphony, man.'

Nobody wanted to talk to the director when he was in this mood. Francis squatted on the bare earth of the mountainside, surrounded by smashed balsawood pine trees, hugging his knees. He wore a Stetson hat, filched from Quincey Morris's wardrobe. Drizzle ran from its brim in a tiny stream. Eleanor, his wife, concentrated on keeping the children out of the way.

'This is the worst fucking film of my career. The worst I'll ever make. The *last* movie.'

The first person to tell Francis to cheer up and that things weren't so bad would get fired and be sent home. At this point, crowded under a leaky lean-to with other surplus persons, Kate was tempted.

'I don't want to be Orson Welles,' Francis shouted at the slate-grey skies, rain on his face, 'I don't want to be David Lean. I just want to make an *Irwin Allen* movie, with violence, action, sex, destruction in every frame. This isn't art, this is atrocity.'

Just before the crew left Bucharest, as the storm was beginning, Marlon Brando had consented to be Dracula. Francis personally wired him a million-dollar down-payment against two weeks' work. Nobody dared remind Francis that if he wasn't ready to shoot Brando's scenes by the end of the year, he would lose the money *and* his star.

The six months was up, and barely a quarter of the film was in the can. The production schedule had been extended and reworked so many times that all forecasts of the end of shooting were treated like forecasts of the end of the War. Everyone said it would be over by Christmas, but knew it would stretch until the last trump.

'I could just stop, you know,' Francis said, deflated. 'I could just shut it down and go back to San Francisco and a hot bath and decent pasta and forget everything. I can still get work shooting commercials, nudie movies, series TV. I could make little films, shot on video with a four-man crew, and show them to my friends. All this D.W. Griffith-David O. Selznick shit just isn't fucking necessary.'

He stretched out his arms and water poured from his sleeves. Over a hundred people, huddled in various shelters or wrapped in orange plastic ponchos, looked at their lord and master and didn't know what to say or do.

'What does this cost, people? Does anybody know? Does anybody care? Is it worth all this? A movie? A painted ceiling? A symphony? Is anything worth all this shit?'

The rain stopped as if a tap were turned off. Sun shone through clouds. Kate screwed her eyes tight shut and fumbled under her poncho for the heavy sunglasses-clip she always carried. She might be the kind of vampire who could go about in all but the strongest sunlight, but her eyes could still be burned out by too much light.

She fixed clip-on shades to her glasses and blinked.

People emerged from their shelters, rainwater pouring from hats and ponchos.

'We can shoot around it,' a co-associate assistant producer said.

Francis fired him on the spot.

Kate saw Ion creep out of the forests and straighten up. He had a wooden staff, newly trimmed. He presented it to his maestro.

'To lean on,' he said, demonstrating. Then, he fetched it up and held it like a weapon, showing a whittled point. 'And to fight with.'

Francis accepted the gift, made a few passes in the air, liking the feel of it in his hands. Then he leaned on the staff, easing his weight onto the strong wood.

'It's good,' he said.

Ion grinned and saluted.

'All doubt is passing,' Francis announced. 'Money doesn't matter, time doesn't matter, we don't matter. This film, this *Dracula*, that is what matters. It's taken the smallest of you,' he laid his hand on Ion's curls, 'to show me that. When we are gone, *Dracula* will remain.'

Francis kissed the top of Ion's head.

'Now,' he shouted, inspired, 'to work, to work.'

11

———◆———

The coach trundles up the mountainside, winding between the tall trees. A blaze of blue light shoots up.

WESTENRA: Treasure!

HARKER's Voice: *They said the blue flames marked the sites of long-lost troves of bandit silver and gold. They also said no good ever came of finding it.*

WESTENRA: Coachman, stop! Treasure.

Swales pulls up the reins, and the team halt. The clatter of hooves and reins dies. The night is quiet.

The blue flame still burns.

Westenra jumps out and runs to the edge of the forest, trying to see between the trees, to locate the source of the light.

HARKER: I'll go with him.

Warily, Harker takes a rifle down from the coach, and breeches a bullet.

Westenra runs ahead into the forest, excited. Harker carefully follows up, placing each step carefully.

WESTENRA: Treasure, man. Treasure.

Harker hears a noise, and signals Westenra to hold back. Both men freeze and listen.

The blue light flickers on their faces and fades out. Westenra is disgusted and disappointed.

Something moves in the undergrowth. Red eyes glow.

A dire wolf leaps up at Westenra, claws brushing his face, enormously furred body heavy as a felled tree. Harker fires. A red flash briefly spotlights the beast's twisted snout.

The wolf's teeth clash, just missing Westenra's face. The huge animal, startled if not wounded, turns and disappears into the forest.

Westenra and Harker run away as fast as they can, vaulting over prominent tree-roots, bumping low branches.

WESTENRA: Never get out of the coach... never get out of the coach.

They get back to the road. Swales looks stern, not wanting to know about the trouble they're in.

HARKER's Voice: *Words of wisdom. Never get out of the coach, never go into the woods... unless you're prepared to become the compleat animal, to stay forever in the forests. Like him, Dracula.*

12

At the party celebrating the 100th Day of Shooting, the crew brought in a coffin bearing a brass plate that read simply DRACULA. Its lid creaked open and a girl in a bikini leaped out, nestling in Francis's lap. She had plastic fangs, which she spit out to kiss him.

The crew cheered. Even Eleanor laughed.

The fangs wound up in the punch bowl. Kate fished them out as she got drinks for Marty Sheen and Robert Duvall.

Duvall, lean and intense, asked her about Ireland. She admitted she hadn't been there in decades. Sheen, whom everyone thought was Irish, was Hispanic, born Ramon Estevez. He was drinking heavily and losing weight, travelling deep into his role. Having surrendered entirely to Francis's 'vision', Sheen was talking with Harker's accent and developing the character's hollow-eyed look and panicky glance.

The real Jonathan, Kate remembered, was a decent but dull sort, perpetually 'umble around brighter people, deeply suburban. Mina, his fiancée and her friend, kept saying that at least he was real, a worker ant not a butterfly like Art or Lucy. A hundred years later, Kate could hardly remember Jonathan's face. From now on, she would always think of Sheen when anyone mentioned Jonathan Harker. The original was eclipsed.

Or erased. Bram Stoker had intended to write about Kate in his book, but left her out. Her few poor braveries during the Terror tended to be ascribed to Mina in most histories. That was probably a blessing.

'What must it have been like for Jonathan,' Sheen said. 'Not even knowing there were such things as vampires? Imagine, confronted with Dracula himself. His whole world upside-down. All he had was himself, and it wasn't enough.'

'He had family, friends,' Kate said.

Sheen's eyes glowed. 'Not in Transylvania. *Nobody* has family and friends in Transylvania.'

Kate shivered and looked around. Francis was showing off martial arts moves with Ion's staff. Fred Forrest was rolling a cigar-sized joint. Vittorio Storaro, the cinematographer, doled out his special spaghetti, smuggled into the country inside film cans, to appreciative patrons. A Romanian official in an ill-fitting shiny suit, liaison with the state studios, staunchly resisted offers of drinks. He probably assumed anything from Hollywood was likely to be laced with Bowles-Ottery ergot, that Western hallucinogen derived from rotten wheat. To be fair, there was a lot of BOP going around the crew, especially since Dennis Hopper showed up with goodies from home. She wondered which of the native hangers-on was the *Securitate* spy, and giggled at the thought that they all might be spies and still not know the others were watching them.

Punch, which she was sipping for politeness's sake, squirted out of her nose as she laughed. Duvall patted her back and she recovered. She was not used to social drinking.

Ion, in a baseball cap given him by one of Francis's kids, was joking with the girl in the bikini, a dancer who played one of the gypsies, his eyes reddening with thirst. Kate decided to leave them be. Ion would control himself with the crew. Besides, the girl might like a nip from the handsome lad.

With a handkerchief, she wiped her face. Her specs had gone crooked with her spluttering and she rearranged them.

'You're not what I expected of a vampire lady,' Duvall said.

Kate slipped the plastic fangs into her mouth and snarled like a kitten.

Duvall and Sheen laughed.

13

For two weeks, Francis had been shooting the 'Brides of Dracula' sequence. The mountainside was as crowded as London's Oxford Street, extras borrowed from the Romanian army salted with English faces recruited from youth hostels and student exchanges. Storaro was up on a dinosaur-necked camera crane, swooping through the skies, getting shots of rapt faces.

The three girls, two warm and one real vampire, had only showed up tonight, guaranteeing genuine crowd excitement in long-shot or blurry background rather than the flatly faked enthusiasm radiated for their own close-ups.

Kate was supposed to be available for the brides, but they didn't need advice. It struck her as absurd that she should be asked to tell the actresses how to be alluring. The vampire Marlene, cast as the blonde bride, had been in films since the silent days and wandered about nearly naked, exposing herself to the winds. Her warm sisters needed to be swathed in furs between shots.

Marlene was one of those vampires who showed up on film and in mirrors; there were more of them around these days. One of those vampire mysteries no one had any real explanation for. Maybe evolution, an adaptation to the twentieth century? Hundreds of years before Kate turned, it was said no artist could paint a vampire's likeness. That belief died out with the development of photography. Now, it seemed most vampires could be filmed.

In a shack-like temporary dressing room, the brides were transformed. Bunty, a sensible Englishwoman, was in charge of their make-up. The living girls, twins from Malta who had appeared in a *Playboy* layout, submitted to all-over pancake that gave their flesh an unhealthy shimmer and opened their mouths like dental patients as false canines were fitted. Their fangs were a hundred times more expensive if hardly more convincing than the joke shop set Kate had kept after the party.

Francis, with Ion in his wake carrying a script, dropped by to cast an eye over the brides. He asked Marlene to open her mouth and examined her dainty pointy teeth.

'We thought we'd leave them as they are,' said Bunty.

Francis shook his head.

'They need to be bigger, more obvious.'

Bunty took a set of dagger-like eye-teeth from her kit and

approached Marlene, who waved them away.

'I'm sorry, dear,' the make-up woman apologised.

Marlene laughed musically and hissed, making Francis jump. Her mouth opened wide like a cobra's, and her fangs extended a full two inches.

Francis grinned.

'Perfect.'

The vampire lady took a little curtsey.

14

Kate mingled with the crew, keeping out of camera-shot. She was used to the tedious pace of filmmaking. Everything took forever and there was rarely anything to see. Only Francis, almost thin now, was constantly on the move, popping up everywhere – with Ion, nick-named 'son of Dracula' by the crew, at his heels – to solve or be frustrated by any one of a thousand problems.

The stands erected for the extras, made by local labour in the months before shooting, kept collapsing. It seemed the construction people, whom she assumed also had the door contract at the Bucharest hotel, had substituted inferior wood, presumably pocketing the difference in lei, and the whole set was close to useless. Francis had taken to having his people work at night, after the Romanians contractually obliged to do the job had gone home, to shore up the shoddy work. It was, of course, ruinously expensive and amazingly inefficient.

The permits to film at Borgo Pass had still not come through. An associate producer was spending all her time at the Bucharest equivalent of the Circumlocution Office, trying to get the trilingual documentation out of the Ministry of Film. Francis would have to hire an entire local film crew and pay them to stand idle while his Hollywood people did the work. That was the expected harassment.

The official in the shiny suit, who had come to represent for everyone the forces hindering the production, stood on one side, eagerly watching the actresses. He didn't permit himself a smile.

Kate assumed the man dutifully hated the whole idea of *Dracula*. He certainly did all he could to get in the way. He could only speak English when the time came to announce a fresh snag, conveniently forgetting the language if he was standing on the spot where Francis wanted camera track laid and he was being told politely to get out of the way.

'Give me more teeth,' Francis shouted through a bullhorn. The actresses responded.

'All of you,' the director addressed the extras, 'look horny as hell.'

Ion repeated the instruction in three languages. In each one, the sentence expanded to a paragraph. Different segments of the crowd were enthused as each announcement clued them in.

Arcs, brighter and whiter than the sun, cast merciless, bleaching patches of light on the crowd, making faces into skulls. Kate was blinking, her eyes watering. She took off and cleaned her glasses.

Like everybody, she could do with a shower and a rest. And, in her case, a decent feed.

Rumours were circulating of other reasons they were being kept away from Borgo Pass. The twins, flying in a few days ago, had brought along copies of the *Guardian* and *Time*. They were passed around the whole company, offering precious news from home. She was surprised how little seemed to have happened while she was out of touch.

However, there was a tiny story in the *Guardian* about the Transylvania Movement. Apparently, Baron Meinster, a disciple of Dracula, was being sought by the Romanian authorities for terrorist outrages. The newspaper reported that he had picked up a band of vampire followers and was out in the forests somewhere, fighting bloody engagements with Ceaușescu's men. The Baron favoured young get; he would find lost children and turn them. The average age of his army was fourteen. Kate knew the type: red-eyed, lithe brats with sharp teeth and no compunctions about anything. Rumour had it that Meinster's kids would descend on villages and murder entire populations, gorging themselves on blood, killing whole families, whole communities, down to the animals.

That explained the nervousness of some of the extras borrowed from the army. They expected to be sent into the woods to fight the devils. Few of them would come near Kate or any other vampire, so any gossip that filtered through was third-hand and had been translated into and out of several languages.

Quite a few civilian observers hung around, keeping an eye on everything, waving incomprehensible but official documentation at anyone who queried their presence. Shiny Suit knew all about them and was their unofficial boss. Ion kept well away from them. She must ask the lad if he knew anything of Meinster. It was a wonder he had not become one of Meinster's Child Warriors. Maybe he had and was trying to get away from that. Growing up.

The crowd rioted on cue but the camera-crane jammed, dumping the operator out of his perch. Francis yelled at the grips to protect the equipment. Ion translated but not swiftly enough to get them into action.

The camera came loose and fell thirty feet, crunching onto rough stone, spilling film and fragments.

Francis looked at the mess, uncomprehending, a child so shocked by the breaking of a favourite toy that he can't even throw a fit. Then, red fury exploded.

Kate wouldn't want to be the one who told Francis that there might be fighting at Borgo Pass.

15

In the coach, late afternoon, Harker goes through the documents he has been given. He examines letters sealed with a red wax

'D', old scrolls gone to parchment, annotated maps, a writ of excommunication. There are pictures of Vlad, woodcuts of the Christian Prince in a forest of impaled infidels, portraits of a dead-looking old man with a white moustache, a blurry photograph of a murk-faced youth in an unsuitable straw hat.

HARKER's Voice: *Vlad was one of the Chosen, favoured of God. But somewhere in those acres of slaughtered foemen, he found something that changed his mind, that changed his soul. He wrote letters to the Pope, recommending the rededication of the Vatican to the Devil. He had two cardinals, sent by Rome to reason with him, hot-collared — red-hot pokers slid through their back passages into their innards. He died, was buried, and came back...*

Harker looks out of the coach at the violent sunset. Rainbows dance around the treetops.

Westenra cringes but Murray is fascinated.

MURRAY: It's beautiful, the light...

Up ahead is a clearing. Coaches are gathered. A natural stone amphitheatre has been kitted out with limelights which fizz and flare.

Crowds of Englishmen take seats.

Harker is confused, but the others are excited.

MURRAY: A musical evening. Here, so far from Piccadilly...

The coach slows and stops. Westenra and Murray leap out to join the crowds.

Warily, Harker follows. He sits with Westenra and Murray. They pass a hipflask between them.

Harker takes a cautious pull, stings his throat.

Into the amphitheatre trundles a magnificent carriage, pulled by a single black stallion. The beast is twelve-hands high. The carriage is black as the night, with an embossed gold and scarlet crest on the door. A red-eyed dragon entwines around a letter 'D'.

The driver is a tall man, draped entirely in black, only his red eyes showing.

There is mild applause.

The driver leaps down from his seat, crouches like a big cat and stands taller than ever. His cloak swells with the night breeze.

Loud music comes from a small orchestra.

'Take a Pair of Crimson Eyes', by Gilbert and Sullivan.

The driver opens the carriage door.

A slim white limb, clad only in a transparent veil, snakes around the door. Tiny bells tinkle on a delicate ankle. The toenails are scarlet and curl like claws.

The audience whoops appreciation. Murray burbles babyish delight. Harker is wary.

The foot touches the carpet of pine needles and a woman swings out of the carriage, shroud-like dress fluttering around her slender form. She has a cloud of black hair and eyes that glow like hot coals.

She hisses, tasting the night, exposing needle-sharp eye-teeth. Writhing, she presses her snake-supple body to the air, as if sucking in the essences of all the men present.

MURRAY: The bloofer lady...

The other carriage door is kicked open and the first woman's twin leaps out. She is less languid, more sinuous, more animal-like. She claws and rends the ground and climbs up the carriage wheel like a lizard, long red tongue darting. Her hair is wild, a tangle of twigs and leaves.

The audience, on their feet, applaud and whistle vigorously. Some of the men rip away their ties and burst their collar-studs, exposing their throats.

FIRST WOMAN: Kisses, sister, kisses for us all...

The hood of the carriage opens, folding back like an oyster to disclose a third woman, as fair as they are dark, as voluptuous as they are slender. She is sprawled in abandon on a plush mountain of red cushions. She writhes, crawling through pillows, her scent stinging the nostrils of the rapt audience.

The driver stands to one side as the three women dance. Some of the men are shirtless now, clawing at their own necks until the blood trickles.

The women are contorted with expectant pleasure, licking their ruby lips, fangs already moist, shrouds in casual disarray, exposing lovely limbs, swan-white pale skin, velvet-sheathed muscle.

Men crawl at their feet, piling atop each other, reaching out just to touch the ankles of these women, these monstrous, desirable creatures.

Murray is out of his seat, hypnotised, pulled towards the vampires, eyes mad. Harker tries to hold him back, but is wrenched forward in his wake, dragged like an anchor.

Murray steps over his fallen fellows, but trips and goes down under them.

Harker scrambles to his feet and finds himself among the women. Six hands entwine his face. Lips brush his cheek, razor-edged teeth drawing scarlet lines on his face and neck.

He tries to resist but is bedazzled.

A million points of light shine in the women's eyes, on their teeth, on their earrings, necklaces, nose-stones, bracelets, veils, navel-jewels, lacquered nails. The lights close around Harker.

BLONDE WOMAN: You never love, you have never loved…

The driver slaps her, dislocating her face. She scrambles away from Harker, who lies sprawled on the ground.

The women are back in the carriage, which does a circuit of the amphitheatre and slips into the forests. There is a massed howl of frustration, and the audience falls upon each other.

Harker, slowly recovering, sits up. Swales is there. He hauls Harker out of the melée and back to the coach. Harker, unsteady, is pulled into the coach.

Westenra and Murray are dejected, gloomy. Harker is still groggy.

HARKER's Voice: *A vampire's idea of a half-holiday is a third share in a juicy peasant baby. It has no other needs, no other desires, no other yearnings. It is mere appetite, unencumbered by morality, philosophy, religion, convention, emotion. There's a dangerous strength in that. A strength we can hardly hope to equal.*

16

Shooting in a studio should have given more control, but Francis was constantly frustrated by Romanians. The inn set, perhaps the simplest element of the film, was still not right, though the carpenters and dressers had had almost a year to get it together. First, they took an office at the studio and turned it into Harker's bedroom. It was too small to fit in a camera as well as an actor and the scenery. Then, they reconstructed the whole thing in the middle of a sound stage, but still bolted together the walls so they couldn't be moved. The only shot Storaro could take was from the ceiling looking down. Now the walls were fly-away enough to allow camera movement, but Francis wasn't happy with the set dressing.

Prominent over the bed, where Francis wanted a crucifix, was an idealised portrait of Ceauşescu. Through Ion, Francis tried to explain to Shiny Suit, the studio manager, that his film took place before the President-for-Life came to power and that, therefore, it was highly unlikely that a picture of him would be decorating a wall anywhere.

Shiny Suit seemed unwilling to admit there had ever been a time when Ceauşescu didn't rule the country. He kept glancing around nervously, as if expecting to be caught in treason and hustled out to summary execution.

'Get me a crucifix,' Francis yelled.

Kate sat meekly in a director's chair − a rare luxury − while the argument continued. Marty Sheen, in character as Harker, sat cross-legged on his bed, taking pulls at a hipflask of potent brandy. She could smell the liquor across the studio.

The actor's face was florid and his movements slow. He had been more and more Harker and less and less Marty the last few days, and Francis was driving him hard, directing with an emotional scalpel that peeled his star like an onion.

Francis told Ion to bring the offending item over so he could show Shiny Suit what was wrong. Grinning cheerfully, Ion squeezed past Marty and reached for the picture, dextrously dropping it onto a bedpost which shattered the glass and speared through the middle of the frame, punching a hole in the Premier's face.

Ion shrugged in fake apology.

Francis was almost happy. Shiny Suit, stricken in the heart, scurried away in defeat, afraid that his part in the vandalism of the sacred image would be noticed.

A crucifix was found from stock and put up on the wall.

'Marty,' Francis said, 'open yourself up, show us your beating heart, then tear it from your chest, squeeze it in your fist and drop it on the floor.'

Kate wondered if he meant it literally.

Marty Sheen tried to focus his eyes, and saluted in slow motion.

'Quiet on set, everybody,' Francis shouted.

17

Kate was crying, silently, uncontrollably. Everyone on set, except Francis and perhaps Ion, was also in tears. She felt as if she was watching the torture of a political prisoner, and just wanted it to stop.

There was no script for this scene.

Francis was pushing Marty into a corner, breaking him down, trying to get to Jonathan Harker.

This would come at the beginning of the picture. The idea was to show the real Jonathan, to get the audience involved with him. Without this scene, the hero would seem just an observer, wandering between other people's set pieces.

'You, Reed,' Francis said, 'you're a writer. Scribble me a voice-over. Internal monologue. Stream-of-consciousness. Give me the real Harker.'

Through tear-blurred spectacles, she looked at the pad she was scrawling on. Her first attempt had been at the Jonathan she remembered, who would have been embarrassed to have been thought capable of stream-of-consciousness. Francis had torn that into confetti and poured it over Marty's head, making the actor cross his eyes and fall backwards, completely drunk, onto the bed.

Marty was hugging his pillow and bawling for Mina.

All for Hecuba, Kate thought. Mina wasn't even in this movie except as a locket. God knows what Mrs Harker would think when and if she saw *Dracula*.

Francis told the crew to ignore Marty's complaints. He was an actor, and just whining.

Ion translated.

She remembered what Francis had said after the storm, *What does this cost, people?* Was anything worth what this seemed to cost? 'I don't just have to make *Dracula*,' Francis had told an interviewer, 'I have to *be* Dracula.'

Kate tried to write the Harker that was emerging between Marty and Francis. She went into the worst places of her past and realised they still burned in her memory like smouldering coals.

Her pad was spotted with red. There was blood in her tears. That didn't happen often.

The camera was close to Marty's face. Francis was intent, bent close over the bed, teeth bared, hands claws. Marty mumbled, trying to wave the lens away.

'Don't look at the camera, Jonathan,' Francis said.

Marty buried his face in the bed and was sick, choking. Kate wanted to protest but couldn't bring herself to. She was worried Martin Sheen would never forgive her for interrupting his Academy Award scene. He was an actor. He'd go on to other roles, casting off poor Jon like an old coat.

He rolled off his vomit and stared up at where the ceiling should have been but wasn't.

The camera ran on. And on.

Marty lay still.

Finally, the camera operator reported, 'I think he's stopped breathing.'

For an eternal second, Francis let the scene run.

In the end, rather than stop filming, the director elbowed the camera aside and threw himself on his star, putting an ear close to Marty's sunken bare chest.

Kate dropped her pad and rushed into the set. A wall swayed and fell with a crash.

'His heart's still beating,' Francis said.

She could hear it, thumping irregularly.

Marty spluttered, fluid leaking from his mouth. His face was almost scarlet.

His heart slowed.

'I think he's having a heart attack,' she said.

'He's only thirty-five,' Francis said. 'No, thirty-six. It's his birthday today.'

A doctor was called for. Kate thumped Marty's chest, wishing she knew more first aid.

The camera rolled on, forgotten.

'If this gets out,' Francis said, 'I'm finished. The film is over.'

Francis grabbed Marty's hand tight, and prayed.

'Don't die, man.'

Martin Sheen's heart wasn't listening. The beat stopped. Seconds passed. Another beat. Nothing.

Ion was at Francis's side. His fang-teeth were fully extended and his eyes were red. It was the closeness of death, triggering his instincts.

Kate, hating herself, felt it too.

The blood of the dead was spoiled, undrinkable. But the blood of the dying was sweet, as if invested with the life that was being spilled.

She felt her own teeth sharp against her lower lip.

Drops of her blood fell from her eyes and mouth, spattering Marty's chin.

She pounded his chest again. Another beat. Nothing.

Ion crawled on the bed, reaching for Marty.

'I can make him live,' he whispered, mouth agape, nearing a pulseless neck.

'My God,' said Francis, madness in his eyes. 'You can bring him back. Even if he dies, he can finish the picture.'

'Yesssss,' hissed the old child.

Marty's eyes sprang open. He was still conscious in his stalling body. There was a flood of fear and panic. Kate felt his death grasp her own heart.

Ion's teeth touched the actor's throat.

A cold clarity struck her. This undead youth of unknown bloodline must not pass on the Dark Kiss. He was not yet ready to be a father-in-darkness.

She took him by the scruff of his neck and tore him away. He fought her, but she was older, stronger.

With love, she punctured Marty's throat, feeling the death ecstasy convulse through her. She swooned as the blood, laced heavily with brandy, welled into her mouth, but fought to stay in control. The lizard part of her brain would have sucked him dry.

But Katharine Reed was not a monster.

She broke the contact, smearing blood across her chin and his chest hair. She ripped open her blouse, scattering tiny buttons, and sliced herself with a sharpening thumbnail, drawing an incision across her ribs.

She raised Marty's head and pressed his mouth to the wound.

As the dying man suckled, she looked through fogged glasses at Francis, at Ion, at the camera operator, at twenty studio staff. A doctor was arriving, too late.

She saw the blank round eye of the camera.

'Turn that bloody thing off,' she said.

18

The principals were assembled in an office at the studio. Kate, still drained, had to be there. Marty was in a clinic with a drip-feed, awaiting more transfusions. His entire bloodstream would have to be flushed out several times over. With luck, he wouldn't even turn. He would just have some of her life in him, some of her in him, forever. This had happened before and Kate wasn't exactly happy about it. But she had no other choice. Ion would have killed the actor and brought him back to life as a new-born vampire.

'There have been stories in the trades,' Francis said, holding up a copy of *Daily Variety*. It was the only newspaper that regularly got through to the company. 'About Marty. We have to sit tight on this, to keep a lid on panic. I can't afford even the rumour that we're in trouble. Don't you understand, we're in the twilight zone here. Anything approaching a shooting schedule or a budget was left behind a long time ago. We can film round Marty until he's ready to do close-ups. His brother is coming over from the States to double him from the back. We can weather this on the ground, but maybe not in the press. The vultures from the trades want us dead. Ever since *Finian's Rainbow*, they've hated me. I'm a smart kid and nobody likes smart kids. From now on, if anybody *dies* they aren't dead until I say so. Nobody is to tell anyone anything until it's gone through me. People, we're in trouble here and we may have to lie our way out of it. I know you think the Ceauşescu regime is fascist but it's nothing compared to the Coppola regime. You don't know anything until I confirm it. You don't do anything until I say so. This is a war, people, and we're losing.'

19

Marty's family was with him. His wife didn't quite know whether to be grateful to Kate or despise her.

He would live. Really live.

She was getting snatches of his past life, mostly from films he had been in. He would be having the same thing, coping with scrambled impressions of her. That must be a nightmare all of its own.

They let her into the room. It was sunny, filled with flowers. The actor was sitting up, neatly groomed, eyes bright.

'Now I know,' he told her. 'Now I really know. I can use that in the part. Thank you.'

'I'm sorry,' she said, not knowing what for.

20

At a way-station, Swales is picking up fresh horses. The old ones, lathered with foamy sweat, are watered and rested.

Westenra barters with a peasant for a basket of apples. Murray smiles and looks up at the tops of the trees. The moon shines down on his face, making him seem like a child.

Harker quietly smokes a pipe.

HARKER's Voice: *This was where we were to join forces with Van Helsing. This stone-crazy double Dutchman had spent his whole life fighting evil.*

VAN HELSING strides out of the mountain mists. He wears a scarlet army tunic and a curly-brimmed top hat, and carries a cavalry sabre. His face is covered with old scars. Crosses of all kinds are pinned to his clothes.

HARKER's Voice: *Van Helsing put the fear of God into the Devil. And he terrified me.*

Van Helsing is accompanied by a band of rough-riders. Of all races and in wildly different uniforms, they are his personal army of the righteous. In addition to mounted troops, Van Helsing has command of a couple of man-lifting kites and a supply wagon.

VAN HELSING: You are Harker?

HARKER: Dr Van Helsing of Amsterdam?

VAN HELSING: The same. You wish to go to Borgo Pass, Young Jonathan?

HARKER: That's the plan.

VAN HELSING: Better you should wish to go to Hades itself, foolish Englishman.

VAN HELSING's AIDE: I say, Prof, did you know Murray was in Harker's crew. The stroke of '84.

VAN HELSING: Hah! Beat Cambridge by three lengths. Masterful.

VAN HELSING's AIDE: They say the river's at its most level around Borgo Pass. You know these mountain streams, Prof. Tricky for the oarsman.

VAN HELSING: Why didn't you say that before, damfool? Harker, we go at once, to take Borgo Pass. Such a stretch of river should be held for the Lord. The Un-Dead, they appreciate it not. *Nosferatu* don't scull.

Van Helsing rallies his men into mounting up. Harker dashes back to the coach and climbs in. Westenra looks appalled as Van Helsing waves his sabre, coming close to fetching off his own Aide's head.

WESTENRA: That man's completely mad.

HARKER: In Wallachia, that just makes him normal. To fight what we have to face, one has to be a little mad.

Van Helsing's sabre shines with moonfire.

VAN HELSING: To Borgo Pass, my angels… charge!

Van Helsing leads his troop at a fast gallop. The coach is

swept along in the wake of the uphill cavalry advance. Man-lifting box-kites carry observers into the night air.

Wolves howl in the distance.

Between the kites is slung a phonograph horn.

Music pours forth. *Swan Lake*, Act 2, Scene 10 – Scene: Moderato.

VAN HELSING: Music. Tchaikovsky. It upsets the devils. Stirs in them memories of things that they have lost. Makes them feel dead. Then we kill them good. Kill them forever.

As he charges, Van Helsing waves his sword from side to side. Dark, low shapes dash out of the trees and slip among the horses' ankles. Van Helsing slashes downwards, decapitating a wolf. The head bounces against a tree, becoming that of a gypsy boy, and rolls down the mountainside.

Van Helsing's cavalry weave expertly through the pines. They carry flaming torches. The music soars. Fire and smoke whip between the trees.

In the coach, Westenra puts his fingers in his ears. Murray smiles as if on a pleasure ride across Brighton Beach. Harker sorts through crucifixes.

At Borgo Pass, a small gypsy encampment is quiet. Elders gather around the fire. A girl hears the Tchaikovsky whining among the winds and alerts the tribe.

The gypsies bustle. Some begin to transform into wolves.

The man-lifting kites hang against the moon, casting vast bat-shadows on the mountainside.

The pounding of hooves, amplified a thousandfold by the trees, thunders. The ground shakes. The forests tremble.

Van Helsing's cavalry explode out of the woods and fall upon the camp, riding around and through the place, knocking over wagons, dragging through fires. A dozen flaming torches are thrown. Shrieking werewolves, pelts aflame, leap up at the riders.

Silver swords flash, red with blood.

Van Helsing dismounts and strides through the carnage, making head shots with his pistol. Silver balls explode in wolf-skulls.

A young girl approaches Van Helsing's Aide, smiling in welcome. She opens her mouth, hissing, and sinks fangs into the man's throat.

Three cavalrymen pull the girl off and stretch her out face-down on the ground, rending her bodice to bare her back. Van Helsing drives a five-foot lance through her ribs from behind, skewering her to the bloodied earth.

VAN HELSING: Vampire bitch!

The cavalrymen congratulate each other and cringe as a barrel of gunpowder explodes nearby. Van Helsing does not flinch.

HARKER's Voice: *Van Helsing was protected by God. Whatever he did, he would survive. He was blessed.*

Van Helsing kneels by his wounded Aide and pours holy water onto the man's ravaged neck. The wound hisses and steams, and the Aide shrieks.

VAN HELSING: Too late, we are too late. I'm sorry, my son.

With a kukri knife, Van Helsing slices off his Aide's head. Blood gushes over his trousers.

The overture concludes and the battle is over.

The gypsy encampment is a ruin. Fires still burn. Everyone is dead or dying, impaled or decapitated or silver-shot. Van Helsing distributes consecrated wafers, dropping crumbs on all the corpses, muttering prayers for saved souls.

Harker sits exhausted, bloody earth on his boots.

HARKER's Voice: *If this was how Van Helsing served God, I was beginning to wonder what the firm had against Dracula.*

The sun pinks the skies over the mountains. Pale light falls on the encampment.

Van Helsing stands tall in the early morning mists.

Several badly wounded vampires begin to shrivel and scream as the sunlight burns them to man-shaped cinders.

VAN HELSING: I love that smell… spontaneous combustion at daybreak. It smells like… salvation.

21

Like a small boy whose toys have been taken away, Francis stood on the rock, orange cagoule vivid against the mist-shrouded pines, and watched the cavalry ride away in the wrong direction. Gypsy extras, puzzled at this reversal, milled around their camp set. Storaro found something technical to check and absorbed himself in lenses.

No one wanted to tell Francis what was going on.

They had spent two hours setting up the attack, laying camera track, planting charges, rigging decapitation effects, mixing Kensington gore in plastic buckets. Van Helsing's troop of ferocious cavalry were uniformed and readied.

Then Shiny Suit whispered in the ear of the captain who was in command of the army-provided horsemen. The cavalry stopped being actors and became soldiers again, getting into formation and riding out.

Kate had never seen anything like it.

Ion nagged Shiny Suit for an explanation. Reluctantly, the official told the little vampire what was going on.

'There is fighting in the next valley,' Ion said. 'Baron Meinster has come out of the forests and taken a keep that stands over a strategic pass. Many are dead or dying. Ceauşescu is laying siege to the Transylvanians.'

'We have an agreement,' Francis said, weakly. 'These are my men.'

'Only as long as they aren't needed for fighting, this man says,' reported Ion, standing aside to let the director get a good look at the Romanian official. Shiny Suit almost smiled, a certain smug attitude suggesting that this would even the score for that dropped picture of the Premier.

'I'm trying to make a fucking movie here. If people don't keep their word, maybe they deserve to be overthrown.'

The few bilingual Romanians in the crew cringed at such sacrilege. Kate could think of dozens of stronger reasons for pulling down the Ceauşescu regime.

'There might be danger,' Ion said, 'if the fighting spreads.'

'This Meinster, Ion. Can he get us the cavalry? Can we do a deal with him?'

'An arrogant elder, maestro. And doubtless preoccupied with his own projects.'

'You're probably right. Fuck it.'

'We're losing the light,' Storaro announced.

Shiny Suit smiled blithely and, through Ion, ventured that the battle should be over in two to three days. It was fortunate for him that Francis only had prop weapons within reach.

In the gypsy camp, one of the charges went off by itself. A pathetic phut sent out a choking cloud of violently green smoke. Trickles of flame ran across fresh-painted flats.

A grip threw a bucket of water, dousing the fire.

Robert Duvall and Martin Sheen, in costume and make-up, stood about uselessly. The entire camera crew, effects gang and support team were gathered, as if waiting for a cancelled train.

There was a long pause. The cavalry did not come riding triumphantly back, ready for the shot.

'Bastards,' Francis shouted, angrily waving his staff like a spear.

22

The next day was no better. News filtered back that Meinster was thrown out of the keep and withdrawing into the forests, but that Ceauşescu ordered his retreat be harried. The cavalry were not detailed to return to their filmmaking duties. Kate wondered how many of them were still alive. The retaking of the keep must have been a bloody, costly battle. A cavalry charge against a fortress position would be almost a suicide mission.

Disconsolately, Francis and Storaro sorted out some pick-up shots that could be managed.

A search was mounted for Shiny Suit, so that a definite time could be established for rescheduling of the attack scene. He had vanished into the mists, presumably to escape the American's wrath.

Kate huddled under a tree and tried to puzzle out a local newspaper. She was brushing up her Romanian, while simultaneously coping with the euphemisms and lacunae of a non-free press. According to the paper, Meinster had been crushed weeks ago and was hiding in a ditch somewhere, certain to be beheaded within the hour.

She couldn't help feeling the real story was in the next valley. As a newspaperwoman, she should be there, not waiting around for this stalled juggernaut to get back on track. Meinster's kids frightened and fascinated her. She should know about them, try to understand. But American Zoetrope had first call on her and she didn't have the heart to be another defector.

Marty Sheen joined her.

He was mostly recovered and understood what she had done for him, though he was still exploring the implications of their blood link. Just now, he was more anxious about working with Brando – due in next week – than his health.

There was still no scripted ending.

23

The day the cavalry – well, most of them – came back, faces drawn and downcast, uniforms muddied, eyes haunted, Shiny Suit was discovered with his neck broken, flopped half in a stream. He must have fallen in the dark, tumbling down the precipitous mountainside.

His face and neck were ripped, torn by the sharp thorns of the mountain bushes. He had bled dry into the water, and his staring face was white.

'It is good that Georghiou is dead,' Ion pronounced. 'He upset the maestro.'

Kate hadn't known the bureaucrat's name.

Francis was frustrated at this fresh delay, but graciously let the corpse be removed and the proper authorities be notified before proceeding with the shoot.

A police inspector was escorted around by Ion, poking at a few broken bushes and examining Georghiou's effects. Ion somehow persuaded the man to conclude the business speedily.

The boy was a miracle, everyone agreed.

'Miss Reed,' Ion interrupted.

Dressed as an American boy, with his hair cut by the make-up department, a light-meter hung around his neck, Ion was unrecognisable as the bedraggled orphan who had come to her hotel room in Bucharest.

Kate laid aside her journal and pen.

'John Popp,' Ion pronounced, tapping his chest. His J-sound was perfect. 'John Popp, the American.'

She thought about it.

Ion — no, John — had sloughed off his nationality and all national characteristics like a snake shedding a skin. Newborn as an American, pink-skinned and glowing, he would never be challenged.

'Do you want to go to America?'

'Oh yes, Miss Reed. America is a young country, full of life. Fresh blood. There, one can be anything one chooses. It is the only country for a vampire.'

Kate wasn't sure whether to feel sorry for the vampire youth or for the American continent. One of them was sure to be disappointed.

'John Popp,' he repeated, pleased.

Was this how Dracula had been when he first thought of moving to Great Britain, then the liveliest country in the world just as America was now? The Count had practised his English pronunciation in conversations with Jonathan, and memorised railway timetables, relishing the exotic names of St Pancras, King's Cross and Euston. Had he rolled his anglicised name – Count DeVille – around his mouth, pleased with himself?

Of course, Dracula saw himself as a conqueror, the rightful ruler of all lands he rode over. Ion-John was more like the Irish and Italian emigrants who poured through Ellis Island at the beginning of the century, certain America was the land of opportunity and that each potato-picker or barber could become a self-made plutocrat.

Envious of his conviction, affection stabbing her heart, wishing she could protect him always, Kate kissed him. He struggled awkwardly, a child hugged by an embarrassing auntie.

24

Mists pool around Borgo Pass. Black crags project from the white sea.

The coach proceeds slowly. Everyone looks around, wary.

MURRAY: Remember that last phial of laudanum... I just downed it.

WESTENRA: Good show, man.

MURRAY: It's like the Crystal Palace.

Harker sits by Swales, considering the ancient castle that dominates the view. Broken battlements are jagged against the boiling sky.

HARKER's Voice: *Castle Dracula. The trail snaked through the forest, leading me directly to him. The Count. The countryside was Dracula. He had become one with the mountains, the trees, the stinking earth.*

The coach halts. Murray pokes his head out of the window, and sighs in amazement.

SWALES: Borgo Pass, Harker. I'll go no further.

Harker looks at Swales. There is no fear in the coachman's face, but his eyes are slitted.

A sliver of dark bursts like a torpedo from the sea of mist. A sharpened stake impales Swales, bloody point projecting a foot or more from his chest.

Swales sputters hatred and takes a grip on Harker, trying to hug him, to pull him onto the sharp point sticking out of his sternum.

Harker struggles in silence, setting the heel of his hand against Swales's head. He pushes and the dead man's grip relaxes. Swales tumbles from his seat and rolls off the precipice, falling silently into the mists.

MURRAY: Good grief, man. That was extreme.

25

———————◆———————

Rising over Borgo Pass was Castle Dracula. Half mossy black stone, half fresh orange timber.

Kate was impressed.

Though the permits had still not come through, Francis had ordered the crew to erect and dress the castle set. This was a long way from Bucharest and without Georghiou, the hand of Ceaușescu could not fall.

From some angles, the castle was an ancient fastness, a fit lair for the vampire King. But a few steps off the path and it was a shell, propped up by timbers. Painted board mingled with stone.

If Meinster's kids were in the forests, they could look up at the mountain and take heart. This sham castle might be their rallying-point. She hummed 'Paper Moon', imagining vampires summoned back to these mountains to a castle that was not a castle and a king who was just an actor in greasepaint.

A grip, silhouetted in the gateway, used a gun-like device to wisp thick cobweb on the portcullis. Cages of imported vermin were stacked up, ready to be unloosed. Stakes, rigged up with bicycle seats that would support the impaled extras, stood on the mountainside.

It was a magnificent fake.

Francis, leaning on his staff, stood and admired the edifice thrown up on his orders. Ion-John was at his side, a faithful Renfield for once.

'Orson Welles said it was the best train set a boy could have,' Francis said. Ion probably didn't know who Welles was. 'But it broke him in the end.'

In her cardigan pocket, she found the joke shop fangs from the 100th Day of Shooting party. Soon, there would be a 200th Day party.

She snapped the teeth together like castanets, feeling almost giddy up here in the mists where the air was thin and the nights cold.

In her pleasant contralto, far more Irish-inflected than her speaking voice, she crooned, 'It's a Barnum and Bailey world, just as phoney as it can be, but it wouldn't be make-believe if you believed in me.'

26

On foot, Harker arrives at the gates of the castle. Westenra and Murray hang back a little way.

A silent crowd of gypsies parts to let the Englishmen through. Harker notices human and wolf teeth strung in necklaces, red eyes and feral fangs, withered bat-membranes curtaining under arms, furry bare feet hooked into the rock. These are the Szgany, the children of Dracula.

In the courtyard, an armadillo noses among freshly severed human heads. Harker is smitten by the stench of decay but tries to hide his distaste. Murray and Westenra groan and complain. They both hold out large crucifixes.

A rat-like figure scuttles out of the crowds.

RENFIELD: Are you English? I'm an Englishman. R.M. Renfield, at your service.

He shakes Harker's hand, then hugs him. His eyes are jittery, mad.

RENFIELD: The Master has been waiting for you. I'm a lunatic, you know. Zoophagous. I eat flies. Spiders. Birds, when I can get them. It's the blood. The blood is the life, as the book says. The Master understands. Dracula. He knows you're coming. He knows everything. He's a poet-warrior in the classical sense. He has the vision. You'll see, you'll learn. He's lived through the centuries. His wisdom is beyond ours, beyond anything we can imagine. How can I make you understand? He's promised me lives. Many lives. Some nights, he'll creep up on you, while you're shaving, and break your mirror. A foul bauble of man's vanity. The blood of Attila flows in his veins. He is the Master.

Renfield plucks a crawling insect from Westenra's coat and gobbles it down.

RENFIELD: I know what bothers you. The heads. The severed heads. It's his way. It's the only language they understand. He doesn't love these things, but he knows he must do them. He knows the truth. Rats! He knows where the rats come from. Sometimes, he'll say, 'They fought the dogs and killed the cats and bit the babies in the cradles, and ate the cheeses out of the vats and licked the soup from the cooks' own ladles.'

Harker ignores the prattle and walks across the courtyard. Scraps of mist waft under his boots.

A huge figure fills a doorway. Moonlight shines on his great, bald head. Heavy jowls glisten as a humourless smile discloses yellow eye-teeth the size of thumbs.

Harker halts.

A bass voice rumbles.

DRACULA: I… am… Dracula.

27

Francis had first envisioned Dracula as a stick-insect skeleton, dried up, hollow-eyed, brittle. When Brando arrived on set, weighing in at 250 pounds, he had to rethink the character as a blood-bloated leech, full to bursting with stolen life, overflowing his coffin.

For two days, Francis had been trying to get a usable reading of the line 'I am Dracula.' Kate, initially as thrilled as anyone else to see Brando at work, was bored rigid after numberless mumbled retakes.

The line was written in three-foot-tall black letters on a large piece of cardboard held up by two grips. The actor experimented with emphases, accents, pronunciations from 'Dorragulya' to 'Jacoolier'. He read the line looking away from the camera and peering straight at the lens. He tried it with false fangs inside his mouth, sticking out of his mouth, shoved up his nostrils or thrown away altogether.

Once he came out with a bat tattooed on his bald head in black lipstick. After considering it for a while, Francis ordered the decal wiped off. You couldn't say that the star wasn't bringing ideas to the production.

For two hours now, Brando had been hanging upside-down in the archway, secured by a team of very tired technicians at the end of two guy-ropes. He thought it might be interesting if the Count were discovered like a sleeping bat.

Literally, he read his line upside-down.

Marty Sheen, over whose shoulder the shot was taken, had fallen asleep.

'I am Dracula. I am Dracula. I am Dracula. I am Dracula. I am Dracula! I am Dracula?

'Dracula am I. Am I Dracula? Dracula I am. I Dracula am. Am Dracula I?

'I'm Dracula.

'The name's Dracula. Count Dracula.

'Hey, I'm Dracula.

'Me… Dracula. You… liquid lunch.'

He read the line as Stanley Kowalski, as Don Corleone, as Charlie Chan, as Jerry Lewis, as Laurence Olivier, as Robert Newton.

Francis patiently shot take after take.

Dennis Hopper hung around, awed, smoking grass. All the actors wanted to watch.

Brando's face went scarlet. Upside-down, he had problems with the teeth. Relieved, the grips eased up on the ropes and the star dropped towards the ground. They slowed before his head cracked like an egg on the ground. Assistants helped him rearrange himself.

Francis thought about the scene.

'Marlon, it seems to me that we could do worse than go back to the book.'

'The book?' Brando asked.

'Remember, when we first discussed the role. We talked about how Stoker describes the Count.'

'I don't quite…'

'You told me you knew the book.'

'I never read it.'

'You said…'

'I lied.'

28

Harker, in chains, is confined in a dungeon. Rats crawl around his feet. Water flows all around.

A shadow passes.

Harker looks up. A grey bat-face hovers above, nostrils elaborately frilled, enormous teeth locked. DRACULA seems to fill the room, black cape stretched over his enormous belly and trunk-like limbs.

Dracula drops something into Harker's lap. It is Westenra's head, eyes white. Harker screams.

Dracula is gone.

29

An insectile clacking emerged from the Script Crypt, the walled-off space on the set where Francis had hidden himself away with his typewriter.

Millions of dollars poured away daily as the director tried to come up with an ending. In drafts Kate had seen – only a fraction of the attempts Francis had made – Harker killed Dracula, Dracula killed Harker, Dracula and Harker became allies, Dracula and Harker were both killed by Van Helsing (unworkable, because Robert Duvall was making another film on another continent), lightning destroyed the whole castle.

It was generally agreed that Dracula should die.

The Count perished through decapitation, purifying fire, running water, a stake through the heart, a hawthorn bush, a giant crucifix, silver bullets, the hand of God, the claws of the Devil, armed insurrection, suicide, a swarm of infernal bats, bubonic plague, dismemberment by axe, permanent transformation into a dog.

Brando suggested that he play Dracula as a Green Suitcase. Francis was on medication.

30

'Reed, what does he mean to you?'

She thought Francis meant Ion-John.

'He's just a kid, but he's getting older fast. There's something…'

'Not John. Dracula.'

'Oh, him.'

'Yes, him. Dracula. Count Dracula. King of the Vampires.'

'I never acknowledged that title.'

'In the 1880s, you were against him?'

'You could say that.'

'But he gave you so much, eternal life?'

'He wasn't my father. Not directly.'

'But he brought vampirism out of the darkness.'

'He was a monster.'

'Just a monster? In the end, just that?'

She thought hard.

'No, there was more. He was more. He was… he *is*, you know… big. Huge, enormous. Like the elephant described by blind men. He had many aspects. But all were monstrous. He didn't bring us out of the darkness. He was the darkness.'

'John says he was a national hero.'

'John wasn't born then. Or turned.'

'Guide me, Reed.'

'I can't write your ending for you.'

---•---

At the worst possible time, the policeman was back. There were questions about Shiny Suit. Irregularities revealed by the autopsy.

For some reason, Kate was questioned.

Through an interpreter, the policeman kept asking her about the dead official, what had their dealings been, whether Georghiou's prejudice against her kind had affected her.

Then he asked her when she had last fed, and upon whom?

'That's private,' she said.

She didn't want to admit that she had been snacking on rats for months. She'd had no time to cultivate anyone warm. Her powers of fascination were thinning.

A scrap of cloth was produced and handed to her.

'Do you recognise this?' she was asked.

It was filthy, but she realised that she did.

'Why, it's my scarf. From Biba. I...'

It was snatched away from her. The policeman wrote down a note.

She tried to say something about Ion, but thought better of it. The translator told the policeman Kate had almost admitted to something.

She felt distinctly chilled.

She was asked to open her mouth, like a horse up for sale. The policeman peered at her sharp little teeth and tutted.

That was all for now.

32

---•---

'How are monsters made?'

Kate was weary of questions. Francis, Marty, the police. Always questions.

Still, she was on the payroll as an advisor.

'I've known too many monsters, Francis. Some were born, some were made all at once, some were eroded, some shaped themselves, some twisted by history.'

'What about Dracula?'

'He was the monster of monsters. All of the above.'

Francis laughed.

'You're thinking of Brando.'

'After your movie, so will everybody else.'

He was pleased by the thought.

'I guess they will.'

'You're bringing him back. Is that a good idea?'

'It's a bit late to raise that.'

'Seriously, Francis. He'll never be gone, never be forgotten. But your Dracula will be powerful. In the next valley, people are fighting over the tatters of the old, faded Dracula. What will your Technicolor, 70mm, Dolby stereo Dracula *mean*?'

'Meanings are for the critics.'

33

Two Szgany gypsies throw Harker into the great hall of the castle. He sprawls on the straw-covered flagstones, emaciated and wild-eyed, close to madness.

Dracula sits on a throne which stretches wooden wings out behind him. Renfield worships at his feet, tongue applied to the Count's black leather boot. Murray, a blissful smile on his face and scabs on his neck, stands to one side, with Dracula's three vampire brides.

DRACULA: I bid you welcome. Come safely, go freely and leave some of the happiness you bring.

Harker looks up.
HARKER: You... were a Prince.

DRACULA: I am a Prince still. Of Darkness.

The brides titter and clap. A frown from their Master silences them.

DRACULA: Harker, what do you think we are doing here, at the edge of Christendom? What dark mirror is held up to our unreflecting faces?

By the throne is an occasional table piled high with books and periodicals. *Bradshaw's Guide to Railway Timetables in England, Scotland and Wales*, George and Weedon Grossmith's *Diary of a Nobody*, Sabine Baring-Gould's *The Book of Were-Wolves*, Oscar Wilde's *Salomé*.
Dracula picks up a volume of the poetry of Robert Browning.

DRACULA: 'I must not omit to say that in Transylvania there's a tribe of alien people that ascribe the outlandish ways and dress on which their neighbours lay such stress, to their fathers and mothers having risen out of some subterraneous prison into which they were trepanned long time ago in a mighty band out of Hamelin town in Brunswick land, but how or why, they don't understand.'

Renfield claps.

RENFIELD: Rats, Master. Rats.

Dracula reaches down with both hands and turns the madman's head right around. The brides fall upon the madman's twitching body, nipping at him greedily before he dies and the blood spoils.
Harker looks away.

At the airport, she was detained by officials. There was some question about her passport.

Francis was worried about the crates of exposed film. The negative was precious, volatile, irreplaceable. He personally, through John, argued with the customs people and handed over disproportionate bribes. He still carried his staff, which he used to point the way and rap punishment. With his stomach swelling again, he looked like Friar Tuck.

The film, the raw material of *Dracula*, was to be treated as if it were valuable as gold and dangerous as plutonium. It was stowed on the aeroplane by soldiers.

A blank-faced woman sat across the desk.

Stirrings of panic ticked inside Kate. The scheduled time of departure neared.

The rest of the crew were lined up with their luggage, joking despite tiredness. After over a year, they were glad to be gone for good from this backward country. They talked about what they would do when they got home. Marty Sheen seemed healthier, years younger. Francis was bubbling again, excited to be on to the next stage.

Kate looked from the Romanian woman to the portraits of Nicolae and Elena on the wall behind her. All eyes were cold, hateful. The woman wore a discreet crucifix and a Party badge clipped to her uniform lapel.

A rope barrier was removed and the eager crowd of the *Dracula* company stormed towards the aeroplane, mounting the steps, squeezing into the cabin.

The flight was for London, then New York, then Los Angeles. Half a world away.

Kate wanted to stand up, to join the plane, to add her own jokes and fantasies to the rowdy chatter, to fly away from here. Her luggage, she realised, was in the hold.

A man in a black trenchcoat (*Securitate?*) and two uniformed policemen arrived and exchanged terse phrases with the woman.

Kate gathered they were talking about Shiny Suit. And her. They used old, cruel words: leech, *nosferatu*, parasite. The *Securitate* man took her passport.

'It is impossible that you be allowed to leave.'

Across the tarmac, the last of the crew – Ion-John among them, baseball cap turned backwards, bulky kit-bag on his shoulder – disappeared into the sleek tube of the aeroplane. The door was pulled shut.

She was forgotten, left behind.

How long would it be before anyone noticed? With different sets of people debarking in three cities, probably forever. It was easy to miss one mousy advisor in the excitement, the anticipation, the triumph of going home with the movie shot. Months of post-production, dialogue looping, editing, rough cutting, previews, publicity and release lay ahead, with box office takings to be crowed over and prizes to be competed for in Cannes and on Oscar night.

Maybe when they came to put her credit on the film, someone would think to ask what had become of the funny little old girl with the thick glasses and the red hair.

'You are a sympathiser with the Transylvania Movement.'

'Good God,' she blurted, 'why would anybody want to live here?'

That did not go down well.

The engines were whining. The plane taxied towards the runway.

'This is an old country, Miss Katharine Reed,' the *Securitate* man sneered. 'We know the ways of your kind, and we understand how they should be dealt with.'

All the eyes were pitiless.

The giant black horse is led into the courtyard by the gypsies. Swords are drawn in salute to the animal. It whinnies slightly, coat glossy ebony, nostrils scarlet.

Inside the castle, Harker descends a circular stairway carefully, wiping aside cobwebs. He has a wooden stake in his hands.

The gypsies close on the horse.

HARKER's Voice: *Even the castle wanted him dead, and that's what he served at the end. The ancient, blood-caked stones of his Transylvanian fastness.*

Harker stands over Dracula's coffin. The Count lies, bloated with blood, face puffy and violet.

Gypsy knives stroke the horse's flanks. Blood erupts from the coat.

Harker raises the stake with both hands over his head.

Dracula's eyes open, red marbles in his fat, flat face. Harker is given pause.

The horse neighs in sudden pain. Axes chop at its neck and legs. The mighty beast is felled.

Harker plunges the stake into the Count's vast chest.

The horse jerks spastically as the gypsies hack at it. Its hooves scrape painfully on the cobbles.

A gout of violently red blood gushes upwards, splashing directly into Harker's face, reddening him from head to waist. The flow continues, exploding everywhere, filling the coffin, the room, driving Harker back.

Dracula's great hands grip the sides of the coffin and he tries to sit. Around him is a cloud of blood droplets, hanging in the air like slo-mo fog.

The horse kicks its last, clearing a circle. The gypsies look with respect at the creature they have slain.

Harker takes a shovel and pounds at the stake, driving it deeper into Dracula's barrel chest, forcing him back into his filthy sarcophagus.

At last, the Count gives up. Whispered words escape from him with his last breath.

DRACULA: The horror… the horror…

36

Kate supposed there were worse places than a Romanian jail. But not many.

They kept her isolated from the warm prisoners. Rapists and murderers and dissidents were afraid of her. She found herself penned with uncommunicative Transylvanians, haughty elders reduced to grime and resentful new-borns.

She had seen a couple of Meinster's kids. Their calm, purposeful, blank-eyed viciousness disturbed her. Their definition of enemy was terrifyingly broad, and they believed in killing. No negotiation, no surrender, no accommodation. Just death, on an industrial scale.

The bars were silver. She fed on insects and rats. She was weak.

Every day, she was interrogated.

They were convinced she had murdered Georghiou. His throat had been gnawed and he was completely exsanguinated.

Why her? Why not some Transylvanian terrorist?

Because of the bloodied once-yellow scrap in his dead fist. A length of thin silk, which she had identified as her Biba scarf. The scarf she had thought of as civilisation. The bandage she had used to bind Ion's wound.

She said nothing about that.

Ion-John was on the other side of the world, making his way. She was left behind in his stead, an offering to placate those who would pursue him. She could not pretend even to herself that it was not deliberate. She understood all too well how he had survived so many years underground. He had learned the predator's trick: to be loved, but never to love. For that, she pitied him even as she could cheerfully have torn his head off.

There were ways out of jails. Even jails with silver bars and garlic hung from every window. The Romanian jailers prided themselves on knowing vampires, but they still treated her as if she were feeble-minded and fragile.

Her strength was sapping, and each night without proper feeding made her weaker.

Walls could be broken through. And there were passes out of the country. She would have to fall back on skills she had thought never to exercise again.

But she was a survivor of the night.

As, quietly, she planned her escape from the prison and from the country, she tried to imagine where the 'Son of Dracula' was, to conceive of the life he was living in America, to count the used-up husks left in his wake. Was he still at his maestro's side, making himself useful? Or had he passed beyond that, found a new patron or become a maestro himself?

Eventually, he would build his castle and enslave a harem. What might he become: a studio head, a cocaine baron, a rock promoter, a media mogul, a *star*? Truly, Ion-John was what Francis had wanted of Brando: Dracula reborn. An old monster, remade for the new world and the next century, meaning all things, tainting everything he touched.

She would leave him be, this new monster of hers, this creature born of Hollywood fantasy and her own thoughtless charity. With Dracula gone or transformed, the world needed a fresh monster. And John Popp would do as well as anyone else. The world had made him and it could deal with him.

Kate extruded a fingernail into a hard, sharp spar, and scraped the wall. The stones were solid, but between them was old mortar, which crumbled easily.

Harker, face still red with Dracula's blood, is back in his room at the inn in Bistritz. He stands in front of the mirror.

HARKER's Voice: *They were going to make me a saint for this, and I wasn't even in their fucking church any more.*

Harker looks deep into the mirror.
  He has no reflection.
  Harker's mouth forms the words, but the voice is Dracula's.
  The horror... the horror...

INTERLUDE

CASTLE IN THE DESERT

Anno Dracula 1977

The man who had married my wife cried when he told me how she died. Junior – Smith Ohlrig Jr, of the oil and copper Ohlrigs – hadn't held on to Linda much longer than I had, but their marriage had gone one better than ours. They had a daughter.

Whatever relation you are to a person who was once married to one of your parents, Racquel Loring Ohlrig was to me. In Southern California, it's such a common family tie you'd think there'd be a nice tidy name for it, pre-father or potential-parent.

The last time I'd seen her was at the Poodle Springs bungalow her mother had given me in lieu of alimony. Thirteen or fourteen years old going on 108, with a micro-halter top and frayed jean-shorts, stretch of still-chubby tummy in between, honey-coloured hair past the small of her back, an underlip that couldn't stop pouting without surgery, binary star sunglasses and a leather headband with Aztec symbols. She looked like a pre-schooler dressed up as a squaw for a costume party, but had the vocabulary of a sailor in Tijuana and the glittery eyes of a magpie with three convictions for aggravated burglary.

She'd asked for money, to gas up her boyfriend's 'sickle', and took my television (no great loss) while I was in the atrium telephoning her mother. In parting, she scrawled 'Fuck you, piggy-dad' in red lipstick on a Spanish mirror. Piggy-Dad, that was me. She still had prep school penmanship, with curly-tails on her ys and a star over the i.

Last I'd heard, the boyfriend was gone with the rest of the Wild Angels. Racquel was back with Linda, taking penicillin shots and going with someone in a rock band.

Now, things were serious.

'My little girl,' Junior kept repeating, 'my little girl…'

He meant Racquel.

'They took her away from me,' he said. 'The vipers.'

All our lives, we've known about the vampires, if only from books and movies. Los Angeles was the last place they were likely to settle. After all, California is known for the sunshine. Vipers would frazzle like burgers on a grill. Now, it was changing. And not just because of affordable prescription sunglasses.

The dam broke in 1959, about the time Linda was serving me papers, when someone in Europe finally destroyed Dracula. Apparently, all vipers remembered who they were biting when they heard the news. It was down to the Count that so many of them lived openly in the world, but his example kept them in their coffins, confined to joyless regions of the old world like Transylvania and England. With the wicked old witch dead, they didn't have to stay on the plantation any longer. They spread.

The first vipers in California were elegant European predators, rotten with old money and thirsty for more than blood. In the early sixties, they bought up real estate, movie studios, talent agencies (cue lots of gags), orange groves, restaurant franchises, ocean-front properties, parent companies. Then their get began to appear: American vampires, new-borns with wild streaks. Just as I quit the private detective business, bled-dry bodies turned up all over town as turf wars erupted and were settled out of court. For some reason, drained corpses were often dumped on golf courses. Vipers made more vipers, but they also made viper-killers – including such noted humanitarians as the Manson

Family – and created new segments of the entertainment and produce industry.

As the Vietnam War escalated, things went quiet on the viper front. Word was that the elders of the community began ruthless policing of their own kind. Besides, the cops were more worried about draft-dodgers and peace-freak protesters. Now, vampires were just another variety of Los Angeles fruitcake. Hundred-coffin mausoleums opened up along the Strip, peddling shelter from the sun at five bucks a day. A swathe of Bay City, boundaried by dried-up canals, started to be called Little Carpathia, a ghetto for the poor suckers who didn't make it up to castles and estates in Beverly Hills. I had nothing real against vipers, apart from a deep-in-the-gut crawly distrust it was impossible for anyone of my generation – the World War II guys – to quell entirely. Linda's death, though, hit me harder than I thought I could be hit, a full-force ulcer-bursting right to the gut. Ten years into retirement, I was at war.

To celebrate the Bicentennial Year, I'd moved from Poodle Springs, back into my old Los Angeles apartment. I was nearer the bartenders and medical practitioners to whom I was sole support. These days, I knocked about, boring youngsters in the profession with the Sternwood case or the Lady in the Lake, doing light sub-contract work for Lew Archer – digging up family records at county courthouses – or Jim Rockford. All the cops I knew were retired, dead or purged by Chief Exley. I hadn't had any pull with the D.A.'s office since Bernie Ohls' final stroke. I admitted I was a relic, but so long as my lungs and liver behaved at least eight hours a day I was determined not to be a shambling relic.

I was seriously trying to cut down on the Camels, but the damage was done back in the puff-happy '40s when no one outside the cigarette industry knew nicotine was worse for you than heroin. I told people I was drinking less, but never really kept score. There were times, like now, when Scotch was the only soldier that could complete the mission.

* * *

Junior, as he talked, drank faster than I did. His light tan suit was the worse for a soaking. It had been worn until dry, wrinkling and staining around the saggy shape of its owner. His shirtfront had ragged tears where he had caught on something.

Since his remarriage to a woman nearer Racquel's age than Linda's, Junior had been a fading presence in the lives of his ex-wife and daughter (ex-daughter?). I couldn't tell how much of his story was from experience and how much filtered through what others had told him. It was no news that Racquel was running with another bad crowd, the Anti-Life Equation. They weren't all vipers, Junior said, but some, the ringleaders, were. Racquel, it appears, got off on being bitten. Not something I wanted to know, it hardly came as a surprise. With the motorcycle boy, who went by the name of Heavenly Blues but liked his friends to address him as 'Mr President', she'd been sporting a selection of bruises which didn't come from taking a bad spill off the pillion of his hog. For tax purposes, the Anti-Life Equation was somewhere between religious and political. I had never heard of them, but it's impossible to keep up with all the latest cults.

Two days ago, at his office – Junior made a pretence of still running the company, though he had to clear every paper-clip purchase with Riyadh and Tokyo – he'd taken a phone call from his daughter. Racquel sounded agitated and terrified, and claimed she'd made a break with the ALE, who wanted to sacrifice her to some elder vampire. She needed money – that same old refrain, haunting me again – to make a dash for Hawaii or, oddly, the Philippines (she thought she'd be safe in a Catholic country, which suggested she'd never been to one). Junior, tower of flab, had written a cheque. His new wife, smart doll, talked him out of sending it. Last night, at home, he had gotten another call from Racquel, hysterical this time, with screaming and other background effects. They were coming for her, she said. The call was cut off.

To his credit, Junior ignored his lawfully married flight attendant and drove over to Linda's place in Poodle Springs, the big house where I'd been uncomfortable. He found the doors open, the house extensively trashed and no sign of Racquel. Linda was at the bottom of the kidney-shaped swimming pool, bitten all over, eyes white. To set a seal on the killing, someone had driven an iron spike through her forehead. A croquet mallet floated above her. I realised he had gone into the pool fully-dressed and hauled Linda out. Strictly speaking, that was violating the crime scene but I would be the last person to complain.

He had called the cops, who were very concerned. Then, he'd driven to the city to see me. It's not up to me to say whether that qualified as a smart move or not.

'This Anti-Life Equation,' I asked Junior, feeling like a shamus again, 'did it come with any names?'

'I'm not even sure it's called that. Racquel mostly used just the initials, ALE. I think it was Anti-Life Element once. Or Anti-Love. Their guru or nabob or whatever he calls himself is some kind of hippie Rasputin. He's one of them, a viper. Khorda. Someone over at one of the studios – Traeger or Bob Evans or one of those kids, maybe Bruckheimer – fed this Khorda some money on an option, but it was never-never stuff. So far as I know, they never killed anyone before.'

Junior cried again and put his arms around me. I smelled chlorine on his ragged shirt. I felt all his weight bearing me down, and was afraid I'd break, be no use to him at all. My bones are brittle these days. I patted his back, which made neither of us feel any better. At last, he let me go and wiped his face on a wet handkerchief.

'The police are fine people,' he said. He got no argument from me. 'Poodle Springs has the lowest crime rate in the state. Every contact I've had with the PSPD has been cordial, and I've always been impressed with their efficiency and courtesy.'

The Poodle Springs Police Department were tigers when it came to finding lost kittens and discreetly removing drunken ex-spouses from floodlit front lawns. You can trust me on this.

'But they aren't good with murder,' I said. 'Or vipers.'

Junior nodded. 'That's just it. They aren't. I know you're

retired. God, you must be I don't know how old. But you used to be connected. Linda told me how you met, about the Wade-Lennox case. I can't even begin to imagine how you could figure out that tangle. For her, you've got to help. Racquel is still alive. They didn't kill her when they killed her mother. They just took her. I want my little girl back safe and sound. The police don't know Racquel. Well, they do… and that's the problem. They said they were taking the kidnap seriously, but I saw in their eyes that they knew about Racquel and the bikers and the hippies. They think she's run off with another bunch of freaks. It's only my word that Racquel was even at the house. I keep thinking of my little girl, of sands running out. Desert sands. You've got to help us. You've just got to.'

I didn't make promises, but I asked questions.

'Racquel said the ALE wanted to sacrifice her? As in tossed into a volcano to appease the Gods?'

'She used a bunch of words. "Elevate", was one. They all meant "kill". Blood sacrifice, that's what she was afraid of. Those vipers want my little girl's blood.'

'Junior, I have to ask, so don't explode. You're sure Racquel isn't a part of this?'

Junior made fists, like a big boy about to get whipped by someone half his size. Then it got through to the back of his brain. I wasn't making assumptions like the PSPD, I was asking an important question, forcing him to prove himself to me.

'If you'd heard her on the phone, you'd know. She was terrified. Remember when she wanted to be an actress? Set her heart on it, nagged for lessons and screen tests. She was – what? – eleven or twelve? Cute as a bug, but froze under the lights. She's no actress. She can't fake anything. She can't tell a lie without it being written all over her. You know that as well as anyone else. My daughter isn't a perfect person, but she's a kid. She'll straighten out. She's got her mom's iron in her.'

I followed his reasoning. It made sense. The only person Racquel had ever fooled was her father, and him only because he let himself be fooled out of guilt. She'd never have come to me for gas money if Junior were still giving in to his princess's every whim. And he was right – I'd seen Racquel Ohlrig (who had wanted to call herself Amber Valentine) act, and she was on the Sonny Tufts side of plain rotten.

'Khorda,' I said, more to myself than Junior. 'That's a start. I'll do what I can.'

Mojave Wells could hardly claim to come to life after dark, but when the blonde viper slid out of the desert dusk, all four living people in the diner – Mom and Pop behind the counter, a trucker and me on stools – turned to look. She smiled as if used to the attention but deeming herself unworthy of it, and walked between the empty tables.

The girl wore a white mini-dress belted on her hips with interlocking steel rings, a blue scarf that kept her hair out of the way, and square black sunglasses. Passing from purple twilight to fizzing blue-white neon, her skin was white to the point of colourlessness, her lips naturally scarlet, her hair pale blonde. She might have been Racquel's age or God's.

I had come to the desert to find vampires. Here was one.

She sat at the end of the counter, by herself. I sneaked an eyeful. She was framed against the 'No Vipers' sign lettered on the window. Mom and Pop – probably younger than me, I admit – made no move to throw her out on her behind, but also didn't ask for her order.

'Get the little lady whatever she wants and put it on my check,' said the trucker. The few square inches of his face not covered by salt-and-pepper beard were worn leather, the texture and colour of his cowboy hat.

'Thank you very much, but I'll pay for myself.'

Her voice was soft and clear, with a long-ago ghost of an accent. Italian or Spanish or French.

'R.D., you know we don't accommodate vipers,' said Mom. 'No offence, ma'am, you seem nice enough, but we've had bad ones through here. And out at the castle.'

Mom nodded at the sign and the girl swivelled on her stool. She genuinely noticed it for the first time and the tiniest flush came to her cheeks.

Almost apologetically, she said, 'You probably don't have the fare I need?'

'No, ma'am, we don't.'

She slipped off her stool and stood up. Relief poured out of Mom like sweat.

R.D., the trucker, reached out for the viper's slender, bare arm, for a reason I doubt he could explain. He was a big man, not slow on the draw. However, when his fingers got to where the girl had been when his brain sparked the impulse to touch, she was somewhere else.

'Touchy,' commented R.D.

'No offence,' she said.

'I've got the *fare* you need,' said the trucker, standing up. He scratched his throat through beard.

'I'm not that thirsty.'

'A man might take that unkindly.'

'If you know such a man, give him my condolences.'

'R.D.,' said Mom. 'Take this outside. I don't want my place busted up.'

'I'm leaving,' said R.D., dropping dollars by his coffee cup and cleaned plate. 'I'll be honoured to see you in the parking lot, Missy Touchy.'

'My name is Geneviève,' she said, 'accent grave on the third e.'

R.D. put on his cowboy hat. The viper darted close to him and lightning-touched his forehead. The effect was something like the Vulcan nerve pinch. The light in his eyes went out. She deftly sat him down at a table, like a floppy rag doll. A yellow toy duck squirted out of the top pocket of his denim jacket and thumped against a plastic ketchup tomato in an unheard of mating ritual.

'I am sorry,' she said to the room. 'I have been driving for a long time and could not face having to cripple this man. I hope you will explain this to him when he wakes up. He'll ache for a few days, but an icepack will help.'

Mom nodded. Pop had his hands out of sight, presumably on a shotgun or a baseball bat.

'For whatever offence my kind has given you in the past, you have my apologies. One thing, though: your sign – the word "viper". I hear it more and more as I travel west, and it strikes me as insulting. "No Vampire Fare on Offer" will convey your message, without provoking less gentle *vipers* than myself.'

She looked mock-sternly at the couple, with a hint of fang. Pop pulled his hold-out pacifier and I tensed, expecting fireworks. He raised a gaudy Day of the Dead crucifix on a lamp-flex, a glowing-eyed Christ crowned by thorny lightbulbs.

'Hello, Jesus,' said Geneviève, then added, to Pop, 'Sorry, sir, but I'm not that kind of girl.'

She did the fast-flit thing again and was at the door.

'Aren't you going to take your trophy?' I asked.

She turned, seeing me for the first time, and lowered her glasses. Green-red eyes like neons. I could see why she kept on the lens caps. Otherwise, she'd pick up a train of mesmerised conquests.

I held up the toy and squeezed. It gave a quack.

'Rubber Duck,' said Mom, with reverence. 'That's his CB handle.'

'He'll need new initials,' I said.

I flew the duck across the room and Geneviève took it out of the air, an angel in the outfield. She made it quack, experimentally. When she laughed, she looked the way Racquel ought to have looked. Not just innocent, but solemn and funny at the same time.

R.D. began moaning in his sleep.

'May I walk you to your car?' I asked.

She thought a moment, sizing me up as a potential geriatric Duckman, and made a snap decision in my favour, the most encouragement I'd had since Kennedy was in the White House.

I made it across the diner to her without collapsing.

I had never had a conversation with a vampire before. She told me straight off she was over 550 years old. She had lived

97

in the human world for hundreds of years before Dracula changed the rules. From her face, I'd have believed her if she said she was born under the shadow of Sputnik and that her ambition was to become one of Roger Vadim's ex-wives.

We stood on Main Street, where her fire-engine-red Plymouth Fury was parked by my Chrysler. The few stores and homes in sight were shuttered up tight, as if an air raid was due. The only place to go in town was the diner and that seemed on the point of closing. I noticed more of those ornamental crucifixes, attached above every door as if it were a religious holiday. Mojave Wells was wary of its new neighbours.

Geneviève was coming from the East and going to the West. Meagre as it was, this was the first place she'd hit in hours that wasn't a government proving ground. She knew nothing about the Anti-Life Equation, Manderley Castle or a viper named Khorda, let alone Racquel Ohlrig.

But she was a vampire and this was all about vampires.

'Why all the questions?' she asked.

I told her I was a detective. I showed my licence, kept up so I could at least do the sub-contract work, and she asked to see my gun. I opened my jacket to show the shoulder-holster. It was the first time I'd worn it in years, and the weight of the Smith & Wesson .38 Special had pulled an ache in my shoulder.

'You are a private eye? Like in the movies.'

Everyone said that. She was no different.

'We have movies in Europe, you know,' she said. The desert wind was trying to get under her scarf, and she was doing things about it with her hands. 'You can't tell me why you're asking questions because you have a client. Is that not so?'

'Not so,' I said. 'I have a man who might think he's a client, but I'm doing this for myself. And a woman who's dead. Really dead.'

I told the whole story, including me and Linda. It was almost confessional. She listened well, asking only the smart questions.

'Why are you here? In… what is the name of this village?'

'Mojave Wells. It calls itself a town.'

We looked up and down the street and laughed. Even the tumbleweeds were taking it easy.

'Out there in the desert,' I explained, 'is Manderley Castle, brought over stone by stone from England. Would you believe it's the wrong house? Back in the '20s, a robber baron named Noah Cross wanted to buy the famous Manderley – the one that later burned down – and sent agents over to Europe to do the deal. They came home with Manderley Castle, another place entirely. Cross still put the jigsaw together, but went into a sulk and sold it back to the original owners, who emigrated to stay out of the War. There was a murder case there in the '40s, nothing to do with me. It was one of those locked-room things, with Borgia poisons and disputed wills. A funny little Chinaman from Hawaii solved it by gathering all the suspects in the library. The place was abandoned until a cult of moon-worshippers squatted it in the '60s, founded a lunatic commune. Now, it's where you go if you want to find the Anti-Life Equation.'

'I don't believe anyone would call themselves that.'

I liked this girl. She had the right attitude. I was also surprised to find myself admitting that. She was a bloodsucking viper, right? Wasn't Racquel worried that she was to be sacrificed to a vampire elder? Someone born in 1416 presumably fitted the description. I wanted to trust her, but that could be part of her trick. I've been had before. Ask anyone.

'I've been digging up dirt on the ALE for a few days,' I said, 'and they aren't that much weirder than the rest of the local kooks. If they have a philosophy, this Khorda makes it all up as he goes along. He cut a folk rock album, *Deathmaster*. I found a copy for ninety-nine cents and feel rooked. "Drinking blood/Feels so good", that sort of thing. People say he's from Europe, but no one knows exactly where. The merry band at the ALE includes a Dragon Lady called Diane LeFanu, who may actually own the castle, and L. Keith Winton, who used to be a pulp writer for *Astounding Stories* but has founded a new religion that involves the faithful giving him all their money.'

'That's not a *new* religion.'

I believed her.

'What will you do now?' she asked.

'This town's dead as far as leads go. Dead as far as anything else, for that matter. I guess I'll have to fall back on the dull old business of going out to the castle and knocking on the front door, asking if they happen to have my wife's daughter in the dungeon. My guess is they'll be long gone. With a body left back in Poodle Springs, they have to figure the law will snoop for them in the end.'

'But we might find something that'll tell us where they are. A clue?'

'"We"?'

'I'm a detective, too. Or have been. Maybe a detective's assistant. I'm in no hurry to get to the Pacific. And you need someone who knows about vampires. You may need someone who knows about other things.'

'Are you offering to be my muscle? I'm not that ancient I can't take care of myself.'

'I *am* that ancient, remember. It's no reflection on you, but a new-born vampire could take you to pieces. And a new-born is more likely to be stupid enough to want to. They're mostly like that Rubber Duck fellow, bursting with impulses and high on their new ability to get what they want. I was like that once myself, but now I'm a wise old lady.'

She quacked the duck at me.

'We take your car,' I said.

Manderley Castle was just what it sounded like. Crenellated turrets, arrow-slit windows, broken battlements, a drawbridge, even a stagnant artificial moat. It was sinking slowly into the sands and the tower was noticeably several degrees out of the vertical. Noah Cross had skimped on foundation concrete. I wouldn't be surprised if the minion who mistook this pile for the real Manderley was down there somewhere, with a divot sticking out of his skull.

We drove across the bridge into the courtyard, home to a VW bus painted with glow-in-the-dark fanged devils, a couple of pick-up trucks with rifle racks, the inevitable Harley-Davidsons and a fleet of customised dune buggies with batwing trimmings and big red-eye lamps.

There was music playing. I recognised Khorda's composition, 'Big Black Bat in a Tall Dark Hat'.

The Anti-Life Equation was home.

I tried to get out of the Plymouth. Geneviève was out of her driver's side door and around (over?) the car in a flash, opening the door for me as if I were her great-grandmama.

'There's a trick to the handle,' she said, making me feel no better.

'If you try and help me out, I'll shoot you.'

She stood back, hands up. Just then, my lungs complained. I coughed a while and red lights went off behind my eyes. I hawked up something glistening and spat it at the ground. There was blood in it.

I looked at Geneviève. Her face was flat, all emotion contained.

It wasn't pity. It was the blood. The smell did things to her personality.

I wiped off my mouth, did my best to shrug, and got out of the car like a champion. I even shut the door behind me, trick-handle or no.

To show how fearless I was, how unafraid of hideous death, I lit a Camel and punished my lungs for showing me up in front of a girl. I filled them with the smoke I'd been fanning their way since I was a kid.

Coffin nails, they called them then.

We fought our aesthetic impulses and went towards the music. I felt I should have brought a mob of Mojave Wells villagers with flaming torches, sharpened stakes and silvered scythes.

'"What a magnificent pair of knockers,"' said Geneviève, nodding at a large square door.

'There's only one,' I said.

'Didn't you see *Young Frankenstein*?'

Though she'd said they had movies in Europe, somehow I didn't believe vipers – vampires, I'd have to get used to calling them if I didn't want Geneviève ripping my throat out one fine night – concerned themselves with dates at the local passion pit. Obviously, the undead read magazines, bought underwear, grumbled about taxes and did crossword puzzles like everyone else. I wondered if she played chess.

She took the knocker and hammered to wake the dead.

Eventually the door was opened by a skinny old bird dressed as an English butler. His hands were knots of arthritis and he could do with a shave.

The music was mercifully interrupted.

'Who is it, George?' boomed a voice from inside the castle.

'Visitors,' croaked George the butler. 'You are visitors, aren't you?'

I shrugged. Geneviève radiated a smile.

The butler was smitten. He trembled with awe.

'Yes,' she said, 'I'm a vampire. And I'm very, very old and very, very thirsty. Now, aren't you going to invite me in? Can't cross the threshold unless you do.'

I didn't know if she was spoofing him.

George creaked his neck, indicating a sandy mat inside the doorway. It was lettered with the word 'WELCOME'.

'That counts,' she admitted. 'More people should have those.' She stepped inside. I didn't need the invite to follow.

George showed us into the big hall. Like all decent cults, the ALE had an altar and thrones for the bigwigs and cold flagstones with the occasional mercy rug for the devoted suckers.

In the blockiest throne sat Khorda, a vampire with curly fangs, the full long-hair-and-tangled-beard hippie look and an electric guitar. He wore a violent purple and orange kaftan, and his chest was covered by bead necklaces hung with diamond-eyed skulls, plastic novelty bats, Austro-Hungarian military medals, inverted crosses, a 'Nixon in '72' button, gold marijuana leaves and a dried human finger. By his side was a wraith-thin vision in velvet I assumed to be Diane LeFanu, who claimed – like a lot of vipers – to be California's earliest vampire settler. I noticed she wore discreet little ruby earplugs.

At the feet of these divines was a crowd of kids, of both varieties, all with long hair and fangs. Some wore white shifts, while others were naked. Some wore joke-shop plastic fangs, while others had real ones. I scanned the congregation, and spotted Racquel at once, eyes a red daze, kneeling on stone with her shift tucked under her, swaying her ripe upper body in time to the music Khorda had stopped playing.

I admitted this was too easy. I started thinking about the case again, taking it apart in my mind and jamming the pieces together in new ways. Nothing made sense, but that was hardly breaking news at this end of the century.

Hovering like the Wizard of Oz between the throne-dais and the worshipper-space was a fat living man in a 1950s suit and golf hat. I recognised L. Keith Winton, author of 'Robot Rangers of the Gamma Nebula' (1946) and other works of serious literature, including *Plasmatics: The New Communion* (1952), founding text of the Church of Immortology. If ever there was a power-behind-the-throne bird, this was he.

'We've come for Racquel Loring Ohlrig,' announced Geneviève. I should probably have said that.

'No one of that name dwells among us,' boomed Khorda. He had a big voice.

'I see her there,' I said, pointing.

'Sister Red Rose,' said Khorda.

He stuck out his arm and gestured. Racquel stood. She did not move like herself. Her teeth were not a joke. She had real fangs. They fitted badly in her mouth, making it look like an ill-healed red wound. Her red eyes were puffy.

'You turned her,' I said, anger in my gut.

'Sister Red Rose has been elevated to the eternal.'

Geneviève's hand was on my shoulder.

I thought of Linda, bled empty in her pool, a spike in her head. I wanted to burn this castle down, and sew the ground with garlic.

'I am Geneviève Dieudonné,' she announced, formally.

'Welcome, Lady Elder,' said the LeFanu woman. Her eyes held no welcome for Geneviève. She made a gesture, which unfolded membrane-like velvet sleeves. 'I am Diane LeFanu. And this is Khorda, the Deathmaster.'

Geneviève squared up against the guru viper.

'General Iorga, is it not? Late of the Carpathian Guard. We met in 1888, at the palace of Prince Consort Dracula. Do you remember?'

Khorda/Iorga was not happy.

I realised he was wearing a wig and a false beard. He might have immortality, but was well past youth. I saw him as a tubby, ridiculous fraud. He was one of those elders who had been among Dracula's toadies, but was lost in a world without a King Vampire. Even for California, he was a sad soul.

'Racquel,' I said. 'It's me. Your father wants…'

She spat hissing red froth.

'It would be best if this new-born were allowed to leave with us,' Geneviève said, not to Khorda but Winton. 'There's the small matter of a murder charge.'

Winton's plump, bland, pink face wobbled. He glared at Khorda. The guru trembled on his throne, and boomed without words.

'Murder, Khorda?' asked Winton. 'Murder? Who told you we could afford murder?'

'None was done,' said Khorda/Iorga.

I wanted to skewer him with something. But I went beyond anger. He was too afraid of Winton – not a person you'd immediately take as a threat, but clearly the top dog at the ALE – to lie.

'Take the girl,' Winton said to me.

Racquel howled in rage and despair. I didn't know if she was the same person we had come for. As I understood it, some vampires changed entirely when they turned, burned out their previous memories and became sad blanks, reborn with dreadful thirsts and the beginnings of a mad cunning.

'If she's a killer, we don't want her,' said Winton. 'Not yet.'

I approached Racquel. The other cultists shrank away from her. Her face shifted, bloating and smoothing as if flatworms were passing just under her skin. Her teeth were ridiculously expanded, fat pebbles of sharp bone. Her lips were torn and split.

She hissed as I reached out to touch her.

Had this girl, in the throes of turning, battened on her mother, on Linda, and gone too far, taken more than her human mind had intended, glutting herself until her viper thirst was assuaged?

JOHNNY ALUCARD

I saw the picture only too well. I tried to fit it with what Junior had told me.

He had sworn Racquel was innocent.

But his daughter had never been innocent, not as a warm person and not now as a new-born vampire.

Geneviève stepped close to Racquel and managed to slip an arm round her. She cooed in the girl's ear, coaxing her to come, replacing the Deathmaster in her mind.

Racquel took her first steps. Geneviève encouraged her. Then Racquel stopped as if she'd hit an invisible wall. She looked to Khorda/Iorga, hurt and betrayal in her eyes, and to Winton, with that pleading moué I knew well. Racquel was still herself, still trying to wheedle love from unworthy men, still desperate to survive through her developing wiles.

Her attention was caught by a noise. Her nose wrinkled, quizzically.

Geneviève had taken out her rubber duck and quacked it.

'Come on, Racquel,' she said, as if to a happy dog. 'Nice quacky-quacky. Do you want it?'

She quacked again.

Racquel attempted a horrendous smile. A baby-tear of blood showed on her cheek.

We took our leave of the Anti-Life Equation.

Junior was afraid of his daughter. And who wouldn't be?

I was back in Poodle Springs, not a place I much cared to be. Junior's wife had stormed out, enraged that this latest drama didn't revolve around her. Their house was decorated in the expensive-but-ugly mock Spanish manner, and called itself ranch-style though there were no cattle or crops on the grounds.

Geneviève sat calmly on Junior's long grey couch. She fitted in like a piece of Carrera marble at a Tobacco Road yard sale. I was helping myself to Scotch.

Father and daughter looked at each other.

Racquel wasn't such a fright now. Geneviève had driven her here, following my lead. Somehow, on the journey, the

elder vampire had imparted grooming tips to the new-
born, helping her through the shock of turning. Racquel
had regular-sized fangs, and the red in her eyes was just
a tint. Outside, she had been experimenting with her
newfound speed, moving her hands so fast they seemed not
to be there.

But Junior was terrified. I had to break the spell.

'It's like this,' I said, setting it out. 'You both killed Linda.
The difference is that one of you brought her back.'

Junior covered his face and fell to his knees.

Racquel stood over him.

'Racquel has been turning for weeks, joining up with that
crowd in the desert. She felt them taking her mind away,
making her part of a harem or a slave army. She needed
someone strong in her corner, and Daddy didn't cut it. So
she went to the strongest person in her life, and made her
stronger. She just didn't get to finish the job before the Anti-
Life Equation came to her house. She called you, Junior, just
before she went under, became part of their family. When
you got to the house, it was just as you said. Linda was at the
bottom of the swimming pool. She'd gone there to turn. You
didn't even lie to me. She was dead. You took a mallet and a
spike – what was it from, the tennis net? – and made her truly
dead. Did you tell yourself you did it for her, so she could be
at peace? Or was it because you didn't want to be in a town
– a world – with a *stronger* Linda Loring? She was a fighter. I
bet she fought you.'

There were deep scratches on his wrists, like the rips in his
shirt I had noticed that night. If I were a gather-the-suspects-
in-the-library type of dick, I would have spotted that as a clue
straight off.

Junior sobbed a while. Then, when nobody killed him,
he uncurled and looked about, with the beginnings of an
unattractive slyness.

'It's legal, you know,' he said. 'Linda was dead.'

Geneviève's face was cold. I knew California law did not
recognise the state of undeath. Yet. There were enough
vampire lawyers on the case to get that changed soon.

'That's for the cops,' I said. 'Fine people. You've always been impressed with their efficiency and courtesy.'

Junior was white under the tear-streaks. He might not take a murder fall on this, but Tokyo and Riyadh weren't going to like the attention the story would get. That was going to have a transformative effect on his position in Ohlrig Oil and Copper. And the PSPD would find something to nail him with: making false or incomplete statements, mutilating a corpse for profit (no more alimony), contemptible gutlessness.

Another private eye might have left him with Racquel.

She stood over her father, fists swollen by the sharp new nails extruding inside, dripping her own blood – the blood that she had made her mother drink – onto the mock-mission-style carpet.

Geneviève was beside her, with the duck.

'Come with me, Racquel,' she said. 'Away from the dark red places.'

Days later, in a bar on Cahuenga just across from the building where my office used to be, I was coughing over a shot and a Camel.

They found me.

Racquel was her new self, flitting everywhere, flirting with men of all ages, sharp eyes fixed on the pulses in their necks and the blue lines in their wrists.

Geneviève ordered bull's blood.

She made a face.

'I'm used to fresh from the bull,' she said. 'This is rancid.'

'We're getting live piglets from next week,' said the bartender. 'The straps are already fitted, and we have the neck-spigots on order.'

'See,' Geneviève told me. 'We're here to stay. We're a market. Consumers.'

I coughed some more.

'You could get something done about that,' she said, softly.

I knew what she meant. I could become a vampire. Who

knows: if Linda had made it, I might have been tempted. As it was, I was too old to change.

'You remind me of someone,' she said. 'Another detective. In another country, a century ago.'

'Did he catch the killer and save the girl?'

An unreadable look passed over her face. 'Yes,' she said, 'that's exactly what he did.'

'Good for him.'

I drank. The Scotch tasted of blood. I could never get used to drinking that.

According to the newspapers, there'd been a raid on the castle in the desert. General Iorga and Diane LeFanu were up on a raft of abduction, exploitation and murder charges; with most of the murder victims undead enough to recite testimony in favour of their killers, they would stay in court forever. No mention was made of L. Keith Winton, though I had noticed a storefront on Hollywood Boulevard displaying nothing but a stack of Immortology tracts. Outside, fresh-faced new-born vampires smiled under black parasols and invited passersby in for 'a blood test'. Picture this: followers who are going to give you all their money *and* live forever. And they said Dracula was dead.

'Racquel will be all right,' Geneviève assured me. 'She's so good at this that she frightens me. She won't make get again in a hurry.'

I looked at the girl, surrounded by eager warm bodies. She'd use them up by the dozen. I saw the last of Linda in her, and regretted that there was none of me.

'What about you?' I asked Geneviève.

'I've seen the Pacific. Can't drive much further. I'll stay around for a while, maybe get a job. I used to know a lot about being a doctor. Perhaps I'll try to get into med school, and requalify. I'm tired of jokes about leeches. Then again, I have to unlearn so much. Mediaeval knowledge is a handicap, you know.'

I put my licence on the bar.

'You could get one like it,' I said.

She took off her glasses. Her eyes were still startling.

'This was my last case, Geneviève. I got the killer and I saved the girl. It's been a long goodbye and it's over. I've met my own killers, in bottles and soft-packs of twenty. Soon, they'll finish me and I'll be sleeping the big sleep. There's not much more I can do for people. There are going to be a lot more like Racquel. Those kids at the castle in the desert. The customers our bartender is expecting next week. The suckers drawn into Winton's nets. Some are going to need you. And some are going to be real vipers, which means other folk are going to need you to protect them from the worst they can do. You're good, sweetheart. You could do good. There, that's my speech over.'

She dipped a fingertip in her glass of congealing blood and licked it clean, thinking.

'You might have an idea there, gumshoe.'

I drank to her.

PART TWO

———————◆———————

ANDY WARHOL'S DRACULA

ANNO DRACULA 1978-79

1

As Nancy snuffed, her blood curdled. The taste of vile scabs flooded his mouth. He pushed her away, detaching fangs from her worn wounds. Ropes of bloody spittle hung from her neck to his maw. He wiped his mouth on his wrist, breaking their liquid link. A last electric thrill shuddered, arcing between them. Her heart stopped.

He had pulled her backward onto the bed, holding her down to him as he worked at her throat, her hands feebly scrabbling his sides. Empty, she was deadweight on top of him. He was uncomfortably aware of the quilt of garbage they lay on: magazines, bent spoons, hypodermic needles, used Kleenex, ripped and safety-pinned clothes, banknotes, congealed sandwiches, weeks of uneaten complimentary mints. A package of singles – Sid's 'My Way' – had broken under them, turning the much-stained mattress into a fakir's bed of nails. Vinyl shards stabbed his unbroken skin.

Johnny Pop was naked but for leopard-pattern briefs and socks, and the jewellery. Prizing his new clothes too much to get them gory, he had neatly folded and placed the suit and shirt on a chair well away from the bed. His face and chest were sticky with blood and other discharges.

As the red rush burst in his eyes and ears, his senses flared, more acute by a dozenfold. Outside, in the iced velvet October night, police sirens sounded like the wailings of the bereaved mothers of Europe. Distant shots burst as if they were fired in the room, stabs of noise inside his skull. Blobby TV light painted neon a cityscape across ugly wallpaper, populated by psychedelic cockroaches.

He tasted the ghosts of the Chelsea Hotel: drag queens and vampire killers, junkies and pornographers, artists and freaks, visionaries and wasters. Pressing into his mind, they tried to make of his undead body a channel through which they could claw their way back to this plane of existence. Their voices shrieked, clamouring for attention. Cast out of Manhattan, they lusted for restoration to their paved paradise.

Though his throat protested, Johnny forced himself to swallow. Nancy's living blood had scarcely been of better quality than this dead filth. Americans fouled their bodies. Her habits would have killed her soon, even if she hadn't invited a vampire into Room 100. He didn't trouble himself with guilt. Some people were looking for their vampires, begging all their lives for death. His *nosferatu* hold upon the world was tenuous. He could only remain on sufferance. Without the willing warm, he would starve and die. They fed him. They were to blame for him.

Dead blood, heavy with tuinol and dilaudid, smote his brain, washing away the ghosts. He had to be careful; this city was thronged with the truly dead, loitering beyond the ken of the warm, desperate for attention from those who could perceive them. When he was feeding, they crowded around. Having been dead, however briefly, he was a beacon for them.

He yowled and threw the meat-sack off him. He sat up in the bed, nerves drawn taut, and looked at the dead girl. She was ghost-white flesh in black underwear. The flowering neck wound was the least of the marks on her. Scarifications criss-crossed her concave stomach. Pulsing slits opened like gills in her sides, leaking the last of her. The marks of his talons, they were dead mouths, beseeching more kisses from him.

Since arriving in America, he'd been careful to take only those who asked for it, who already lived like ghosts. There were relatively few vampires here. Drained corpses attracted attention. Already, he knew, he'd been noticed. To prosper, he must practise the skills of his father-in-darkness. First, to hide; then, to master.

The Father was always with him, first among the ghosts. He watched over Johnny and kept him from real harm.

Sid, Belsen-thin but for his Biafra-bloat belly, was slumped in a ratty chair in front of blurry early morning television. He looked at Johnny and at Nancy, incapable of focusing. Earlier, he'd shot up through his eyeball. Colours slid and flashed across his bare, scarred-and-scabbed chest and arms. His head was a skull in a spiky fright-wig, huge eyes swarming as *Secret Squirrel* reflected on the screen of his face. The boy tried to laugh but could only shake. A silly little knife, not even silver, was loosely held in his left hand.

Johnny pressed the heels of his fists to his forehead, and jammed his eyes shut. Blood-red light shone through the skin curtains of his eyelids. He had felt this before. It wouldn't last more than a few seconds. Hell raged in his brain. Then, as if a black fist had struck him in the gullet, peristaltic movement forced fluid up through his throat. He opened his mouth, and a thin squirt of black liquid spattered across the carpet and against the wall.

'Magic spew,' said Sid, in amazement.

The impurities were gone. Johnny was on a pure blood-high now. He contained all of Nancy's short life. She had been an all-American girl. She had given him everything.

He considered the boy in the chair and the girl on the bed, the punks. Their tribes were at war, his and theirs. Clothes were their colours, Italian suits versus safety-pinned PVC pants. This session at the Chelsea had been a truce that turned into a betrayal, a rout, a massacre. The Father was proud of Johnny's strategy.

Sid looked at Nancy's face. Her eyes were open, showing only veined white. He gestured with his knife, realising something had happened. At some point in the evening, Sid had stuck his knife into himself a few times. The tang of his rotten blood filled the room. Johnny's fangs slid from their gum-sheaths, but he had no more hunger yet. He was too full.

He thought of the punks as Americans, but Sid was English. A musician, though he couldn't really play his guitar. A singer, though he could only shout.

America was a strange new land. Stranger than Johnny had imagined in the Old Country, stranger than he could have imagined. If he drank more blood, he would soon be an American. Then he would be beyond fear, untouchable. It was what the Father wanted for him.

He rolled the corpse off his shins and cleaned himself like a cat, contorting his supple back and neck, extending his foot-long tongue to lick off the last of the bloodstains. He unglued triangles of vinyl from his body and threw them away. Satisfied, he got off the bed and pulled on crusader white pants, immodestly tight around crotch and rump, loose as a sailor's below the knee. The dark-purple shirt settled on his back and chest, sticking to him where his saliva was still wet. He rattled the cluster of gold chains and medallions – Transylvanian charms, badges of honour and conquest – that hung in the gap between his hand-sized collar-points.

With the white jacket, lined in blood-red silk, Johnny was a blinding apparition. He didn't need a strobe to shine in the dark. Sid raised his knife-hand, to cover his eyes. The boy's reaction was better than any mirror.

'Punk sucks,' said Johnny, inviting a response.

'Disco's stupid,' Sid sneered back.

Sid was going to get in trouble. Johnny had to make a slave of the boy, to keep himself out of the story.

He found an unused needle on the bed. Pinching the nipple-like bulb, he stuck the needle into his wrist, spearing the vein perfectly. He let the bulb go and a measure of his blood – of Nancy's? – filled the glass phial. He unstuck himself. The tiny wound was invisibly healed by the time he'd smeared away the bead of blood and licked his thumbprint. He tossed the Syrette to Sid, who knew exactly what to do with it, jabbing it into an old arm-track and squirting. Vampire blood slid into Sid's system, something between a virus and a drug. Johnny felt the hook going into Sid's brain, and fed him some line.

Sid stood, momentarily invincible, teeth sharpening, eyes reddened, ears bat-flared, movements swifter. Johnny shared his sense of power, almost paternally. The vampire buzz wouldn't last long, but Sid would be a slave as long as he lived, which was unlikely to be forever. To become *nosferatu*, you had to give and receive blood; for centuries, most mortals had merely been giving; here, a fresh compact between the warm and the undead was invented.

Johnny nodded towards the empty thing on the bed. Nobody's blood was any good to her now. He willed the command through the line, through the hook, into Sid's brain. The boy, briefly possessed, leaped across the room, landing on his knees on the bed, and stuck his knife into the already dead girl, messing up the wounds on her throat, tearing open her skin in dozens of places. As he slashed, Sid snarled, black fangs splitting his gums.

Johnny let himself out of the room.

2

He stepped out of the Chelsea Hotel onto the sidewalk of West 23rd Street and tasted New York. It was the dead time, the thick hours before dawn, when all but the most committed night owls were home abed, or at least crashed out on a floor, their blood sluggish with coffee, cigarettes or drugs. This was the vampire afternoon. Johnny understood how alone he was. There were other vampires in this city – he was almost ready to seek them out – but none like him, of his line.

America was vast, bloated with rich, fatty blood. The fresh country supported only a few ticks that tentatively poked prosboces through thick hide, sampling without gorging. By comparison, Johnny was a hungry monster. Minutes after taking Nancy, he could have fed again, and again. He had to take more than he needed. He could handle dozens of warm bodies a night without bursting, without choking on the ghosts. Eventually, he would make children-in-darkness, slaves to serve him, to shield him. He must pass on the bloodline of the Father. But not yet.

He hadn't intended to come to this city of towers, with its moat of running water. His plan was to stick to the film people he had hooked up with in the Old Country and go to fabled Hollywood on the Pacific. But there was a mix-up at JFK and he was detained in Immigration while the rest of the company, American passports brandished like protective banners, were waved on to catch connecting flights to Los Angeles or San Francisco. He was stuck at the airport in a crowd of overeager petitioners, dark-skinned and warm, as dawn edged threateningly closer. The Father was with him then, as he slipped into a men's room and bled a Canadian flight attendant who gave him a come-on, invigorating himself with something new and wild. Buzzing with fresh blood, first catch of this new land, he concentrated his powers of fascination to face down the officials who barred his way. It was beneath him to bribe those who could be overpowered by force of will.

America was disorienting. To survive, he must adapt swiftly. The pace of change in this century was far more rapid than the glacial shifts of the long years the Father spent in his Carpathian fastness. Johnny would have to surpass the Father to keep ahead, but bloodline would tell. Though of an ancient line, he was a twentieth-century creature, turned only thirty-four years earlier, taken into the dark before he was formed as a living man. In Europe, he had been a boy, hiding in the shadows, waiting. Here, in this bright America, he could fulfil his potential. People took him for a young man, not a child.

Johnny Pop had arrived.

He knew he had been noticed. He was working hard to fit in, recognising how gauche he had been a few short weeks ago. On his first nights in New York, he had made mistakes. Blood in the water excited the sharks.

Someone stood on the corner, watching him. Two black men in long leather coats. One wore dark glasses despite the hour, the other had a slim-brimmed hat with a tiny feather in the band. Not vampires, but there was something of the predator about them. They were well armed. Silver shoe-buckles and buttons, coats loose over guns. And their bodies were weapons, a finished blade, an arrow shaft. From inside his coat, the black man in sunglasses produced a dark knife. Not silver, but polished hardwood.

Johnny tensed, ready to fight and kill. He had just fed. He was at his strongest.

The knifeman smiled. He balanced his weapon by its point, and tapped his forehead with its hilt, a warrior salute. He would not attack yet. His presence was an announcement, a warning. He was showing himself. This man had seen Johnny before he was seen. His night skills were sharp.

Then, the knifeman and his partner were gone. They seemed to disappear, to step into a shadow even Johnny's night eyes could not penetrate.

He suppressed a shudder. This city was not yet his jungle and he was exposed here – out on the street in a white suit that shone like a beacon – as he had not been in the Old Country.

The black men should have destroyed him now. When they had a chance. Johnny would do his best to see they did not get another.

It was time to move on, to join the crowd.

A mustard-yellow taxi cruised along the street, emerging like a dragon from an orange-pink groundswell of steam. Johnny hailed the cab and slid into its cage-like interior. The seat was criss-crossed with duct tape, battlefield dressings on a fatal wound. The driver, a gaunt white man with a baggy military jacket, glanced instinctively at the rear-view mirror, expecting to lock eyes with his fare. Johnny saw surprise in the young man's face as he took in the reflection of an empty hack. He twisted to look into the dark behind him and saw Johnny there, understanding at once what he had picked up.

'You have a problem?' Johnny asked.

After a moment, the taxi driver shrugged.

'Hell, no. A lot of guys won't even take spooks, but I'll take anyone. They all come out at night.'

Behind the driver's gun-sight eyes, Johnny saw jungle twilight, purpled by napalm blossoms. He heard the reports of shots fired years ago. His nostrils stung with dead cordite.

Uncomfortable, he broke the connection.

Johnny told the driver to take him to Studio 54.

3

Even now, this late in the night, a desperate line lingered outside the club. Their breath frosted in a cloud and they stamped unfashionably shoed feet against the cold. Losers with no chance, they would cajole and plead with Burns and Stu, the hard-faced bouncers, but never see the velvet rope lifted. An invisible sign was on their foreheads. Worse than dead, they were boring.

Johnny paid off the cab with sticky bills lifted from Nancy's purse, and stood on the sidewalk, listening to the throb of the music from inside. 'Pretty Baby', Blondie. Debbie Harry's living-dead voice called to him.

The taxi did not move off. Was the driver hoping for another fare from among these damned? No, he was fixing Johnny in his mind. A man without a reflection should be remembered.

'See you again soon, Jack,' said the white man.

Like the black men outside the Chelsea, the taxi driver was a danger. Johnny had marked him. It was good to know who would come for you, to be prepared. The white man's name was written on his licence just as his purpose was stamped on his face. It was Travis. In Vietnam, he had learned to look monsters in the face, even in the mirror.

The cab snarled to life and prowled off.

Moving with the music, Johnny crossed the sidewalk towards the infernal doorway, reaching out with his mind to reconnect with the bouncers, muscular guys with Tom of Finland leather caps and jackets. Burns was a moonlighting cop with sad eyes and bruises, Stu a trust-fund kid with his own monster father in his head; Johnny's hooks were in both of them, played out on the thinnest of threads. They were not, would never be, his get, but they were his. First, he would have warm chattels; get would come later.

He enjoyed the wails and complaints from the losers as he breezed past the line, radiating an 'open sesame' they could never manage. Stu clicked the studded heels of his motorcycle boots and saluted, fingers aligned with the peak of his black-leather forage cap with Austro-Hungarian precision. Burns smartly lifted the rope, the little sound of the hook being detached from the eye exciting envious sighs, and stood aside. To savour the moment, Johnny paused in the doorway, knowing the spill of light from inside made his suit shine like an angelic raiment, and surveyed those who would never get in. Their eyes showed such desperation that he almost pitied them.

Two weeks ago, he had been among them, drawn to the light but kept away from the flame. Like some older creatures of his kind, he could not force his way into a place until he had been invited across the threshold. Then, his clothes – found in a suitcase chosen at random from the carousel at the airport – had not been good. Being *nosferatu* was unusual enough to get him attention. Steve Rubell, passing the door, took note of Johnny's sharp, beautiful face. Possessed of the knack of seeing himself as others saw him, Johnny understood the owner-manager was intrigued by the vampire boy on his doorstep. But Shining Lucifer himself couldn't get into 54 with a Bicentennial shirt, cowboy boots and black hair flattened like wet sealskin to his skull.

When he came back, the next night, he wore clothes that fitted: a Halston suit – black outside in the dark, with a violet weave that showed under the lights – and a Ralph Lauren shirt with fresh bloodstains across the polo player. They still smelled faintly of their previous owner, Tony from Brooklyn. The bouncers didn't even need to check with Steve to let Johnny in. He took the opportunity, later that night in the back rooms, to lay a tiny smear of his blood on them both, apparently a token of gratitude, actually a sigil of ownership. Johnny was saving them for later, knowing they would be needed.

As he ducked past the curtains and slid into 54, Johnny felt Tony's ghost in his limbs. He had taken much from Tony Manero, whom he had exsanguinated on Brooklyn Bridge. From the boy, he had caught the blood rhythms that matched the music of the month. Tony had been a dancer; Johnny had inherited that from him, along with his fluffed-up but flared-back hairstyle and clothes that were not just a protective cover but a style, a display.

Tony was with him most nights now, a ghost. The kid had never made it to 54, but he'd been better than Brooklyn, good enough for Manhattan. Johnny thought Tony, whose empty carcass he had weighted and tossed off the bridge, would be happy that some of him at least had made it in the real city. When the blood was still fresh in him, Johnny had followed its track, back to Tony's apartment, and slipped in – unnoticed by the kid's family, even the fallen priest – to take away his wardrobe, the night-clothes that were now his armour.

He let the music take him, responding to it with all his blood. Nancy's ghost protested, making puking motions at the sound of the disco despised by all true punks. By taking her, Johnny had won a great victory in the style wars. He liked killing punks. No one noticed when they were gone. They were all committing slow suicide anyway; that was the point, for there was no future. To love disco was to want to live forever, to aspire to an immortality of consumption. Punks didn't believe in anything beyond death, and loved nothing, not even themselves.

He wondered what would happen to Sid.

A man in the moon puppet, spooning coke up his nose, beamed down from the wall, blessing the throng with a 1978 benediction. As Johnny stepped onto the illuminated floor and strutted through the dancers, his suit shone like white flame. He had the beat with his every movement. Even his heart pulsed in time to the music. He smiled as he recognised the song, fangs bright as neons under the strobe, eyes red glitter balls. This was the music he had made his own, the song that meant the most of all the songs.

'Staying Alive', The Bee Gees.

In its chorus, he heard the wail of the warm as they died under his kisses, ah-ah-ah-ah, staying alive. In its lyric, he recognised himself: a woman's man with no time to talk.

His dancing cleared a circle.

It was like feeding. Without even taking blood, he drew

in the blood of the crowd to himself, loosening the ghosts of those who danced with him from their bodies. Tulpas stretched out through mouths and noses and attached to him like ectoplasmic straws. As he danced, he sucked with his whole body, tasting minds and hearts, outshining them all. No one came near, to challenge him. The Father was proud of him.

For the length of the song, he *was* alive.

4

'Gee, who is that boy?' asked Andy, evenly. 'He is fantastic.'

Penelope was used to the expression. It was one of Andy's few adjectives. Everyone and everything was either 'fantastic' or 'a bore' or something similar, always with an elongated vowel early on. All television was 'fa-antastic'; World War II was 'a bo-ore'. Vintage cookie tins were 'si-imply wonderful'; income taxes were 'ra-ather old'. Famous people were 've-ery interesting'; living daylight was 'pra-actically forgotten'.

She turned to look down on the dance floor. They were sitting up on the balcony, above the churning masses, glasses of chilled blood on the table between them, at once shadowed enough to be mysterious and visible enough to be recognisable. There was no point in coming to Studio 54 unless it was to be seen, to be noticed. At tomorrow's sunset, when they both rose from their day's sleep, it would be Penny's duty to go through the columns, reading out any mentions of their appearances, so Andy could cluck and crow over what was said about him, and lament that so much was left out.

It took her a moment to spot the object of Andy's attention.

For once, he was right. The dancer in the white suit was fantastic. Fa-antastic, even. She knew at once that the boy was like Andy and her, *nosferatu*. His style was American, but she scented a whiff of European gravemould. This was no new-born, no *nouveau*, but an experienced creature, practised in his dark skills. Only a vampire with many nights behind him could seem so *young*.

It had to happen. She was not the first to come here. She had known an invasion was inevitable. America could not hold out forever. She had not come here to be unique, but to be away from her kind, from her former lives. Though she had inevitably hooked up with Andy, she did not want to be sucked back into the world of the undead. But what she wanted meant very little any more, which was as it should be. Whatever came, she would accept. It was her duty, her burden.

She looked back at Andy. An American vampire icon. He'd died in 1968, shot by the demented Valerie Solanas... but rallied in hospital, mysteriously infused with new blood, and come out of his coma as a walking, thirsty ghost.

It took sharp senses indeed to distinguish his real enthusiasms from his feigned ones. He had worked hard – and it did not do to underestimate this languid scarecrow's capacity for hard work – to become as inexpressive as he was, to cultivate what passed in America for a lack of accent. His chalk-dusted cheeks and cold mouth gave nothing away. His wig was silver tonight, thick and stiff as a knot of fox-tails. His suit was quiet, dark and Italian, worn with a plain tie.

They both wore goggle-like black glasses to shield their eyes from the club's frequent strobes. But, unlike some of his earlier familiars, Penny made no real attempt to look like him.

She watched the dancer spin, hip cocked, arm raised in a disco heil, white jacket flaring to show scarlet lining, a snarl of concentration on his cold lovely face.

How could Andy not be interested in another of the undead? Especially one like this.

At least the dancing boy meant the night wasn't a complete wash-out. It had been pretty standard so far: two openings, three parties and a reception. One big disappointment: Andy had hoped to bring Miz Lillian, the President's mama, to the reception for Princess Ashraf, twin sister of the Shah of Iran, but the White House got wind and scuttled the plan. Andy's fall-back date, Lucie Arnaz, was hardly a substitute, and

JOHNNY ALUCARD

Penny was forced to make long conversation with the poor girl – of whom she had never heard – while Andy did the silent act most people thought of as deliberate mystification but which was actually simple sulking. The Princess, sharp ornament of one of the few surviving vampire ruling houses, was not exactly on her finest fettle, either – preoccupied by the troubles of her absolutist brother, who was currently back home surrounded by Mohammedan fanatics screaming for his impalement.

In the car between Bianca Jagger's party at the Tea Rooms and L.B. Jeffries's opening at the Photographers' Gallery, Paloma Picasso rather boringly went on about the tonic properties of human blood as face cream. Penny would have told the warm twit how stupid she was being about matters of which she plainly knew nothing, but Andy was frozen enough already without his faithful vampire companion teeing off someone so famous – Penny wasn't sure what exactly the painter's daughter was famous *for* – she was sure to get his name in *Vanity Fair*. At Bianca's, Andy thought he'd spotted David Bowie with Catherine Deneuve, but it turned out to be a far less interesting couple. Another disappointment.

Bob Colacello, editor of *Inter/VIEW* and Andy's connection with the Princess, wittered on about how well she was bearing up, and how she was trying to sell Andy on committing to an exhibition in the new museum of modern art the Shah had endowed in Teheran. Penny could tell Andy was chilling on the idea, sensing – quite rightly – that it would not do well to throw in with someone on the point of losing everything. Andy elaborately ignored Bob, and that meant everyone else did too. He had been delighted to learn from Penny what 'sent to Coventry' meant and redoubled his use of that ancient schoolboy torture. There was a hurt desperation in Bob's chatter, but it was all his own fault and she didn't feel a bit sorry for him.

At the Photographers', surrounded by huge blow-ups of war orphans and devastated Asian villages, Andy got on one of his curiosity jags and started quizzing her about Oscar Wilde. What had he been like, had he really been amusing all the time, had he been frightened when the wolves gathered, how much had he earned, how famous had he really been, would he have been recognised everywhere he went? After nearly a hundred years, she remembered Wilde less well than many others she had known in the '80s. Like her, the poet was one of the first modern generation of new-born vampires. He was one of those who turned but didn't last more than a decade, eaten up by disease carried over from warm life. She didn't like to think of contemporaries she had outlived. But Andy insisted, nagging, and she dutifully coughed up anecdotes and aphorisms to keep him contented. She told Andy that he reminded her of Oscar, which was certainly true in some ways. Penny dreaded being recategorised from 'fascinating' to 'a bore', with the consequent casting into the outer darkness.

All her life, all her afterlife, had been spent by her own choice in the shadows cast by a succession of tyrants. She supposed she was punishing herself for her sins. Even Andy had noticed; in the Factory, she was called 'Penny Penance' or 'Penny Penitent'. However, besotted with titles and honours, he usually introduced her to outsiders as 'Penelope Churchward, Lady Godalming'. She had never been married to Lord Godalming (or, indeed, anyone), but Arthur Holmwood had been her father-in-darkness, and some vampire aristos did indeed pass on titles to their get.

She was not the first English rose in Andy's entourage. She had been told she resembled the model Jane Forth, who had been in Andy's movies. Penny knew she had only become Andy's Girl of the Year after Catherine Guinness left the Factory to become Lady Neidpath. She had an advantage over Andy's earlier debs, though: she was never going to get old. As Girl of the Year, it was her duty to be Andy's companion of the night and to handle much of the organisational and social business of the Factory, of Andy Warhol Enterprises, Incorporated. It was something she was used to, from her Victorian years as an 'Angel in the Home' to her nights as last governess of the House of Dracula. She could even keep track of the money.

She sipped her blood, decanted from some bar worker who was 'really' an actor or a model. Andy left his drink untouched, as usual. He didn't trust blood that showed up in a glass. Nobody ever saw him feeding. Penny wondered if he was an abstainer. Just now, the red pinpoints in his dark glasses were fixed. He was still watching the dancer.

The vampire in the white suit hooked her attention too.

For a moment, she was sure it was *him*, come back yet again, young and lethal, intent on murderous revenge.

She breathed the name, 'Dracula.'

Andy's sharp ears picked it up, even through the dreadful guff that passed for music these days. It was one of the few names guaranteed to provoke his interest.

Andy prized her for her connection to the late King Vampire. Penny had been at the Palazzo Otranto at the end. She was one of the few who knew the truth about the last hours of *il principe*, though she jealously kept that anecdote to herself. So far as she knew, only Katie Reed and the Dieudonné chit shared the story. The three of them had earned scars that wouldn't show on their pale vampire skins, the lash-marks of Vlad Bloody Dracula, dastard and dictator, and stalwart, dauntless, forgiving, gone-and-not-coming-back Charles Bloody Beauregard.

'The boy looks like him,' she said. 'He might be the Count's get, or of his bloodline. Most vampires Dracula made came to look like him. He spread his doppelgangers throughout the world.'

Andy nodded, liking the idea.

The dancer had Dracula's red eyes, his aquiline nose, his full mouth. But he was clean-shaven and had a bouffant of teased black hair, like a Broadway actor or a teenage idol. His features were as Roman as Romanian.

Penny had understood on their first meeting that Andy Warhol didn't want to be just a vampire. He wanted to be *the* vampire, Dracula. Even before his death and resurrection, his coven had called him 'Drella': half Dracula, half Cinderella. It was meant to be cruel: he was the Count of the night hours, but at dawn he changed back into the girl who cleared away the ashes.

'Find out who he is, Penny,' Andy said. 'We should meet him. He's going to be famous.'

She had no doubt of that.

5

Flushed from dancing and still buzzed with Nancy's blood, Johnny moved on to the commerce of the night. The first few times he had set up his shop in men's rooms, like the dealers he was rapidly putting out of business. Spooked by all the mirrors, he shifted from striplit johns to the curtained back rooms where the other action was. All the clubs had such places.

In the dark room, he felt the heat of the busy bodies and tasted ghosts, expelled on yo-yo strings of ectoplasm during orgasm. He threaded his way through writhing limbs to take up his habitual spot in a leather armchair. He slipped off his jacket, draping it carefully over the back of his seat, and popped his cufflinks, rolling his sleeves up to his elbows. His white lower arms and hands shone in the dark.

Burns, on a break, came to him first. The hook throbbed in his brain, jones throbbing in his bones like a slow drumbeat. The first shot of drac had been free, but now it was a hundred dollars a pop. The bouncer handed Johnny a crisp C-note. With the nail of his little finger, Johnny jabbed a centimetre-long cut in the skin of his left arm. Burns knelt down in front of the chair and licked away the welling blood. He began to suckle the wound, and Johnny pushed him away.

There was a plea in the man's eyes. The drac jolt was in him, but it wasn't enough. He had the strength and the senses, but also the hunger.

'Go bite someone,' Johnny said, laughing.

The bouncer's hook was in deep. He loved Johnny and hated him, but he'd do what he said. For Burns, hell would be to be expelled, to be denied forever the taste.

A girl in a shimmering fringed dress replaced the bouncer. She had violent orange hair.

'Is it true?' she asked.

'Is what true?'

'That you can make people like you?'

He smiled, sharply. He could make people *love* him.

'A hundred dollars and you can find out,' he said.

'I'm game.'

She was very young, a child. She had to scrape together the notes, in singles and twenties. Usually he had no patience for that and pushed such small-timers out of the way to find someone with the right money, as curt as a bus driver. But he needed small bills too, for cab fares and tips.

As her mouth fixed on his fresh wound, he felt his barb sink into her. She was a virgin, in everything. Within seconds, she was his slave. Her eyes widened as she found she was able to see in the dark. She touched fingertips to her suddenly sharp teeth.

It would last such a pathetically short time, but for now she was a princess of the shadows. He named her Nocturna and made her his daughter until dawn. She floated out of the room, to hunt.

He drew more cuts across his arm, accepted more money, gave more drac. A procession of strangers, all his slaves, passed through. Every night there were more.

After an hour, he had $8,500 in bills. Nancy's ghost was gone, stripped away from him in dribs and drabs, distributed among his children of the night. His veins were sunken and tingling. His mind was crowded with impressions that faded to nothing as fast as the scars on his milky skin. All around, in the dark, his temporary get bit each other. He relished the musical yelps of pain and pleasure.

Now, he thirsted again.

6

A red-headed vampire girl bumped into her and hissed, displaying pearly fangs. Penelope lowered her dark glasses and gave the chit a neon glare. Cowed, the creature backed away. Intrigued, Penny took the girl by the bare upper arm and looked into her mouth like a dentist. Her fangs were real, but shrank as she quivered in Penny's *nosferatu* grip. Red swirls dwindled in her eyes, and she was warm again, a frail thing.

Penny understood what the vampire boy was doing in the back room. At once, she was aghast and struck with admiration. She had heard of the warm temporarily taking on vampire attributes by drinking vampire blood without themselves being bitten. There was a story about Katie Reed and a flier in World War I. But it was rare and dangerous.

Well, it used to be rare.

All around her, mayfly vampires darted. A youth blundered into her arms and tried to bite her. She firmly pushed him away, breaking the fingers of his right hand to make a point. They would heal instantly but ache like the Devil when he turned back into a real boy.

A worm of terror curled in her heart. To do such a thing meant having a vision. Vampires, made conservative by centuries, were rarely innovators. She was reminded, again, of Dracula, who had risen among the *nosferatu* by virtue of his willingness to venture into new, large-scale fields of conquest. Such vampires were always frightening.

Would it really be a good thing for Andy to meet this boy?

She saw the white jacket shining in the darkness. The vampire stood at the bar, with Steve Rubell, ringmaster of 54, and the movie actress Isabelle Adjani. Steve, as usual, was flying, hairstyle falling apart above his bald spot. His pockets bulged with petty cash taken from the overstuffed tills.

Steve spotted her, understood her nod of interest, and signalled her to come over.

'Penny darling,' he said, 'look at me. I'm like you.'

He had fangs too. And red-smeared lips.

'I… am… a vampiah!'

For Steve, it was just a joke. There was a bite mark on Adjani's neck, which she dabbed with a bar napkin.

'This is just the biggest thing evah,' Steve said.

'Fabulous,' she agreed.

Her eyes fixed the vampire newcomer. He withstood her gaze. She judged him no longer a new-born but not yet an elder. He was definitely of the Dracula line.

'Introduce me,' she demanded, delicately.

Steve's red eyes focused.

'Andy is interested?'

Penny nodded. Whatever was swarming in his brain, Steve was sharp.

'Penelope, this is Johnny Pop. He's from Transylvania.'

'I am an American, now,' he said, with just a hint of accent.

'Johnny, my boy, this is the witch Penny Churchward.'

Penny extended her knuckles to be kissed. Johnny Pop took her fingers and bowed slightly, an Old World habit.

'You cut quite a figure,' she said.

'You are an elder?'

'Good grief, no. I'm from the class of '88. One of the few survivors.'

'My compliments.'

He let her hand go. He had a tall drink on the bar, blood concentrate. He would need to get his blood count up, to judge by all his fluttering get.

Some fellow rose off the dance floor on ungainly, short-lived wings. He made it a few feet into the air, flapping furiously. Then, there was a ripping and he collapsed onto the rest of the crowd, yelling and bleeding.

Johnny smiled and raised his glass to her.

She would have to think about this development.

'My friend Andy would like to meet you, Johnny.'

Steve was delighted, and slapped Johnny on the arm.

'Andy Warhol is the Vampire Queen of New York City,' he said. 'You have arrived, my deah!'

Johnny wasn't impressed. Or was trying hard not to be.

Politely, he said, 'Miss Churchward, I should like to meet your friend Mr Warhol.'

7

So, this ash-faced creature was coven master of New York. Johnny had seen Andy Warhol before, here and at the Mudd Club, and knew who he was, the man who painted soup cans and made the dirty movies. He hadn't known Warhol was a vampire, but now it was pointed out, it seemed obvious. What else could such a person be?

Warhol was not an elder but he was unreadable, beyond Johnny's experience. He would have to be careful, to pay proper homage to this master. It would not do to excite the enmity of the city's few other vampires; at least, not yet. Warhol's woman – consort? mistress? slave? – was intriguing, too. She danced on the edge of hostility, radiating prickly suspicion, but he had a hook of a kind in her too. Born to follow, she would trot after him as faithfully as she followed her artist master. He had met her kind before, stranded out of their time, trying to make a way in the world rather than reshape it to suit themselves. It would not do to underestimate her.

'Gee,' Warhol said, 'you must come to the Factory. There are things you could do.'

Johnny didn't doubt it.

Steve made a sign and a photographer appeared. Johnny noticed Penelope edging out of shot just before the flash went off. Andy, Steve and Johnny were caught in the bleached corner. Steve, grinning with his fresh teeth.

'Say, Johnny,' Steve said, 'we will show up, won't we? I mean, I've still got my image.'

Johnny shrugged. He had no idea whether the drac suck Steve had taken earlier would affect his reflection. That had as much to do with Nancy as him. Andy had an image, though. Bloodline – go figure.

'Wait and see what develops,' Johnny said.

'If that's the way it has to be, that's the way it is.'

It didn't do to think too hard about what Americans said.

'Gee,' mused Andy, 'that's, uh, fa-antastic, that's a thought.'

Within months, Johnny would rule this city.

8

He fed often, less for sustenance than for business. This one, seized just before sunrise, was the last of three taken throughout a single April night. He had waylaid the Greek girl, a seamstress in the garment district, on her way to a long day's work. She was too terrified to make a sound as Johnny ripped into her throat. Blood poured into his gaping mouth, and he swallowed. He fed his lust, his need. It wasn't just blood, it was money.

The girl, dragged off the street into an alley, had huge, startled eyes. Her ghost was in him as he bled her. She was called Thana, Death. The name stuck in his craw, clogging the lizard stem of his brain that always came alive as he fed. She should have been called Zoë, Life. Was something wrong with her blood? She had no drugs, no disease, no madness. She started to fight him, mentally. The girl knew about her ghost, could struggle with him on a plane beyond the physical. Her unexpected skill shocked him.

He broke the bloody communion and dropped her onto some cardboard boxes. He was exhilarated and terrified. Thana's ghost snapped out of his mind and fell back into her. She sobbed soundlessly, mouth agape.

'Death,' he said, exorcising her.

Her blood made him full to the point of bursting. The swollen veins around his mouth and neck throbbed like painful erections. Just after a big feed, he was unattractively jowly, turgid sacs under his jawline, purplish flush to his cheeks and chest. He couldn't completely close his mouth, crowded as it was with blocky, jagged fangs.

He thought about wasting Thana, fulfilling the prophecy of her name.

No. He must not kill while feeding. Johnny was taking more victims but drinking less from each, holding back from killing. If people had to be killed, he'd do it without taking blood, much as it went against the Father's warrior instinct that subjugation of the vanquished should be commemorated at least by a mouthful of hot blood. This was America and things were different.

Who'd have thought there'd be such a fuss about Nancy and Sid? He was surprised by the extensive news coverage of another drab death at the Chelsea. Sid, a slave who could never finger Johnny without burning out his brain completely, was charged with murder. Out on bail, he was remanded back to jail for bottling Patti Smith's brother. On Rikers Island, he found out 'punk' had another meaning in prison.

Kicked loose again, he had turned up dead of an overdose, with a suntan that struck witnesses as being unusual for February. It was either down to the political situation in Iran or Johnny's own enterprise: in the weeks Sid was locked up and kicking, heroin had become infinitely purer, perhaps thanks to Persians getting their money out in drugs, perhaps dealers competing with drac. Because Sid was well known, the ragged end of his life was picked apart by a continuing police investigation. Loose ends could turn up; someone like Rockets Redglare, who had dealt in Room 100, might remember seeing Sid and Nancy with a vampire on the night of the killing. Johnny had no idea a singer who couldn't sing would be so famous. Even Andy was impressed by the headlines, and wondered whether he should do a Sid picture to catch the moment.

He knelt by Thana, holding her scarf to her throat wound. He took her hand and put it up to the makeshift dressing, indicating where she should press. In her hating eyes, he had no reflection. To her, he was nothing.

Fine.

Johnny left the girl and looked for a cab.

9

He had a penthouse apartment now, rent paid in cash every month, at the Bramford, a Victorian brownstone of some reputation. A good address was important. He needed somewhere to keep his clothes and a coffin lined with Transylvanian dirt. At heart, Johnny was a traditionalist. Andy was the same, prizing American antique furniture – American antique, hah! – and art deco bric-a-brac, filling his town house with the prizes of the past while throwing out the art of the future in his Factory.

Johnny had over $11.5 million in several accounts, and cash stashes in safe deposit boxes all over the city. He intended to pay income taxes on some of it, quite soon. In a moment of candour, he had discussed his business with the Churchward woman. She was the only vampire of real experience in the city, besides Andy.

Open about so much, Andy was closemouthed about business and blood. He clammed shut when asked about feeding, though Johnny guessed he took nips from all his assistants. He talked a lot about how much money he made from art, but was vague about what he did with it.

Johnny and Penelope couldn't decide whether what Johnny did was against the law or not. But while selling his own blood was a legal grey area, assault and murder weren't. He was reluctant to relinquish those tools entirely, but accepted that standards of behaviour in America were ostensibly different from those of his European backwater homeland. It wasn't that assault and murder were less common here than in Romania, but the authorities made more noise about it.

Those like Thana, left alive after his caresses, might argue that his powers of fascination constituted coercion, that he had

135

perpetrated upon them a form of rape or robbery. Statutes against organ-snatching might even be applicable. Penelope said that soon it wouldn't be safe to pick up a Mr Goodbar and suck him silly without getting a signature on a consent form.

The first real attempt to destroy him had come not from the church or the law, but from criminals. He was cutting into their smack and coke action. A couple of oddly dressed black men came for him with silver razors. The iron of the Father rose up within him and he killed them both, shredding their clothes and faces to make a point. He found out their names from the *Daily Bugle*, Youngblood Priest and Tommy Gibbs. He wondered if the black men he had seen outside the Chelsea on the night he met Andy were in with that Harlem crowd. He had glimpsed them again, several times, singly and as a pair. They were virtual twins, though one was further into the dark than the other. The knifeman's partner packed a crossbow under his coat. They would not be so easy to face down.

The Mott Street Triads had found a vampire of their own – one of those hopping Mandarins, bound by prayers pasted to his forehead – and tried feeding and milking him, cooking their own drac. Markedly inferior, their product was exhausted within a month, an entire body gone to dust and sold on the street. Soon, such *nosferatu* slaves, captured and used up fast, would be common. Other vampires would sell their own drac, in America or their homelands. If the craze could take off in New York, then it would eventually spread everywhere.

Johnny had repeatedly turned down offers of 'partnership' from the established suppliers of drugs. A cash payment of $6 million to the Prizzi family eliminated most of the hassle his people had been getting on the street. The Harlem rogues were off his case. He could pass for Italian, which meant he was to be respected for the moment. Mafia elders like Corrado Prizzi were men of rough honour; younger wiseguys like John Gotti and Frank White, on the rise even as the dons were fading, were of a different stripe. Gotti, or someone like him, would eventually move into drac. By then, Johnny intended to be retired and in another city.

The cops were interested. He had spotted them at once, casually loitering around crime scenes, chatting with dazed witnesses, giving penetrating stares. He had them marked down: the bogus hippie with the woolly vest, the completely bald man with the good suit, the maniac driver in the battered porkpie hat. Like the Father, he knew when to be careful, when to be daring. The police meant nothing in this land. They didn't even have silver bullets, like *Securitate* in the Old Country.

His own children – the dhampires – were busy. With his blood in them, they changed for a while. The first few times, they just relished the new senses, the feel of fangs in their mouths, the quickening of reflexes. Then, red thirst pricked. They needed to assuage it, before the suck wore off.

Apparently, the biting had started in the semi-underground gay clubs, among the leather-and-chains community. Johnny guessed one of the Studio 54 bouncers was the fountainhead. Both Burns and Stu were denizens of those cruising places. Within a few months, the biting had got out of hand. Every week, there were deaths, as dhampires lost control during the red rush, took too much from their lovers of the moment.

The money, however, kept coming in.

10

In the lobby, already brightening with dawn light, an unnerving twelve-year-old clacked together two pink perspex eggs on a string. Johnny understood he was trying to get into the *Guinness Book of Records*. The child was a holy terror, allowed to run loose by his indulgent parents and their adoring circle. More than one resident of the Bramford had expressed a desire to be around when little Adrian Woodhouse 'got his come-uppance', but Johnny knew it would not do to cross the boy. If you intend to live forever, do not make enemies of children.

He hurried towards the cage elevator, intent on getting out of ear-range of the aural water torture.

'Johnny, Johnny…'

As he spun around, excess blood dizzied him. He felt it sloshing around inside. Everything was full: his stomach, his heart, his veins, his bladder, his lungs. It was practically backing up to his eyeballs.

The dhampire was cringing in a shrinking shadow.

'Johnny,' she said, stepping into the light.

Her skin darkened and creased, but she ignored it. She had crumpled bills in her hand, dirty money. He could imagine what she had done to get it.

It was the girl he had once called Nocturna. The Virgin of 54. She wasn't fresh any more, in any way.

'Please,' she begged, mouth open and raw.

'Things have changed,' he said, stepping into the elevator, drawing the mesh across between them. He saw her red-rimmed eyes.

'Take it,' she said, rolling the bills into tubes and shoving them through the grille. They fell at his feet.

'Talk to Rudy or Elvira,' he said. 'They'll fix you up with a suck.'

She shook her head, desperately. Her hair was a mess, singed white in patches. She grabbed the grille, fingers sticking through like worms.

'I don't want a suck, I want *you*.'

'You don't want me, darling. You can't afford me. Now, pull in your claws or you'll lose them.'

She was crying rusty tears.

He wrenched the lever and the elevator began to rise. The girl pulled her hands free. Her face sank and disappeared. She had pestered him before. He would have to do something about her.

It wasn't that he didn't do business that way any more, but that he had to be more selective about the clientele. For the briefest of suckles from the vein, the price was now $10,000. He was choosy about the mouths he spurted into.

Everyone else could just buy a suck.

11

Rudy and Elvira were waiting in the foyer of the apartment, red-eyed from the night, coming down slowly. They were dhampires themselves, of course. The Father had known the worth of warm slaves, his gypsies and madmen, and Johnny had taken some care in selecting the vassals he needed.

As Johnny entered the apartment, peeling off his floor-length turquoise suede coat and tossing away his black-feathered white Stetson hat, Rudy leaped up from the couch, almost to attention. Elvira, constricted inside a black sheath dress low-necked enough to show her navel, raised a welcoming eyebrow and tossed aside *The Sensuous Woman*. Rudy took his coat and hat and hung them up. Elvira rose like a snake from a basket and air-kissed his cheeks. She touched black nails to his face, feeling the bloat of the blood.

They proceeded to the dining room.

Rudy Pasko, a hustler Johnny had picked up on the A-train, dreamed of turning, becoming like his master. Jittery, nakedly ambitious, *American*, he would be a real monster, paying everybody back for ignoring him in life. For the moment, he had his uses.

Elvira, this year's compleat Drac Hag, was a better bet for immortality. She knew when to run cool or hot, and took care to keep a part of herself back, even while snuffing mountains of drac and chewing on any youth who happened to be passing. She liked to snack on gay men, claiming – with her usual dreadful wordplay – that they had better taste than straights. Andy had passed her on from the Factory.

The money was on the polished oak dining table, in attaché cases. It had already been counted, but Johnny sat down and did it again. Rudy called him 'the Count', almost mockingly. The boy didn't understand; the money wasn't Johnny's until it was counted. The obsessive-compulsive thing was a trick of the Dracula bloodline. Some degenerate, mountain-dwelling distant cousins could be distracted from their prey by a handful of pumpkin seeds, unable to pass by without counting every one. That was absurd, this was important. Andy understood about money, why it was essential not for what it could buy but in itself. Numbers were beautiful.

Johnny's fingers were so sensitive that he could make the count just by riffling the bundles, by caressing the cash. He picked out the dirty bills, the torn or taped or stained notes, and tossed them to Rudy.

There was $158,591 on the table, a fair night's takings. His personal rake would be an even $100,000.

'Where does the ninety-one dollars come from, Rudy?'

The boy shrugged. The non-negotiable price of a suck was $500. There shouldn't be looser change floating around.

'Boys and girls have expenses,' Rudy said.

'They are not to dip into the till,' Johnny said, using an expression he had recently learned. 'They are to hand over the takings. If they have expenses, they must ask you to cover them. You have enough for all eventualities, have you not?'

Rudy looked at the heap of messy bills and nodded. He had to be reminded of his hook sometimes.

'Now, things must be taken care of.'

Rudy followed him into the reception room. The heart of the penthouse, the reception room was windowless but with an expanse of glass ceiling. Just now, with the sun rising, the skylight was curtained by a rolling metal blind drawn by a hand-cranked winch.

There was no furniture, and the hardwood floor was protected by a plastic sheet. It was Rudy's duty to get the room ready for Johnny by dawn. He had laid out shallow metal trays in rows, like seed-beds in a nursery.

Johnny undid his fly and carefully pissed blood onto the first tray. The pool spread, until it lapped against the sides. He paused his flow, and proceeded to the next tray, and the next. In all, he filled thirty-seven trays to a depth of about a quarter of an inch. He lost his bloat, face smoothing and tightening, clothes hanging properly again.

Johnny watched from the doorway as Rudy worked the winch, rolling the blind. Rays of light speared down through the glass ceiling, falling heavily on the trays. Morning sun was the best, the purest. The trays smoked slightly, like vats of tomato soup on griddles. There was a smell he found offensive, but which the warm – even dhampires – could not distinguish. Like an elder exposed to merciless daylight, the blood was turning to granulated material. Within a few hours it would all be red dust, like the sands of Mars. Drac.

12

In the afternoon, as he slept in his white-satin-lined coffin, a troop of good Catholic boys whose fear of Johnny was even stronger than the blood-hooks in their brains came to the apartment and, under Elvira's supervision, worked on the trays, scooping up and measuring out the powdered blood into foil twists ('sucks' or 'jabs') that retailed for $500 each. After sunset, the boys (and a few girls) took care of the distribution, spreading out to the clubs and parties and street corners and park nooks where the dhampires hung out.

Known on the street as drac or bat's blood, the powder could be snuffed, swallowed, smoked or heated to liquid and injected. With a fresh user, the effect lasted the hours of the night and was burned out of the system at sunrise. After a few weeks, the customer was properly hooked – a dhampire – and needed three or four sucks a night to keep sharp. No one knew about long-term effects yet, though serious dhampires like Nocturna were prone to severe sunburn and even showed signs of being susceptible to spontaneous combustion. Besides a red thirst for a gulp or two of blood, the dhampire also had a need, of course, to raise cash to feed the habit. Johnny didn't care much about that side of the business, but the *Daily Bugle* had run editorials about the rise in mugging, burglary, car crime and other petty fund-raising activities.

Thus far, Johnny was sole supplier of the quality stuff. During their short-lived venture, the Triads had cut their dwindling drac with cayenne pepper, tomato paste and powdered cat shit. The Good Catholics were all dhampires themselves, though he kicked them out and cut them off if they exceeded their prescribed dosage – which kept them scrupulously honest about cash. His major expenses were kickbacks to the families, club owners, bouncers, street cops and other mildly interested parties.

Johnny Pop would be out of the business soon. He was greedy for more than money. Andy had impressed on him the importance of being famous.

13

Johnny Pop was certainly the social success of the summer. He had just showed up at Trader Vic's with *Margaret Trudeau* on his elegant arm. Penelope was not surprised and Andy was silently ecstatic. An inveterate collector of people, he delighted in the idea of the Transylvanian hustler and the Canadian Prime Minister's ex getting together. Margaux Hemingway would be furious: she had confided in Andy and Penny that she thought it was serious with Johnny. Penny could have told her what was serious with Johnny, but she didn't think any warm woman would understand.

From across the room, as everyone turned to ogle the couple, Penny observed Johnny, realising again why no one else saw him as she did. He had Olde Worlde charm by the bucketful. That thirsty edge that had made him seem a rough beast was gone. His hair was an improbable construction, teased and puffed every which way, and his lips were a girl's. But his eyes were Dracula's. It had taken her a while to notice, for she had really known *il principe* only after his fire had dwindled. This was what the *young* Dracula, freshly *nosferatu*, must have been like. This was the bat-cloaked creature of velvet night who with sheer smoking magnetism had overwhelmed flighty Lucy, virtuous Mina and stately Victoria, who had bested Van Helsing and stolen an empire. He didn't dance so often now that he had the city's attention, but all his moves were like dancing, his gestures so considered, his looks so perfect.

He had told several versions of the story, but always insisted he was Dracula's get, perhaps the last to be turned personally by the King Vampire in his 500-year reign. Johnny didn't like to give dates, but Penny put his conversion at somewhere during the last war. Who he had been when warm was another matter. He claimed to be a lineal descendant as well as get, the last modern son of some bye-blow of the Impaler, which was why the dying bloodline had fired in him, making him the true Son of Dracula. She could almost believe it. Though he was proud to name his Father-in-Darkness, he didn't like to talk about the Old Country and what had brought him to America. There were stories there, she would wager. Eventually, it would all come out. He had probably drained a commissar's daughter and got out one step ahead of red vampire killers.

There was trouble in the Carpathians now. The Transylvania Movement, wanting to claim Dracula's ancient fiefdom as a homeland for all the displaced vampires of the world, were in open conflict with Ceauşescu's army. The only thing Johnny had said about that mess was that he would prefer to be in America than Romania. After all, the modern history of vampirism – so despised by the Transylvanians – had begun when Dracula left his homeland for what was in 1885 the most exciting, modern city in the world. She conceded the point: Johnny Pop was displaying the real Dracula spirit, not TM reactionaries like Meinster and Crainic who wanted to retreat to their castles and pretend it was still the Middle Ages.

Andy got fidgety as Johnny worked the room, greeting poor Truman Capote or venerable Paulette Goddard, sharp Ivan Boesky or needy Liza Minnelli. He was deliberately delaying his inevitable path to Andy's table. It was like a Renaissance court, Penny realised. Eternal shifts of power and privilege, of favour and slight. Three months ago, Johnny had needed to be in with Andy; now, Johnny had risen to such a position that he could afford to hold himself apart, to declare independence. She had never seen Andy on the hook this badly, and was willing to admit she took some delight in it. At last, the master was mastered.

Eventually, Johnny arrived and displayed his prize.

Penny shook Mrs Trudeau's hand and felt the chill coming from her. Her scarlet choker didn't quite match her crimson evening dress. Penny could smell the musk of her scabs.

Johnny was drinking well, these nights.

Andy and Johnny sat together, close. Mrs Trudeau frowned, showing her own streak of jealousy. Penny wouldn't be able to explain to her what Andy and Johnny had, why everyone else was superfluous when they were together. Despite the fluctuations in their relationship, they were one being with two bodies. Without saying much, Johnny made Andy choke with laughter he could never let out. There was a reddish flush to Andy's albino face.

'Don't mind them,' Penny told Mrs Trudeau. 'They're bats.'

14

'I don't suppose this'd do anything for you,' said the girl from *Star Wars* whose real name Penny had forgotten, cutting a line of red powder on the coffee table with a silver razorblade.

Penny shrugged.

Vampires did bite each other. If one were wounded almost to death, an infusion of another's *nosferatu* blood could have restorative powers. Blood would be offered by an inferior undead to a coven master to demonstrate loyalty. Penny had no idea what, if any, effect drac would have on her and wasn't especially keen on finding out. The scene was pretty much a bore.

Princess Leia was evidently a practised dhampire. She snorted through a tubed $100 bill and held her head back. Her eyes reddened and her teeth grew points.

'Arm wrestle?' she asked.

Penny wasn't interested. Dhampires all had this rush of vampire power but no real idea of what to do with it. Except nibble. They didn't even feed properly.

Most of the people at this party were drac addicts. They went for the whole bit, black capes and fingerless black widow web gloves, Victorian cameos at the throat, lots of velvet and leather, puffy mini-dresses over thigh-boots.

Half this lot had dracced themselves up completely for a midnight screening of *The Rocky Horror Picture Show* at the Waverly, and were just coming down, which meant they were going around the room pestering anyone they thought might be holding out on a stash, desperate to get back up there. There was a miasma of free-floating paranoia, which Penny couldn't keep out of her head.

'Wait 'til this gets to the Coast,' said Princess Leia. 'It'll be monstrous.'

Penny had to agree.

She had lost Andy and Johnny at CBGBs and fallen in with this crowd. The penthouse apartment apparently belonged to some political big-wig she had never heard of, Hal Philip Walker, but he was out of town. Brooke Hayward was staying here with Dennis Hopper. Penny had the idea that Johnny knew Hopper from some foreign debauch, and wanted to avoid him – which, if true, was unusual.

She was welcome here, she realised, because she was a vampire.

It hit her that if the drac ran out, there was a direct source in the room. She was stronger than any warm person, but it was a long time since she had fought anyone. The sheer press of dhampires would tell. They could hold her down and cut her open, then suck her dry, leaving her like crushed orange pulp. For the first time since turning, she understood the fear the warm had of her kind. Johnny had changed things permanently.

Princess Leia, fanged and clawed, eyed her neck slyly, and reached out to touch her.

'Excuse me,' said Penny, slipping away.

Voices burbled in her mind. She was on a wavelength with all these dhampires, who didn't know how to communicate. It was just background chatter, amplified to skull-cracking levels.

In the bedroom where she had left her coat, a Playmate of the Month and some rock n' roll guy were messily performing dhampire sixty-nine, gulping from wounds in each other's wrists. Penny had fed earlier and the blood did nothing for her.

A Broadway director tried to talk to her.

Yes, she had seen *Pacific Overtures*. No, she didn't want to invest in *Sweeney Todd*.

Where had anybody got the idea that she was rich?

That fat Albanian from *Animal House*, fangs like sharpened cashew nuts, claimed newfound vampire skills had helped him solve Rubik's cube. He wore a black Inverness cape over baggy Y-fronts. His eyes flashed red and gold like a cat's in headlights.

Penny had a headache.

She took the elevator down to the street

15

While looking for a cab, she was accosted by some dreadful drac hag. It was the girl Johnny called Nocturna, now a snowy-haired fright with yellow eyes and rotten teeth.

The creature pressed money on her, a crumpled mess of notes.

'Just a suck, precious,' she begged.

Penny was sickened.

The money fell from the dhampire's hands, and was swept into the gutter.

'I think you'd better go home, dear,' advised Penny.

'Just a suck.'

Nocturna laid a hand on her shoulder, surprisingly strong. She retained some *nosferatu* attributes.

'Johnny still loves me,' she said, 'but he has business to take care of. He can't fit me in, you see. But I need a suck, just a little kiss, nothing serious.'

Penny took Nocturna's wrist but couldn't break the hold.

The dhampire's eyes were yolk yellow, with shots of blood. Her breath was foul. Her clothes, once fashionable, were ragged and gamey.

Penny glanced up and down the street. She could use a cop, or Spider-Man. People were passing, but in the distance. No one noticed this little scene.

Nocturna brought out something from her reticule. A Stanley knife. Penny felt a cold chill as the blade touched her cheek, then a venomous sting. The tool was silvered. She gasped in pain, and the dhampire stuck her mouth over the cut.

Penny struggled, but the dhampire was suddenly strong, juiced up by pure drac. She would make more cuts and take more sucks.

'You're his friend,' Nocturna said, lips red. 'He won't mind. I'm not being unfaithful.'

Penny supposed she deserved this.

But, as the red rush dazed Nocturna, Penny broke free of the dhampire. She dabbed her cheek. Because of the silver, the cut would stay open, perhaps even leave a scar. This one would be where it showed.

There were people nearby, watching. Penny saw their red eyes. More dhampires, out for drac, out for her blood. She backed towards the lobby, cursing Johnny Pop.

Nocturna staggered after her.

A taxi cab stormed down the street, scattering dhampires. Penny stuck out her hand and flagged it down. Nocturna howled, and flew at her. Penny wrenched open the cab door and threw herself in. She told the driver to drive off, anywhere, fast.

Nocturna and the others hissed at the window, nails scratching the glass.

The cab sped up and left them behind.

Penny was resolved. Penance was one thing, but enough was enough. She would get out of this city. The Factory could run itself. She would leave Andy to Johnny, and hope they were satisfied with each other.

'Someday a red rain's gonna come,' said the taxi driver. 'And wash the scum off the streets.'

She wished she could agree with him.

16

---◆---

Johnny was one of the privileged few allowed into Andy's town house to witness the artist's levée. At high summer, it was impractical to wait for sundown before venturing out – so Johnny had to be ferried the short distance from the Bramford to East 66th Street in a sleek limo with tinted windows and hustle under a parasol up to the door of Number 57.

With the Churchward woman's desertion, there was a blip in the smooth running of Andy's social life and he was casting around for a replacement Girl of the Year. Johnny was wary of being impressed into taking on too many of Penny Penitent's duties. There were already so many demands on his time, especially with that mad Bella Abzug whipping the NYPD into a frenzy about 'the drac problem'. It wasn't even illegal yet, but his dealers were rousted every night. His pay-offs to the families and the cops ratcheted up every week, which pushed him to raise the price of a suck, which meant the dhamps had to peddle more ass or bust more head to scrape together cash for their habit. The papers were full of vampire murders, and real vampires weren't even suspects.

The two-storey lobby of Number 57 was dominated by imperial busts – Napoleon, Caesar, Dracula – and still-packed crates of sculptures and paintings. Things were everywhere, collected but uncatalogued, most still in the original wrapping.

Johnny sat on an upholstered *chaise longue* and leafed through a male pornographic magazine that was on top of a pile of periodicals that stretched from *The New York Review of Books* to *The Fantastic Four*. He heard Andy moving about upstairs and glanced at the top of the wide staircase. Andy made an entrance, a skull-faced spook-mask atop a floor-length red velvet dressing gown which dragged like Scarlett O'Hara's train as he descended.

In this small, private moment – with no one else around to see – Andy allowed himself to smile, a terminally ill little boy indulging his love of dressing-up. It wasn't just that Andy was a poseur, but that he let everyone know it and still found the reality in the fakery, making the posing the point. When Andy pretended, he just showed up the half-hearted way everyone else did the same thing. In the months he had been in New York, Johnny had learned that being an American was just like being a vampire, to feed off the dead and to go on and on and on, making a virtue of unoriginality, waxing a corpse-face to beauty. In a country of surfaces, no one cared about the rot that lay beneath the smile, the shine and the dollar. After the persecutions of Europe, it was an enormous relief.

Andy extended a long-nailed hand towards an occasional table by the *chaise longue*. It was heaped with the night's invitations, more parties and openings and galas than even Andy could hit before dawn.

'Choose,' he said.

Johnny took a handful of cards, and summarised them for Andy's approval or rejection. Shakespeare in the Park, Paul Toombes in *Timon of Athens* ('gee, misa-anthropy'). A charity ball for some new wasting disease ('gee, sa-ad'). An Anders Wolleck exhibit of metal sculptures ('gee, fa-abulous'). A premiere for the latest Steven Spielberg film, *1941* ('gee, wo-onderful'). A screening at Max's Kansas City of a work in progress by Scott and Beth B, starring Lydia Lunch and Teenage Jesus ('gee, u-underground'). A nightclub act by Divine ('gee, na-aughty'). Parties by and for John Lennon, Tony Perkins ('ugh, *Psycho*'), Richard Hell and Tom Verlaine, Jonathan and Jennifer Hart ('ick!'), Blondie ('the cartoon character or the band?'), Malcolm McLaren ('be-est not'), David Johansen, Edgar Allan Poe ('ne-evermore'), Frank Sinatra ('Old Hat Rat Pack Hack!').

The night had some possibilities.

17

Andy was in a sulk. Truman Capote, lisping through silly fangs, had spitefully told him about an Alexander Cockburn parody, modelled on the lunch chatter of Warhol and Colacello with Imelda Marcos as transcribed in *Inter/VIEW*. Andy, of course, had to sit down in the middle of the party and pore through the piece. In Cockburn's version, Bob and Andy took Count Dracula to supper at Mortimer's Restaurant on the Upper East Side and prodded him with questions like 'Don't you wish you'd been able to spend Christmas in Transylvania?' and 'Is there still pressure on you to think of your image and act a certain way?'

Johnny understood the real reason that the supposedly unflappable artist was upset was that he had been scooped. After this, Andy wouldn't be able to run an interview with Dracula. He'd been hoping Johnny would channel the Father's ghost, as others had channelled such *Inter/VIEW* subjects as the Assyrian wind demon Pazuzu and Houdini. Andy didn't prize Johnny just because he was a vampire; it was important that he was of the direct Dracula line.

He didn't feel the Father with him so much, though he knew he was always there. It was as if he had absorbed the great ghost almost completely, learning the lessons of the Count, carrying on his mission on Earth. The past was fog, now. His European life and death were faint, and he told varying stories because he remembered differently each time. But in the fog stood the red-eyed, black-caped figure of Dracula, reaching out to him, reaching out through him.

Sometimes, Johnny Pop thought he *was* Dracula. The Churchward woman had almost believed it, once. And Andy would be so delighted if it were true. But Johnny wasn't *just* Dracula.

He was no longer unique. There were other vampires in the country, the city, at this party. They weren't the Olde Worlde seigneurs of the Transylvania Movement, at once arrogant and pitiful, but Americans, if not by birth then inclination. Their extravagant names had a copy-of-a-copy paleness, suggesting hissy impermanence: Sonja Blue, Santanico Pandemonium, Skeeter, Scumbalina. Metaphorical (or actual?) children-in-darkness of Andy Warhol, the first thing they did upon rising from the dead was – like an actor landing a first audition – change their names. Then, with golden drac running in their veins, they sold themselves to the dhamps, flooding to New York where the most suckheads were. In cash, they were richer than most castle-bound TM elders, but they coffined in camper vans or at the Y, and wore stinking rags.

Andy snapped out of his sulk. A vampire youth called Whistler paid homage to him as the Master, offering him a criss-crossed arm. Andy stroked the kid's wounds, but held back from sampling the blood.

Johnny wondered if the hook he felt was jealousy.

18

Johnny and Andy lolled on the backseat of the limo with the sun-roof open, playing chicken with the dawn.

The chatter of the night's parties still ran around Johnny's head, as did the semi-ghosts he had swallowed with his victims' blood. He willed a calm cloud to descend upon the clamour of voices and stilled his brain. For once, the city was quiet.

He was bloated with multiple feedings – at every party, boys and girls offered their necks to him – and Andy seemed flushed enough to suggest he had accepted a few discreet nips somewhere along the course of the night. Johnny felt lassitude growing in him, and knew that after relieving himself and letting the Good Catholics go to work, he would need to hide in the refrigerated coffin unit that was his New York summer luxury for a full day.

The rectangle of sky above was starless pre-dawn blue-grey. Red tendrils were filtering through, reflected off the glass frontages of Madison Avenue. The almost-chill haze of four a.m. had been burned away in an instant, like an ancient elder, and it would be another murderously hot day, confining them both to their lairs for a full twelve hours.

They said nothing, needed to say nothing.

19

The Hallowe'en party at 54 was desperately lavish. Steve made him Guest of Honour, naming him the Official Spectre at the Feast.

In a brief year, Johnny had become this town's favourite monster. Andy was Vampire Master of New York, but Johnny Pop was Prince of Darkness, father and furtherer of a generation of dhamps, scamps and vamps. There were songs about him ('Fame, I'm Gonna Live Forever'), he had been in a movie (at least his smudge had) with Andy (Ulli Lommel's *Drac Queens*), he got more neck than a giraffe, and there was a great deal of interest in him from the Coast.

Cakes shaped like coffins and castles were wheeled into 54, and the Man in the Moon sign was red-eyed and fang-toothed in homage. Liberace and Elton John played duelling pianos, while the Village People – the Indian as the Wolf Man, the Cowboy as the Creature From the Black Lagoon, the Construction Worker as the Monster, the Biker as Dracula, the Cop as the Thing From Another World, the Soldier as the Hunchback of Notre Dame – belted out a cover of Bobby 'Boris' Pickett's 'The Monster Mash'.

The day drac became a proscribed drug by act of Congress, Johnny stopped manufacturing it personally and impressed a series of down-on-their-luck *nosferatu* to be undead factories. The price of the product shot up again, as did the expense of paying off the cops and the mob, but his personal profits towered almost beyond his mind's capacity to count. He knew the bubble would burst soon, but was ready to diversify, to survive into another era. It would be the eighties soon. That was going to be a different time. The important thing was going to be not drac or fame or party invites, but money. Numbers would be his shield and his castle, his spells of protection, invisibility and fascination.

He didn't dance so much, now. He had made his point. But he was called onto the floor. Steve set up a chant of 'Johnny Pop, Johnny Pop' that went around the crowd. Valerie Perrine and Steve Guttenberg gave him a push. Nastassja Kinski and George Burns slapped his back. Peter Bogdanovich and Dorothy Stratten kissed his cheeks. He slipped his half-caped Versace jacket off and tossed it away, cleared a space, and performed, not to impress or awe others as before, but for himself, perhaps for the last time. He had never had such a sense of his own power. He no longer heard the Father's voice, for he was the Father. All the ghosts of this city, of this virgin continent, were his to command and consume.

Here ended the American Century. Here began, again, the Anni Draculae.

20

Huge, lovely eyes fixed him from the crowd. A nun in full penguin suit. Red, red heart-shaped lips and ice-white polished cheeks. Her pectoral cross, stark silver against a white collar, smote him with a force that made him stagger. She wasn't a real nun, of course, just as the Village People weren't real monsters. This was a party girl in a costume, trying to probe the outer reaches of bad taste.

She touched his mind and an electricity sparked.

He remembered her. The girl whose name was Death, whom he had bitten and left holding a scarf to a leaking neck wound. He had taken from her but now, he realised, she had taken from him. She was not a vampire, but he had turned her, changed her, made her a huntress.

She daintily lifted her cross and held it up. Her face was a gorgeous blank.

Her belief gave the symbol power and he was smitten, driven back across the flashing dance floor, between stumbling dancers. Death glided after him like a ballet dancer, instinctively avoiding people, face red and green and purple and yellow with the changing light. At the dead centre of the dance floor, she held her cross up high above her head. It was reflected in the glitter ball, a million shining cruciforms dancing over the crowds and the walls.

Johnny felt each reflected cross as a whiplash.

All his friends were here. Andy was up there on a balcony, somewhere, looking down with pride. And Steve had planned this whole evening for him. This was where his rise had truly begun, where he had sold his first suck, made his first dollars. But he was not safe here. Death had consecrated Studio 54 against him.

Other vampires in the crowd writhed in pain. Johnny saw the shredded-lace punk princess who called herself Scumbalina holding her face, smoking crosses etched on her cheeks and chin. Even the dhampires were uncomfortable, haemorrhaging from noses and mouths, spattering the floor and everyone around with their tainted blood.

Death was here for him, not the others.

He barged through the throng, and made it to the street. Dawn was not far off. Death was at his heels.

A taxi was waiting for him.

21

———◆———

Inside the hack, he told the driver to take him to the Bramford.

He saw the nun step out of 54 as the vehicle moved off. He searched inside himself for the Father, willing the panic he had felt to subside. His flight from the party would be remembered. It did not do to show such weakness.

Something was still wrong. What was it?

The nun had shaken him. Had the girl become a real nun? Was she despatched by some Vatican bureau to put an end to him? The church had always had its vampire killers. Or was she working with the mafia? To evict him from the business he had created, so the established crime families could claim drac fortunes for their own. Perhaps she was a minion of one of his own kind, a cat's paw of the Transylvania Movement? At the moment, Baron Meinster – the treacherous dandy, still desperate to be King of the Cats – was petitioning the UN for support. TM elders considered Johnny an upstart who was bringing vampirism into disrepute by sharing it so widely.

Throughout the centuries, Dracula had faced and bested enemies almost without number. To be a visionary was always to excite the enmity of inferiors. Johnny felt the Father in him, and sat back in the cab, planning.

He needed soldiers. Vampires. Dhampires. Get. An army, to protect him. Intelligence, to foresee new threats. He would start with Rudy and Elvira. It was time he gave them what they wanted, and turned them. Patrick Bateman, his young investment advisor, was another strong prospect. Men like Bateman, made vampires, would be perfect for the coming era. The Age of Money.

The cab parked outside the Bramford. It was full night, and a thin frost of snow lay on the sidewalks, slushing in the gutters.

Johnny got out and paid off the cab driver.

Familiar mad eyes. This was someone else he had encountered in the past year. Travis. The man had changed: the sides of his head were shaved and a Huron ridge stood up like a thicket on top of his skull.

The cabbie got out of the vehicle.

Johnny could tear this warm fool apart if he tried anything. He could not be surprised.

Travis extended his arm, as if to shake hands. Johnny looked down, and suddenly there was a pistol – shot out on a spring device – in the man's hand.

'Suck on this,' said Travis, jamming the gun into Johnny's stomach and pulling the trigger.

The first slug passed painlessly through him as if he were made of water. There was an icy shock, but no hurt, no damage. An old-fashioned lead bullet. Johnny laughed out loud. Travis pulled the trigger again.

This time, it was silver.

The bullet punched into his side, under his ribs, and burst through his back, tearing meat and liver. A hurricane of fire raged in the tunnel carved through him. The worst pain of his *nosferatu* life brought him to his knees, and he could *feel* the cold suddenly – his jacket was back at 54 – as the wet chill of the snow bit through his pants and at the palm of his outstretched hand.

Another silver bullet, through the head or the heart, and he would be finished.

The cab driver stood over him. There were others, in a circle. A crowd of Fearless Vampire Killers. The silent nun. The black man with wooden knives. The black man with the crossbow. The cop who'd sworn to break the Transylvania Connection. An architect, on his own crusade to avenge a family bled dead by dhamps. The ageing beatnik from the psychedelic van, with his smelly tracking dog. A red-skinned turncoat devil boy with the tail and sawn-off horns. The exterminator with the skull on his chest and a flame-thrower in his hands.

This company of stone loners was brought together by a single mission, to put an end to Johnny Pop. He had known about them all, but never guessed they might connect with each other. This city was so complicated.

The cop, Doyle, took Johnny's head and made him look at the Bramford.

Elvira was dead on the front steps, stake jutting from her cleavage, strewn limbs like the arms of a swastika. Rudy scuttled out of the shadows, avoiding Johnny's eyes. He hopped from one foot to another, a heavy briefcase in his hands. The arrow man made a dismissive gesture, and Rudy darted off, hauling what cash he could take. The Vampire Killers hadn't even needed to bribe him with their own money.

There was a huge crump, a rush of hot air, and the top floor windows all exploded in a burst of flame. Glass and burning fragments rained all around. His lair, his lieutenants, his factory, a significant amount of money, his coffin of earth. All gone in a moment.

The Vampire Killers were grimly satisfied.

Johnny saw people filling the lobby, rushing out onto the streets.

Again, he would have an audience.

The Father was strong in him, his ghost swollen, stiffening his spine, deadening his pain. His fang-teeth were three inches long, distending his jaw. All his other teeth were razor-edged lumps. Fresh rows of piranha-like fangs sprouted from buds he had never before suspected. His nails were poison daggers. His shirt tore at the back as his shoulders swelled, loosing the beginnings of black wings. His shoes burst and rips ran up the sides of his pants.

He stood up, slowly. The hole in his side was healed over, scabbed with dragonscales. A wooden knife lanced at him, and he batted it out of the air. Flame washed against his legs, melting the snow on the sidewalk, burning away his ragged clothes, hurting him not a bit.

Even the resolute Killers were given pause.

He fixed all their faces in his mind.

'Let's dance,' Johnny hissed.

22

Johnny lay broken on the sidewalk, a snow angel with cloak-like wings of pooled, scarlet-satin blood. He was shot through with silver and wood, and smoking from a dousing in flame. He was a ghost, locked in useless, fast-spoiling meat. The Father was loosed from him, standing over his ruin, eyes dark with sorrow and shame, a pre-dawn penumbra around his shoulders.

The Vampire Killers were dead or wounded or gone. They had not bought his true death easily. They were like him in one way: they had learned the lesson of *Dracula*, that only a family could take him down. He had known there were hunters on his track; he should have foreseen they would band together and taken steps to break them apart, as the Father would have done, had done with his own persecutors.

With the New York sunrise, he would crumble to nothing, to a scatter of drac on the snow.

Bodies moved nearby, on hands and knees, faces to the wet stone, tongues lapping. Dhampires. Johnny would have laughed. As he died, he was being sucked up, his ghost snorted by addicts.

The Father told him to reach out, to take a hold.

He could not. He was surrendering to the cold. He was leaving the Father, and letting himself be taken by Death. She was a huge-eyed fake nun.

The Father insisted.

It wasn't just Johnny dying. He was the last link with the Father. When Johnny was gone, it would be the end of Dracula too.

Johnny's right hand twitched, fingers clacking like crab-claws. It had almost been cut through at the wrist, and even his rapid healing couldn't undo the damage.

The Father instructed.

Johnny reached out, fingers brushing a collar, sliding around a throat, thumbnail resting against a pumping jugular. He turned his head, and focused his unburst eye.

Rudy Pasko, the betrayer, the dhampire.

He would kill him and leave the world with an act of vengeance.

No, the Father told him.

Rudy's red eyes were balls of fear. He was swollen with Johnny's blood, overdosing on drac, face shifting as muscles under the skin writhed like snakes.

'Help me,' Johnny said, 'and I'll kill you.'

Rudy had boosted a car and gathered Johnny together to pour him into the passenger seat. The dhampire was on a major drac trip and saw the light at the end of his tunnel. If he were to be bitten by Johnny in his current state, he would die, would turn, would be a dhampire no longer. Like all the dhamps, his dearest wish was to be more, to be a full vampire. It wasn't as easy as some thought. They had to be bitten by the vampire whose blood they had ingested. Most street drac was cut so severely that the process was scrambled. Dhampires had died. But Rudy knew where the blood in him had come from. Johnny realised that his Judas had betrayed him not just for money, but because Rudy thought that if he spilled enough of Johnny's blood, he could work the magic on his own. In the British idiom Johnny had learned from Sid, Rudy was a wanker.

They arrived at Andy's town house just before dawn.

If Johnny could get inside, he could survive. It wasn't easy, even with Rudy's help. During the fight, he had shapeshifted too many times, sustained too many terrible wounds, even lost body parts. He had grown wings, and they'd been shredded by silver bullets, then ripped out by the roots. Important bones were gone from his back. One of his feet was lopped off and lost in the street. He hoped it was hopping after one of his enemies.

He had tasted some of them, the Vampire Killers. In Doyle's blood, he found a surprise: the drac-busting cop was a secret dhampire, and had dosed himself up to face Johnny. The knifeman, who had vampire blood in him from a strange birth, had stuffed himself with garlic, to make his blood repulsive.

The blood was something. He was fighting now.

Rudy hammered on Andy's door, shouting. Johnny had last seen Andy at 54, at the party he had left. He should be home by now, or would be home soon. As dawn approached, Johnny felt himself smoking. It was a frosty All Hallows' morn, but the heat building up like a fever inside him was monsoon-oppressive and threatened to explode in flames.

Johnny's continued life depended on Andy having made it home.

The door was opened. It was Andy himself, not yet out of his party clothes, dazzled by the pinking end of night. Johnny felt waves of horror pouring off the artist and understood exactly how he must look.

'It's just red, Andy. You use a lot of red.'

Rudy helped him into Andy's hallway. The gloom was like a welcoming cool in midsummer. Johnny collapsed on the *chaise longue* and looked at Andy, begging.

Only one thing could cure him. Vampire blood.

His first choice would have been the Churchward woman, who was almost an elder. She had survived a century and was of a fresh bloodline. But Penny was gone, fleeing the city and leaving them all in the bloody lurch.

It would have to be Andy. He understood and backed away, eyes wide.

Johnny realised he didn't even know what Andy's bloodline was. Who had made him?

Andy was horrified. He hated to be touched. He hated to give anything, much less himself.

Johnny had no choice. He reached out with what was left of his mind and took a hold of the willing Rudy. He made the dhamp, still hopped up on prime drac, grab Andy by the arms and force him across the lobby, bringing him to the *chaise longue* as an offering for his Master.

'I'm sorry, Andy,' said Johnny.

He didn't prolong the moment. Rudy exposed Andy's neck, stringy and chalky, and Johnny pounced like a cobra, sinking his teeth into the vein, opening his throat for the expected gush of life-giving, mind-blasting vampire blood. He didn't just need to take blood, he needed a whole ghost, to replace the tatters he had lost.

Johnny nearly choked.

He couldn't keep Andy's blood down. His stomach heaved, and gouts poured from his mouth and nose.

How had Andy done it? For all these years?

Rudy looked down on them both, wondering why Johnny was trying to laugh, why Andy was squealing and holding his neck. What the frig was going down in the big city?

Andy wasn't, had never been, a vampire.

He was still alive.

Johnny at last understood just how much Andy Warhol was his own invention.

Andy was dying now and so was Johnny.

Andy's blood did Johnny some good. He could stand up. He could take hold of Rudy, lifting him off his feet. He could rip open Rudy's throat with his teeth and gulp down pints of the dhamp's drac-laced blood. He could toss Rudy's corpse across the lobby.

That taken care of, he cradled Andy, trying to get the dying man's attention. His eyes were still moving, barely. His neck wound was a gouting hole, glistening with Johnny's vampire spittle. The light was going out.

Johnny stuck a thumbnail into his own wrist and poured his blood into Andy's mouth, giving back what he had taken. Andy's lips were as red as rubies. Johnny coaxed him and finally, after minutes, Andy swallowed, then relaxed and let go, taking his first and final drac trip.

In an instant, as it happens sometimes, Andy Warhol died and came back. It was too late, though. Valerie Solanas had hurt him very badly and there were other problems. The turning would not take.

Johnny was too weak to do anything more.

Andy, Warhola the Vampyre at last, floated around his hallway, relishing the new sensations. Did he miss being a magnificent fake?

Then, the seizures took him and he began to crumble. Shafts of light from the glass around the door pierced him, and he melted away like the Wicked Witch of the West.

Andy Warhol was a vampire for only fifteen minutes.

Johnny would miss him. He had taken some of the man's ghost, but it was a quiet spirit. It would never compete with the Father for mastery.

Johnny waited. In a far corner, something stirred.

25

Rudy could have been a powerful vampire. He rose, turned, full of *nosferatu* vigour, eager for his first feeding, brain a-buzz with plans of establishing a coven, a drac empire, a place in the night.

Johnny was waiting for him.

With the last of his strength, he took Rudy down and ripped him open in a dozen places, drinking his vampire blood. Finally, he ate the American boy's heart. Rudy hadn't thought it through. Johnny spat out his used-up ghost. Sad little man.

He exposed Rudy's twice-dead corpse to sunlight, and it powdered. The remains of two vampires would be found in Andy's house, the artist and the drac dealer. Johnny Pop would be officially dead. He had been just another stage in his constant turning.

It was time to quit this city. Hollywood beckoned. Andy would have liked that.

At nightfall, bones knit and face reforming, he left the house. He went to Grand Central Station. There was a cash stash in a locker there, enough to get him out of the city and set him up on the Coast.

The Father was proud of him. Now, he could acknowledge his bloodline in his name. He was no longer Ion Popescu, no longer Johnny Pop; he was Johnny Alucard.

And he had an empire to inherit.

INTERLUDE

———————◆———————

WHO DARES WINS

ANNO DRACULA 1980

Palace Green was blocked, an armoured car emphasising a point she would have thought established sufficiently well by police vans. Uniformed coppers – the Special Patrol Group, of recent ill reputation – and camo-clad squaddies were kitted up for riot, and locals kept out of their homes and offices muttered themselves towards a resentful shade of disgruntled. To Kate Reed, this patch of Kensington felt too much like Belfast for comfort, though passing trade on Embassy Row – veiled woman-shapes with Harrods bags, indignant diplomats of all nations, captains of endangered industries – was of a different quality from the bottle-throwers and -dodgers of the Garvachy Road.

TV crews penned beyond the perimeter had to make do with stories about the crowds rather than the siege. Kate saw the TV reporter Anne Diamond, collar turned up and microphone thrust out, sorting through anxious faces at the barrier, thirsty for someone with a husband or girlfriend trapped inside the Embassy or, better yet, among the terrorists.

'Evenin' Miss Reed,' said a vampire bobby she remembered from the Met's old B Division, which used to handle vampire-related crime.

'It's been a funny old week at Palace Green…'

Sensing the imminence of an anecdote with a moral, Kate showed Sergeant Dixon her NUJ card and was let through.

'We've been waiting for you,' said the sergeant, with fatherly concern, lifting a plank from the barrier. 'This is a rum old do and no mistake.'

Anne Diamond and a dozen other broadcast and print hopefuls were furious that one of the least significant of their number had a free ticket to the big carnival. It wasn't even as if Kate were the only vampire hack on the street. She'd spotted Paxman, drifting incorporeally in mist-form through the crowds. She was, however, the only journo Baron Meinster would talk with.

For two years, she had been waiting for the Transylvanian to call in the favour he'd granted by spiriting her out of Romania via his underground railway. She knew he'd helped her to spite the Ceauşescus, with whom he had a long-standing personal feud, but his intervention still saved her life. This was not what she had expected, but the development didn't surprise her either. Since Teheran, embassy sieges had become a preferred means of the powerless lording it over the powerful. Not that the Baron, *soi-disant* First Elder of the Transylvania Movement, would consider himself powerless.

A tall, moustached vampire in police uniform took a firm grip on Kate's upper arm. Dixon retreated without offering the traditional cup of tea.

'Daniel Dravot,' she said, 'it has been a long time.'

'Yes, Miss Reed,' said the vampire, unsmiling.

'Still *Sergeant* Dravot, I see. Though not truly of the Metropolitan Police, I'll wager.'

'All in the service of the Queen, Miss Reed.'

'Indeed.'

Dravot had been in the shadows as long as she could remember – in Whitechapel in 1888, in France in 1918. Last she'd heard, he'd been training and turning new generations of vampire secret agents. He was back in the field, apparently.

She was walked over to the command post, a large orange workman's hut erected over a hole in the pavement. Dravot lifted a flap-door and ushered her inside.

* * *

She found herself among uncomfortable men of power.

A plainclothes copper sat on a stool, hunched over a field telephone whose wires were crocodile-clamped into an exposed circuit box. Down in the pit, ear-phones worn like a stethoscope under long hair, was a thin warm man of undetermined age. He wore New Romantic finery – full-skirted sky-blue highwayman's coat, knee-boots and puffy mauve britches, three-cornered hat with a feather – and jotted notes on a pad in violet ink. Above them, literally and figuratively, hovered three vampires: a death-faced *eminence grise* in a gravemould-grubby Gannex mac, a human weapon in a black jump-suit and balaclava, and a willowy youth in elegant grey.

She recognised all of these people.

The policeman was Inspector Cherry, who often wound up with the cases involving vampires. A solid, if somewhat whimsical plod, he was an old B Division hand, trained by Bellaver. The dandy in the ditch was Richard Jeperson, chairman of the Ruling Cabal of the Diogenes Club, longest-lived and most independent branch of British Intelligence. He had inherited Dravot, not to mention Kate, from his late predecessors, both of whom she had been close to, Charles Beauregard and Edwin Winthrop. It had been some time since she had last been called to Pall Mall and asked to look into something, but you were never dropped from the club's lists. The vampires were: Caleb Croft, high up in whatever the United Kingdom called its Secret Police these days; Hamish Bond, a spy whose obituaries she never took seriously; and Lord Ruthven, the Home Secretary.

'Katie Reed, good evening,' said Ruthven. 'How charming to see you again, though under somewhat trying circumstances. Very nice piece in the *Grauniad* about the royal fiancée. Gave us all the giggles.'

Ruthven, once a fixture as Prime Minister, was back in the cabinet after a generation out of government. Rumoured to be Margaret Thatcher's favourite vampire, he was horribly likely to succeed her in Number Ten by the next ice age, reclaiming his old job. He brought a century of political experience to the ministerial post and a considerably longer lifetime of survival against the odds.

As Ruthven rose, so did Croft. The grey man had resigned his teaching position to return to secret public service. Kate's skin crawled in his presence. He affected not to remember her. Among monsters, there were monsters – and Croft was the worst she knew. He had a high opinion of her, too... 'Kate Reed was – is – a terrorist, space kidettes,' he'd said when he last set eyes on her. Then, he was just an academic, though he'd used her to clear up one of his messes. Soon, he'd be in a position to tidy her away and no questions asked.

'She's here,' said Cherry, into the phone.

The policeman passed her the set, hand over the mouthpiece.

'Try to find out how many of them there are,' said Jeperson in a stage-whisper. 'But don't be obvious about it.'

'I don't think we need teach Katie Reed anything,' said the Home Secretary. 'She has a wealth of varied experience.'

Unaccountably, that verdict made her self-conscious. She knew about all these men, but they also knew quite a bit about her. Like them all, she had wound in and out of the century, as often covered in blood as glory. Ever since her turning, she had been close to the Great Game of power and intelligence.

Kate put the phone to her ear and said, 'Hello.'

'Katharine,' purred Baron Meinster. His unretractable fangs gave him a vaguely slushy voice, as if he were speaking through a mouthful of blood.

'I'm here, Baron.'

'Excellent. I'm glad to hear it. Is Ruthven there?'

'I'm fine, thank you, and how are you?'

'He is. How delicious. Ten years of dignified petitions and protests, when all I needed to do to get attention was take over a single building. How do you like the banners? Do you think He would appreciate them?'

She knew who Meinster meant when he said 'He'.

The flags of the Socialist Republic had been torn down, and two three-storey banners unfurled from the upper windows of the Embassy. They were blazoned with a tall black dragon, red-eyed and fanged.

'It's time to revive the Order of the Dragon,' said Meinster. 'It's how He got His name.'

She knew that, of course.

'People here want to know what you want, Baron.'

'People there know what I want. I've been telling them for years. I want what is ours. I want a homeland for the undead. I want Transylvania.'

'I think they mean immediately. Blankets? Food?'

'I want Transylvania, immediately.'

She covered the mouthpiece and spoke.

'He wants Transylvania, Home Secretary.'

'Not in our gift, more's the pity. Would he take, say, Wales? I'm sure I can swing Margaret on that. The taffs are all bloody Labour voters anyway, so we'd be glad to turn them over to that drac-head dandy. Or, I don't know, what about the Falkland Islands? They're far distant enough to get shot of without much squawking at home. The Baron could spend his declining years nipping sheep. That's all they ever do up in the Carpathians, anyway.'

'There might be a counter-offer, Baron,' she told him. 'In the South Atlantic.'

'Good God, woman, I'm not serious,' said Ruthven. 'Tell him to be a nice little bat and give up. We'll slap his wrist and condemn him for inconveniencing our old mucka Ceaușescu and his darling Elena, then let him do an hour-long interview with Michael Parkinson on the BBC, just before *Match of the Day*. He should know we like him a lot more than the bloody Reds.'

'Is that an official offer?'

'Not in my lifetime, Miss Reed. Will he talk to me?'

'Would you talk with the Home Secretary?'

A pause. 'Don't think so. He's an upstart. Not of the Dracula line.'

'I heard that,' said Ruthven. 'I've been a vampire far longer than Vladdy-Come-Lately Meinster. He was turned in the 1870s and he's basically little more than a Bucharest bum boy. I was already an elder when he was sucking off his first smelly barmaid.'

They might be of different bloodlines, but Ruthven and Meinster were of a similar type. Turned in their golden youth, they remained petulant boys forever, even as they amassed power and wealth. To them, the world would always be a giant train set. Engineering crashes was great fun.

'Katharine,' said Meinster, 'you had better come visit.'

She really wasn't keen. 'He wants me to go inside.'

'Out of the question,' said Croft.

'Not wise, Kate,' said the spy. 'Meinster's a mad dog. A killer.'

'Commander Bond, your concern is most touching. Are you with the SAS now? Or is everybody dressed up in the wrong uniform these days? What do they call it, "deniability"?'

'Aren't you supposed to be a *secret* agent, Bond,' sniped the Home Secretary. 'Does *everybody* know who you are?'

'I met Miss Reed on an earlier mission, sir.'

'That's one way of putting it, Hamish Bond.'

'Rome, 1959,' said Jeperson, from the pit. 'Not one of the club's notable successes. The Crimson Executioner business. And the death of Dracula.'

Lord Ruthven ummed. 'You were mixed up in that too, weren't you? How you do show up, Katie. Literally all over the map. A person might think you did it on purpose.'

'Not really.'

'We can't let a civilian – an Irish national at that – compromise the situation,' said Croft. 'Give the word, and I'll send in Bond and settle Meinster's hash. Set-ups like this are why we have people like him.'

Bond stood at attention, ready to kill for England.

'Margaret would have our heads on poles, Croft. And I'm not ready to become an ornament just yet. Katie Reed, do you solemnly promise not to succumb to the Stockholm Syndrome? Meinster's a fearful rotter, you know. Good clothes and a boyish charm are no guarantee of good character.'

'I've met him before. I was not entirely captivated.'

'Good enough for me. Any other opinions?' Everyone looked as if they were about to say something, but the Home Secretary cut them all off. 'I thought so. Katie, our hearts go with you.'

'Wouldn't you rather have a gun?' asked Jeperson.

'Ugh. No. Nasty things.'

'A shadow? I can have Nezumi here in fifteen minutes. You've worked with her before.'

Kate remembered the Japanese vampire girl who used to live in the flat upstairs from hers. An elder, and an instrument of the Diogenes Club.

'Isn't it a school night?'

Meinster would have someone who'd notice even a shadow as mouse-like as Nezumi. It was safer to go into the Embassy alone.

Safer, but still stupid.

She was marched again, with Dravot taking hold of her arm in exactly the same place, to the front line, the pavement outside the Embassy. Power was cut off to the street lamps as well as the building, but large floodlights illuminated the dragon banners, projecting human silhouettes against the walls. It must be very dramatic on television, though she overheard Paxman arguing down the line with a BBC controller who wanted, if no one was being murdered just now, to cut back to the snooker finals. As she approached the Embassy, there was some excitement among the crowd, mostly from people asking who the hell she was.

Kate saw no faces at the windows. SAS snipers with silver bullets in their rifles were presumably concealed on the nearest rooftops. Men like Hamish Bond were trained to use crossbows with silver-tipped quarrels. There were even English longbowmen schooled in Agincourt skills, eager to skewer an undead with a length of sharpened willow.

On one side, Jeperson suavely ran down what they knew about the situation inside the Embassy. On the other, Croft brutally gave bullet points about the things they'd like to know.

So far as they understood, there were about twenty-five hostages, including the Romanian Ambassador, whom no one would really miss since he was a faceless apparatchik, and Patricia Rice, a pretty upper-middle class student who had been visiting in order to arrange a tour of collective farms by her Marxist Student Group. As a bled-dry corpse, Rice would be a public relations nightmare: her great-great uncle or someone had once been a famous comedian, and news stories were already homing in on her. The viewers were following the siege just to see if the posh bird made it through the night. Besides Meinster, there were perhaps five vampire terrorists. It was imperative she confirm the numbers, and find out what kind of ordnance they were packing besides teeth and claws. From what she remembered of Meinster's kids up in the Carpathians, they didn't need that much more.

As they reached the front doorstep, Dravot let her go.

Everyone backed away from her in a semi-circle, skinny shadows growing on the Embassy frontage.

In theory, Kate could be arrested if she crossed the threshold. The Embassy was legally Romanian turf and she remained a fugitive from state justice. It occurred to her that this would be a needlessly elaborate way of whisking her back to the prison she had clawed her way out of. Which didn't mean the *Securitate*, besides whom the SPG were lollipop men, weren't up to it.

She thought of pressing the bell-button, but remembered the power was off. She rapped smartly on the door.

The report was surprisingly loud. Weapons were rattled, and she turned to hiss reassurance. If anything would be worse than being bound in a diplomatic pouch and sunk in a Bucharest dungeon, it would be getting shot dead by some jittery squaddie.

The door opened and she was pulled inside.

In the dark lobby, her eyes adjusted instantly. Candles had been stuck up all around and lit.

She had been grabbed by two vampires. A rat-faced fright who scuttled like an insect, his unnaturally elongated torso tightly confined by a long musty jacket with dozens of bright little buttons like spider-eyes. And a new-born girl with a headscarf, bloody smears on her chin, a man's pinstripe jacket, Dr Martens boots and a sub-machine gun. The girl's red eyes told Kate exactly how she felt about her: hatred, mistrust, envy and fear.

'Patricia Rice?' Kate asked.

The new-born hissed. She had been turned recently, in the four days since the siege began.

No one had told her Meinster was making vampires of the hostages. It was the surest way of triggering the Stockholm Syndrome, she supposed. Rice had given up Marxism and pledged herself to a new cause.

She remembered Meinster in the mountains, explaining why the Transylvania Movement would win. 'We can make more of us,' he had said. 'We can drown them.'

Rice took her hand and tugged. Kate stood her ground.

She had been a vampire for nearly a century. This fresh immortal needed a lesson in seniority. Meinster was a fanatic for bloodline, pecking order and respect for elders. It was one reason he was wrong about long-term strategy: he could easily make more vampires, but not more like him. As Ruthven said, he was a parvenu anyway, a pretend-elder barely older than Kate. If Dracula was still King of the Cats, Meinster would never be taken seriously by anyone.

She broke Rice's hold.

'Just take me to your leader,' she said.

The rat-*nosferatu* led the way. He moved jerkily, like a wrong-speed silent movie. He was one of the very old ones, far beyond the human norm. Kate had met creatures like him before and knew they were among the most dangerous of vampirekind. They were all red thirst, and no pretence about civilisation.

She was taken upstairs to a high-ceilinged conference room. Free-standing candelabra threw active shadows on the walls. Hostages were tied up, huddled against the walls: their arms were striped with scabs, but not their necks. Meinster was conserving his resources.

The Baron stood in one corner with his lieutenants. They were vampire kids, child-shaped but old-eyed. These were his favoured troops, not least because he wasn't himself very tall or broad. On *Not the Nine O'Clock News*, he was impersonated (very well) by Pamela Stephenson.

Meinster wore a very smart grey cloak, over a slightly darker grey frock coat and riding boots. His ruffled shirt would have looked better on Adam Ant. His hair was improbably gold, gelled into a fixed wave. His smile was widened by his fangs.

One of his lieutenants had a gun to match Rice's; the other held Meinster's two poodles. In the forest, Kate had seen Meinster kill another vampire for ridiculing his beloved dogs. They were vampire pets, little canine monsters with sharpened fangs, fattened on drops of baby's blood. They must have been smuggled into the country despite quarantine regulations designed to keep undead animals like them out – a more serious crime than terrorism in the opinion of many Home Counties pet owners.

'Katharine, well met.'

'Baron,' she acknowledged.

'She was insolent,' hissed Rice. 'I hate her already.'

'Shush up, Patty-Pat,' said Meinster.

'We don't need her. We only need me. You said so, when you turned me. You said you only needed me. Me.'

'Am I beginning to detect a theme tune?' suggested Kate. '"The Me Song"?'

Rice raised a hand to slap, but Kate snatched her wrist out of the air and bent her arm around her back. She got snarled up on the strap of her gun.

'You turned this girl, Baron?'

Meinster smiled artfully, a boy caught out.

'Things must be desperate.'

She let Rice go. The new-born sulked, face transforming into a bloated mask of resentment and self-pity. She should watch that tendency to shapeshift, or her scowl might really stick. She only had to look at Mr Rat-features to see a dire example of the syndrome.

'May I offer you someone to drink, Katharine. We've a fine selection of fusty old bureaucrats. Oh, and three cultural attachés who admit that they're spies.'

'Only three?'

'So far. We can offer Ruthven some interesting documents from the secret files. Nicolae and Elena tell the world about modernisation and harmony with the West, but we both know they play a different hand at home. My old comrade has much to hide. I'd be most willing to share it with your lovely Mrs Thatcher.'

'She's not mine. I'm Irish, remember.'

'Of course, Katharine. Potato famines, Guinness, Dana. I am well up on the West. As a coming man, I have to learn all these things. Just as He did, a century ago.'

When he so much as hinted at the name, his eyes were radiant. She thought she saw tiny twin bats flapping in his pupils.

'You so want to be him, Baron. How well did you know him?'

'He was more a father to me than any human family. More a mother. More anything.'

On the subject, Meinster was blind. To him, Dracula was the King of the Cats, the fount of wisdom and destiny, a God and a champion. Kate knew too many vampires like the Baron, forcing themselves to be what they imagined Dracula had been, hoping to become everything he was but not knowing the whole story.

'At the end, he wanted to die,' she said. 'I saw that.'

'You saw what you wanted to see, Katharine. You are not of his direct bloodline.'

'I wish that were true.'

'Heresy,' shouted Rice, raising her gun and fiddling with anything that might be a safety catch. 'She defiles the name of the Father-in-Darkness.'

Meinster nodded, snake-swift. The old *nosferatu*, rodent-ears twitching, took the new-born's gun away from her.

'Thank you, Orlok,' acknowledged Meinster.

Kate looked again at the reeking thing. She knew who Graf von Orlok was. During the Terror, when London rose against the rule of Dracula, he had been in command of the Tower where the 'traitors' were kept. If she had been less fortunate during her underground period, she might have met Orlok before. Several of her friends had, and not survived.

Sometimes, she forgot to be afraid of vampires. After all, she was a bloodsucking leech too and no one was ever afraid of her. Sometimes, she remembered.

Now, looking at the spark in Orlok's grubby eyes, she remembered the first vampires she had seen, when she was a warm girl and the dead were rising all around.

In her heart, nightmare spasmed.

'Katharine, I will prevail,' said the Baron.

'How? The British government doesn't negotiate with terrorists.'

Meinster laughed.

'What's a terrorist, Katharine? You were a terrorist. And you've just had a conversation with the Home Secretary. Once upon a time, you were a wanted insurrectionist and Orlok was a lawful authority. Once Nicolae Ceaușescu was a terrorist, my partisan comrade, and the Nazis were our enemy.'

That was true.

'And, in our homeland, you were unjustly accused of murder, hunted by corrupt police. Then, when you came to me in the mountains, we had common cause. Nothing has really changed. We have been adrift, I'll admit. Since He passed, we have pretended to be humans, to be just another of the many races of mankind, but we are not. You've never lived with your own kind, Katharine. You've spent a century working with *them*, fighting for the cattle. Yet they still fear and loathe you. Here in England, the warm are polite and pretend not to despise us; but in our homeland, you must have seen the truth. Vampires are hated. And we *must* be hated. Our inferiors must hate and fear and respect us. He knew that. His was the vision we must struggle to bring about. We must be the princes of the earth, not the servants of men. Then, believe me, He will rise again. What you saw was an illusion. Dracula does not die and become dust.'

Meinster was trembling with excitement, a boy dreaming of Christmas morning.

Kate saw Patricia Rice, adoring her father-lover-fiend.

'First, Transylvania…'

Meinster let it hang.

'I've seen who's out there,' said Kate. 'I know what they can do. Having hostages won't help. You had one card, and you've played it badly.'

She nodded at Patricia Rice.

'On the contrary, she was my masterstroke. Are you not, dearest Patty-Pat?'

He reached out and touched Rice's face. She squirmed against his hand, like one of his fanged poodles.

'She will be my Elena, when I rule. The first of my Elenas.'

The Baron gave orders to Orlok, in rapid Romanian. Kate only picked up a few words. One of them, of course, was *moarte* – 'death'.

'First, the fire,' said the Baron, sweeping over a candelabrum. Flames caught a tablecloth and swarmed over the furniture. The hostages began screaming. 'Now, we make a dramatic departure.'

He leaped up onto a windowsill and posed against the tall opening. Searchlights outside swung to light him up. He was a swashbuckling figure, cloak swept back over his shoulders.

'To me, my brides.'

Rice hopped up to nestle under one arm. He stretched the other out, beckoning to Kate.

'Become a bride of Dracula, my fiery Irish colleen.'

'That's far too presumptuous, Baron.'

Orlok picked her up and tossed her to Meinster.

'Comfy?' he asked the two. Kate saw Rice almost swoon in delight, but didn't understand it herself.

Apart from all other considerations, she knew Meinster was gay.

He leaned against the windows and smashed through.

For a moment, Kate assumed the Baron, like his supposed father-in-darkness, could grow wings and fly. Then gravity and reality took over.

They plummeted to the pavement.

Meinster sprang up like a cat. Kate, badly shaken, rolled into the gutter. Rice, knees and ankles broken, howled as the bones knit back together.

People rushed forward.

'I have surrendered,' Meinster announced, 'to these flowers

177

of English and Irish vampire maidenhood.'

A black-clad figure swarmed up the front of the Embassy, to the broken window. Flames were already pouring out, blackening the sill.

There was gunfire inside the building.

Richard Jeperson helped her stand and brush herself down, showing real concern. His style was more Charles Beauregard than Edwin Winthrop: she wondered how long he could last under the likes of Ruthven and Croft, not to mention Margaret Thatcher.

Along with the police, TV crews surged forward.

She heard commentators chattering, speculating on the rapid pace of events.

Another vampire was tossed out of the window, turning to a rain of ashes. Hamish Bond was doing his job. Kate thought Orlok might give him a fight, then she saw Dravot, out of his police helmet, signalling a cadre of black ninja-suited men, vampires all, to move in. Britain had been working for a century to create the vampires it needed rather than the ones imposed upon it.

The front door was smashed. Vampires crawled head-down from the flat roof and lizard-swarmed in through upper-storey windows. It was over in moments.

Jeperson and she were separated from the action by a press of people. Between riot shields, she saw Meinster and Ruthven facing each other, warily but without going for the throat. It was as if they were looking in reflecting mirrors for the first time since their turning.

'What was the point?' she asked. 'This was all arranged between them. This wasn't a siege, it was a pantomime. It's not about vampires, it's about communism.'

Jeperson was sad-eyed.

'You of all people know Romania,' he said. 'You've seen what happens in the satellite countries. There's no real *detente*. We have to get rid of the whole shoddy system. Nicolae Ceauşescu is a monster.'

'And Meinster is better?'

'He isn't worse.'

'Richard, *you* don't know. You weren't there during the Terror. When people like Meinster, and people like Ruthven, are in charge, people like you, and people like me, get shoved into locked boxes. It happens slowly, without a revolution, without fireworks, and the world grows cold and hard. Ruthven's back and you're supporting Meinster. How long will it be before we start praying for Dracula?'

'I'm sorry, Kate. I *do* understand.'

'Why was I here?'

'To be a witness. For history. Beauregard said that about you. Someone outside the Great Game has to know. Someone has to judge.'

'And approve?'

Jeperson was chilled. 'Not necessarily.'

Then, he was pulled away too. She was in a crowd.

A cheer rose up. A line of people, hands on heads, bent over, scurried out of the Embassy door. The hostages. Among them was Orlok, with the poodles. She would have bet he'd survive.

She tripped over thick cable, and followed it back out of the press of bodies. A BBC OB van hummed with activity.

This was news. She was a newspaperwoman.

Somewhere near, she would find a phone. It was time to call her editor.

PART THREE

THE OTHER SIDE OF MIDNIGHT

ANNO DRACULA 1981

1

At midnight, 1980 flew away across the Pacific and 1981 crept in from the East. A muted cheer rose from the pretty folk around the barbecue pit, barely an echo of the raucous welcome to a new decade, which had erupted at the last Paradise Cove New Year party.

Of this company, only Geneviève clung to the old – the proper – manner of reckoning decades, centuries and (when they came) millennia. The passing of time was important to her; born in 1416, she'd let more time pass than most. Even among vampires, she was an elder. Five minutes ago – last year, last decade – she'd started to explain proper dating to a greying California boy, an ex-activist they called 'the Dude'. His eyes, already glazed from the weed he'd been toking throughout the party, grew heavy-lidded. She doubted he'd drawn a straight breath since Jefferson Airplane changed their name. She quite liked the Dude's eyes, in any condition.

'It's as simple as this,' she reiterated, hearing the French in her accent ('eet's', 'seemple', 'ziss') which only came out when she was tipsy ('teep-see') or trying for effect. 'Since there was no Year Nothing, the first decade ended with the end of Year Ten AD; the first century with the end of AD 100; the first millennium with the end of AD 1000. Now, at this moment, a new decade is to begin. 1981 is the first year of the 1980s, as 1990 will be the last.'

Momentarily, the Dude looked as if he understood, but he

was just concentrating to make out her accented words. She saw insight spark in his mind, a vertiginous leap which made him want to back away from her. He held out his twisted, tufted joint.

'Man, if you start questioning time,' he said, 'what have you got left? Physical matter? Maybe you question that next, and the mojo won't work any more. You'll think holes between molecules and sink through the surface of the Earth. Drawn by gravity. Heavy things should be left alone. Fundamental things, like the ground you walk on, the air you breathe. You do breathe, don't you, man? Suddenly it hits me, I don't know if you do.'

'Yes, I breathe,' she said. 'When I turned, I didn't die. That's not common.'

She proved her ability to inhale by taking a toke from the joint. She didn't get a high like his; for that, she'd have to sample his blood as it channelled the intoxicants from his alveoli to his brain. She had the mellow buzz of him, from saliva on the roach as much as from the dope smoke. It made her thirsty.

Because it was just after midnight on New Year's Eve, she kissed him. He enjoyed it, non-committally. Tasting straggles of tobacco in his beard and the film of a cocktail – white Russian – on his teeth and tongue, she sampled the ease of him, the defiant crusade of his back-burnered life. She understood now precisely what the expression 'ex-activist' meant. If she let herself drink, his blood would be relaxing.

Breaking the kiss, she saw more sparks in his eyes where her face was not reflected. Her lips were sometimes like razors, even more than her fang-teeth. She'd cut him slightly, just for a taste, not even thinking, and left some of herself on his tongue. She swallowed: mostly spit, but with tiny ribbons of blood from his gums.

French kissing was the kindest form of vampirism. From the minute exchange of fluid, she could draw a surprising sustenance. For her, just now, it was enough. It took the edge off her red thirst.

'Keep on breathing, man,' said the Dude, reclaiming his

joint, smiling broadly, drifting back towards the rest of the party, enjoying the unreeling connection between them. 'And don't question time. Let it pass.'

Licking her lips daintily, she watched him amble. He wasn't convinced 1980 had been the last year of the old decade and not the first of the new. Rather, he wasn't convinced that it mattered. Like a lot of Southern Californians, he'd settled on a time that suited him and stayed in it. Many vampires did the same thing, though Geneviève thought it a waste of longevity. In her more pompous moments, she felt the whole point was to embrace change while carrying on what was of value from the past.

When she was born and when she was turned, time was reckoned by the Julian Calendar, with its annual error of eleven minutes and fourteen seconds. Thinking of it, she still regretted the ten days – the 5th to the 14th of October, 1582 – Pope Gregory XIII had stolen from her, from the world, to make his sums add up. England and Scotland, ten days behind Rome, held out against the Gregorian Calendar until 1752. Other countries stubbornly stuck with Julian dating until well into the twentieth century: Russia had not chimed in until 1918, Greece until 1923. Before the modern era, those ten-day shifts made diary-keeping a complex business for a necessarily much-travelled creature. In his 1885 journal, maintained while travelling on the continent and later excerpted by Bram Stoker, Jonathan Harker refers to May the 4th as the eve of St George's Day, which would have been April the 22nd back home in England. Those leap-frogged weeks had been far much more jarring than the time-zone-hopping she sometimes went through as an air passenger.

The Paradise Cove Trailer Park Colony had been her home for all of four years, an eyeblink which made her a senior resident among the constitutionally impermanent peoples of Malibu. Here, ancient history was Sonny and Cher and *Leave It to Beaver*, anything on the 'golden oldies' station or in off-prime time re-run.

Geneviève – fully, Geneviève Sandrine de l'Isle Dieudonné, though she went by Gené Dee for convenience – had once paddled in the Atlantic and *not known* what lay between France and China. She was older than the name 'America'; had she not turned, she'd probably have been dead before Columbus brought back the news. In all those years, ten days shouldn't matter, but supposedly significant dates made her aware of that fold in time, that wrench which pulled the future hungrily closer, which had swallowed one of her birthdays. By her internal calendar, the decade would not fully turn for nearly two weeks. This was a limbo between unarguable decades. She should have been used to limbos by now. For her, Paradise Cove was the latest of a long string of pockets out of time and space, cosy coffins shallowly buried away from the rush of the world.

She was the only one of her kind at the party; if she took 'her kind' to mean vampires – there were others in her current profession, private investigation, even other incomers from far enough out of state to be considered foreign parts. Born in Northern France under the rule of an English king, she'd seen enough history to recognise the irrelevance of nationality. To be Breton in 1416 was to be neither French nor English, or both at the same time. Much later, during the Revolution, France had scrapped the calendar again, ducking out of the 1790s, even renaming the months. In the long term, the experiment was not a success. That was the last time she – Citizen Dieudonné – had really lived in her native land; the gory business soured her not only on her own nationality, but humanity in general. Too many eras earned names like 'the Terror'. Vampires were supposed to be obscenely bloodthirsty and she wasn't blind to the excesses of her kind, but the warm drank just as deeply from open wounds and usually made more of a mess of it.

From the sandy patio beside her chrome-finished airstream trailer, she looked beyond the gaggle of folks about the pit, joking over franks impaled on skewers. The Dude was mixing a pitcher of white Russians with his bowling buddies, resuming a months-long argument over the precise wording of the opening narration/song of *Branded*. An eight-track in an open-top car played 'Hotel California', The Eagles' upbeat but ominous song about a vampire and her victims. Some were dancing on the sand, shoes in a pile that would be hard to sort out later. White rolls of surf crashed on the breakers, waves edged delicately up the beach.

Out there was the Pacific Ocean and the curve of the Earth, and beyond the blue horizon, as another shivery song went, was a rising sun. Setting, rather – she was looking west. Dawn didn't worry her: at her age, as long as she dressed carefully – sunglasses, a floppy hat, long sleeves – she wouldn't even catch a severe tan, let alone frazzle up into dust and essential salts like some *nosferatu* of the Dracula bloodline. She had grown out of the dark. To her owl eyes, it was no place to hide, which meant she had to be careful where she looked on party nights like this. She liked living by the sea: its depths were still impenetrable to her, still a mystery.

'Hey, Gidget,' came a rough voice, 'need a nip?'

It was one of the surfers, a shaggy bear of a man she had never heard called anything but Moondoggie. He wore frayed shorts, flip-flops and an old blue shirt, and probably had done since the 1950s. He was a legendary veteran of tubes and pipes and waves long gone. He seemed young to her, though his friends called him an old man.

His offer was generous. She had fed off him before, when the need was strong. With his blood came a salt rush, the sense of being enclosed by a curl of wave as his board torpedoed across the surface of the water.

Just now, she didn't need it. She still had the taste of the Dude. Smiling, she waved him away. As an elder, she didn't have the red thirst so badly. Since Charles, she had fed much less. That wasn't how it was with many vampires, especially those of the Dracula line. Some *nosferatu* got thirstier and thirstier with passing ages, and were finally consumed by their own raging red needs. Those were the ones who got to be called monsters. Beside them, she was a minnow.

Moondoggie tugged at his open collar, scratching below his salt-and-pepper beard. The LAPD had wanted to hang a murder rap on him two years ago, when a runaway turned up dead in his beach hut. She had investigated and cleared his name. He would always be grateful to his 'Gidget', which she learned was a contraction of 'Girl Midget'. Never tall, she had turned – frozen – at sixteen. Recently, after centuries of being treated like a child, she was most often taken for a woman in her twenties. That was: by people who didn't know she wasn't warm, wasn't entirely living. She'd have examined her face for the beginnings of lines, but mirrors were no use to her.

Shots were fired in the distance. She looked at the rise of the cliffs and saw the big houses, decks lit by fairy light UFO constellations, seeming to float above the beach, heavy with heavy hitters. Firing up into the sky was a Malibu New Year tradition. Reputedly started by the film director John Milius, a famous surf and gun nut, it was a stupid, dangerous thing to do. Gravity and momentum meant bullets came down somewhere, and not always into the water. In the light of New Year's Day, she found spent shells in the sand or pocked holes in driftwood. One year, someone's head would be under a slug. Milius had made her cry with *Big Wednesday*, though. Movies with coming-of-age, end-of-an-era romanticism crawled inside her heart and melted her. She would have to tell Milius it got worse and worse with centuries.

So, the 1980s?

Some thought her overly formal for always using the full form, but she'd lived through decades called 'the eighties' before. For the past hundred years 'the eighties' had meant the Anni Draculae, the 1880s. Among other things, the founding of Dracula's brief empire had drawn her out of the shadow of eternal evening into something approaching the light. That brought her together with Charles, the warm man with whom she had spent seventy-five years, until his death in 1959, the warm man who had shown her that she, a vampire, could still love, that she had turned without dying inside.

She wasn't unique, but she was rare. Most vampires lost more than they gained when they turned; they died and came back as different people, caricatures of their former selves, compelled to extremes by an inner drive. Creatures like that were one of the reasons why she was here, at the far western edge of a continent where 'her kind' were still comparatively rare.

Other vampires had nests in the Greater Los Angeles area. Don Drago Robles, a landowner before the incorporation of the state into the Union, had quietly waited for the city to close around his *hacienda*, and was rising as a political figure with a growing constituency, a Californian answer to Baron Meinster's European Transylvania Movement. A few long-lived movie or music people, the sort with reflections in silver and voices that registered on recording equipment, had Spanish-style castles along Sunset Boulevard, like eternal child rock god Timmy V or silent movie star David Henry Reid. More, small sharks mostly, swam through Angelino sprawl, battening on marginal people to leech them dry of dreams as much as blood, or − in that ghastly new thing − selling squirts of their own blood ('drac') to sad addicts ('dhampires') who wanted to be a vampire for the night but didn't have the heart to turn all the way.

She should be grateful to the rogues; much of her business came from people who got mixed up with bad egg vampires. Her reputation for extricating victims from predators was like gold to distressed parents or cast-aside partners. Sometimes she worked as a deprogrammer, helping kids out of all manner of cults. They grew beliefs stranger than Catholicism, or even vampirism, out here among the orange groves: the Moonies, the Esoteric Order of Dagon, Immortology, Psychoplasmics.

As always, she stuck it out until the party died. All the hours of the night rolled away and red light cast the shadows of clifftop homes onto the beach. January cold gathered, driving those warmer folks who were still sensible from their barbecues and beach-towels to their beds.

Marty Burns, sometime sit-com star and current inhabitant of a major career slump, was passed out face down on the chilling sands in front of her trailer space. She found a blanket to throw over him. He murmured in liquor-and-pills lassitude. She tucked the blanket comfortably around his neck. Marty was hilarious in person, even when completely off his face, but *Salt & Pepper*, the star-making show he was squandering residuals from, was puzzlingly free of actual humour. The dead people on the laugh-track audibly split sides at jokes deader than they were. The year was begun with a moderate good deed, though purging the kid's system and dragging him to AA might have been a more lasting solution to whatever was inside him, chewing away.

She would sleep later, in the morning, locked in her sleek trailer, a big metal coffin equipped with everything she needed. Of all her homes over the years, this was the one she cherished the most. The trailer was chromed everywhere it could be, and customised with steel shutters that bolted over the windows and the never-used sun roof. Economy of space forced her to limit her possessions – so few after so long – to those that really meant the most to her: ugly jewellery from her mediaeval girlhood, some of Charles's books and letters, a Dansette gramophone with an eclectic collection of sides, her beloved answering machine, a tacky Mexican crucifix with light-up eyes that she kept on show just to prove she wasn't one of *those* vampires, a rubber duck with a story attached, two decent formal dresses and four pairs of Victorian shoes (custom-cobbled for her tiny feet) which had outlasted everything made this century and would do for decades more. On the road, she could kink herself double and rest in the trunk of her automobile, a pillar-box red 1958 Plymouth Fury, but the trailer was more comfortable.

She wandered towards the sea-line, across the disturbed sands of the beach. There had been dancing earlier, grown-ups who had been in Frankie and Annette movies trying to fit their old moves to current music. *Le freak, c'est chic.*

She trod on a hot pebble that turned out to be a bullet, and saluted Big John up on his A-list Hollywood deck. Milius had written *Dracula* for Francis Ford Coppola, from the novel she was left out of. Not wanting to have the Count brought back to mind, she'd avoided the movie, though her vampire journalist friend Kate Reed, also not mentioned in Stoker's fiction, had worked on it.

She hadn't heard from Kate in too long; Geneviève knew she'd spent some time behind the Iron Curtain, on the trail of the Transylvania Movement, that odd faction of the Baron Meinster's which wanted Dracula's estates as a homeland for vampires. God, if that ever happened, she would get round to re-applying for American citizenship; they were accepting *nosferatu* now, which they hadn't been in 1917 when she last looked into it. Meinster was one of those Dracula wannabes who couldn't quite carry off the opera cloak and ruffle shirt, with his prissy little fangs and his naked need to be the new King of the Cats. She'd already seen him make a grab for the title once, and get bloody egg on his face – but the absence of Dracula made even a metaphorical empty throne a temptation to the ambitious.

Wavelets lapped at her bare toes. Her nails sparkled under water.

1970s music hadn't been much, not after the 1960s. Glam rock. The Bee Gees. The Carpenters. Disaster movies. *M*A*S*H*. Burt Reynolds. The zipless fuck. Watergate. An oil crisis. The Bicentennial Summer. The Iran hostage crisis. No Woodstock. No Swinging London. No one like Kennedy. Nothing like the Moon Landing.

If she were to fill a diary page for every decade, the 1970s would be heavily padded. She'd been to some parties and helped some people, settled into the slow, pastel, dusty ice-cream world of Southern California, a little to one side of the swift stream of human history. She wasn't even much bothered by memories, the curse of the long-lived.

Not bad, not good, not anything.

She wasn't over Charles, never would be really. He was a constant, silent presence in her heart, an ache and a support and a joy. He was a memory she would never let slip. And Dracula, finally destroyed soon after Charles's death, still cast a long cloak-shadow over her life. And Kate's, and Penelope Churchward's too – and who knew what Penny was up to these days? Without Charles – without Dracula – they were all three adrift. It struck Geneviève that if anyone rose to take the place of the two dead men they'd spent their lives clinging to or running from, she, Kate and Penny would end up together, like the three witches in *Macbeth* – prophesying, misleading and anointing, in thunder, lightning or in rain. Once, it'd have been a tragedy. Now, it'd be a sit-com.

Like Bram Stoker, she wondered what her life, what the world, would have been like if Vlad Tepes had never turned or been defeated before his rise to power.

Might-have-beens and the dead. Bad company.

John Lennon was truly dead, too. Less than a month ago, in New York, he'd taken a silver bullet through the heart, a cruel full stop for the 1970s, for what was left of the 1960s. Annie Wilkes, Lennon's killer, said she was the musician's biggest fan, but that he had to die for breaking up the Beatles. Geneviève didn't know how long Lennon had been a vampire, but she sadly recognised in the dirge 'Imagine' that copy-of-a-copy voidishness characteristic of creatives who turned to prolong their artistic lives, but found the essential thing that made them who they were, that powered their talent, gone, and that the best they could hope for was a kind of rarefied self-plagiarism. Mad Annie might have done John a favour, making him immortal again. Currently the most famous vampire-slayer in the world, she was a heroine to the bedrock strata of warm America which would never accept vampirekind as even kissing cousins to humanity.

What, she wondered as the sun touched the sky, would this new decade bring?

2

COUNT DRACULA
A SCREENPLAY

by Herman J. Mankiewicz and Orson Welles
Based on the novel of Bram Stoker

Nov 30, 1939

Fade In

1. EXT. TRANSYLVANIA – FAINT DAWN – 1885

Window, very small in the distance, illuminated. All around this an almost totally black screen. Now, as the camera moves slowly towards this window, which is almost a postage stamp in the frame, other forms appear: spiked battlements, vast granite walls, and now, looming up against the still-nighted sky, enormous iron grillwork.

Camera travels up what is now shown to be a gateway of gigantic proportions and holds on the top of it – a huge initial 'D' showing darker and darker against the dawn sky. Through this and beyond we see the gothic-tale mountaintop of Dracula's estate, the great castle a silhouette at its summit, the little window a distant accent in the darkness.

Dissolve

(A series of setups, each closer to the great window, all telling something of:)

2. EXT. THE LITERALLY INCREDIBLE DOMAIN OF VLAD, COUNT DRACULA

Its right flank resting for forty miles along the Borgo Pass, the estate truly extends in all directions farther than the eye can see. An ocean of sharp tree-tops, with occasionally a deep rift where there is a chasm. Here and there are silver threads where the rivers wind in deep gorges through the forests. Designed by nature to be almost completely vertical and jagged – it was, as will develop, primordial forested mountain when Dracula acquired and changed its face – it is now broken and shorn, with its fair share of carved peaks and winding paths, all man-made.

Castle Dracula itself – an enormous pile, compounded of several demolished and rebuilt structures of varying architecture, with broken battlements and many towers – dominates the scene from the very peak of the mountain. It sits on the edge of a very terrible precipice.

Dissolve

3. EXT. THE VILLAGE

In the shadows, literally the shadows, of the mountain. As we move by, we see that the peasant doors and windows are shuttered and locked, with crucifixes and obscene clusters of garlic as further protection and sealing. Eyes peep out, timid, at us. The camera moves like a band of men: purposeful, cautious, intrepid, curious.

Dissolve

4. EXT. FOREST OF STAKES

Past which we move. The sward is wild with mountain weeds, the stakes tilted at a variety of Dutch angles, the execution field unused and not seriously tended for a long time.

Dissolve

5. EXT. WHAT WAS ONCE A GOOD-SIZED PRISON STOCKADE

All that now remains, with one exception, are the individual plots, surrounded by thorn fences, on which the hostages were kept, free and yet safe from each other and the landscape at large. (Bones in several of the plots indicate that here there were once human cattle, kept for blood.)

Dissolve

6. EXT. A WOLF PIT

In the f.g., a great shaggy dire wolf, bound by a silver chain, is outlined against the fawn murk. He raises himself slowly, with more thought than an animal should display, and looks out across the estates of Count Dracula, to the distant light glowing in the castle on the mountain. The wolf howls, a child of the night, making sweet music.

Dissolve

7. EXT. A TRENCH BELOW THE WALLS

A slow-scuttling armadillo. A crawling giant beetle. Reflected in the muddy water – the lighted window.

Dissolve

8. EXT. THE MOAT

Angled spears sag. An old notebook floats on the surface of the water – its pages covered in shorthand scribble. As it moves across the frame, it discloses again the reflection of the window in the castle, closer than before.

Dissolve

9. EXT. A DRAWBRIDGE

Over the wide moat, now stagnant and choked with weeds. We move across it and through a huge rounded archway into a formal courtyard, perhaps thirty feet wide and one hundred yards deep, which extends right up to the very wall of the castle. Let's see Toland keep all of it in focus. The landscaping surrounding it has been sloppy and casual for centuries, but this particular courtyard has been kept up in perfect shape. As the camera makes its way through it, towards the lighted window of the castle, there are revealed rare and exotic blooms of all kinds: *Mariphasa lupino lumino*, strange orchid, *Audriensis junior, Triffidus celestus*. The dominating note is one of almost exaggerated wildness, sprouting sharp and desperate – rot, rot, rot. The Hall of the Mountain King, the night the last troll died. Some of the plants lash out, defensively.

Dissolve

10. EXT. THE WINDOW

Camera moves in until the frame of the window fills the frame of the screen. Suddenly the light within goes out. This stops the action of the camera and cuts the music (Bernard Herrmann) which has been accompanying the sequence. In the glass panes of the window we see reflected the stark, dreary mountainscape of the Dracula estate behind and the dawn sky.

Dissolve

11. INT. CORRIDOR IN CASTLE DRACULA – FAINT DAWN – 1885

Ornate mirrors line both walls of the corridor, reflecting arches into infinity. A bulky shadow figure – Dracula – proceeds slowly, heavy with years, through the corridor. He pauses to look into the mirror, and has no reflection, no reflections, to infinity. It seems at last that he is simply not there.

Dissolve

12. INT. DRACULA'S CRYPT – FAINT DAWN – 1885

A very long shot of Dracula's enormous catafalque, silhouetted against the enormous window.

Dissolve

13. INT. DRACULA'S CRYPT – FAINT DAWN – 1885

An eye. An incredible one. Big impossible drops of bloody tears, the reflections of figures coming closer, cutting implements raised. The jingling of sleigh bells in the musical score now makes an ironic reference to Indian temple bells – the music freezes –

DRACULA'S OLD VOICE: *Rose's blood!*

The camera pulls back to show the eye in the face of the old Dracula, bloated with blood but his stolen youth lost again, grey skin parchmented like a mummy, fissures cracking open in the wrinkles around his eyes, fangteeth too large for his mouth, pouching his cheeks and stretching his lips, the nose an improbable bulb. A flash – the descent of a guillotine-like kukri knife, which has been raised above Dracula's neck – across the screen. The head rolls off the neck and bounds down two carpeted steps leading to the catafalque, the camera following. The head falls off the last step onto the marble floor where it cracks, snaky tendrils of blood glittering in the first ray of the morning sun. This ray cuts an angular pattern across the floor, suddenly crossed with a thousand cruciform bars of light as a dusty curtain is wrested from the window.

14. INT. THE FOOT OF DRACULA'S CATAFALQUE

The camera very close. Outlined against the uncurtained window we can see a form – the form of a man, as he raises a bowie knife over his head. The camera moves down along the catafalque as the knife descends into Dracula's heart, and rests on the severed head. Its lips are still moving. The voice, a whisper from the grave

DRACULA'S OLD VOICE: *Rose's blood!*

In the sunlight, a harsh shadow cross falling upon it, the head lap-dissolves into a fanged, eyeless skull.

Fade Out

Count Dracula Cast and Credits, as of January, 1940.

Production Company: Mercury Productions. Distributor: RKO Radio Pictures. Executive Producer: George J. Schaefer. Producer: Orson Welles. Director: Orson Welles. Script: Herman J. Mankiewicz, Orson Welles. From the novel by Bram Stoker. Director of Photography: Gregg Toland. Editors: Mark Robson, Robert Wise. Art Director: Van Nest Polglase. Special Effects: Vernon L. Walker. Music/Musical Director: Bernard Herrmann.

Orson Welles (Dracula), Joseph Cotten (Jedediah Renfield), Everett Sloane (Van Helsing), Dorothy Comingore (Mina Murray), Robert Coote (Artie Holmwood), William Alland (Jon Harker), Agnes Moorehead (Mrs Westenra), Lucille Ball (Lucy), George Couloris (Dr Walter Parkes Seward), Paul Stewart (Raymond, Asylum Attendant), Alan Ladd (Quincey P. Morris), Fortunio Bonanova (Inn-Keeper at Bistritz), Vladimir Sokoloff (Szgany Chieftain), Dolores Del Rio, Ruth Warrick, Rita Cansino (Vampire Brides), Gus Schilling (Skipper of the *Demeter*).

———————————◆———————————

'Mademoiselle Dieudonné,' intoned the voice on her answering machine, half-way between a growl and a purr, 'this is Orson Welles.'

The voice was deeper even than it had been in the 1930s, when he was a radio star. Geneviève had been in America over Hallowe'en, 1938, when Welles and the Mercury Theatre of the Air broadcast their you-are-there dramatisation of H.G. Wells's 'The Flowering of the Strange Orchid' and convinced half the Eastern seaboard that the country was disappearing under a writhing plague of vampire blossoms. She remembered also the whisper of 'Who *knows* what evil *lurks* in the hearts of *men*?' followed by the triumphant declaration, 'the *Shadow* knows!' and the low chuckle which rose by terrifying lurches to a fiendish, maniacal shriek of insane laughter.

When she had first met the man himself, in Rome in 1959, the voice hadn't disappointed. Now, even on cheap tape and through the tinny, tiny amplifier, it was a call to the soul. Even hawking brandy or frozen peas, the voice was a powerful instrument. That Welles had to compete with Welles imitators for gigs as a commercial pitchman was one of the tragedies of the modern age. Then again, she suspected he drew a deal of sly enjoyment from his long-running role as a ruined titan. As an actor, his greatest role was always himself. Even leaving a message on a machine, he invested phrases with the weight – a quality he had more than a sufficiency of – of a Shakespearean deathbed speech.

'There is a small matter upon which I should like your opinion, in your capacities as a private detective and a member of the undead community. If you would call on me, I should be most grateful.'

She thought about it. Welles was as famous for being broke as for living well. It was quite likely he wouldn't even come

through with her modest rate of a hundred dollars a day,
let alone expenses. And gifts of rare wine or Cuban cigars
weren't much use to her, though she supposed she could
redeem them for cash.

Still, she was mildly bored with finding lost children or bail
jumpers. And no one ever accused Welles of being boring. He
had left the message while she was resting through the hours
of the day. This was the first of the ten or so days between
the Gregorian 1980s and the Julian 1980s. She could afford
to give a flawed genius – his own expression – that much time.

She would do it.

In leaving a message, Welles had given her a pause to think.
She heard heavy breaths as he let the tape run on, his big man's
lungs working. Then, confident that he had won her over, he
cut in with address details, somewhere in Beverly Hills.

'I do so look forward to seeing you again. Until then,
remember... *the weed of crime bears bitter fruit!*'

It was one of his old radio catchphrases.

He did the laugh, the King Laugh, the Shadow Laugh. It
properly chilled her bones, but made her giggle too.

4

She discovered Orson Welles at the centre of attention, on the
cracked bottom of a drained swimming pool behind a rented
bungalow. Three nude vampire girls waved objects – a luminous
skull, a Macbethian bloodied dagger, a fully-articulated monster
bat puppet – at him, darting swiftly about his bulky figure,
nipping at his head with their Hallowe'en props. The former
Boy Wonder was on his knees, enormous Russian shirt open
to the waist, enormous (and putty) nose glistening under the
lights, enormous spade-beard flecked with red syrup. A man
with a hand-held camera, the sort of thing she'd seen used to
make home movies, circled the odd quartet, not minding if the
vampires got between him and his director-star.

A few other people stood around the pool, holding up lights. No sound equipment though: this was being shot silent. Geneviève hung back by the bungalow, keeping out of the way of the work. She had been on film sets before, at Cinecittà and in Hollywood, and knew this crew would be skeletal for a student short. If anyone else had been directing, she'd have supposed he was shooting make-up tests or a rehearsal. But with Welles, she knew that this was the real film. It might end up with the dialogue out of sync, but it would be extraordinary.

Welles was rumbling through a soliloquy.

It took her a moment to realise what the undead girls were doing, then she had to swallow astonished laughter. They were nude not for the titillation of an eventual audience, for they wouldn't be seen. Non-reflecting *nosferatu* would be completely invisible when the footage was processed. The girls were naked because clothes would show up on film, though some elders – Dracula had been one – so violated the laws of optics that they robbed any costume they wore of its reflection also, sucking even that into their black hearts. In the final film, Welles would seem to be persecuted by malignly animated objects – the skull, the dagger and the bat. Now, he tore at his garments and hair like Lear, careful to leave his nose alone, and called out to the angry heavens. The girls flitted, slender and deathly white, not feeling the cold, faces blank, hands busy.

This was the cheapest special effect imaginable.

Welles fell forward on his face, lay still for a couple of beats and hefted himself upright, out of character, calling 'cut'. His nose was mashed.

A dark woman with a clipboard emerged from shadows to confer with the master. She wore a white fur coat and a matching hat. The vampire girls put the props down and stood back, nakedness ignored by the crew members. One took a cloak-like robe from a chair and settled it over her slim shoulders. She climbed out of the pool.

Geneviève had not announced herself. The vampire girl fixed her eye. She radiated a sense of being fed up with the supposed glamour of show business.

'Turning was supposed to help my career,' she said. 'I was going to stay pretty forever and be a star. Instead, I lost my image. I had good credits. I was up for the last season of *Charlie's Angels*. I'd have been the blonde.'

'There's always the theatre,' Geneviève suggested.

'That's not being a star,' the girl said.

She was obviously a new-born, impatient with an eternity she didn't yet understand. She wanted all her presents *now*, and no nonsense about paying dues or waiting her turn. She had cropped blonde hair, very pale, almost translucent skin stretched over bird-delicate bones and a tight, hard, cute little face, with sharp angles and glinting teeth, small reddish eyes. Her upper arm was marked by parallel claw-marks, not yet healed, like sergeant's stripes. Geneviève stored away the detail.

'Who's that up there, Nico?' shouted one of the other girls.

Nico? Not the famous one, Geneviève supposed.

'Who?' the girl asked, out loud. 'Famous?'

Nico – indeed, not the famous one – had picked the thought out of Geneviève's mind. That was a common elder talent, but unusual in a new-born. If she lasted, this girl might do well. She'd have to pick a new name though, to avoid confusion with the singer of 'All Tomorrow's Parties'.

'Another one of us,' the starlet said to the girl in the pool. 'An invisible.'

'I'm not here for a part,' Geneviève explained. 'I'm here to see Mr Welles.'

Nico looked at her askew. Why would a vampire who wasn't an actress be here? Tumblers worked in the new-born's mind. It worked both ways: Nico could pick words up, but she also sent them out. The girls in the pool were named Mink and Vampi (please!), and often hung with Nico.

'You're old, aren't you?'

Geneviève nodded. Nico's transparent face showed eagerness.

'Does it come back? Your face in the mirror?'

'Mine hasn't.'

Her face fell, a long way. She was a loss to the profession. Her feelings were all on the surface, projected to the back stalls.

'Different bloodlines have different qualities,' Geneviève said, trying to be encouraging.

'So I heard.'

Nico wasn't interested in faint hopes. She wanted instant cures.

'Is that Mademoiselle Dieudonné?' roared the familiar voice.

'Yes, Orson, it's me,' she said.

Nico reacted, calculating. She was thinking that Geneviève might be an important person.

'Then that's a wrap for the evening. Thank you, people. Submit your expenses to Oja and be back here tomorrow night, at midnight sharp. You were all stupendous.'

Oja was the woman with the clipboard: Oja Kodar, Welles's companion and collaborator. She was from Yugoslavia, another refugee washed up on this California shore.

Welles seemed to float out of the swimming pool, easily hauling his enormous girth up the ladder by the strength of his own meaty arms. She was surprised at how light he was on his feet.

He pulled off his putty nose and hugged her.

'Geneviève, Geneviève, you are welcome.'

The rest of the crew came up, one by one, carrying bits of equipment.

'I thought I'd get Van Helsing's mad scene in the can,' explained Welles.

'Neat trick with the girls.'

The twinkle in his eye was almost Santa Clausian. He gestured hypnotically.

'Elementary movie magic,' he said. 'Georges Méliès could have managed it in 1897.'

'Has it ever been done before? I don't recall seeing a film with the device.'

'As a matter of fact, I think it's an invention of my own. There are still tricks to be teased out of the cinema. Even after so many years – a single breath for you, my dear – the talkies are not quite perfected. My little vampires may have careers as puppeteers, animators. You'd never see their hands. I should shoot a short film for children.'

'You've been working on this for a long time?'

'I had the idea at about seven o'clock this evening,' he said, with a modest chuckle. 'This is Hollywood, my dear, and you can get anything with a phone call. I got my vampires by ordering out, like pizza.'

Geneviève guessed the invisible girls were hookers, a traditional career option for those who couldn't make a showing in the movies. Some studio execs paid good money to be roughed up by girls they'd pass over with contempt at cattle calls. And vampires, properly trained, could venture into areas of pain and pleasure a warm girl would find uncomfortable, unappetising or unhealthy.

She noticed Nico had latched on to a young male assistant and was alternately flirting with him and wheedling at him for some favour. Welles was right: she could have a career as a puppet-mistress.

'Come into the house, Geneviève,' said Welles. 'We must talk.'

The crew and the girls bundled together. Oja, as production manager, arranged for them to pool up in several cars and be returned to their homes or – in the case of Nico, Mink and Vampi – to a new club where there were hours to be spent before the dawn. Gary, the cameraman, wanted to get the film to the lab and hurried off on his own to an all-night facility. Many movie people kept vampire hours without being undead.

There was an after-buzz in the air. Geneviève wondered if it was genius, or had some of the crew been sniffing drac to keep going. She had heard it was better than speed. She assumed she would be immune to it, and anyway even as a blood drinker – like all of her kind, she had turned by drinking vampire blood – she found the idea of dosing her system with another vampire's powdered blood, diluted with the Devil knew what, disgusting.

Welles went ahead of her, into the nondescript bungalow, turning on lights as he went. She looked back for a moment at the cast-off nose by the pool.

Van Helsing's mad scene?

She knew the subject of Welles's current project. He had mentioned to her that he had always wanted to make *Dracula*. Now, it seemed, he was acting on the impulse. It shouldn't have, but it frightened her a little. She was in two minds about how often that story should be told.

5

Welles did not so much live in the bungalow as occupy it. She recognised the signs of high-end, temporary tenancy. Pieces of extremely valuable antique furniture, imported from Spain, stood among ugly, functional, modern sticks that had come with the let. The den, the largest space in the building, was made aesthetically bearable by a hanging she put at sixteenth century, nailed up over the open fireplace like a curtain. The tapestry depicted a knight trotting in full armour through forest greenery, with black-faced, red-eyed-and-tongued devils peeping from behind tall, straight trees. The piece was marred by a bad burn that had caught at one corner and spread evil fingers upwards. All around were stacks of books, square-bound antique volumes and bright modern paperbacks, and rickety towers of film cans.

Geneviève wondered why Welles would have cases of good sherry and boxes of potato chips stacked together in a corner, then realised he must have been part-paid in goods for his commercial work. He offered her sherry and she surprised him by accepting.

'I do sometimes drink wine, Orson. Dracula wasn't speaking for us all.'

He arched an eyebrow and made a flourish of pouring sherry into a paper cup.

'My glassware hasn't arrived from Madrid,' he apologised.

She sipped the stuff, which she couldn't really taste, and sat on a straight-backed gothic chair. It gave her a memory-flash of hours spent in churches when she was a warm girl. She wanted to fidget.

Welles plumped himself down with a Falstaffian rumble and strain on a low couch that had a velvet curtain draped over it. He was broad enough in the beam to make it seem like a throne.

Oja joined them and silently hovered. Her hair was covered by a bright headscarf.

A pause.

Welles grinned, expansively. Geneviève realised he was protracting the moment, relishing a role. She even knew who he was doing, Sydney Greenstreet in *The Maltese Falcon*. The ambiguous mastermind enjoying himself by matching wits with the perplexed private eye. If Hollywood ever remade *Falcon*, which would be a sacrilege, Welles would be in the ring for Gutman. Too many of his acting jobs were like that, replacing another big personality in an inferior retread of something already got right.

'I'll be wondering why you asked me here tonight,' she prompted.

'Yes,' he said, amused.

'It'll be a long story.'

'I'm rather afraid so.'

'There are hours before dawn.'

'Indeed.'

Welles was comfortable now. She understood he had been switching off from the shoot, coming down not only from his on-screen character but from his position as backyard god.

'You know I've been playing with *Dracula* for years? I wanted to make it at RKO in 1940, did a script, designed sets, cast everybody. Then it was dropped.'

She nodded.

'We even shot some scenes. I'd love to steal in some night and rescue the footage from the vaults. Maybe for use in the current project. But the studio has the rights. Imagine if paintings belonged to whoever mixed the paints and wove the canvas. I'll have to abase myself, as usual. The children who inherited RKO after Hughes ran it aground barely know who I am, but they'll enjoy the spectacle of my contrition, my pleading, my total dejection. I may even get my way in the end.'

'Hasn't *Dracula* been made? I understand that Francis…'

'I haven't seen that. It doesn't matter to me or the world. I didn't do the first stage productions of *Macbeth* or *Caesar*, merely the best. The same goes for the Stoker. A marvellous piece, you know.'

'Funnily enough, I have read it,' she put in.

'Of course you have.'

'And I met Dracula.'

Welles raised his eyes, as if that were news to him. Was this all about picking her brains? She had spent all of fifteen minutes in the Royal Presence, nearly a hundred years ago, but was quizzed about that (admittedly dramatic) occasion more than the entire rest of her five hundred and sixty-five years. She'd seen the Count again, after his true death – as had Welles, she remembered – and been at his last funeral, seen his ashes scattered. She supposed she had wanted to be sure he was really finally dead.

'I've started *Dracula* several times. It seems like a cursed property. This time, maybe, I'll finish it. I believe it has to be done.'

Oja laid hands on his shoulders and squeezed. There was an almost imperial quality to Welles, but he was an emperor in exile, booted off his throne and cast out, retaining only the most loyal and long-suffering of his attendants.

'Does the name Alucard mean anything to you?' he asked. 'John Alucard?'

'This may come as a shock to you, Orson, but "Alucard" is "Dracula" spelled backwards.'

He gave out a good-humoured version of his Shadow laugh.

'I had noticed. He is a vampire, of course.'

'Central and Eastern European *nosferatu* love anagrams as much as they love changing their names,' she explained. 'It's a real quirk. My late friend Carmilla Karnstein ran through at least half a dozen scramblings of her name before running out. Millarca, Marcilla, Allimarc, Carl Liam…'

'My name used to be Olga Palinkas,' put in Oja. 'Until Orson thought up "Oja Kodar" for me, to sound Hungarian.'

'The promising sculptor "Vladimir Zagdrov" is my darling Oja too. You are right about the undead predilection for *noms des plumes*, alter egos, secret identities, anagrams and palindromes and acrostics. Just like actors. A hold-over from the Byzantine mindset, I believe. It says something about the way the creatures think. Tricky but obvious, as it were. The back-spelling might also be a compensation: a reflection on parchment for those who have none in the glass.'

'This Alucard? Who is he?'

'That's the exact question I'd like answered,' said Welles. 'And you, my dear Mademoiselle Dieudonné, are the person I should like to provide that answer.'

'Alucard says he's an independent producer,' said Oja. 'With deals all over town.'

'But no credits,' said Welles.

Geneviève could imagine.

'He has money, though,' said Welles. 'No credits, but a line of credit. Cold cash and the Yankee dollar banish all doubt. That seems unarguable.'

'Seems?'

'Sharp little word, isn't it? Seems and is, syllables on either side of a chasm of meaning. This Mr Alucard, a *nosferatu*, wishes to finance my *Dracula*. He has offered me a deal the likes of which I haven't had since RKO and *Kane*. An unlimited budget, major studio facilities, right of final cut, control over everything from casting to publicity. The only condition he imposes is that I must make this subject. He wants not my *Don Quixote* or my *Around the World in 80 Days*, but my *Dracula*, only.'

'The Coppola,' – a glare from Welles made her rephrase – 'that other film, with Brando as the Count? That broke even in the end, didn't it? Made back its budget. *Dracula* is a box office subject. There's probably room for another version. Not to mention sequels, a spin-off TV series and imitations. Your Mr Alucard makes sense. Especially if he has deep pockets and no credits. Being attached to a good, to a *great*, film would do him no harm. Perhaps he wants the acclaim?'

Welles rolled the idea around his head.

'No,' he concluded, almost sadly. 'Gené, I have never been accused of lack of ego. My largeness of spirit, my sense of self-worth, is part of my act, as it were. The armour I must needs haul on to do my daily battles. But I am not blind to my situation. No producer in his right mind would bankroll me to such an extent, would offer me such a deal. Not even these kids, this Spielberg and that Lucas, could get such a sweetheart deal. I am as responsible for that as anyone. The studios of today may be owned by oil companies and hotel magnates, but there's a race memory of that contract I signed when I was twenty-four and of how it all went wrong, for me and for everyone. When I was kicked off the lot in 1943, RKO took out ads in the trades announcing their new motto, "showmanship, not genius"! Hollywood doesn't want to have me around. I remind the town of its mistakes, its crimes.'

'Alucard is an independent producer, you say. Perhaps he's a fan?'

'I don't think he's seen any of my pictures.'

'Do you think this is a cruel prank?'

Welles shrugged, raising huge hands. Oja was more guarded, more worried. Geneviève wondered whether she was the one who had insisted on calling in an investigator.

'The first cheques have cleared,' said Welles. 'The rent is paid on this place.'

'You are familiar with the expression…'

'The one about equine dentistry? Yes.'

'But it bothers you? The mystery?'

'The Mystery of Mr Alucard. That is so. If it blows up in my face, I can stand that. I've come to that pass before and I shall venture there again. But I should like some presentiment, either way. I want you to make some discreet inquiries about our Mr Alucard. At the very least, I'd like to know his real name and where he comes from. He seems very American at the moment, but I don't think that was always the case. Most of all, I want to know what he is up to. Can you help me, Mademoiselle Dieudonné?'

6

'You know, Gené,' said Jack Martin wistfully, contemplating the melting ice in his empty glass through the wisps of cigarette smoke that always haloed his head, 'none of this matters. It's not important. Writing. It's a trivial pursuit, hardly worth the effort, inconsequential on any cosmic level. It's just blood and sweat and guts and bone hauled out of our bodies and fed through a typewriter to slosh all over the platen. It's just the sick soul of America turning sour in the sunshine. Nobody really reads what I've written. In this town, they don't know Flannery O'Connor or Ray Bradbury, let alone Jack Martin. Nothing will be remembered. We'll all die and it'll be over. The sands will close over our civilisation and the sun will turn into a huge red fireball and burn even you from the face of the earth.'

'That's several million years away, Jack,' she reminded him.

He didn't seem convinced. Martin was a writer. In high school, he'd won a national competition for an essay entitled 'It's Great to Be Alive'. Now in his grumbling forties, the sensitive but creepy short stories that were his most personal work were published in small science fiction and men's magazines, and put out in expensive limited editions by fan publishers who went out of business owing him money. He had made a living as a screenwriter for ten years without ever seeing anything written under his own name get made. He had a problem with happy endings.

However, he knew what was going on in 'the industry' and was her first port of call when a case got her mixed up with the movies. He lived in a tar-paper shack on Beverly Glen Boulevard, wedged between multi-million-dollar estates. He told everybody that at least it was earthquake-proof.

Martin rattled the ice. She ordered him another Coca-Cola. He stubbed out one cigarette and lit another.

The girl behind the hotel bar, dressed as a magician, sloshed ice into another glass and reached for a small chromed hose. She squirted Coke into the glass, covering the ice.

Martin held up his original glass.

'Wouldn't it be wonderful if you could slip the girl a buck and have her fill up *this* glass, not go through all the fuss of getting a fresh one and charging you all over again. There should be infinite refills. Imagine that, a utopian dream, Gené. It's what America needs. A *bottomless* Coke!'

'It's not policy, sir,' said the girl. With the Coke came a quilted paper napkin, an unhappy edge of lemon and a plastic stirrer.

Martin looked at the bar girl's legs. She was wearing black fishnets, high-heeled pumps, a tight white waistcoat, a tail coat and top hat.

The writer sampled his new, bottomed, Coke. The girl went to cope with other morning customers.

'I'll bet she's an actress,' he said. 'I think she does porno.'

Geneviève raised an eyebrow.

'Most X-rated films are better directed than the slop that comes out of the majors,' Martin insisted. 'I could show you a reel of something by Gerard Damiano or Jack Horner that you'd swear was Bergman or Don Siegel. Except for the screwing.'

Martin wrote 'scripts' for adult movies, under well-guarded pseudonyms to protect his Writer's Guild membership. The Guild didn't have any moral position on porno, but members weren't supposed to take jobs which involved turning out a full-length feature script in two afternoons for three hundred dollars. Martin claimed to have invented Jamie Gillis's catchphrase, 'Suck it, bitch!'

'What can you tell me about John Alucard?'

'The name is…'

'Besides that his name is "Dracula" written backwards.'

'He's from New York. Well, that's where he was last. I heard he ran with that art crowd. You know, Warhol and Jack Smith. He's got a first-look deal at United Artists, and something cooking with Fox. There's going to be a story in the trades that he's set up an independent production company with Griffin Mill, Julia Phillips and Don Simpson.'

'But he's never made a movie?'

'The word is that he's never *seen* a movie. That doesn't stop him calling himself a producer. Say, are you working for him? If you could mention that I'm available. Mention my rewrite on *Can't Stop the Music*. No, don't. Say about that TV thing that didn't happen. I can get you sample scripts by sundown.'

Martin was gripping her upper arm.

'I've never met Alucard, Jack. I'm checking into him for a client.'

'Still, if you get the chance, Gené. You know what it would mean to me. I'm fending off bill-collectors and Sharkko Press still hasn't come through for the *Tenebrous Twilight* limiteds. A development deal, even a rewrite or a polish, could get me through winter and spring. Buy me time to get down to Ensenada and finish some stories.'

She would have to promise. She had learned more than the bare facts. The light in Jack Martin's eyes told her something about John Alucard. He had some sort of magic effect, but she didn't know whether he was a conjurer or a wizard.

Now, she would have to build on that.

7

Short of forcing her way into Alucard's office and asking outright whether he was planning on leaving Orson Welles in the lurch, there wasn't much more she could do. After Martin, she made a few phone calls to industry contacts, went through recent back numbers of *Variety* and the *Hollywood Reporter* and hit a couple of showbiz watering holes, hoping to soak up gossip.

Now, Geneviève was driving back along the Pacific Coast Highway to Paradise Cove. The sun was down and a heavy, unstarred darkness hung over the sea. The Plymouth, which she sometimes suspected of having a mind of its own, handled gently, taking the blind curves at speed. She twiddled the radio past a lot of disco, and found a station pumping out two-tone. That was good, that was new, that was a culture still alive.

'...*mirror in the bathroom, recompense*
all my crimes of self-defence...'

She wondered about what she had learned.

It wasn't like the old days when the studios were tight little fiefdoms and a stringer for Louella Parsons would know everything going on in town and all the current scandal. Most movies weren't even made in Hollywood any more, and the studios were way down on the lists of interests owned by multi-national corporations with other primary concerns. The buzz was that United Artists might well be changing its name to TransAmerica Pictures.

General word confirmed most of what Martin had told her, and turned up surprisingly few extra details. Besides the Welles deal, financed off his own line of credit with no studio production coin as yet involved, John Alucard had projects in development all over town, with high-end talent attached. He was supposed to be in bed with Michael Cimino – still hot off *The Deer Hunter* – on *The Lincoln County Wars*, a Western about the vampire outlaw Billy the Kid and a massacre of settlers in Roswell, New Mexico, in the 1870s. With the Mill-Simpson-Phillips set-up, he was helping the long in-development Anne Rice project, *Interview With the Mummy*, which Elaine May was supposed to be making with Cher and Ryan O'Neal – unless it was Nancy Walker, with Diana Ross and Mark Spitz.

In an interview in the *Reporter*, Alucard said: 'The pursuit of making money is the only reason to make movies. We have no obligation to make history. We have no obligation to make art. We have no obligation to make a statement. Our obligation is to make money.' A lot of execs, and not a few directors and writers, found his a refreshing and invigorating stance, though Geneviève had the impression Alucard was parroting someone else's grand theory. If he truly believed what he said, and was not just laying down something the studios' corporate owners wanted to hear, then John Alucard did not sound like someone who would happily want to be in business with Orson Welles. Apart from anything else, his manifesto was a 1980s rewrite, at five times the length with in-built repetition to get through to the admass morons at the back of the hall, of 'showmanship, not genius'.

What she couldn't find out was what his projects really were. Besides Welles's *Dracula*, which wasn't mentioned by anyone she had talked with, and the long-gestating shows he was working on with senior production partners, he had half a dozen other irons in the fire. Directors and stars were attached, budgets set, start dates announced, but no titles ever got mentioned, and the descriptions in the trades – 'intense drama', 'romantic comedy' – were hardly helpful. That was interesting and unusual. John Alucard was making a splash, waves radiating outwards, but surely he would have to say eventually what the pictures were. Or had that become the least important part of the package? An agent at CAA told her that for men like Alucard, the art was in the deal not on the screen.

That did worry her.

Could it be that there wasn't actually a pot of gold at the end of this rainbow? The man was a vampire, but was he also a phantom? No photographs existed, of course. Everyone had a second-hand description, always couched as a casting suggestion: a young Louis Jourdan, a smart Jack Palance, a rough trade David Niven. It was agreed that the man was European, a long time ago. No one had any idea how long he had been a vampire, even. He could be a new-born fresh-killed and risen last year, or a centuried elder who had changed his face a dozen times. His name always drew the same reaction: excitement, enthusiasm, fear. There was a sense that John Alucard was getting things on the road, and that it'd be a smart career move to get close, to be ready to haul out of the station with him.

She cruised across sandy tarmac into the trailer park. The seafood restaurant was doing a little New Year's Day business. She would be thirsty soon.

Someone sat on the steps of her trailer, leaning back against the door, hands loose in his lap, legs in chinos, cowboy boots.

Someone dead.

8

The someone on her steps was *truly* dead. Over his punctured heart a star-shaped blotch was black in the moonlight.

Geneviève felt no residue. The intangible thing – immortal soul, psychic energy, battery power – which kept mind and body together in both *nosferatu* and the warm was gone.

Broken is the golden bowl, the spirit flown forever.

She found she was crying. She touched her cheek and looked at the thick, salt, red tears, then smeared them away on her handkerchief.

It was Moondoggie. In repose his face seemed older, his smile lines turned to slack wrinkles.

She took a moment with him, remembering the taste of the living man, that he was the only one who called her 'Gidget', his inability to put in words what it was about surfing that made him devote his life to it (he'd been in pre-med once, long, long ago and when there was a crack-up or a near-drowning, the doctor he might have been would surface and take over), and the rush of the seas that came with his blood.

That man was gone. Besides sorrow at the waste, she was angry. And afraid.

It was easy to see how it had happened. The killer had come close, face to face, and stuck Moondoggie through the heart. The wound was round, not a slit. The weapon was probably a wooden stake or a sharpened metal pole. The angle of the puncture was upwards, so the killer was shorter than the rangy surfer. Stuck through, Moondoggie had been carefully propped up on her doorstep. She was being sent a message.

Moondoggie was a warm man, but he'd been killed as if he were a vampire.

He was not cold yet. The killing was recent.

Geneviève turned in a half-circle, looking out across the beach. Like most vampires, she had above average night vision for a human being – without sun glare bleaching everything bone-white, she saw better than by day – but no hawk-like power of distinguishing far-off tiny objects or magical X-ray sight.

It was likely that the assassin was nearby, watching to see that the message was received. Counting on the popular belief that vampires did have unnatural eyesight, she moved slowly enough that anyone in concealment might think she was staring directly at them, that they had been seen.

A movement.

The trick worked. A couple of hundred yards off, beyond the trailer park, out on the beach, something – someone – moved, clambering upright from a hollow depression in the dry sand.

As the probable murderer stood, Geneviève saw a blonde pony-tail whipping. It was a girl, mid-to-late teens, in a halter-top and denim shorts, with a wispy gauze neckscarf and – suggestive detail – running shoes and knee-pads. She was undersized but athletic. Another girl midget: no wonder she'd been able to get close enough to Moondoggie, genial connoisseur of teen dreams, to stab him in the heart.

She assumed the girl would bolt. Geneviève was fast enough to run her down, but the killer ought to panic. In California, what people knew about vampires was scrambled with fantasy and science fiction.

For once, Geneviève was tempted to live up to her image. She wanted to rip out the silly girl's throat.

(And drink.)

She took a few long steps, flashing forwards across the beach.

The girl stood her ground, waiting.

Geneviève paused. The stake wasn't in the dead man's chest. The girl still had it. Her right hand was out of sight behind her back.

Closer, she saw the killer's face in the moonlight. Doll-pretty, with an upturned nose and the faintest fading traces of freckles. She was frowning with concentration now but probably had a winning smile, perfect teeth. She should be a cheerleader, not an assassin.

She wasn't a vampire, but Geneviève knew she was no warm creampuff, either. She had killed a strong man twice her weight with a single thrust and was prepared for a charging *nosferatu*.

Geneviève stood still, twenty yards from the girl.

The killer produced her stake. It was stained.

'Meet Simon Sharp,' she said in a clear, casual voice. Geneviève found her flippancy terrifying.

'You killed a man,' Geneviève said, trying to get through to her, past the madness.

'Not a man, a viper. One of you, undead vermin.'

'He was alive.'

'You'd snacked on him, Frenchie. He would have turned.'

'It doesn't work like that.'

'That's not what I hear, not what I *know*.'

From her icy eyes, this teenager was a fanatic. There could be no reasoning with her.

Geneviève would have to take her down, hold her until the police got here.

Whose side would the cops take? A vampire or a prom queen? Geneviève had fairly good relations with the local law, who were more uneasy about her as a private detective than as a vampire, but this might stretch things.

The girl smiled. She did look awfully cute.

Geneviève knew the mad bitch could probably get away with it. At least once. She had the whole Tuesday Weld thing going for her.

'You've been warned, not spared,' said the girl. 'My A plan was to skewer you on sight, but the Overlooker thinks this is better strategy. It's some English kick, like cricket. Go figure.'

The Overlooker?

'It'd be peachiest all around if you left the state, Frenchie. The country, even. Preferably, the planet. Next time we meet, it won't be a warning. You'll get a formal introduction to the stalwart Simon. *Capisce*?'

'Who are you?'

'The Slayer,' said the girl, gesturing with her stake. 'Barbie, the Vampire Slayer.'

Despite herself, despite everything, Geneviève had to laugh. That annoyed Barbie.

Geneviève reminded herself that this silly girl, playing dress-up-and-be-a-heroine, was a real live murderess.

She laughed more calculatedly.

Barbie wanted to kill her, but made no move. Whoever this Overlooker – bloody silly title – was, his or her creature didn't want to exceed the brief given her.

(Some English kick, like cricket.)

Geneviève darted at the girl, nails out. Barbie had good reactions. She pivoted to one side and launched a kick. A cleated shoe just missed Geneviève's midriff but raked her side painfully. She jammed her palm-heel at Barbie's chin, and caught her solidly, shutting her mouth with a click.

Simon Sharp went flying. That made Geneviève less inhibited about close fighting.

Barbie was strong, trained and smart. She might have the brain of a flea, but her instincts were panther-like and she went all out for a kill. But Geneviève was still alive after five hundred and fifty years as a vampire.

Barbie tried the oldest move in girly martial arts and yanked her opponent's hair, cutting her hand open. Geneviève's hair was fine but strong and sharp, like pampas grass to the touch. The burst of hot blood was a distraction, sparking lizardy synapses in Geneviève's brain, momentarily blurring her thoughts. She threw Barbie away, skittering her across the sand on her can in an undignified tangle.

Mistake.

Barbie pulled out something like a Mace spray and squirted at Geneviève's face.

Geneviève backed away from the cloud, but got a whiff of the mist. Garlic, water and silver salts. Garlic and (holy?) water didn't bother her – more mumbo-jumbo, ineffective against someone not of Dracula's bloodline – but silver was deadly to all *nosferatu*. This spray might not kill her, but it could scar her for a couple of centuries. It was vanity, she supposed, but she had got used to people telling her she was pretty.

She scuttled away backwards across the sand. The cloud dissipated in the air. She saw the droplets, shining under the moon, falling with exaggerated slowness, pattering onto the beach.

When the spray was gone, so was Barbie the Vampire Slayer.

9

'And, uh, this is exactly where you found Mr Griffin, miss?' asked the LAPD homicide detective.

Geneviève was distracted. Even just after dawn the sun was fatiguing her. In early daylight, on a gurney, Moondoggie – whose name turned out to have been Jeff Griffin – looked colder and emptier, another of the numberless dead stranded in her past, while she went on and on and on.

'Miss Dew-dun-ee?'

'Dieudonné,' she corrected, absent-mindedly.

'Ah yes, Dieudonné. Acute accent over the e. That's French, isn't it? I have a French car. My wife says…'

'Yes, this is where I found the body,' she answered, catching up.

'Ah. There's just one thing I don't understand.'

She paid attention to the crumpled little man. He had curly hair, a gravel voice and a raincoat. He was working on the first cigar of the day. One of his eyes was glass, and aimed off to the side.

'And what might that be, Lieutenant?'

'This girl you mentioned, this…' he consulted his notebook, or pretended to, 'this "Barbie". Why would she hang around after the murder? Why did she have to make sure you found the body?'

'She implied that she was under orders, working for this Overlooker.'

The detective touched his eyebrow as if to tuck his smelly cigar behind his ear like a pen, and made great play of thinking hard, trying to work through the story he had been told. He was obviously used to people lying to him, and equally obviously unused to dealing with vampires. He stood between her and the sun as she inched into the shrinking shadow of her trailer.

She wanted to get a hat and dark glasses but police tape still barred her door.

'"Overlooker", yes. I've got a note of that, miss. Funny expression, isn't it. Gives the impression the "Overlooker" is supposed *not* to see something, that the whole job is about, ah, overlooking. Not like my profession, miss. Or yours either, I figure. You're a PI, like on TV?'

'With fewer car chases and shoot-outs.'

The detective laughed. He was a funny little duck. She realised he used his likability as a psychological weapon, to get close to people he wanted to nail. She couldn't mistake the situation: she was in the ring for the killing, and her story about Barbie the Slayer didn't sound straight in daylight. What sane professional assassin gives a name, even a partial name, to a witness?

'A vampire private eye?' The detective scratched his head.

'It makes sense. I don't mind staying up all night. And I've got a wealth of varied experience.'

'Have you solved any big cases? Really big ones?'

Without thinking, she told a truth. 'In 1888, I half-way found out who Jack the Ripper was.'

The detective was impressed.

'I thought no one knew how that panned out. Scotland Yard still have it open. What with you folk living longer and longer, it's not safe to close unsolved files. The guy who took the rap died, didn't he? These days, the theorists say it couldn't have been him.'

'I said I half-way found out.'

She had a discomfiting memory flash, of her and Charles in an office in Whitechapel in 1888, stumbling over the last clue, all the pieces falling into place. The problem was that solving the mystery hadn't meant sorting everything out. The case had continued to spiral out of control. There was a message there.

'That wouldn't be good enough for my captain, I'm afraid, miss. He has to answer to Police Chief Exley, and Chief Exley insists on a clearance and conviction rate. I can't just catch them, I have to prove they did it. I have to go to the courts. You'd be surprised how many guilty parties walk free. Especially the rich ones, with fancy lawyers. In this town, it's hard to get a conviction against a rich man.'

'This girl looked like a high-school kid.'

'Even worse, miss. Probably has rich folks.'

'I've no idea about that.'

'And pretty is as good as being rich. Better. Juries like pretty girls as much as lawyers like rich men.'

There was a shout from the beach. One of the uniformed cops who had been combing the sand held up a plastic evidence bag. Inside was Barbie's bloody stake.

'Simon Sharp,' Geneviève said. The detective's eyebrows rose. 'That's what she called it. What kind of person gives a pet name to a murder weapon?'

'You think you've heard everything in this business and then something else comes along and knocks you flat. Miss, if you don't mind me asking, I know it's awkward for some women, but, um, well, how old are you?'

'I was born in 1416,' she said.

'That's five hundred and, um, sixty-five.'

'Thereabouts.'

The detective shook his head again and whistled.

'Tell me, does it get easier? Everything?'

'Sadly, no.'

'You said you had – uh, how did you put it? – "a wealth of varied experience". Is that like getting cleverer every year? Knowing more and more of the answers?'

'Would that it did, Lieutenant. Sometimes I think it just means having more and more questions.'

He chuckled. 'Ain't that the truth.'

'Can I get into my trailer now?' she asked, indicating the climbing sun.

'We were keeping you out?' he asked, knowing perfectly well he had been. 'That's dreadful, with your condition and everything. Of course you can go inside, miss. We'll be able to find you here if any more questions come up? It's a trailer, isn't it? You're not planning on hitching it up to your car and driving off, say, out of state?'

'No, Lieutenant.'

'That's good to know.'

He gallantly tore the police tape from her door. She had her keys out. Her skin tingled, and the glare off the sea turned everything into blobby, indistinct shapes.

'Just one more thing,' said the detective, hand on her door.

The keys were hot in her fingers.

'Yes,' she said, a little sharply.

'You're on a case, aren't you? Like on TV?'

'I'm working on several investigations. May I make a bet with you, Lieutenant? For a dime?'

The detective was surprised by that. But he fished around in his raincoat pocket and, after examining several tissues and a book of matches, came up with a coin and a smile.

'I bet I know what you're going to ask me next,' she said. 'You're going to ask me who I'm working for?'

He was theatrically astonished.

'That's just incredible, miss. Is it some kind of vampire mind-reading power? Or are you like Sherlock Holmes, picking up tiny hints from little clues, like the stains on the cigar-band or the dog not howling in the night?'

'Just a lucky guess,' she said. Her cheeks were really burning, now.

'Well, see if I can luckily guess your answer. Client confidentiality privilege, like a lawyer or a doctor, eh?'

'See. You have hidden powers too, Lieutenant.'

'Well, Miss Dieudonné, I do what I can, I do what I can. Any idea what I'm going to say next?'

'No.'

His smile froze slightly and she saw ice in his real eye.

'Don't leave town, miss.'

On rising, she found Jack Martin had left a message on her machine. He had something for her on 'Mr A'. Geneviève listened to the brief message twice, thinking it over.

She had spent only a few hours asking about John Alucard, and someone had got killed. A connection? It would be strange if there wasn't. Then again, as the detective had reminded her, she'd been around for a long time. In her years, she'd ticked off a great many people, not a few as long-lived as she was herself. Also, this was Southern California, La-La Land, where the nuts came from: folk didn't necessarily need a reason to take against you, or to have you killed.

Could this Overlooker be another Manson? Crazy Charlie was a vampire-hater too, and used teenage girls as assassins. Everyone remembered the death of Sharon Tate, but the Manson Family had also destroyed a vampire elder, Ferdinand von Krolock, up on La Cienaga Drive and painted bat symbols on the walls with his old blood. Barbie the Slayer was cutie-pie where the Family chicks had been skaggy, but that could be a 1980s thing as opposed to a 1960s one.

Geneviève knew she could take care of herself, but the people who talked to her might be in danger. She must mention it to Martin, who wasn't long on survival skills. He could at least scurry down to Mexico for a couple of months. In the meantime, she was still trying to earn her hundred dollars a day, so she returned Martin's call. The number he had left was (typically) a bar. The growling man who picked up had a message for her, giving an address in the valley where she could find the writer.

This late in the afternoon, the sun was low in the sky. She loved the long winter nights.

In a twist-tied plastic bag buried among the cleaning products and rags under her sink unit was a gun, a ladylike palm-sized automatic. She considered fishing it out and transferring it to the Plymouth Fury, but resisted the impulse. No sense in escalating. As yet, even the Overlooker didn't want her dead.

That was not quite a comfort.

11

The address was an anonymous house in an anonymous neighbourhood out in the diaspora-like sprawl of ranchos and villas and vistas. More cars and vans were outside than a single family should run to. Either there was a party on or this was a suburban commune. She parked on the street and watched for a moment. The lights from the windows and the patio were a few candles brighter than they needed to be. Cables ran out of a side-door and round to the backyard.

She got out of the Plymouth and followed the hose-thick cables, passing through a cultivated arbour into a typical yard space, with an oval pool covered by a heavy canvas sheet that was damp where it rested on water, and a white wooden gazebo, made up with strands of dead ivy and at the centre of several beams of light. A lot of people were around but this was no party. She should have guessed: another film set. She saw lights on stands and a camera crew, plus the usual assortment of hangers-on, gophers, rubberneckers, fluffers, runners and extras.

This was more like a 'proper' movie set than the scene she had found at Welles's bungalow, but she knew from the naked people in the gazebo that this was a far less proper movie. Again, she should have guessed. This was a Jack Martin lead, after all.

'Are you here for "Vampire Bitch, Number Three"?'

The long-haired, chubby kid addressing her wore a tie-dyed T-shirt and a fisherman's waistcoat, pockets stuffed with goodies. He carried a clipboard.

Geneviève shook her head. She didn't know whether to be flattered or offended. Then again, in this town, everyone thought everyone else was an actor or actress. They were usually more or less right.

She didn't like the sound of the part. If she had a reflection that caught on film and was going to prostitute herself for a skinflick, she would at least hold out for 'Vampire Bitch, Number One'.

'The part's taken, I'm afraid,' said the kid, not exactly dashing her dreams of stardom. 'We got Seka at the last minute.'

He nodded towards the gazebo where three warm girls in pancake make-up hissed at a hairy young man. They undid his Victorian cravat and waistcoat.

'I'm here to see Jack Martin?' she said.

'Who?'

'The writer?'

She remembered Martin used pseudonyms for this kind of work, and spun off a description: 'Salt and pepper beard, *Midnight Cowboy* jacket with the fringes cut off, smokes a lot, doesn't believe in positive thinking.'

The kid knew who she meant. 'That's "Mr Stroker". Come this way. He's in the kitchen doing rewrites. Are you sure you're not here for a part? You'd make a groovy vampire chick.'

She thanked him for the compliment, and followed his lead through a mess of equipment to the kitchen, torn between staring at what was going on between the three girls and one guy in the gazebo and keeping her eyes clear. About half the crew were of the madly ogling variety, while the others were jaded enough to stick to their jobs and look at their watches as the shoot edged towards golden time.

'Vampire Bitch Number Two, put more tongue in it,' shouted an intense bearded man whose megaphone and beret marked him as the director. 'I want to see fangs, Samantha. You've got a jones for that throbbing vein, you've got a real lust for blood. Don't slobber. That's in bad taste. Just nip nicely. That's it. That's colossal. That's the cream.'

'What is the name of this picture?' Geneviève asked.

'*Debbie Does Dracula*,' said the kid. 'It's going to be a four-boner classic. Best thing Boris Adrian has ever shot. He goes for production values, not just screwing. It's got real crossover potential as a "couples" movie. Uh oh, there's a gusher.'

'Spurt higher, Ronny,' shouted the director, Boris Adrian. 'I need the arc to be high lit. Thank you, that's perfect. Seka, Samantha, Désirée, you can writhe in it if you like. That's outstanding. Now, collapse in exhaustion, Ronny. That's perfect. Cut, and print.'

The guy in the gazebo collapsed in real exhaustion, and the girls called for assistants to wipe them off. Some of the crew applauded and congratulated the actors on their performances, which Geneviève supposed was fair enough. One of the 'Vampire Bitches' had trouble with her false fang-teeth.

The director got off his shooting-stick and sat with his actors, talking motivation.

The kid held a screen door open and showed her into the kitchen. Martin sat at a tiny table, cigarette in his mouth, hammering away at a manual typewriter. Another clipboard kid, a wide girl with a frizz of hair and Smiley badges fastening her overall straps, stood over him.

'Gené, excuse me,' said Martin. 'I'll be through in a moment.'

Martin tore through three pages, working the carriage return like a gunslinger fanning a Colt, and passed them up to the girl, who couldn't read as fast as he wrote.

'There's your Carfax Abbey scene,' Martin said, delivering the last page.

The girl kissed his forehead and left the kitchen.

'She's in love with me.'

'The assistant?'

'She's the producer, actually. Debbie W. Griffith. Had a monster hit distributing *Throat Sprockets* in Europe. You should see that. It's the first real adult film for the vampire market. Plays at midnight matinees.'

'She's "D.W. Griffith", and you're…?'

Martin grinned. 'Meet "Bram Stroker".'

'And why am I here?'

Martin looked around, to make sure he wasn't overheard, and whispered, 'This is it, this is his. Debbie's a front. This is *un film de* John Alucard.'

'It's not Orson Welles.'

'But it's a start.'

A dark girl, kimono loose, walked through the kitchen carrying a couple of live white rats in one hand, muttering to herself about 'the Master'. Martin tried to say hello, but she breezed past, deeply into her role, eyes drifting. She lingered a moment on Geneviève, but wafted out onto the patio and was given a mildly sarcastic round of applause.

'That's Kelly Nicholls,' said Martin. 'She plays Renfield. In this version, it's not *flies* she eats, not in the usual sense. This picture has a great cast: Dirk Diggler as Dracula, Annette Haven as Mina, Holly Body as Lucy, John Leslie as Van Helsing.'

'Why didn't you tell me about this yesterday?'

'I didn't know then.'

'But you're the screenwriter. You can't have been hired and written the whole thing to be shot this afternoon.'

'I'm the rewriter. Even for the adult industry their first pass at the script blew dead cats. It was called *Dracula Sucks*, and boy did it ever. They couldn't lick it, as it were. It's the subject: *Dracula*. You know what they say about the curse, the way it struck down Coppola in Romania. I've spent the day doing a page one rewrite.'

Someone shouted 'Quiet on set,' and Martin motioned Geneviève to come outside with him to watch the shooting.

'The next scene is Dracula's entrance,' he murmured to her. 'He hauls the three vampire bitches – pardon the expression – off Jonathan and, ah, well, you can imagine, *satiates* them, before tossing them baby in a bag.'

'I was just offered a role in the scene. I passed.'

Martin harrumphed. Unsure about this whole thing, she began to follow.

A movement in an alcove distracted her. A pleasant-faced warm young man sat in there, hunched over a sideboard. He wore evening dress trousers and a bat-winged black cloak but nothing else. His hair was black and smoothed back, with a prominent widow's peak painted on his forehead. For a supposed vampire, he had a decent tan.

He had a rolled up ten-dollar bill stuck in his nose.

A line of red dust was on the sideboard. He bent over and snuffed it up. She had heard of drac, but never seen it.

The effect on the young man was instant. His eyes shone like bloodied marbles. Fang-teeth shot out like switchblades.

'Yeah, that's it,' he said. 'Instant vamp!'

He flowed upright, unbending from the alcove, and slid across the floor on bare feet. He wasn't warm, wasn't a vampire, but something in between – a dhampire – that wouldn't last more than an hour.

'Where's Dracula?' shouted Boris Adrian. 'Has he got the fangs-on yet?'

'I am Dracula,' intoned the youth, as much to convince himself. 'I *am* Dracula!'

As he pushed past her, Geneviève noticed the actor's trousers were held together at the fly and down the sides by strips of velcro. She could imagine why.

She felt obscurely threatened. Drac – manufactured from vampire blood – was extremely expensive and highly addictive. In her own veins flowed the raw material of many a valuable fangs-on instant vamp fugue. In New York, where the craze came from, vampires had been kidnapped and slowly bled empty to make the foul stuff.

Geneviève followed the dhampire star. He reached out his arms like a wingspread, cloak billowing, and walked across the covered swimming pool, almost flying, as if weightless, skipping over sagging puddles and, without toppling or using his hands, made it over the far edge. He stood at poolside and let the cloak settle on his shoulders.

'I'm ready,' he hissed through fangs.

The three fake vampire girls in the gazebo huddled together, a little afraid. They weren't looking at Dracula's face, his hypnotic eyes and fierce fangs, but at his trousers. Geneviève realised there were other properties of drac that she hadn't read about in the newspapers.

The long-haired kid who had spoken to her was working a pulley. A shiny cardboard full moon rose above the gazebo. Other assistants held bats on fishing lines. Boris Adrian nodded approval at the atmosphere.

'Well, Count, go to it,' the director ordered. 'Action.'

The camera began to roll as Dracula strode up to the gazebo, cloak rippling. The girls writhed over the prone guy, Jonathan Harker, and awaited the coming of their dark prince.

'This man is mine,' said Dracula, in a Californian drawl that owed nothing to Transylvania. 'As you all are mine, you vampire bitches, you horny vampire bitches.'

Martin silently recited the lines along with the actor, eyes alight with innocent glee.

'You never love,' said the least-fanged of the girls, who had short blonde hair, 'you yourself have never loved.'

'That is not true, as you know well and as I shall prove to all three of you. In succession, and together. Now.'

The rip of velcro preceded a gasp from the whole crew. Dirk Diggler's famous organ was blood-red and angry. Geneviève wondered if he could stab a person with it and suck their blood. Or was that just a rumour, like the Tijuana werewolf show Martin spent his vacations trying to track down?

The 'vampire bitches' huddled in apparently real terror.

'Whatever he's taking, I want some of it,' breathed Martin.

12

———————◆———————

Later, in an empty all-night diner, Martin was still excited about *Debbie Does Dracula*. Not really sexually, though she didn't underestimate his prurience, but mostly high on having his words read out, caught on film. Even as 'Bram Stroker', he had pride in his work.

'It's a stopgap till the real projects come through,' he said, waving a deadly cigarette. 'But it's cash in hand, Gené. Cash in hand. I don't have to hock the typewriter. Debbie wants me for the sequel they're making next week, *Taste the Cum of Dracula*, with Vanessa Del Rio as Marya Zaleska. But I may pass. I've got something set up at Universal, near as damn it. A remake of *Buck Privates*, with Belushi and Dan Aykroyd. It's between me and this one other guy, Lionel Fenn, and Fenn's a drac-head from the East with a burn-out date stamped on his forehead. I tell you, Gené, it's adios to "Bram Stroker" and "William Forkner" and "Charles Dickings". You'll be my date for the premiere, won't you? You pretty up good, don't you? When the name Jack Martin means something in this town, I want to direct.'

He was tripping on dreams. She brought him down again.

'Why would John Alucard be in bed with Boris Adrian?' she asked.

'And Debbie Griffith,' he said. 'I don't know. There's an invisible barrier between adult and legit. It's like a parallel world. The adult industry has its own stars and genres and awards shows. No one ever crosses. Oh, some of the girls do bit parts. Kelly was in *The Toolbox Murders*, with Cameron Mitchell.'

'I missed that one.'

'I didn't. She was the chickie in the bath who gets it with a nail-gun. Anyway, that was a fluke. You hear stories that Stallone made a skinflick once, and that some on-the-skids directors take paying gigs under pseudonyms.'

'Like "Bram Stroker"?'

Martin nodded, in his flow. 'But it's not an apprenticeship, not really. Coppola shot nudies, but that was different. Just skin, no sex. Tame now. Nostalgia bait. You've got to trust me, Gené, don't tell anyone, and I mean not anyone, that I'm "Bram Stroker". It's a crucial time for me, a knife-edge between the big ring and the wash-out ward. I really need this *Buck Privates* deal. If it comes to it, I want to hire you to scare off Fenn. You do hauntings, don't you?'

She waved away his panic, her fingers drifting through his nicotine cloud.

'Maybe Alucard wants to raise cash quickly?' she suggested.

'Could be. Though the way Debbie tells it, he isn't just a sleeping partner. He originated the whole idea, got her and Boris together, borrowed Dirk from Jack Horner, even – and I didn't tell you this – supplied the bloody nose candy that gave Dracula's performance the added *frisson*.'

It was sounding familiar.

'Did he write the script?' she asked. 'The first script?'

'Certainly, no writer did. It might be Mr A. There was no name on the title page.'

'It's not a porno movie he wants, not primarily,' she said. 'It's a Dracula movie. Another one. Yet another one.'

Martin called for a coffee refill. The ancient, slightly mouldy character who was the sole staff of the Nighthawks Diner shambled over, coffee sloshing in the glass jug.

'Look at this guy,' Martin said. 'You'd swear he was a goddamned reanimated corpse. No offence, Gené, but you know what I mean. Maybe he's a dhamp. I hear they zombie out after a while, after they've burned their bat-cells.'

Deaf to the discussion, the shambler sloshed coffee in Martin's mug. Here, in Jack Martin Heaven, there were infinite refills. He exhaled contented plumes of smoke.

'Jack, I have to warn you. This case might be getting dangerous. A friend of mine was killed yesterday night, as a warning. And the police like me for it. I can't prove anything, but it might be that asking about Alucard isn't good for your health. Still, keep your ears open. I know about two John Alucard productions now, and I'd like to collect the set. I have a feeling he's a one-note musician, but I want that confirmed.'

'You think he only makes Dracula movies?'

'I think he only makes Dracula.'

She didn't know exactly what she meant by that, but it sounded horribly right.

13

There was night enough left after Martin had peeled off home to check in with the client. Geneviève knew Welles would still be holding court at four in the morning.

He was running footage.

'Come in, come in,' he boomed.

Most of the crew she had met the night before were strewn on cushions or rugs in the den, along with a few newcomers, movie brats and law professors and a very old, very grave black man in a bright orange dashiki. Gary, the cameraman, was working the projector.

They were screening the scene she had seen shot, projecting the picture onto the tapestry over the fireplace. Van Helsing tormented by vampire symbols. It was strange to see Welles's huge, bearded face, the luminous skull, the flapping bat and the dripping dagger slide across the stiff, formal image of the mediaeval forest scene.

Clearly, Welles was in mid-performance, almost holding a dialogue with his screen self, and wouldn't detach himself from the show so she could report her preliminary findings to him any time soon.

She found herself drifting into the yard. There were people there, too. Nico, the vampire starlet, had just finished feeding and lay on her back looking up at the stars, licking blood from her lips and chin. She was a messy eater. A too-pretty young man staggered upright, shaking his head to dispel dizziness. His clothes were Rodeo Drive, but last year's in a town where last week was another era. She didn't have to sample Nico's broadcast thoughts to put him down as a rich kid who had found a new craze to blow his trust fund money on, and her crawling skin told her it wasn't a sports car.

'Your turn,' he said to Nico, nagging.

She kept to the shadows. Nico had seen her but her partner was too preoccupied to notice anyone. The smear on his neck gave Geneviève a little prick of thirst.

Nico sat up with great weariness, the moment of repletion spoiled. She took a tiny paring knife from her clutch-purse. It glinted, silvered. The boy sat eagerly beside her and rolled up the left sleeve of her loose muslin blouse, exposing her upper arm. Geneviève saw the row of scars she had noticed last night. Carefully, the vampire girl opened a stripe and let her blood trickle. The boy fixed his mouth over the wound. She held his hair in her fist.

'Remember, lick,' she said. 'Don't suck. You won't be able to take a full fangs-on.'

His throat pulsed, as he swallowed.

With a roar, the boy let the girl go. He had the eyes and the fangs, even more than Dirk Diggler's Dracula. He moved fast, a temporary new-born high on all the extra senses and the sheer sense of power.

The dhampire put on wraparound mirror shades, ran razor-nailed hands through his gelled hair and stalked off to haunt the La-La night. Within a couple of hours, he would be a real live boy again. By that time, he could have got himself into all manner of scrapes.

Nico squeezed shut her wound. Geneviève caught her pain. The silver knife would be dangerous if it flaked in the cut. For a vampire, silver rot was like bad gangrene.

'It's not my place to say anything,' began Geneviève.

'Then don't,' said Nico, though she clearly received what Geneviève was thinking. 'You're an elder. You can't know what it's like.'

She had a flash that this new-born would never be old. What a pity.

'It's a simple exchange,' said the girl. 'Blood for blood. A gallon for a scratch. The economy is in our favour. Just like the President says.'

Geneviève joined Nico at the edge of the property.

'This vampire trip really isn't working for me,' said Nico. 'That boy, Julian, will be warm again in the morning, mortal and with a reflection. And when he wants to, he'll be a vampire. If I'm not here, there are others. You can score drac on Hollywood Boulevard for twenty-five dollars a suck. Vile stuff, powdered, not from the tap, but it works.'

Geneviève tidied Nico's hair. The girl lay on her lap, sobbing silently. She hadn't just lost blood.

This happened when you became an elder. You were mother and sister to the whole world of the undead.

The girl's despair passed. Her eyes were bright, with Julian's blood.

'Let's hunt, elder, like you did in Transylvania.'

'I'm from France. I've never even been to Romania.'

Now she mentioned it, that was odd. She'd been almost everywhere else. Without consciously thinking of it, she must have been avoiding the supposed *nosferatu* homeland. Kate Reed had told her she wasn't missing much, unless you enjoyed political corruption and paprika.

'There are human cattle out there,' said Nico. 'I know all the clubs. X is playing at the Roxy, if you like West Coast punk. And the doorman at After Hours always lets us in, vampire girls. There are so few of us. We go to the head of the line. Powers of fascination.'

'Human cattle' was a real new-born expression. This close to dawn, Geneviève was thinking of her cosy trailer and shutting out the sun, but Nico was a race-the-sun girl, staying out until it was practically light, bleeding her last as the red circle rose in the sky.

She wondered if she should stick close to the girl, keep her out of trouble. But why? She couldn't protect everyone. She barely knew Nico, probably had nothing in common with her.

She remembered Moondoggie. And all the other dead, the ones she hadn't been able to help, hadn't tried to help, hadn't known about in time. The old gumshoe had told her she should get into her current business because there were girls like this, vampire girls, that only she could understand.

This girl really was none of her business.

'What's that?' said Nico, head darting. There was a noise from beyond the fence at the end of the garden.

Dominating the next property was a three-storey wooden mansion, California cheesecake. Nico might have called it old. Now Geneviève's attention was drawn to it, her night-eyes saw how strange the place was. A rusted-out pick-up truck was on cinderblocks in the yard, with a pile of ragged auto tyres next to it. The windshield was smashed out, and dried streaks – which any vampire would have scented as human blood, even after ten years – marked the hood.

'Who lives there?' Geneviève asked.

'In-bred backwoods brood,' said Nico. 'Orson says they

struck it rich down in Texas and moved to Beverly Hills. You know, swimming pools, movie stars...'

'Oil?'

'Chilli sauce recipe. Have you heard of Sawyer's Sauce?' Geneviève hadn't. 'I guess not. I've not taken solid foods since I turned, though if I don't feed for a night or two I get this terrible phantom craving for those really shitty White Castle burgers. I suppose that if you don't get to the market, you don't know the brand-names.'

'The Sawyers brought Texas style with them,' Geneviève observed. 'That truck's a period piece.'

The back porch was hung with mobiles of bones and nail-impaled alarm clocks. She saw a napping chicken, stuffed inside a canary cage.

'What's that noise?' Nico asked.

There was a wasp-like buzzing, muted. Geneviève scented burning gas. Her teeth were on edge.

'Power tool,' she said. 'Funny time of the night for warm folks to be doing carpentry.'

'I don't think they're all entirely warm. I saw some gross Grandpaw peeping out the other night, face like dried leather, licking livery lips. If he isn't undead, he's certainly nothing like alive.'

There was a stench in the air. Spoiled meat.

'Come on, let's snoop around,' said Nico, springing up. She vaulted over the low fence dividing the properties and crept across the yard like a four-legged crab.

Geneviève thought that was unwise, but followed, standing upright and keeping to the shadows.

This really was none of her business.

Nico was on the porch now, looking at the mobiles. Geneviève wasn't sure whether it was primitive art or voodoo. Some of the stick-and-bone dangles were roughly man-shaped.

'Come away,' she said.

'Not just yet.'

Nico examined the back door. It hung open, an impenetrable dark beyond. The buzzing was still coming from inside the ramshackle house.

Geneviève *knew* sudden death was near, walking like a man. She called to Nico, more urgently.

Something small and fast came, not from inside the house but from the flatbed of the abandoned truck. The shape cartwheeled across the yard to the porch and collided purposefully with Nico. A length of wood pierced the vampire girl's thin chest. An expression, more of surprise than pain or horror, froze on her face.

Geneviève felt the thrust in her own heart, then the silence in her mind. Nico was gone, in an instant.

'How do you like your stake, ma'am?'

It was Barbie. Only someone truly witless would think stake puns the height of repartee.

'Just the time of night for a little viper-on-a-spit,' said the Slayer, lifting Nico's deadweight so that her legs dangled. 'This really should be you, Frenchie. By the way, I don't think you've met Simon's brother, Sidney. Frenchie, Sidney. Sidney, hellbitch creature of the night fit only to be impaled and left to rot in the light of the sun. That's the formalities out of the way.'

She threw Nico away, sliding the dead girl off Sidney the Stake. The new-born, mould already on her startled face, flopped off the porch and fell into the yard.

Geneviève, still shocked by the passing, almost turned to ice. Nico had been in her mind, just barely and with tiny fingers, and her death was a wrench. She thought her skull might be leaking.

'They don't cotton much to trespassers down Texas way,' said Barbie, in a bad cowboy accent. 'Nor in Beverly Hills, neither.'

Geneviève doubted the Sawyers knew Barbie was here.

'Next time, the Overlooker says I can do you too. I'm wishing and hoping and praying you ignore the warning. You'd look so fine on the end of a pole, Frenchie.'

An engine revved, like a signal. Barbie was bounding away, with deer-like elegance.

Geneviève followed.

She rounded the corner of the Sawyer house and saw Barbie climbing into a sleek black Jaguar. In the driver's seat was a man wearing a tweed hunting jacket with matching bondage hood. He glanced backwards as he drove off.

The sports car had vanity plates. OVRLKER1.

Gravel flew as the car sped off down the drive.

'What's all this consarned ruckus?' shouted someone, from the house.

Geneviève turned and saw an American gothic family group on the porch. Blotch-faced teenage boy, bosomy but slack-eyed girl in a polka-dot dress, stern patriarch in a dusty black suit, and hulking elder son in a stained apron and crude leather mask. Only the elder generation was missing, and Geneviève was sure they were up in rocking chairs on the third storey, peeking through the slatted blinds.

'That a dead'n?' asked the patriarch, nodding at Nico.

She conceded that it was.

'*True* dead'n?'

'Yes,' she said, throat catching.

'What a shame and a waste,' said Mr Sawyer, in a tone that made Geneviève think he wasn't referring to a life but to flesh and blood that was highly saleable.

'Shall I call the Sheriff, Paw?' asked the girl.

Mr Sawyer nodded, gravely.

Geneviève knew what was coming next.

14

—————◆—————

'There's just one thing I don't understand, miss.'

'Lieutenant, if there was "just one thing" I didn't understand, I'd be a very happy old lady. At the moment, I can't think of "just one thing" I do understand.'

The detective smiled craggily.

'You're a vampire, miss. Like this dead girl, this, ah, Nico.'

Orson Welles had lent her a crow-black umbrella, which she was using as a parasol.

'And this Barbie, who again nobody else saw, was, ah, a

living person?'

'Warm.'

'Warm, yes. That's the expression. That's what you call us.'

'It's not offensive.'

'That's not how I take it, miss. No, what I'm wondering is: aren't vampires supposed to be faster than the warm, harder to catch hold of in a tussle?'

'Nico was a new-born, and weakened. She'd lost some blood.'

'That's one for the books.'

'Not any more.'

The detective scratched his head, lit cigar-end dangerously near his hair. 'So I hear. It's called "drac" on the streets. I have friends on the Narco Squad. They say it's worse than heroin.'

'Where is this going, Lieutenant?'

He shut his notebook and pinned her with his eye.

'You could have, ah, *taken* Miss Nico? If you got into a fight with her?'

'I didn't.'

'But you could have.'

'I could have killed the Kennedys and Sanford White, but I didn't.'

'Those are closed cases, as far as I'm concerned. This is open.'

'I gave you the number plate.'

'Yes, miss. OVRLKER1. A Jaguar.'

'Even if it's a fake plate, there can't be that many English sports cars in Los Angeles.'

'There are, ah, one thousand, seven hundred and twenty-two registered Jaguars. Luxury vehicles are popular in this city, in some parts of it. Not all the same model.'

'I don't know the model. I don't follow cars. I just know it was a Jaguar. It had the cat on the bonnet, the hood.'

'Bonnet? That's the English expression, isn't it?'

'I lived in England for a long time.'

With an Englishman. The detective's sharpness reminded her of Charles, with a witness or a suspect.

Suspect.

He had rattled the number of Jaguars in Greater Los Angeles off the top of his head, with no glance at the prop notebook. Gears were turning in his mind.

'It was a black car,' she said. 'That should make it easier to find.'

'Most automobiles look black at night. Even red ones.'

'Not to me, Lieutenant.'

Uniforms were off grilling the Sawyers. Someone was even talking with Welles, who had let slip that Geneviève was working for him. Since the client had himself blown confidentiality, she was in an awkward position; Welles still didn't want it known what exactly she was doing for him.

'I think we can let you go now, miss,' said the detective.

She had been on the point of presenting him her wrists for the cuffs.

'There isn't "just one more thing" you want to ask?'

'No. I'm done. Unless there's anything you want to say.'

She didn't think so.

'Then you can go. Thank you, miss.'

She turned away, knowing it would come, like a hand on her shoulder or around her heart.

'There is one thing, though. Not a question. More like a circumstance, something that has to be raised. I'm afraid I owe you an apology.'

She turned back.

'It's just that I had to check you out, you know. Run you through the books. As a witness, yesterday. Purely routine.'

Her umbrella seemed heavier.

'I may have got you in trouble with the state licensing board. They had all your details correctly, but it seems that every time anyone looked at your licence renewal application, they misread the date. As a European, you don't write an open four. It's easy to mistake a four for a nine. They thought you were born in 1916. Wondered when you'd be retiring, in fact. Had you down as a game old girl.'

'Lieutenant, I am a game old girl.'

'They didn't pull your licence, exactly. This is really embarrassing and I'm truly sorry to have been the cause of it, but they want to, ah, review your circumstances. There aren't any other vampires licensed as private investigators in the State of California, and there's no decision on whether a legally dead person can hold a licence.'

'I never died. I'm not legally dead.'

'They're trying to get your paperwork from, ah, France.'

She looked up at the sky, momentarily hoping to burn out her eyes. Even if her original records existed, they'd be so old as to be protected historical documents. Photostats would not be coming over the wire from her homeland.

'Again, miss, I'm truly sorry.'

She just wanted to get inside her trailer and sleep the day away.

'Do you have your licence with you?'

'In the car,' she said, dully.

'I'm afraid I'm going to have to ask you to surrender it,' said the detective. 'And that until the legalities are settled, you cease to operate as a private investigator in the State of California.'

15

At sunset she woke to another limbo, with one of her rare headaches. She was used to knowing what she was doing that night, and the next night, if not specifically then at least generally. Now, she wasn't sure what she *could* do.

Geneviève wasn't a detective any more, not legally. Welles had not paid her off, but if she continued working on John Alucard for him she'd be breaking the law. Not a particularly important one, in her opinion… but vampires lived in such a twilight world that it was best to pay taxes on time and not park in tow-away zones. After all, this was what happened when she drew attention to herself.

She had two other ongoing investigations, neither promising. She should make contact with her clients, a law firm and an

Orange County mother, and explain the situation. In both cases, she hadn't turned up any results and so would not in all conscience be able to charge a fee. She didn't even have that much Welles could use.

Money would start to be a problem around Valentine's Day. The licensing board might have sorted it out by then.

(In some alternate universe.)

She should call Beth Davenport, her lawyer, to start filing appeals and lodging complaints. That would cost, but anything else was just giving up.

Two people were truly dead. That bothered her too.

She sat at her tiny desk by a slatted window, considering her telephone. She had forgotten to switch her answering machine on before turning in, and any calls that might have come today were lost. She had never done that before.

Should she re-record her outgoing message, stating that she was (temporarily?) out of business? The longer she was off the bus, the harder it would be to get back on.

On TV, suspended cops, disbarred private eyes and innocent men on the run never dropped the case. And this was Southern California, where the TV came from.

She decided to compromise. She wouldn't work Alucard, which was what Welles had been paying her for. But, as a concerned – indeed, involved – citizen, no law said she couldn't use her talents unpaid to go after the slayer.

Since this was a police case, word of her status should have filtered down to her LAPD contacts but might not yet have reached outlying agencies. She called Officer Baker, a contact in the Highway Patrol, and wheedled a little to get him to run a licence plate for her.

OVRLKER1.

The call back came within minutes. Excellent service, she admitted, was well worth a supper and cocktails one of these nights. Baker teased her a while about that, then came over.

Amazingly, the plate *was* for a Jaguar. The car was registered in the name of Ernest Ralph Gorse, to an address in a town up the coast, Shadow Bay. The only other forthcoming details were that Gorse was a British subject – not citizen, of course – and held down a job as a high school librarian.

The Overlooker? A school librarian and a cheerleader might seem different species, but they swam in the same tank.

She thanked Baker and rang off.

If it was that easy, she could let the cops handle it. The Lieutenant was certainly sharp enough to run Gorse down and scout around to see if a Barbie popped up. Even if the detective hadn't believed her, he would have been obliged to run the plate, in order to puncture her story. Now, he was obliged to check it out.

But wasn't it all too easy?

Since when did librarians drive Jaguars?

It had the air of a trap.

She was where the Lieutenant must have been seven hours ago. She wouldn't put the crumpled detective on her list of favourite people, but didn't want to hear he'd run into another of the Sharp brothers. Apart from the loss of a fine public servant who was doubtless also an exemplary husband, it was quite likely that if the cop sizing her up for two murders showed up dead, she would be even more suitable for framing.

Shadow Bay wasn't more than an hour away.

16

She parked on the street but took the trouble to check out the Shadow Bay High teachers' parking lot. Two cars: a black Jaguar (OVRLKER1) and a beat-up silver Peugeot ('I have a French car'). Geneviève checked the Peugeot and found LAPD ID on display. The interior was a mess. She caught the after-whiff of cigars.

The school was as unexceptional as the town, with that faintly unreal movie-set feel that came from newness. The oldest building in sight was put up in 1965. To her, places like this felt temporary.

A helpful map by the front steps of the main building told her where the library was, across a grassy quadrangle. The school grounds were dark. The kids wouldn't be back from their Christmas vacation. And no evening classes. She had checked Gorse's address first, and found no one home.

A single light was on in the library, like the cover of a gothic romance paperback.

Cautious, she crossed the quad. Slumped in the doorway of the library was a raincoated bundle. Her heart plunging, she knelt and found the Lieutenant insensible but still alive. He had been bitten badly and bled. The ragged tear in his throat showed he'd been taken the old-fashioned way – a strong grip from behind, a rending fang-bite, then sucking and swallowing. Non-consensual vampirism, a felony in anyone's books, without the exercise of powers of fascination to cloud the issue. It was hard to mesmerise someone with one eye, though some vampires worked with whispers and could even put the fluence on a blind person.

There was another vampire in Shadow Bay. By the look of the leavings, one of the bad 'uns. Perhaps that explained Barbie's prejudice. It was always a mistake to extrapolate a general rule from a test sample of one.

She clamped a hand over the wound, feeling the weak pulse, pressing the edges together. Whoever had bitten the detective hadn't even had the consideration to shut off the faucet after glutting themselves. The smears of blood on his coat and shirt collar overrode her civilised impulses: her mouth became sharp-fanged and full of saliva. That was a good thing. A physical adaptation of her turning was that her spittle had antiseptic properties. Vampires of her bloodline were evolved for gentle, repeated feedings. After biting and drinking, a full-tongued lick sealed the wound.

Angling her mouth awkwardly and holding up the Lieutenant's lolling head to expose his neck, she stuck out her tongue and slathered saliva over the long tear. She tried to ignore the euphoric if cigar-flavoured buzz of his blood. She had a connection to his clear, canny mind.

He had never thought her guilty. Until now.

'Makes a pretty picture, Frenchie,' said a familiar girlish voice. 'Classic Bloodsucker 101, viper and victim. Didn't your father-in-darkness warn you about snacking between meals? You won't be able to get into your party dresses if you bloat up. Where's the fun in that?'

Geneviève knew Barbie wasn't going to accept her explanation. For once, she understood why.

The wound had been left open for her.

'I've been framed,' she said, around bloody fangs.

Barbie giggled, a teen vision in a red ra-ra skirt, white ankle socks, mutton-chop short-sleeved top and faux metallic choker. She had sparkle glitter on her cheeks and an Alice band with artificial antennae that ended in bobbling stars.

She held up her stake and said, 'Scissors cut paper.'

Geneviève took out her gun and pointed it. 'Stone blunts scissors.'

'Hey, no fair,' whined Barbie.

Geneviève set the wounded man aside as carefully as possible and stood up. She kept the gun trained on the slayer's heart.

'Where does it say vampires have to do kung fu fighting? Everyone else in this country carries a gun, why not me?'

For a moment, she almost felt sorry for Barbie the Slayer. Her forehead crinkled into a frown, her lower lip jutted like a sulky five-year-old's and tears of frustration started in her eyes. She had a lot to learn about life. If Geneviève got her wish, the girl would complete her education in Tehachapi Women's Prison.

A silver knife slipped close to her neck.

'Paper wraps stone,' suaved a British voice.

17

'Barbie doesn't know, does she? That you're *nosferatu*?'

Ernest Ralph Gorse, high school librarian, was an epitome

of tweedy middle-aged stuffiness, so stage English that he made Alistair Cooke sound like a Dead End Kid. He arched an elegant eyebrow, made an elaborate business of cleaning his granny glasses with his top-pocket hankie, and gave out a little I'm-so-wicked moué that let his curly fangs peep out from beneath his stiff upper lip.

'No, 'fraid not. Lovely to look at, delightful to know, but frightfully thick, that's our little Barbara.'

The Overlooker – 'Yes,' he had admitted, 'bloody silly name, means nothing, just sounds "cool" if you're a twit.' – had sent Barbie the Slayer off with the drained detective, to call at the hospital ER and the Sheriff's office. Geneviève was left in the library, in the custody of Gorse. He had made her sit in a chair, and kept well beyond her arms' length.

'You bit the Lieutenant?' she stated.

Gorse raised a finger to his lips and tutted.

'Shush now, old thing, mustn't tell, don't speak it aloud. Jolly bad show to give away the game and all that rot. Would you care for some instant coffee? Ghastly muck, but I'm mildly addicted to it. It's what comes of being cast up on these heathen shores.'

The Overlooker pottered around his desk, which was piled high with unread and probably unreadable books. He poured water from an electric kettle into an oversized green ceramic apple. She declined his offer with a headshake. He quaffed from his apple-for-the-teacher mug, and let out an exaggerated ahh of satisfaction.

'That takes the edge off. Washes down *cop au nicotin* very nicely.'

'Why hasn't she noticed?'

Gorse chuckled. 'Everything poor Barbara knows about the tribes of *nosferatu* comes from me. Of course, a lot of it I made up. I'm very creative, you know. It's always been one of my skills. Charm and persuasion, that's the ticket. The lovely featherhead hangs on my every word. She thinks all vampires are gruesome creatures of the night, demons beyond hope of redemption, frothing beasts fit only to be put down like mad dogs. I'm well aware of the irony, old thing. Some cold evenings, the hilarity becomes almost too much to handle. Oh, the stories

I've spun for her, the wild things she'll believe. I've told her she's the Chosen One, the only girl in the world who can shoulder the burden of the crusade against the forces of Evil. Teenage girls adore that I'm-a-secret-Princess twaddle, you know. Especially the Yanks. I copped a lot of it from *Star Wars*. Bloody awful film, but very revealing about the state of the national mind.'

Gorse was enjoying the chance to explain things. Bottling up his cleverness had been a trial for him. She thought it was the only reason she was still alive for this performance.

'But what's the point?'

'Originally, expedience. I've been "passing" since I came to America. I'm not like you, sadly. I can't flutter my lashes and have pretty girls offer their necks for the taking. I really am one of those hunt-and-kill, rend-and-drain sort of *nosferatu*. I tried the other way, but courtship dances just bored me rigid and I thought, well, why not? Why not just rip open the odd throat. So, after a few months here in picturesque Shadow Bay, empties were piling up like junk mail. Then the stroke of genius came to me: I could hide behind a Vampire Slayer, and since there were none in sight I made one up. I checked the academic records to find the dimmest dolly bird in school, and recruited her for the Cause. I killed her lunk of a boyfriend – captain of the football team, would you believe it? – and a selection of snack-sized teenagers. Then, I revealed to Barbara that her destiny was to be the Slayer. Together, we tracked and destroyed that first dread fiend – the school secretary who was nagging me about getting my employment records from Jolly Old England, as it happens – and staked the bloodlusting bitch. However, it seems she spawned before we got to her, and ever since we've been doing away with her murderous brood. You'll be glad to know I've managed to rid this town almost completely of real estate agents. When the roll is called up yonder, that must count in the plus column, though it's my long-term plan not to ever get there.'

Actually, Gorse was worse than the vampires he had made up. He'd had a choice, and *decided* to be evil. He worked hard on fussy geniality, modelling his accent and speech patterns on *Masterpiece Theatre*, but there was ice inside him, a complete vacuum.

'So, you have things working your way in Shadow Bay?' she said. 'You have your little puppet theatre to play with. Why come after me?'

Gorse was trying to decide whether to tell her more. He pulled a half-hunter watch from his waistcoat pocket and pondered. She wondered if she could work her trick of fascination on him. Clearly, he loved to talk, was bored with dissimulation, had a real need to be appreciated. The sensible thing would have been to get this over with, but Gorse had to tell her how brilliant he was. Everything up to now had been his own story; now, there was more important stuff and he was wary of going on.

'Still time for one more story,' he said. 'One more *ghost* story.'

Click. She had him.

He was an instinctive killer, probably a sociopath from birth, but she was his elder. The silver-bladed letter-opener was never far from his fingers. She would have to judge when to jump.

'It's a lonely life, isn't it? Ours, I mean,' he began. 'Wandering through the years, wearing out your clothes, lost in a world you never made? There was a golden age for us once, in London when Dracula was on the throne. 1888 and all that. You, famous girl, did your best to put a stop to it, turned us all back into nomads and parasites when we might have been masters of the universe. Some of us want it that way again, my darling. We've been getting together lately, sort of a pressure group. Not like those Transylvania fools who want to go back to the castles and the mountains, but like Him, battening onto a new, vital world, making a place for ourselves. An exalted place. He's still our inspiration, old thing. Let's say I did it for Dracula.'

That wasn't enough, but it was all she was going to get now. People were outside, coming in.

'Time flies, old thing. I'll have to make this quick.'

Gorse took his silver pig-sticker and stood over her. He thrust.

Faster than any eye could catch, her hands locked around

his wrist.

'Swift filly, eh?'

She concentrated. He was strong but she was old. The knife-point dimpled her blouse. He tipped back her chair and put a knee on her stomach, pinning her down.

The silver touch was white hot.

She turned his arm and forced it upwards. The knife slid under his spectacles and the point stuck in his left eye.

Gorse screamed and she was free of him. He raged and roared, fangs erupting from his mouth, two-inch barbs burst from his fingertips. Bony spars, the beginnings of wings, sprouted through his jacket around the collar and pierced his leather elbow-patches.

The doors opened and people came in. Barbie and two crucifix-waving Sheriff's Deputies.

The Slayer saw (and recognised?) the vampire and rushed across the room, stake out. Gorse caught the girl and snapped her neck, then dropped her in a dead tangle.

'Look what you made me do!' he said to Geneviève, voice distorted by the teeth but echoing from the cavern that was his reshaped mouth. 'She's *broken* now. It'll take ages to make another. I hadn't even got to the full initiation rites. There would have been bleeding and I was making up something about tantric sex. It would have been a real giggle, and you've spoiled it.'

His eye congealed, frothing grey deadness in his face.

She motioned for the deputies to stay back. They wisely kept their distance.

'Just remember,' said Gorse, directly to her. 'You can't stop Him. He's coming back. And then, oh my best beloved, you will be as sorry a girl as ever drew a sorry breath. He is not one for forgiveness, if you get my drift.'

Gorse's jacket shredded and wings unfurled. He flapped into the air, rising above the first tier of bookshelves, hovering at the mezzanine level. His old school tie dangled like a dead snake.

The deputies tried shooting at him. She supposed she would have too.

He crashed through a tall set of windows and flew off, vast

shadow blotting out the moon and falling on the bay.

The deputies holstered their guns. She wondered for about two minutes whether she should stick with her honesty policy.

Letting a bird flutter in her voice, she said, 'That man... he was a v-v-vampire.'

Then she did a pretty fair imitation of a silly girl fainting. One deputy checked her heartbeat while she was 'out', and was satisfied that she was warm. The other went to call for back-up.

Through a crack in her eyelids, she studied 'her' deputy. His hands might have lingered a little too long on her chest for strict medical purposes. The thought that he was the type to cop a feel from a helpless girl just about made it all right to get him into trouble by slipping silently out of the library while he was checking out the dead slayer.

She made it undetected back to her car.

18

———————◆———————

In her trailer, after another day of lassitude, she watched the early evening bulletin on Channel 6. Anchor persons Karen White and Lew Landers discussed the vampire killing in Shadow Bay. Because the primary victim was a cute teenage girl, it was the top story. The wounding of a decorated LAPD veteran – the Lieutenant was still alive, but off the case – also rated a flagged mention. The newscast split-screened a toothpaste commercial photograph of 'Barbara Dahl Winters', smiling under a prom queen tiara, and an 'artist's impression' of Gorse in giant bat-form, with blood tastefully dripping from his fangs. Ernest 'Gory' Gorse turned out to be a fugitive from Scotland Yard, with a record of petty convictions before he turned and a couple of likely murders since. Considering a mug shot from his warm days, Karen said the killer looked like such a nice fellow, even scowling over prisoner numbers, and Lew commented that you couldn't judge a book by its cover.

Geneviève continued paying attention well into the next item – about a scary candlelight vigil by hooded supporters of Annie Wilkes – and only turned the sound down on her portable TV set when she was sure her name was not going to come up in connection with the Shadow Bay story.

Gorse had implied she was being targeted because of her well-known involvement in the overthrow of Count Dracula, nearly a century ago. But that didn't explain why he had waited until now to give her a hard time. She also gathered from what he had let slip in flirtatious hints that he wasn't the top of the totem pole, that he was working with or perhaps for someone else.

Gorse had said: 'You can't stop Him. He's coming back.'

Him? He?

Only one vampire inspired that sort of *quondam rex que futurus* talk. Before he finally died, put out of his misery, Count Dracula had used himself up completely. Geneviève was sure of that. He had outlived his era, several times over, and been confronted with his own irrelevance. His true death was just a formality.

And *he* was not coming back.

A woodcut image of Dracula appeared on screen. She turned the sound up.

The newscast had reached the entertainment round-up, which in this town came before major wars on other continents. A fluffy-haired woman in front of the Hollywood sign was talking about the latest studio craze: Dracula pictures. A race was on between Universal and Paramount to get their biopics of the Count to theatres. At Universal, director Joel Schumacher and writer-producer Jane Wagner had cast John Travolta and Lily Tomlin in *St George's Fire*; at MGM, producer Steven Spielberg and director Tobe Hooper had Peter Coyote and Karen Allen in *Vampirgeist*. There was no mention of Orson Welles – or, unsurprisingly, Boris Adrian – but another familiar name came up.

John Alucard.

'Hollywood dealmakers have often been characterised as bloodsuckers,' said the reporter, 'but John Alucard is the first actually to be one. Uniquely, this vampire executive is involved in *both* these competing projects, as a packager of the Universal production and as associate producer of the MGM film. Clearly, in a field where there are too few experts to go around, John Alucard is in demand. Unfortunately, Mr A – as Steven Spielberg calls him – is unable because of his image impairment to grant interviews for broadcast media, but he has issued a statement to the effect that he feels there is room for far more than two versions of the story he characterises as "the most important of the last two centuries". He goes on to say, "There can be no definitive Dracula, but we hope we shall be able to conjure a different Dracula for every person." For decades Hollywood has stayed away from this hot subject but, with the Francis Coppola epic of a few years ago cropping up on Best of All Time lists, it seems we are due, like the Londoners of 1885, for a veritable *invasion* of Draculas. This is Kimberly Wells, for Channel 6 KDHB *Update News*, at the Hollywood sign.'

She switched the television off. The whole world, and Orson Welles, knew now what John Alucard was doing, but the other part of her original commission – who he was and where he came from – was still a mystery. He had come from the East, with a long line of credit. A source had told her he had skipped New York ahead of an investigation into insider-trading or junk bonds, but she might choose to put that down to typical Los Angeles cattiness. Another whisper had him living another life up in Silicon Valley as a consultant on something hush-hush and sci-fi President Reagan's people were calling the Strategic Defense Initiative. Alucard could also be a Romanian shoe salesman with a line in great patter, who had quit his dull job and changed his name the night he learned his turning vampire wasn't going to take in the long run, and set out to become the new Irving Thalberg before he rotted away to dirt.

There must be a connection between the movie-making

mystery man and the high school librarian. Alucard and Gorse. Two vampires in California. She had started asking around about one of them, and the other had sent a puppet to warn her off.

John Alucard could not *be* Count Dracula.

Not yet, at least.

19

On her way up into the Hollywood Hills to consult the only real magician she knew, she decided to call on Jack Martin, to see if he wanted to come along on the trip. The movie mage would interest him.

The door of Martin's shack hung open.

Her heart skipped. Loose manuscript pages were drifting out of Martin's home, catching on the breeze, and scuttling along Beverly Glen Boulevard, sticking on the manicured hedges of the million-dollar estates.

She knocked on the door, which popped a hinge and hung free.

'Jack?'

Had Gorse got to him?

She ventured inside, prepared to find walls dripping red and a ruined corpse lying in a nest of torn-up screenplays.

Martin lay on a beat-up sofa, mouth open, snoring slightly. He was no more battered than usual. A Mexican wrestling magazine was open on his round stomach.

'Jack?'

He came awake, blearily.

'It's you,' he said, cold.

His tone was like a silver knife.

'What's the matter?'

'As if you didn't know. You're not good to be around, Gené. Not good at all. You don't see it, but you're a wrecker.'

She backed away.

'Someone tipped off the Writers' Guild about the porno. My ticket got yanked, my dues were not accepted. I'm off the list. I'm off all the lists. All possible lists. I didn't get *Buck Privates*. They went with Lionel Fenn.'

'There'll be other projects,' she said.

'I'll be lucky to get *Buck's Privates*.'

Martin had been drinking, but didn't need to get drunk to be in this despair hole. It was where he went sometimes, a mental space like Ensenada, where he slunk to wallow, to soak up the misery he turned into prose. This time, she had an idea he wasn't coming back; he was going lower than ever, and would end up a beachcomber on a nighted seashore, picking broken skulls out of bloody seaweed, trailing bare feet through ink-black surf, becoming the exile king of his own dark country.

'It just took a phone call, Gené. To smash everything. To smash me. I wasn't even worth killing. That hurts. You, they'll kill. I don't want you to be near me when it happens.'

'Does this mean our premiere date is off?'

She shouldn't have said that. Martin began crying, softly. It was a shocking scene, upsetting to her on a level she had thought she had escaped from. He wasn't just depressed, he was scared.

'Go away, Gené,' he said.

20

This was not a jaunt any more. Jack Martin was as lost to her as Moondoggie, as her licence.

How could things change so fast? It wasn't the second week of January, wasn't the Julian 1980s, but everything that had seemed certain last year, last decade, was up for debate or thrown away.

There was a cruelty at work. Beyond Gorse.

She parked the Plymouth and walked across a lawn to a ranch-style bungalow. A cabalist firmament of star-signs decorated the mail-box.

The mage was a trim, fiftyish man, handsome but small, less a fallen angel than a fallen cherub. He wore ceremonial robes to receive her into his *sanctum sanctorum*, an arrangement of literal shrines to movie stars of the 1920s and 30s: Theda Bara, Norma Desmond, Clara Bow, Lina Lamont, Jean Harlow, Blanche Hudson, Marion Marsh, Myrna Loy. His all-seeing amulet contained a long-lashed black and white eye, taken from a still of Rudolph Valentino. His boots were black leather motorcycle gear, with polished chrome buckles and studs.

As a boy, the mage – Kenneth Anger to mortals of this plane – had appeared as the Prince in the 1935 Max Reinhardt film of *A Midsummer Night's Dream*. In later life, he had become a filmmaker, but for himself not the studios (his 'underground' trilogy consisted of *Scorpio Rising*, *Lucifer Rising* and *Dracula Rising*), and achieved a certain notoriety for compiling *Hollywood Babylon*, a collection of scurrilous but not necessarily true stories about the seamy private lives of the glamour gods and goddesses of the screen. A disciple of Aleister Crowley and Adrian Marcato, he was a genuine movie magician.

He was working on a sequel to *Hollywood Babylon*, which had been forthcoming for some years. It was called *Transylvania Babylon*, and contained all the gossip, scandal and lurid factoid speculation that had ever circulated about the elder members of the vampire community. Nine months ago, the manuscript and all his research material had been stolen by minions of a pair of New Orleans-based vampire elders who were the focus of several fascinating, enlightening and perversely amusing chapters. Geneviève had recovered the materials, though the book was still not published as Anger had to negotiate his way through a maze of injunctions and magical threats before he could get the thing in print.

She hesitated on the steps that led down to his slightly sunken *sanctum*. Incense burned before the framed pictures, swirling up to the low stucco ceiling.

'Do you have to be invited?' he asked. 'Enter freely, spirit of dark.'

'I was just being polite,' she admitted.

The mage was a little disappointed. He arranged himself on a pile of harem cushions and indicated a patch of Turkish carpet where she might sit.

There was a very old bloodstain on the weave.

'Don't mind that,' he said. 'It's from a thirteen-year-old movie extra deflowered by Charlie Chaplin at the very height of the Roaring Twenties.'

She decided not to tell him it wasn't hymeneal blood (though it was human).

'I have cast spells of protection, as a precaution. It was respectful of you to warn me this interview might have consequences.'

Over the centuries, Geneviève had grown out of thinking of herself as a supernatural creature, and was always a little surprised to run into people who still saw her that way. It wasn't that they might not be right, it was just unusual and unfashionable. The world had monsters, but she still didn't know if there was magic.

'One man who helped me says his career has been ruined because of it,' she said, the wound still fresh. 'Another, who was just my friend, was killed.'

'My career is beyond ruination,' said the mage. 'And death means nothing. As you know, it's a passing thing. The lead-up, however, can be highly unpleasant, I understand. I think I'd opt to skip that experience, if at all possible.'

She didn't blame him.

'I've seen some of your films and looked at your writings,' she said. 'It seems to me that you believe motion pictures are rituals.'

'Well put. Yes, all real films are invocations, summonings. Most are made by people who don't realise that. But I do. When I call a film *Invocation of My Demon Brother*, I mean it exactly as it sounds. It's not enough to plop a camera in front of a ceremony. Then you only get religious television, God help you. It's in the lighting, the cutting, the music. Reality must be banished, channels opened to the beyond. At screenings, there are always manifestations. Audiences might not realise on a conscious level what is happening, but they always know. Always. The amount of ectoplasm poured into the auditorium by drag queens at a West Hollywood revival of a Joan Crawford picture would be enough to embody a minor djinn in the shape of the Bitch Goddess, with a turban and razor cheekbones and shoulderpads out to here.'

She found the image appealing, but also frightening.

'If you were to make a dozen films about, say, the Devil, would the Prince of Darkness appear?' she asked.

The mage was amused. 'What an improbable notion! But it has some substance. If you made twelve ordinary films about the Devil, he might seem more real to people, become more of a figure in the culture, get talked about and put on magazine covers. But, let's face it, the same thing happens if you make one ordinary film about a shark. It's the thirteenth film that makes the difference, that might work the trick.'

'That would be your film? The one made by a director who understands the ritual?'

'Sadly, no. A great tragedy of magick is that to be most effective it must be worked without conscious thought, without intent. To become a master mage, you must pass beyond the mathematics and become a dreamer. My film, of the Devil you say, would be but a tentative summoning, attracting the notice of a spirit of the beyond. Fully to call His Satanic Majesty to Earth would require a work of surpassing genius, mounted by a director with no other intention but to make a wonderful illusion, a von Sternberg or a Frank Borzage. That thirteenth film, a *Shanghai Gesture* or a *History is Made at Night*, would be the perfect ritual. And its goaty hero could leave his cloven hoofprint in the cement outside Grauman's Chinese.'

21

Geneviève parked the Plymouth near Bronson Caverns, in sight of the Hollywood Sign, and looked out over Los Angeles, the city transformed by distance into a carpet of Christmas lights. MGM used to boast 'More stars than there were in the

Heavens', and there they were, twinkling individually, a fallen constellation. Car lights on the freeways were glowing platelets flowing through neon veins. From up here, you couldn't see the hookers on Hollywood Boulevard, the endless limbo motels and real estate developments, the lost, lonely and desperate. You couldn't hear the laugh track, or the screams.

It came down to magic. And whether she believed in it.

Clearly, Kenneth Anger did. He had devoted his life to rituals. A great many of them, she had to admit, had worked. And so did John Alucard and Ernest Gorse, vampires who thought themselves magical beings. Dracula had been another of the breed, thanking Satan for eternal night-life.

She just didn't know.

Maybe she was still undecided because she had never slipped into the blackness of death. Kate Reed, her Victorian friend, had done the proper thing. Kate's father-in-darkness, Harris, had drunk her blood and given of his own, then let her die and come back, turned. Chandagnac, Geneviève's mediaeval father-in-darkness, had worked on her for months. She had transformed slowly, coming alive by night, shaking off the warm girl she had been.

In the last century, since Dracula came out of his castle, there had been a lot of work done on the subject. It was no longer possible to disbelieve in vampires. With the *nosferatu* in the open, vampirism had to be incorporated into the prevalent belief systems and this was a scientific age. These days, everyone generally accepted the 'explanation' that the condition was a blood-borne mutation, an evolutionary quirk adapting a strain of humankind for survival. But, as geneticists probed ever further, mysteries deepened: vampires retained the DNA pattern they were born with as warm humans, and yet they were *different* creatures. And, despite Max Planck's Black Blood Refractive Postulate of 1902, the laws of optics still seemed broken by the business with mirrors.

If there were vampires, there could be magic.

And Alucard's ritual – the mage's thirteen movies – might work. He could come back, worse than ever.

Dracula.

She looked up from the city-lights to the stars.

Was the Count out there, on some intangible plane, waiting to be summoned? Reinvigorated by a spell in the beyond, thirsting for blood, vengeance, power? What might he have learned in Hell, that he could bring to the Earth?

She hated to think.

22

She drove through the studio gates shortly before dawn, waved on by the uniformed guard. She was accepted as a part of Orson's army, somehow granted an invisible arm-band by her association with the genius.

The Miracle Pictures lot was alive again. 'If it's a good picture, it's a Miracle!' had run the self-mocking, double-edged slogan, all the more apt as the so-called fifth-wheel major declined from mounting Technicolor spectacles like the 1939 version of *The Duelling Cavalier*, with Errol Flynn and Fedora, to financing drive-in dodos like *Machete Maidens of Mora Tau*, with nobody and her uncle. In recent years, the fifty-year-old sound stages had mostly gone unused as Miracle shot their product in the Philippines or Canada. The standing sets seen in so many vintage movies had been torn down to make way for bland office buildings where scripts were 'developed' rather than shot. There wasn't even a studio tour.

Now, it was different.

Orson Welles was in power and legions swarmed at his command, occupying every department, beavering away in the service of his vision. They were everywhere: gaffers, extras, carpenters, managers, accountants, make-up and effects technicians, grips, key grips, boys, best boys, designers, draughtsmen, teamsters, caterers, guards, advisors, actors, writers, planners, plotters, doers, movers, shakers.

Once Welles had said this was the best train-set a boy could have. It was very different from three naked girls in an empty swimming pool.

She found herself on Stage 1, the Transylvanian village set. Faces she recognised were on the crew: Jack Nicholson, tearing through his lines with exaggerated expressions; Oja Kodar, handing down decisions from above; Debbie W. Griffith (in another life, she presumed), behind the craft services table; Dennis Hopper, in a cowboy hat and sunglasses.

The stage was crowded with on-lookers. Among the movie critics and TV reporters were other directors – she spotted Spielberg, DePalma and a shifty Coppola – intent on kibbitzing on the master, demonstrating support for the abused genius or suppressing poisonous envy. Burt Reynolds, Gene Hackman and Jane Fonda were dressed up as villagers, rendered unrecognisable by make-up, so desperate to be in this movie that they were willing to be unbilled extras.

Somewhere up there, in a platform under the roof, sat the big baby. The visionary who would give birth to his Dracula. The unwitting magician who might, this time, conjure more than even he had bargained for.

She scanned the rafters, a hundred feet or more above the studio floor. Riggers crawled like pirates among the lights. Someone abseiled down into the village square.

She was sorry Martin wasn't here. This was his dream.

A dangerous dream.

23

---◆---

THE OTHER SIDE OF
MIDNIGHT
A SCRIPT

by Orson Welles
Based on *Dracula* by Bram Stoker

Revised final, January 6, 1981

1. An ominous chord introduces an extreme CU of a crucifix held in a knotted fist. It is sunset, we hear sounds of village life. We see only the midsection of the VILLAGE WOMAN holding the crucifix. She pulls tight the rosary-like string from which the cross hangs, as if it were a strangling cord. A scream is heard off camera, coming from some distance. The Woman whirls around abruptly to the left, in the direction of the sound. Almost at once the camera pans in this direction too, and we follow a line of PEASANT CHILDREN, strung out hand in hand and dancing, towards the INN of the Transylvanian Village of Bistritz. We close on a leaded window and pass through – the set opening up to let in the camera – to find JONATHAN HARKER, a young Englishman with a tigerish smile, in the centre of a tableau Breughel interior, surrounded by peasant activity, children, animals, etc. He is framed by dangling bulbs of garlic, and the Village Woman's crucifix is echoed by one that hangs on the wall. Everyone, including the animals, is frozen, shocked. The scream is still echoing from the low wooden beams.

HARKER: What did I say?

The INN-KEEPER crosses himself. The peasants mutter.

HARKER: Was it the place? Was it [relishing each syllable] Castle Dra-cu-la?

More muttering and crossing. Harker shrugs and continues with his meal. Without a cut, the camera pans around the cramped interior, to find MINA, Harker's new wife, in the doorway. She is huge-eyed and tremulous, more impressed by 'native superstitions' than her husband, but with an inner steel core which will become apparent as Jonathan's outward bluff crumbles. Zither and fiddle music conveys the bustle of this border community.

MINA: Jonathan dear, come on. The coach.

Jonathan flashes a smile, showing teeth that wouldn't shame a vampire. Mina doesn't see the beginnings of his viperish second face, but smiles indulgently, hesitant. Jonathan pushes away his plate and stands, displacing children and animals. He joins Mina and they leave, followed by our snake-like camera, which almost jostles them as they emerge into the twilight. Some of the crowd hold aloft flaming torches, which make shadow-featured flickering masks of the worn peasant faces. Jonathan, hefting a heavy bag, and Mina, fluttering at every distraction, walk across the village square to a waiting COACH. Standing in their path, a crow-black figure centre-frame, is the Village Woman, eyes wet with fear, crucifix shining. She bars the Harkers' way, like the Ancient Mariner, and extends the crucifix.

VILLAGE WOMAN: If you must go, wear this. Wear it for your mother's sake. It will protect you.

Jonathan bristles, but Mina defuses the situation by taking the cross.

MINA: Thank you. Thank you very much.

The Woman crosses herself, kisses Mina's cheek, and departs. Jonathan gives an eyebrows-raised grimace, and Mina shrugs, placatory.

COACHMAN: All aboard for Borgo Pass, Visaria and Klausenburg.

We get into the coach with the Harkers, who displace a fat MERCHANT and his 'secretary' ZITA, and the camera gets comfortable opposite them. They exchange looks, and Mina holds Jonathan's hand. The Coach lurches and moves off – it is vital that the camera remain fixed on the

Harkers to cover the progress from one sound stage to the next, with the illusion of travel maintained by the projection of reflected Transylvanian mountain road scenery onto the window. We have time to notice that the Merchant and Zita are wary of the Harkers; he is middle-aged and balding, and she is a flashy blonde. The coach stops.

COACHMAN (v.o.): Borgo Pass.

JONATHAN: Mina, here's our stop.

MERCHANT: Here?
MINA (proud): A carriage is meeting us here, at midnight. A nobleman's.
MERCHANT: Whose carriage?

JONATHAN: Count Dracula's.

Jonathan, who knows the effect it will have, says the name with defiance and mad eyes. The Merchant is terror-struck, and Zita hisses like a cat, shrinking against him. The Harkers, and the camera, get out of the coach, which hurries off, the Coachman whipping the horses to make a quick getaway. We are alone in a mountain pass, high above the Carpathians. Night-sounds: wolves, the wind, bats. The full moon seems for a moment to have eyes, DRACULA's hooded eyes.

JONATHAN (pointing): You can see the castle.

MINA: It looks so... desolate, lonely.

JONATHAN: No wonder the Count wants to move to London. He must be raging with cabin fever, probably ready to tear his family apart and chew their bones. Like Sawney Beane.

MINA: The Count has a family?

JONATHAN (delighted): Three wives. Like a Sultan.

Imagine how that'll go down in Piccadilly.

Silently, with no hoof- or wheel-sounds, a carriage appears, the DRIVER a black, faceless shape. The Harkers climb in, but this time the camera rises to the top of the coach, where the Driver has vanished. We hover as the carriage moves off, a LARGE BAT flapping purposefully over the lead horses, and trundles along a narrow, vertiginous mountain road towards the castle. We swoop ahead of the carriage, becoming the eyes of the Bat, and take a flying detour from the road, allowing us a false perspective view of the miniature landscape to either side of the full-size road and carriage, passing beyond the thick rows of pines to a whited scrape in the hillside that the Harkers do not see, an apparent chalk quarry which we realise consists of a strew of complete human skeletons in agonised postures, skulls and rib-cages broken, the remains of thousands and thousands of murdered men, women, children and babies. Here and there, skeletons of armoured horses and creatures between wolf or lion and man. This gruesome landscape passes under us and we close on CASTLE DRACULA, a miniature constructed to allow our nimble camera to close on the highest tower and pass down a stone spiral stairway that affords covert access to the next stage...

...and the resting chamber of Dracula and his BRIDES. We stalk through a curtain of cobweb, which parts unharmed, and observe as the three shroud-clad Brides rise from their boxes, flitting about before us. Two are dark and feral, one is blonde and waif-like. We have become Dracula and stalk through the corridors of his castle, brassbound oaken doors opening before us. Footsteps do not echo and we pass mirrors that reveal nothing – reversed sets under glass, so as not to catch our crew – but a spindle-fingered, almost animate shadow is cast, impossibly long arms reaching out, pointed head with bat-flared ears momentarily sharp against a tapestry. We move faster and faster through the Castle, coming out into the great HALLWAY at the very top of a wide staircase. Very small, at the bottom of the steps, stand Jonathan and Mina, beside their luggage. Sedately, we fix on them and move downwards, our cloaked shadow contracting. As we near the couple, we see their faces: Jonathan awe-struck, almost in love at first sight, ready to become our slave; Mina horrified, afraid for her husband, but almost on the point of pity. The music, which has passed from lusty human strings to ethereal Theremin themes, swells, conveying the ancient, corrupt, magical soul of Dracula. We pause on the steps, six feet above the Harkers, then leap forwards as Mina holds up the crucifix, whose blinding light fills the frame. The music climaxes, a sacred choral theme battling the eerie Theremin.

2: CU on the ancient face, points of red in the eyes, hair and moustaches shocks of pure white, pulling back to show the whole stick-thin frame wrapped in unrelieved black.

THE COUNT: I… am… Dracula.

The Other Side of Midnight Cast and Credits, as of January 1981

Production Company: Mercury Productions. Distributor: Miracle Pictures. Executive Producer: John Alucard. Producer: Orson Welles. Director: Orson Welles. Script: Orson Welles. From the novel by Bram Stoker. Director of Photography: Gary Graver. Production Designer: Ken Adam. Special Make-Up Effects: Rick Baker. Optical Effects: ILM. Music: John Williams.

Jack Nicholson (Jonathan Harker), Richard Gere (Arthur Holmwood), Orson Welles (Van Helsing/Swales), Shelley Duvall (Mina), Susan Sarandon (Lucy), Cameron Mitchell (Renfield), Dennis Hopper (Quincey), Jason Robards (Dr Seward), Joseph Cotten (Mr Hawkins), Jeanne Moreau (Peasant Woman), Anjelica Huston, Marie-France Pisier, Kathleen Turner (Vampire Brides), John Huston (The Count).

24

Welles had rewritten the first scenes – the first *shot* – of the film to make full use of a new gadget called a Louma Crane, which gave the camera enormous mobility and suppleness. Combined with breakaway sets and dark passages between stages, the device meant that he could open *The Other Side of Midnight* with a single tracking shot longer and more elaborate than the one he had pulled off in *Touch of Evil*.

Geneviève found Welles and his cinematographer on the road to Borgo Pass, a full-sized mock-up dirt track complete with wheelruts and milestones. The night-black carriage, as yet not equipped with a team of horses, stood on its marks, the crest of Dracula on its polished doors. To either side were forests, the nearest trees half life-size and those beyond getting smaller and smaller as they stretched out to the studio backdrop of a Carpathian night. Up ahead was Dracula's castle, a nine-foot-tall edifice, currently being sprayed by a technician who seemed like the Colossal Man, griming and fogging the battlements.

The two men were debating a potentially thorny moment in the shot when the camera would be detached from the coach and picked up by an aerial rig. Hanging from the ceiling was a contraption that looked like a Wright Brothers-Georges Méliès collaboration, a man-shaped flying frame with a camera hooked onto it, and a dauntless operator inside.

She hated to think what all this was costing.

Welles saw her, and grinned broadly.

'Gené, Gené,' he welcomed her. 'You must see this cunning bit of business. Even if I do say so myself, it's an absolute stroke of genius. A simple solution to a complex problem. When *Midnight* comes out, they'll all wonder how I did it.'

He chuckled.

'Orson,' she said, 'we have to talk. I've found some things out. As you asked. About Mr Alucard.'

He took that aboard. He must have a thousand and one mammoth and tiny matters to see to, but one more could be accommodated. That was part of his skill as a director, being a master strategist as well as a visionary artist.

She almost hated to tell him.

'Where can we talk in private?' she asked.

'In the coach,' he said, standing aside to let her step up.

25

The prop coach, as detailed inside as out, creaked a lot as Welles shifted his weight. She wondered if the springs could take it.

She had laid out the whole thing.

She still didn't know who John Alucard was, though she supposed him some self-styled last disciple of the King Vampire, but she told Welles what she thought he was up to.

'He doesn't want a conjurer,' Welles concluded, 'but a sorcerer, a magician.'

Geneviève remembered Welles had played Faustus on stage.

'Alucard needs a genius, Orson,' she said, trying to be a comfort.

Welles's great brows knit in a frown. This was too great a thing to get even his mind around.

He asked the forty-thousand-dollar question: 'And do you believe it will work? This conjuring of Dracula?'

She dodged it. 'John Alucard does.'

'Of that I have no doubt, no doubt at all,' rumbled Welles. 'The colossal conceit of it, the enormity of the conception, boggles belief. All this, after so long, all this can be mine, a real chance to, as the young people so aptly say, do my thing. And it's part of a Black Mass. A film to raise the Devil Himself. No mere charlatan could devise such a warped, intricate scheme.'

With that, she had to agree.

'If Alucard is wrong, if magic doesn't work, then there's no harm in taking his money and making my movie. That would truly be beating the Devil.'

'But if he's right…'

'Then I, Orson Welles, would not merely be Faustus, nor even Prometheus, I would be Pandora, unloosing all the ills of the world to reign anew. I would be the father-in-darkness of a veritable Bright Lucifer.'

'It could be worse. You could be cloning Hitler.'

Welles shook his head.

'And it's my decision,' he said, wearily. Then he laughed, so loud that the interior of the prop carriage shook as with a thunderbolt from Zeus.

She didn't envy the genius his choice. After such great beginnings, no artist of the twentieth century had been thwarted so consistently and so often. Everything he had made, even *Kane*, was compromised as soon as it left his mind and ventured into the marketplace. Dozens of unfinished or unmade films, unstaged theatrical productions, projects stolen away and botched by lesser talents, often with Welles still around as a cameo player to see the potential squandered. And here, at the end of his career, was the chance to claw everything back, to make good on his promise, to be a Boy Wonder again, to prove at last that he was the King of his World.

And against that, a touch of brimstone. Something she didn't even necessarily believe.

Great tears emerged from Welles's clear eyes and trickled into his beard. Tears of laughter.

There was a tap at the coach door.

'All ready on the set now, Mr Welles,' said an assistant.

'This shot, Gené,' said Welles, ruminating, 'will be a marvel, one for the books. And it'll come in under budget. A whole reel, a quarter of an hour, will be in the can by the end of the day. Months of planning, construction, drafting and setting up. Everything I've learned about the movies since 1939. It'll all be there.'

Had she the heart to plead with him to stop?

'Mr Welles,' prompted the assistant.

Suddenly firm, decided, Welles said, 'We take the shot.'

26

On the first take, the sliding walls of the Bistritz Inn jammed, after only twenty seconds of exposure. The next take went perfectly, snaking through three stages, with over a hundred performers in addition to the principals and twice that many technicians focusing on fulfilling the vision of one great man. After lunch, at the pleading of Jack Nicholson – who thought he could do better – Welles put the whole show on again. This time, there were wobbles as the flying camera went momentarily out of control, plunging towards the toy forest, before the operator (pilot?) regained balance and completed the stunt with a remarkable save.

Two good takes. The spontaneous chaos might even work for the shot.

Geneviève had spent the day just watching, in awe.

If it came to a choice between a world without this film and a world with Dracula, she didn't know which way she would vote. Welles, in action, was a much younger man, a charmer and a tyrant, a cheerleader and a patriarch. He was everywhere, flirting in French with Jeanne Moreau, the peasant woman, and hauling ropes with the effects men. Dracula wasn't in the shot, except as a subjective camera and a shadow-puppet, but John Huston was on stage for every moment, when he could have been resting in his trailer, just amazed by what Welles was doing, a veteran as impressed as parvenus like Spielberg and DePalma, who were taking notes like trainspotters in locomotive heaven.

Still unsure about the outcome of it all, she left without talking to Welles again.

Driving up to Malibu, she came down from the excitement.

In a few days, it would be the Julian 1980s. And she should start working to get her licence back. Considering everything, she should angle to get paid by Welles, who must have enough of John Alucard's money to settle her bill.

When she pulled into Paradise Cove, it was full dark. She took a moment after parking the car to listen to the surf, an eternal sound, pre- and post-human.

She got out of the car and walked towards her trailer. As she fished around in her bag for her keys, she sensed something that made quills of her hair.

As if in slow motion, her trailer exploded.

A burst of flame in the sleeping section spurted through the shutters, tearing them off their frames, and then a second, larger fireball expanded from the inside as the gas cylinders in the kitchen caught, rending the chromed walls apart, wrecking the integrity of the vessel.

The light hit her a split-second before the noise.

Then the blast lifted her off her feet and threw her back across the sandy lot.

Everything she owned rained around her in flames.

27

'Do you know what's the funny side of the whole kit and kaboodle?' said Ernest Gorse. 'I didn't even think it would work. Johnny Alucard has big ideas and he is certainly making something of himself on the coast, but this Elvis Lives nonsense is potty. Then again, you never know with the dear old Count. He's been dead before.'

She was too wrung out to try to get up yet.

Gorse, in a tweed ulster and fisherman's hat, leaned on her car, scratching the finish with the claws of his left hand. A gangrene growth festered in his empty eye-socket. His face was demonised by the firelight.

'You must have said something persuasive, love,' Gorse continued. 'Orson Welles has walked off his comeback picture, shut it down after a single day's shooting. He can't be found. The project's dead. No other genius would dare take over.'

Everything she owned.

That's what it had cost her.

'But, who knows, maybe Fatty wasn't the genius?' suggested Gorse. 'Maybe it was Boris Adrian. Alucard backed all those Dracula pictures equally. Perhaps you haven't thwarted him after all. Perhaps He really is coming back.'

All the fight was out of her. Gorse must be enjoying this.

'You should leave the city, maybe the state,' he said. 'There is nothing here for you, old thing. Be thankful we've left you the motor. Nice roadboat, by the way, but it's not a Jag, is it? Consider the long lines, all the chrome, the ostentatious muscle. D'you think the Yanks are trying to prove something? Don't trouble yourself to answer. It was a rhetorical question.'

She pushed herself up on her knees.

Gorse had a gun. 'Paper wraps stone,' he said. 'With silver foil.'

She got to her feet, not brushing the sand from her clothes. There was ash in her hair. People had come out of the other trailers, fascinated and horrified. Her trailer was a burning shell.

That annoyed her, gave her a spark.

With a swiftness Gorse couldn't match, she took his gun. She broke his wrist and tore off his hat too. He was surprised in a heart-dead British sort of way, raising his eyebrows as far as they would go. His quizzical, ironic expression begged to be scraped off his face, but it would just grow back crooked.

'Jolly well done,' he said, going limp. 'Really super little move. Didn't see it coming at all.'

She could have thrown him into the fire, but just gave his gun to one of the on-lookers, the Dude, with instructions that he was to be turned over to the police when they showed up.

'Watch him, he's a murderer,' she said. Gorse looked hurt. 'A common murderer,' she elaborated.

The Dude understood and held the gun properly. People gathered round the shrinking vampire, holding him fast. He was no threat any more: he was cut, wrapped and blunted.

There were sirens. In situations like this, there were always sirens.

She kissed the Dude goodbye, got into the Plymouth, and drove north away from Hollywood along the winding coast road, without a look back. She wasn't sure whether she was lost or free.

INTERLUDE

YOU ARE THE WIND
BENEATH MY WINGS

ANNO DRACULA 1986

1

———————◆———————

'Eyes front, pledges,' said Captain Gardner, commanding attention. 'This is Miss Churchward. She will be your etiquette instructress.'

There were grins. This little lot didn't think they needed lessons in manners. They were about to learn they were wrong.

Penelope perched on a desk, arranging herself decorously. She smoothed her immaculate cream skirt over her upper flank, drawing attention to her long, long legs.

All the class stared. Men *and* women. Penny was inches taller than she'd been when she died. A slight shapeshift, worked over decades. She'd exercised powers of fascination even before turning vampire. Now, she was mistress of sex fu.

Folding chairs noisily aligned. The pledges, sprawling and slobbish a moment ago, sat up straight. This class had been through Purgatory basic and were parade-drilled. They wore casual clothes with no rank or service insignia. Hot shots and cool customers. Pushovers, really.

Slipping off her sunglasses, she shook out her full, heavy hair. She tapped the diamond-sharp nail of her littlest finger against her fang-teeth.

She made a fan gesture in front of her neck. The top two buttons of her watered silk blouse were undone. What was the point of pricey underthings unless they were glimpsable? Though she didn't need to breathe, she did.

After a century of clothing buttoned-to-the-throat, she was

experimenting with cleavage. The leech-scars on her breasts and neck – left by quack doctoring in her new-born days – had faded to milky vaccination circles, almost imperceptible.

Some of the guys awkwardly crossed their legs. Others tented clipboards over their laps. The women were as interested, if not uniformly friendly.

Penny had sunk hooks in them all. Without even bleeding them. Just by walking into the room.

She tugged.

As one, the class shuffled forwards, scraping chairs across linoleum.

She put out a hand in a stop sign, then signalled a come-on to one of the pledges. An all-American youth was pulled from his seat, as if on strings. Code Name: Banshee. He wore an eye-abusing Hawaiian shirt over chinos and lace-up combat boots. Instead of regulation shades, he wore a New Wavy mirrored purple visor. He had about forty-eight teeth. She had him pegged as class clown. Did he know banshees were supposed to be women?

He began to sing to her, off-key and loud. Now she gathered how he got his call sign. The others were astonished, mouths open like goldfish.

'I can't li-i-ive,' he warbled, 'if living is without you…'

She laughed and cut him off with a gesture. Outside, a dog howled, presumably bleeding from the ears.

'Elementary glamour,' she announced, letting Banshee fall back in his chair like an unfisted muppet. 'A little show, a little tell, a lot of imagination. If you're to be vampires, you have to learn this. I am not the most seductive, dangerous person in the world. I am rarely the most attractive woman in any given room. But, if I concentrate, I can be. Any questions?'

A woman at the back, in short-sleeved dress whites, raised a cautious hand.

'Can we learn how to do… that?'

Penny looked at her. Code Name: Desire. A fluffy blonde with a crooked smile and a killer body. Her time over the assault course was the best among the women. Third overall.

'By the end of this course,' Penny said, 'you will have

learned how to turn it on and off like a tap. A faucet, as you Americans say.'

'Does it work on, ah, babes too, ma'am?' asked Banshee.

She turned it all back on and aimed at him. Full force.

'I am given to understand, pledge, that it does.'

The jock punched the air and whooped, 'All ri-i-ight!'

2

By the end of her first week, every one of the nine men and three women on the course had propositioned Penelope. Six of the guys and one of the girls wanted to sleep with her as well as get bitten. She took up none of the offers. They told themselves she'd done it to them, that she was working on their minds. But she'd just opened them to the possibilities and let them do the rest.

She'd washed four men and one woman out of her class. Her word alone wasn't enough but other instructors concurred. These pledges didn't have the red stuff. Jedburgh, director of the Program, rubber-stamped the termination orders. They were back on the bus, bound to silence by confidentiality agreements. If they ever talked about Purgatory, they'd end up in court – or Arlington. Would any settle for less and become dhampires? There must be contingency plans. She'd learned not to ask about such things.

She spent time with Captain Gardner, a veteran of the US Bat-Soldier Program. Code Name: America. Turned shortly before America's entry into World War II, he'd been maintained ever since. A defence asset. The Pentagon liked to keep its vampires in a glass coffin marked 'In the event of war, break'. Gardner's 1940s swing pace was a contrast with the 1980s MTV zoom of the pledges. He was blond, handsome, plastic. A Muscle Beach body. An Arrow Collar face. Wrapped in a flag. Andy would have loved him.

In his quarters, they drank from purebred army-issue cats.

That mellowed her out nicely. Only on active duty would the Captain take human blood.

Gardner was as much out of his time as she was hers: Artie Shaw and Glenn Miller gramophone records filed in a purpose-built cabinet, signed photos of Franklin Roosevelt and Ernie Pyle framed on the wall, Stars and Stripes shield hung over the bedboard. She, at least, made an effort to embrace the new, and had a boxful of ruinously expensive little silver discs by Whitney Houston, Genesis and Bruce Springsteen. After her up-and-down turn-of-the-decade New York adventures (which she associated with spiky, unlistenable punk), mainstream rock suited her mid-'80s mood. It went with the tailored earth-tones suits – sharp shoulders, little skirt to speak of, worn at all times with high-heeled pumps and seamed stockings – and an even tan cultivated by exposing her face and arms to the sun in three-second bursts.

Gardner didn't offer her his vampire blood and hadn't made an effort to get her into his militarily-perfect bed. It was in the corner, blanket-folds as sharp as coffin-corners, tight enough to bounce dimes off.

The folders lay on the table between them.

Seven survivors. Five men and two women.

Tomorrow, Gardner would make them all his sons- and daughters-in-darkness, passing on his bloodline. His code name would mark the group. America. She hadn't volunteered her own perhaps-dubious blood, though she supposed her contract meant the Shop could tap her if they wanted to. The pledges would be test-tube vampires. Their transformation would be passionless. A measured injection of blood direct to the vein. Very unlike the hot confusion of her own turning. Gardner wouldn't even be in the room with his get as they were reborn.

She still had questions.

If the Program was such a success and had been for fifty years, why were there so few Bat-Soldiers? This inter-services training facility (outside Purgatory, New Mexico) had turned out a trickle of graduates over the decades, but nothing like an all-conquering vampire army. No undead legions had been unloosed on the Vietcong, no creature commandos sent in after the Iran hostages.

Word was that the Program was being stepped up. Her own recruitment by the Shop – a government agency she'd never heard of – suggested this was true. Besides the warm pledges, a group of already-established vampires were here in training. They were kept separate from her class. She understood most weren't even American. Some were elders, veterans of Dracula's Carpathian Guard.

Gardner looked through the folders, passing them to Penny for a second glance.

Real names were listed, but came as news to her. On the courses, code names were used: Banshee, Desire, the Confessor, Iceman, Nikita, the Angel, Velcro.

Their pre-course careers were outlined. The class was drawn from different forces: two Marines, a Navy SEAL, two regular army, a transfer from NASA's astronaut programme and a CIA agent. All had home towns, parents, reasons for joining the services, employment histories, school and medical records, a tangle of living relationships and interests.

Tomorrow, at sunset, they would all change.

'Do you ever regret turning?' she asked Gardner. 'Do you miss growing old, having conventional offspring, passing the torch?'

Gardner was firm. 'No, ma'am.'

3

The class, whom she thought of as in part her get, were mostly coming along.

Nikita was in the infirmary with an unpredictable reaction like the infection which had laid Penelope low nearly a hundred years ago. An undetectable bug carried over from warm life into her new-born vampire state mutated into a dangerous parasite. Unlike Penny, the CIA girl was not treated with leeches. Paul Beecher, the Program's vampire physician, had the patient on a regular drip of 'golden'. Scuttlebutt had it that the high-quality blood was harvested entirely from virgin altar boys the night before their first wet dream. Dr Beecher said the prognosis was encouraging.

Otherwise, the 'America' new-borns took to the night with an enthusiasm it was her job to temper. Banshee, Iceman and the Angel – shapeshifters with flight capability – were often out in the desert, soaring aloft like gliders. She was worried they'd fail to learn the lesson of Icarus. If they stayed in the air past dawn, they'd burn up in sunlight. Desire was a mind-worm: she could put anyone under her spell and had a low-level telepathic link with those she sampled. She could potentially be a skull-walker, capable of projecting herself completely into someone whose blood she'd drunk. With the help of Darryl Revok, a Canadian expert, she was puppeteering cats, taking their minds for a spell and guiding them like remote-control spy-cams. There were obvious intelligence applications. The Confessor, who doubled as the group's chaplain, and Velcro, a Grenada combat veteran, were like Penny, just vampires – with no 'talents' apart from living longer, healing faster, moving swifter and surviving on blood alone.

In 1941, Gardner had been bled to death on an operating table, as vampire blood – smuggled out of Europe – dripped into his veins. His heart stopped and restarted. Back then, it was generally believed turning was impossible without death. These new Bat-Soldiers had been slowly exsanguinated, hearts and brains never flatlining. They ingested Gardner's blood in time-release capsules.

It wasn't really new: Geneviève Dieudonné, with whom Penny had a complicated relationship, had gone through something similar in the fifteenth century. But it was still unusual. No one was sure whether the Bat-Soldiers were proper vampires or highly-evolved dhampires. Dr Beecher let slip that the Program was working on making the process reversible. Surviving grads could serve their fifty-year-hitches and muster out, restored to full warmth (and mortality). He foresaw a surprising percentage would opt for 'normal' life, even with ageing and death included in the package.

If the option were open to her, she would have to seriously consider it.

Before staying as she was.

She'd been a vampire much longer than she'd been warm.

One reason for the slow progress of the Program was that the Shop had got hold of extensive documentation of a project carried out during World War I by the Germans, at the direction of Dracula himself. She knew a little about that from Charles, the warm fiancé who'd left her for Geneviève but still opted for old age and death rather than vampirism. He had been with the Diogenes Club, a more gentlemanly British version of the Shop. The Kaiser's mad scientists had created a cadre of fearsome flying shapeshifters, far more mutated than any of the Program's bat-men. Few of those vampire aces came through the war human-minded enough to be of any use to anyone.

The last survivors of the experiment were exterminated by Hitler, whose own dreams of a pureblood German vampire race had fizzled. The Nazi plan was to kill off all extant 'mongrel vampires', whom they classed with gypsies and Jews. Then, a mass communion of Aryan blood would create a new iron bloodline. The War ended before Hitler's vision was realised. Gardner told her he'd faced and bested a couple of the prototype vampire supermen, remarkable only for ugliness. Upon turning, their faces shapeshifted into scarlet skulls or batwing-eared fright masks and stuck that way. Dracula himself supported the Allies and went into Romania on a crusade in 1944, uniting the elder vampires of the region against the Nazis. She'd come into that story late, joining the Count's household after Truman, Stalin and Churchill manoeuvred him out of his castle stronghold and into useless Italian exile at the Palazzo Otranto.

At one time, she'd thought vampires must become masters of the world. Would these new-borns, who could live as vampires but perhaps just switch it off, fulfil that dream? And where would that leave her?

It was good that these new-borns were imprinted on her.

One night, she might need them.

Penelope found out more about the other group.

One night, after visiting the infirmary to lend Nikita some fashion magazines, she bumped into a vampire she recognised from Europe. Baron Alexis Ziska. He pretended not to remember her.

Ziska had been in London in '88 with the Prince Consort's Carpathian Guard. He'd also hung about Otranto, a vague connection of Asa Vajda, Dracula's annoying Moldavian fiancée. One of those carbon copy elders, he had cut his moustache and cloak too obviously in imitation of the Count. Since Dracula's true death, the copy had faded. There were black smudges under his red-rimmed eyes.

'Baron, we must catch up,' she said.

Ziska grunted.

'With each other's news, I mean. What brings you here, to Purgatory?'

The vampire mumbled.

'I have clearance,' Penny reassured him. 'I'm with the Shop.'

At mention of the agency, Ziska suppressed a flush of terror. He was a sender, leaking emotion all over the place. No wonder he was reduced to a hanger-on.

'Have you found a friend, Lex?' shouted someone from the ward. 'Haul her in. She's bound to be better company than you. Did you bring the fat mice, as I requested?'

The voice came from a bed behind black curtains. Ziska's face darkened.

'That sounds like an invitation,' she said.

Ziska stamped into the ward. Penny tagged along and helped open the curtains.

'My my, what a pretty one,' said the thing in the bed. 'You must introduce me.'

The patient was more coal than flesh, a living skeleton clad in black, cooked meat. The eyes were wetly mobile and the teeth sharp and white. Penny took the patient to be male, a vampire and on the way to recovery.

'Baron Lajos Czuczron,' said Ziska, 'this is, ah, Lady Godalming.'

'Penelope Churchward,' she corrected, extending a hand. 'Penny.'

Charcoal fingers took hers. She let Czuczron kiss her hand by pressing lipless teeth to her knuckles.

'Enchanté, mademoiselle.'

Czuczron was another Carpathian, a Hungarian. She remembered the name. A sometime member of Dracula's inner circle, he'd neglected to call on his old master in exile. An invitation to the Royal Wedding, sent care of his old regiment, had been politely declined. She understood he was among the few vampires to prosper under communism. If he was here, he must be on the outs in Budapest.

'I regret offending your eyes with my present person. I am usually reckoned attractive. A dashing blade. I was staked out on a rock by ungrateful peasants and left for sunrise. Only the intervention of my good and faithful friends preserved me from the cruelty of true death.'

He was on a drip, like Nikita. She assumed he was getting 'golden' too.

'Had I known flowers of undeath like yourself were to be found in America, I should have come to this Virgin Land years ago. It has been an awakening, my dear.'

Ziska hissed, trying to shut Czuczron up.

'Come, Lex, we are all comrades. We are all *nosferatu* of the Old World. If this Shop wishes to help our cause, for whatever reasons, it would be impolite to shun them. Dearest Penny, I yearn to rise from this bed and hunt again. I am reinvigorated by our prospects, willing myself back to strength for the night when we return to our homelands, to become the princes we should always have been.'

She recognised the tune. Most popularly associated with Baron Meinster, of the Transylvania Movement.

Dr Beecher came onto the ward and shooed the visitors away from Czuczron. Outside, Ziska was steely and silent. She could taste his distrust and couldn't resist twisting the stake.

'So the Shop is training an army of elders? Carpathians. Intriguing times ahead.'

Ziska actually growled and faded into the shadows.

5

They lost the Angel, not to the sun or bad blood but to ambition. In flying form, he affected white eagle-feathers rather than leathery bat-membranes. He further lived up to his call sign by sporting golden eyes, pre-Raphaelite hippie curls and loose white robes. While unfolding his new wings for an examination, his brain burst from the strain of the shapeshift. Blood squirted in streams out of his eye-sockets.

Penelope was glad she wasn't there to see that. Blood was her sustenance, but she was wearied by endless spilling of the stuff.

The rest of the pledges were sobered by the casualty. Officially, a training accident.

She took the seminar. The others had to learn from this incident.

'Here is the paradox,' she said. 'Vampires are immortal, but most don't last a year beyond turning. In the weeks after my death, I was nearly destroyed. I was fortunate. Many I could name were not. Tigers are an endangered species, too. It doesn't do to be too efficient a predator. They get hunted to extinction. Now, would anyone like to say anything about the Angel?'

Desire sat quietly at the back, inexpressive. The new-born had slept with the pledge, before and after turning. She must also have been in his head, a greater intimacy than sex. Penny couldn't tell if Desire had the Angel's ghost – or psychic echo – tucked in the corner of her skull.

After several long clock-tick moments, Banshee put up his hand. He hadn't ditched the screaming shirts since turning but now wore his weird eyeshade all the time.

'We were blood brothers,' Banshee said. 'All of us, except

Iceman, we've shared blood. After we got through the first week, we had that party…'

After passing blood tests, a gaggle of flashdancers from a town titty bar had been brought in. For the pledges, this was their first chance to drink from a warm neck. One girl died and Velcro was up on a charge for a week.

'Before dawn, we had a ceremony. We cut open our wrists and let the flows go together.'

Penny shuddered. She'd suffered a year of fever after her first warm meal, a sick child. Her leech-spots itched when she remembered.

'Is this true?' she asked the class.

'It was righteous,' said Velcro.

Penny looked at Desire. The girl nodded.

'Dr Beecher will have to check you all over,' Penny said. 'Iceman, congratulations on opting out of the idiot club.'

Iceman, a human-shaped machine even before turning, took the compliment with a nod. A solo hunter, he'd be top of the class if not marked down for straying from the team. He was literally the coldest vampire Penny had ever known, his body temperature corpse-cool even after feeding. He could exhale darts of frost.

'It's not a wrong thing,' said the Confessor.

She didn't understand.

'The Angel lives on,' said Banshee. 'In us.'

Desire blinked, briefly flashing golden eyes.

6

After weeks of public foreplay, Penelope went to bed with Banshee. His quarters were decorated like a teenager's bedroom with pin-ups and pennants. Giorgio Moroder pounded out of a chunky sound system and Madonna screamed in silence on the muted portable TV. The sex was like the entertainment: noise and light but no connection, synthesised orchestration but a banal tune. Banshee pumped to orgasms as if scoring baskets and whooped with each little victory, seeking approval. It was what Penny had expected and, in truth, wanted.

The mechanics of coupling were over and done with. Her mouth bled from the sharpness of her fangs. Banshee lay under her with his eyes closed. He hadn't slept since turning, so he was overdue for a first lapse into death-like lassitude. Even the TV light patterns hurt his dark-adapted eyes, though he wouldn't admit a weakness. She found his shades on the bedside table and fitted them onto his head so he could look at her.

Penny swallowed her own blood.

'Jedburgh has us on an exercise tomorrow,' said Banshee. 'In the Ghost Town.'

An abandoned silver-mining community from the Old West a couple of klicks from Purgatory was often used for war games.

'We're going up against the other group.'

Penny felt cold.

'The real vampires, Penny.'

She'd seen Ziska again, jogging in formation with old-faced killers. Czuczron was up and around, patches of skin forming over the charred meat. The elder was recovering remarkably.

'We have to be better than the old ones, or there's no point, is there? New has to be improved. We've got to be the best.'

She had an overwhelming *need*. The cat in her room wasn't going to meet it. It was foolish, but a hundred years had not taught her how to resist temptation. She let her weight press onto Banshee, surprising and delighting him, then slithered down his body. She fastened her mouth to his sculptured belly, slid in her fangs, and began sucking gently, pressing and teasing with her tongue. She made a wound which seeped sweetly into her mouth.

Banshee slid his hands under her hair, pressing her face to his skin.

'We have to win,' he said.

In her head, dazed by rich half-warm, half-vampire blood, Penny flew. She rolled over, firework display in her back-brain, and watched the ceiling. Movement and sound caught her attention.

A dove had got into the barracks and was fluttering up in the eaves, dislodging clouds of dust motes which danced in the coloured light. Smoky candles burned on all surfaces, adding scent to the grainy air. The bird's wings flapped, making pixillated flash-images in her vision. It seemed like a series of identical doves, appearing and disappearing about the beams and joists.

Penny sprang upright, shocking Banshee. Piloted by the lizard stem, she acted purely on instinct, personality and intellect left on the damp sheets.

Arms by her sides, she snatched with her mouth.

When she fell back to the bed, bouncing Banshee aside, she bit through feathers and bone. In two bites and swallows, the dove was gone, beak and feet and all.

She puffed feathers out of her mouth in a cloud and straddled Banshee like a bronc-buster.

'Try and throw me, howling man,' she said.

7

'Howdy, girls and boys,' said Jedburgh, waving his straw-mesh Stetson for attention. The director was Shop through and through. A large, untidy Texan, he was warm but looked as if he could take down a two-thousand-year-old hopping Chinese elder with his bare hands.

'I reckon most of you have figured somethin' out about the Program. We let you do your little jobs and we take care of the big picture, but you're all smart folks. The Shop don't take any other kind.'

This briefing was for the instructors. Penelope, still woozy from Banshee's blood, sat next to Captain Gardner, who was sternly disappointed in her. Did he expect she'd become a nun for the USA? She was Code Name: Trampire, after all.

Dr Beecher was there, along with Revok of Psi Division and Rainbird of Infiltration and Liquidation. Several unfamiliar men and women, vampire and warm, were also present. They must be with the other group. Up front with Jedburgh was a walking corpse.

'This here's Caleb Croft. A Brit, but don't hold it against him. He's one of the best buddies the Shop has. He's been ridin' herd on Carpathia Group.'

She had heard of Croft from Charles and poor dear Katie. He didn't look much of a threat, but Penny understood he signed a dozen death warrants before every meal. He never bled without killing.

'Y'all heard of Star Wars, I guess,' said Jedburgh. 'Not the kiddie movie, the Strategic Defense Initiative. The High Frontier. Lord God knows how many billions the Prez has flushed down that latrine. Big bucks, but so far no Buck Rogers. Ronnie loves rockets. Spooks the shit out of the Soviets. They're spendin' themselves silly to keep up. One of the few advantages of a space weapons system that don't work is that there ain't no limit to the mazooma your mortal foe has to waste tryin' to duplicate it. But it still ain't gettin' the Job done. You know the Job: the eradication of the mental disorder known as Soviet Communism. The Kremlin gremlins have had it their own way in Eastern Europe since the Big One. They take it slow and steady, invadin' somewhere every twelve years or so. We're all set to toe-to-toe the bastards over Poland, and they sneak into Afghanistan instead. So, while they're looking East, we shit in their front yard. The game plan is to turn the Transylvania Movement from a talkshow joke into a real alternative for the Warsaw Pact satellites. Heard about the domino theory? Well, this time, we're knockin' and they're fallin'. They're all shakin' like Elvis with a burger jones. Czecho-Slovakia, Poland, Yugo-Slavia and, our mostest bestest special favourite, Nicolae Ceauşescu's Romania. Graduates of this Program will take out the puppet apparatchiks and restore the, ah, rightful rulers. Can you dig it? We're puttin' the Counts in the castles and the Barons in the back of the blood bank.'

'Sir,' said Gardner, 'isn't that dangerous? Many elders have bad human rights records. Mightn't they prove worse in the long run than the Reds?'

Jedburgh waved his hat and grinned.

'We thought of that, Captain. You're right. Most of 'em ain't just bloodsuckers, they're scumsuckers. Each and every one out for their own damned self. As soon as we set 'em up, they'll give us the finger. Your vampire elder is no friend of democracy and liberty. No offence, Caleb – I know you're with the Program, all the way to Memphis. That's why we've been mixin' our own bloodline, soldier. That's why FDR had you made way back when. We're trainin' up Carpathia Group to be good, but we have to train America Group to be better. Tragically, however, it would be a morale disaster if Carpathia got its ass kicked in the exercise, so y'all are goin' to have our bright boys and girls lose tomorrow night. They ain't gonna like it but that's the way it is. Anyone who wants to kick up a fuss will just have to cry themselves to sleep.'

Penny knew one pledge who was going to hate this policy decision.

8

Late in the afternoon, three black helicopters came in low out of the desert and landed on the parade ground. Jedburgh introduced Penelope, Gardner and Dr Beecher to the VIPs: Colonel Oliver North of the National Security Council, with his svelte aide Fawn Hall, and Vice-President Bush, accompanied by a CIA analyst named Ryan. George Bush conveyed a message of support from Rocket Ronnie. Ryan gave Jedburgh a golf bag full of bottles of Gentleman Jack, compliments of the boys in Langley.

Out of the third chopper came two vampires she recognised at once: Baron Meinster, figurehead of the Transylvania Movement, and Graf von Orlok, a known extremist.

Meinster was small, dapper and boyish. Orlok slank behind him, a hideous spectre. The Vice-President could not disguise his sour grimace of distaste whenever Orlok's spider-fingered shadow neared him. She was uncomfortable. If prodded, prejudice so naked would extend to far more human-seeming vampires… like her.

Jedburgh was in an expansive mood for the visitors.

Penny knew America Group, fully briefed on the bad news, were less cheerful. Being ordered to put on a good show but take a dive sat badly with their fundamental programming. Jedburgh had told them they were the Best There Was, which meant they ought to be the Best Losers in the World. That hadn't made it any better. Only Iceman showed no outrage.

At sunset, America Group and Carpathia Group filed out of their respective barracks. They had started even, with twelve pledges in each group. Carpathia – experienced vampires all – suffered no wash-outs or casualties, and remained at full strength, while America was five down. Czuczron turned out, face still a ruin but otherwise in fighting form. He was in better shape than Nikita, who was still shaky but insisted on being on the team. To make the imbalance less obvious, Gardner was taking to the field with America.

The objective was Ghost Town. The teams were competing to take and hold the position. Gardner had outlined a gameplan, by which America took the town first then yielded it when Carpathia caught up. That would give America an achievement as a consolation for eating desert dirt.

Penny was with the observers. Bush, Jedburgh and Orlok took a Jeep out into the desert, to take up position in the old saloon on Main Street. Ryan, Fawn Hall and Beecher would remain at the base in the op centre, monitoring communications. She'd be in a helicopter, with North and Meinster. Other interested parties were scattered across the countryside.

War was to start at midnight.

Oliver North complained that he couldn't see anything out of the open door. Andrews, the gaunt pilot, looked back without sympathy, red points shining in his vampire eyes. Penelope and Meinster had night-sight too. This exercise would be carried out in human darkness.

'I'll give a running commentary, Colonel,' she offered.

The little soldier nodded a simulation of gratitude. He was strapped down and buttoned up tight. The pulses in his neck and temples ticked like a Swiss watch.

Meinster hadn't deigned to speak to her yet.

The Baron was one of those slightly too pretty, slightly too dressy fellows she'd once been impressed by. Having inherited one of the great fortunes of Europe, he'd squandered it on shirts and chocolate while he was alive. She remembered him crawling around Palazzo Otranto, trying to wheedle favours. Dracula – no fan of nancy boys – had never taken him seriously. His ex-boyfriend Herbert von Krolock, openly an exquisite invert, got more respect. Always nakedly ambitious, Meinster was cast out of the inner circle when Princess Asa came on the scene. She rid the court of old guard hangers-on to make room for her own largely useless entourage.

Shapes flew below. Banshee and Iceman, wing to wing, coping with bladewash. Showing off. It would have been wiser to stay out of the helicopter's draught.

'America is in the air, Colonel,' she said.

Meinster snarled, showing a dainty fang.

They were over Ghost Town. Down below bonfires burned around the site, almost in a pentagram. She saw old streets, some buildings almost buried under drifting sands. Jedburgh's Jeep was parked by the hitching rail outside the saloon.

Banshee and Iceman touched down and folded their wings.

The two fliers had carried compact loads. Nikita and Desire. The America Group vampires took up positions around the saloon and checked for traps. Banshee, grin visible from space, kicked in the batwing doors and ducked out of the way of any fire. Nothing.

Jedburgh came out, hat clamped to his head, and shook hands with Banshee. Orlok crept in the deepest shadows, well away from the firelight.

In formation, the rest of America Group – Gardner, the Confessor, Velcro – jogged down Main Street. Gardner took point.

'America has taken the saloon,' she said.

North smiled, tightly. Meinster glared.

Shadows came alive. She had good night eyes, but hadn't noticed Carpathia Group's arrival. They moved like ghosts, silently overwhelming their targets, pressing claws to throats. Gardner dodged his shadow and Banshee hid behind Jedburgh. But the rest of America Group went down. Easily.

Meinster smiled and primped.

'Inform Colonel North what has happened,' he ordered.

'America has fallen,' she said, flatly. North blinked.

She didn't even know if America Group had taken their dive. They might just have been taught a lesson about the capabilities of vampire elders.

There was a ruckus.

Nikita was on her feet, the front of her jump-suit torn open, throat bloody. She kicked a Carpathian with smart martial arts moves, jabbing her foot at his stomach and face. Her boot wiped off his blacking. Penny recognised Alex Ziska.

'America won't lie down,' she said.

'This is futile,' declared Meinster. 'The exercise is over. This goes beyond what was agreed.'

'The exercise isn't over until it's over,' said North. 'By now, you Europeans ought to have learned that.'

Ziska dodged Nikita and stepped behind her, mouth open like a shark's. He took a bite out of the America girl and spat it out.

Now, Nikita was down, bone flashing in her neck wound.

Banshee was on Ziska, stabbing his torso with gathered, sharpened dagger-fingers.

Jedburgh waved his hat.

Carpathians rallied to Ziska, which freed up other Americans to get back in the game. Velcro picked up a length of rotten wood to use as a club (a stake?). Orlok – who wasn't even *in* Carpathia Group – took him down from behind with a deadly hug.

Banshee, wings stretched, rose into the sky, trailing Ziska by one leg. Carpathians, shifting in a heartbeat, took to the air after him. The American flier dropped the flailing Ziska, who fell onto the boardwalk and cracked rotten wood.

'That viper'll have an assful of splinters,' said the pilot, chortling.

North signalled Andrews to keep height with the bat-fight.

On the ground, the Carpathian elders were masters, but in the air, Banshee flew loops around them. Bony barbs protruded like horns from his heels, spiking through his boots. He tore holes in the wings of the elders harrying him. He whooped and howled, an aural attack on anyone with oversensitive hearing.

First one, then another, fell out of the sky, wind tearing through ripped wings.

Banshee was one-on-one with a Carpathian, Czuczron.

They wrestled, eyes and arms locked, huge wings beating the air. Then Banshee shapeshifted, losing the wings and becoming a deadweight, wrenching Czuczron out of the sky, dislocating the elder's wing-shoulders. The combatants came apart and Czuczron smashed into the dirt. Banshee – winged again – barely skimmed the ground before dancing upwards with a victory yell. Showoff.

Meinster was not happy.

On the ground, the exercise dissolved into an old-fashioned bar-room brawl. Jedburgh punched out Orlok, who kept bouncing back as if on a board.

This was a fiasco.

'Why can't we all get along?' she asked Meinster.

PART FOUR

'YOU'LL NEVER DRINK BLOOD IN THIS TOWN AGAIN'

ANNO DRACULA 1990

1

From the top deck of his castle, John Alucard looked over Beverly Hills as the arclight in the sky wrought dawn on the downhill properties. Uncovered swimming pools glinted like sapphires on green baize. He wore Foster-Grant 'Nightshades' ($999.95) and a face-film of sun block, but had developed a tolerance to all but the blaze of California noon. In the Old Country even pre-dawn haze would send him shrieking for shadow, greasy smoke boiling from his pores. Now, in this far edge of the world, he was almost a daywalker.

He leaned against battlements transplanted from a Transylvanian castle, took a hit of Los Angeles's smog-and-orange-blossom air, and listened to freeway traffic, already enlivened by the odd angry gunshot. His mouth watered and his fangs sharpened. This place was delicious. The Father approved.

The Father was with him, constantly. Through Alucard, Dracula's will was done on Earth.

His visitors, three Romanian vampires, were less comfortable with the rising sun. Transylvania Movement hacks were in love with useless tradition. They liked to waste their days locked inside easy-seal travel coffins, wriggling on itchy carpets of native soil.

'Coffin-sleep is for wimps,' he declared. 'Know how many deals you miss, scurrying for the crypt at cock-crow?'

None of the visitors answered him. Their eyes were on the shadows shrinking around their feet.

'Have you heard the story about the vampire who went mad?' Alucard asked. 'His native land, from which he was in permanent exile, was a tiny European province endlessly passed back and forth between the great powers. Each colour change on the map invalidated the soil in his lair and he had to scramble for a fresh supply of dirt.'

Alucard laughed. Only one of the three even tried to join in: the pasty new-born, Feraru.

This last year would have been a nightmare for that apocryphal elder. Maps got redrawn every week, if not every day.

'The post-Communist flag industry can't keep up with the demand,' said Alucard. 'Many countries fly old banners with holes where the hammer and sickle used to be. Makes a bad impression. Looks like a cannonball was shot through the flag. When you tear out the symbol you keep the remnant handy in case you have to sew it back in.'

In the long view, Romania was as it had always been. After the revolutions of 1989, it was no longer under the Ceauşescus and within Soviet hegemony, but someone or something would come along to master the land. Before the Reds, it had been Nazis, domestic and foreign; and before that, before Alucard was born or turned, the Austro-Hungarian and Ottoman Empires. For a proudly independent nation, a Latin-Romance enclave in a Slav sea, the Old Country was the whore of Europe, sold over and over again to the highest bidder, taken by force and rapine by the most convenient strongman. Transylvania, sacred soil of the *nosferatu*, was the whore's get, traded back and forth between Romania and Hungary at the behest of whichever foreigners were on the up in Bucharest or Budapest.

Alucard looked at the trio Baron Meinster had despatched on this mission. Crainic, gaunt from slow-incubating blood disease, currently Meinster's Number Two in the movement. Feraru, who spoke with an upper-class English accent, a new-born of ancient bloodline. Striescu, ruddy from a recent (unauthorised) feeding; his well-cut black suit marked him as ex-*Securitate*.

Visser, the warm private detective he kept on a retainer, had assembled dossiers on them. Alucard knew the names of the four people Striescu had killed in the United States, three on earlier state visits and one two nights ago. From the creature's colour, the tally might be up to five.

Striescu was the muscle and Feraru the money; senior academician Crainic was a thinker. Under Ceauşescu, he'd toiled as a haematologist. Competent, but no Sarah Roberts or Michael Morbius. Last Christmas, as revolution – sparked by a general strike in Timişoara – spread throughout Romania, he was pushed into taking a stand. Token vampire on a committee of dissidents, churchmen and out-of-favour army officers. Less strident than Meinster about *nosferatu* supremacy, Crainic also argued that Transylvania should be a state separate from Romania – with a sliver of Hungary claimed to fatten the shape on the map – and that the new country be given over to the undead.

If this happened and Meinster assumed the position to which he felt entitled, the Baron would become the first vampire sovereign since Dracula. The trick would only work if he kept men like Crainic about him. The velvet dandy's idea of rule was sitting on a throne in superb clothes issuing proclamations to scurrying minions. The senior academician had the nit-picking concentration necessary to stay on top of the night-to-night running of even a small government. But Crainic's hard work and cleverness would not be enough. He'd survived so far by keeping his head down. He didn't have the political savvy that had kept Lord Ruthven in or near the office of British Prime Minister for over a hundred years.

Feraru was from money and in it for the money. Raised in Britain, he'd returned to his ancestral castle when the red dominoes tumbled. The Feraru bloodline was founded by a now-enfeebled elder – a revered, mindless patriarch whose blood was siphoned to turn each rising generation of remote descendants. Feraru was one of many pre-Soviet landowners, warm and *nosferatu*, flooding to the Carpathians to reclaim estates formerly appropriated by now-collapsed governments. Hailing themselves the saviours of oppressed peoples, but nakedly intent on bleeding the peasants dry again. Crainic wore a shabby greatcoat and peaked cap like a middle-aged student, but Feraru was City of London yuppie style on the hoof: Savile Row suit-jacket open to show red trader's braces, cowhide Filofax chained to the hip, red-framed round spectacles, skinny tie with a $$$ pin. He also affected the red-lined black opera cape tradition associated with Count Dracula. Alucard didn't believe the Father had worn such a thing except when visiting the opera, but the cloak was an essential accessory for a certain breed of showily militant vampire.

Crainic would try to persuade, Feraru would try to bribe. Striescu was another matter.

Even when he turned away, Alucard knew exactly where Striescu was standing. A wall of burning light lay between the ex-*Securitate* man and his own back. Not an accident. Striescu was a kick-in-the-door-at-four-in-the-morning murder merchant. A habitual turncoat, he'd killed for the fascist Iron Guard in the 1930s and the communist Gheorgiu-Dej in the '40s and '50s, then settled in under Nicolae and Elena for thirty years of brutal grind. Striescu's speciality was taking care of 'counter-revolutionary elements', assassinating dissidents at home and abroad. Late last year, he'd scented blood in the changing winds. Now he murdered on the QT for the strange coalition between President Ion Iliescu's National Salvation Front and Baron Meinster's United *Nosferatu* Party.

Last Boxing Day, the Ceauşescus were hustled into the snowy courtyard of a Târgovişte barracks to be executed. They were puzzled and furious at their conviction by a drumhead court on charges of 'acts of genocide, subordination of state power in actions against the state and the sabotage of the national economy'. Striescu was among the armed spectators who fired from the crowd, competing with a Parachute Regiment firing squad to put bullets into his former bosses.

Alucard dimly recalled a time when Meinster and Nicolae were best buds. His mind skittered away from that past. To him, it was a prehistory, a dream. If he thought of Dinu Pass, he remembered Dracula, not the partisans. In the Keep, an elder vampire turned a warm boy. The Father found a prospective son. Which of these had he been? Now, at heart, he was both.

These three were the supplicants. And he was the elder.

Feraru shaded his face, finding at last a use for his cloak, raising it like a parasol. He was tanning unevenly, freckle-blotches on his bone-white forehead and under his screwed-shut eyes. The others knew better than to look at the light.

Crainic held out a cream envelope, bearing the Meinster seal. Alucard reached into the shadow and took the letter. He opened it one-handed and eased out a stiff sheet of paper. The letterhead was elaborate, in gold and red; the message was conventional. If Meinster connected John Alucard with a boy he'd once sacrificed to the Father, he didn't mention it.

'The Baron recognises you as influential in the international *nosferatu* community,' said Crainic.

'They do say that,' said Alucard. 'And more.'

'Ah y-yes,' got out Feraru, '"King of the Cats".'

Alucard didn't argue with the title. Crainic gave Feraru a sharp side-glance. The Romanian scientist thought the English businessman a twit. Already: divisions in Meinster's ranks.

'Your support would mean much,' continued Crainic.

'What kind of support? Surely, you're not here with a begging bowl?'

Seductive 'elders' with red buckets were a plague at the Viper Room and other vampire hot spots, extorting dollars for 'the Cause'. Most were new-borns with bogus titles who'd never been nearer Transylvania than Toledo, Ohio.

'Support doesn't have to mean money,' said Crainic.

'Though dosh would be ever so nice,' put in Feraru.

Striescu said nothing. Alucard knew, without even snooping, Meinster had given the *Securitate* man provisional orders to kill him. He was unsure of the circumstances which would trigger an assassination attempt. The Baron was ambitious, stupid and ruthless enough to give it a try on the slightest provocation. If Striescu made a move now, Alucard would toss him off the deck and watch him turn into a comet on the long fall to the lawns below.

'Why do you want Transylvania?' he asked. 'Haven't we outgrown the territory?'

'It is our home,' said Crainic. 'It is not just soil. Even you, an American, must feel that.'

Crainic didn't know John Alucard might once have been Ion Popescu. Or was willing to pretend ignorance. Alucard had changed a lot since the Old Country. Meinster would most likely not recognise him, he'd never taken much notice of other, lesser people.

'This is my home,' Alucard said, indicating the city, but meaning America. 'It's a good place for us. Far better than rainy, rocky Transylvania.'

The sun was up. Warm workmen emerged to take care of lawns and pools. A small army of Mexican Morlocks came out of underground cottages to see to the many, many jobs necessary to keep Alucard's *castillo* running. He had imagined and built his estate to exceed the eye-catching magnificence of the palace down the block where Aaron Spelling lived.

'I have the best of the old world and the new,' he said.

'If Transylvania is ours without question, all vampires will be safer,' said Crainic. 'There will always be somewhere for us. Asylum when the warm pass laws we cannot observe, sanctuary when we flee from the justice of cattle.'

'Meinster can guarantee this?'

Crainic nodded.

'Okay,' said Alucard. 'I'll do what I can for the Baron.'

Feraru smiled unguardedly and grabbed Alucard's hand, forgetting the sun for a moment. Crainic looked for a loophole but could see none. Striescu almost imperceptibly stood down.

'I've an idea I think the Baron will go for,' said Alucard, letting Feraru have his hand back. 'A showcase, something to make the world take notice, to raise an enormous amount of money, an occasion for us all.'

Feraru was already interested and enthused.

'Picture this,' said Alucard, raising his hands to frame a Cinerama screen, 'a concert for Transylvania.'

Feraru, who had never lived behind the Iron Curtain, got it at once. Crainic was puzzled.

'I'm not the only vampire in show business. There's a common misconception that to be turned is to lose the creative spark. Some of us have devoted our lives to disproving that.

Right now, the top-selling album and single in the *Billboard* charts is '*Vanitas*', by the vampire Timmy V. His picture is on the bedroom wall of every warm teenager in the world. He's in the frame to play Peter Pan for Steven Spielberg. Timmy's appeal is mainstream, not ghetto. And I can get him. He isn't the only one. All the vampires of rock, *nosferatu* and warm, would claw each other to get on the bill. Those who don't make the cut will be in career limbo for eternity. For this, the Short Lion would come out of his latest retirement. That fop is still the biggest name vampire ever to fill a stadium. I see a dusk-till-dawn concert on the site of the original Castle Dracula, with live link-ups to events all around the world. The Hollywood Bowl. Stonehenge. Opar in Kenya. The world's first Draculathon. TV, pay-cable and theatrical rights. Vinyl, cassette, CD, video and as-yet uninvented new media sales to infinity. Constant repackaging, always holding something back for the next release so the rubes will buy it over and over again. T-shirts, buttons, posters, pogs, tattoo transfers, souvenir programmes, coffee-table books, action figures, comic books. We even get a cut of the backlash, licensing our mutilated logo to jaded cynics turned off by the hype but who will happily wear "I Don't Give a Flying Fox for Transylvania" T-shirts. All profits, after expenses, go to the Transylvania Movement. Think of a number, take it to the power of 999.95, and you'd still be underestimating the money. If Americans are led properly, given a story they can follow with a happy ending in sight, they become insanely generous. This will make them all, warm and *nosferatu*, our sympathisers. I can deliver this.'

'And what do we have to do?'

'Senior academician Crainic, you have to strike with perfect timing – at the climax of the last act, just before dawn,' said Alucard. 'Timmy V and the Short Lion, who have never before shared a stage, duet on the Free Transylvania anthem – John Lennon's "Imagine", the greatest song ever written by a vampire. Then, you must announce that you have taken power. Your Baron must appear among the stars. I know you have trained men and I know the West has covert units to commit to the crusade. I produced *Bat-21*, remember. What you have never had, not until now, is an *occasion*.'

'When would this be?' asked Crainic.

'Let me see, when would be appropriate? We've missed the Eve of Saint George's, April twenty-second. That would only play in Romania, anyway. The point is to bring Transylvania to the mall, not stuff old world guff down American throats like some devil-kissed PBS special. Hallowe'en is over-commercialised these days. We'd have to compete with jack o' lanterns, razor-filled apples, John Carpenter sequels and an extended episode of *Roseanne*. What would you say to December twenty-first? The longest night of the year.'

'The first anniversary of the Timişoara rising.'

Alucard had let Crainic make the connection, buzzed by street-fighting flashbacks. The senior academician had joined warm and *nosferatu* alike in the soccer chant of 'Ole ole ole ole, Ceauşescu nu mai e!' ('Ceauşescu is no more'). He'd covered a startled priest with his own body when the *Securitate* opened fire. The best thing about a December date was that a longer night meant more acts, more commercial breaks, more sponsorship, more material for the boxed set.

'Excuse me, please,' rasped Striescu, 'what are "pogs"?'

'Collectible cardboard discs,' Alucard explained.

'I see,' said the thug, no wiser.

'We have six months to put the show together. That'll be my department. I'll give you the rock. You must guarantee me the soil.'

Crainic, cautious, looked to Feraru, who was ecstatic.

'It'll be bigger than Live Aid,' said the new-born, 'than Woodstock. We could even get Cliff Richard.'

Alucard had no idea who that was, but let it pass.

'I'll speak with Baron Meinster,' ventured Crainic.

'Give him my best regards,' said Alucard.

All three visitors were now fully backed up against the wall of the turret that rose above the deck, shaded only by the crenellated frill of a Spanish-tile overhang. Feraru kept forgetting himself and sticking his hands out into the sun, raising welts and giving out little squeals.

'Now we should get you indoors. I can have company sent

over if you have the red thirst or any other entertainment needs. This town has very discreet services I think you might enjoy.'

The three couldn't step through the door swiftly enough, the prospect of cool shade more exciting than that of warm blood. Alucard lingered a moment to look up at the sun, safely tucked behind a single thin cloud as if the Father were on high, shading his favoured get.

Pleased with himself, he followed his guests inside.

2

Holly and Kit were about set to take Judd down when the floor fell away like a gallows-trap. They dropped into a wet basement. All around, rattles and hisses. Yellow eyes shone in dark. Sharp mouths darted and nipped.

'Best place for vipers,' cackled the old man. 'A genuine snake-pit!'

Holly and Kit hissed back, through fangs.

Holly felt Kit's embarrassment and rage. Kit felt Holly's acceptance and determination. Inside seconds, Kit was fang-jabbed half-a-dozen times. Holly shifted, thickening her skin, changing her skeleton, raising scales on her arms and legs. She could be a reptile if she took it in mind, and snakes didn't often bite each other. Kit caught some of her calm, but venom burned in his arms, which swelled like Popeye's after spinach.

'Thought you'd happened on free lunch in Tombstone, didn't ya?' Judd called down at them. 'Took me for a foolhead old man with a rinky-dink museum, just begging to be rent and drained like unto a lost sheep.'

Judd, wooden leg stiff and creaking, peered into the pit. He tapped his grizzled temple.

'I ain't so simple, deadfolks. You figured I was a couple of cowboys short of a posse, but I'm up here and you're down there. Says it all, don't it? Sketches the parameters of our relationship. Left my leg on Guadalcanal, back in the Big War.

Since I been messing with the slitherers, I been bit a hundred times. Too ornery to die, that's me. I spit the venom back.'

Holly tried to keep Kit from thrashing and over-exciting the snakes.

The pit was full of rattlers, diamondbacks, copperheads, whatever. Neither knew one serpent from another, though they could tell which beasts were deadly. Everything down here was venomous.

Doctor Porthos, their father-in-darkness and first teacher, had listed things that could hurt them: direct sunlight, silver bullet, stake through the heart. Five nights after he turned them, they'd proved him right. Kit and Holly didn't care to be anyone's 'disciples', not after all the church they'd swallowed back in South Dakota.

Porthos hadn't said anything about snakebite. It might not kill Kit, but it was surely hurting him. Holly put her hand on his fever-hot brow, trying to pull the hurt out of him.

'For live folks, the pit'd be enough. But you're special guests. I got to fetch a prime exhibit. I have Doc Holliday's boots, the ones he wasn't wearing when he died. Bat Masterton's cane and derby hat. Liberty Valance's quirt. You'd sure have appreciated seeing those, I bet. And the shotgun Bob Ollinger used to try to kill the viper Billy the Kid. Ollinger ground up sixteen silver dollars for shot. Billy got the gun away from him and blasted him in the face. "Keep the change, Bob!" That's a true story, deadfolks. An authentic piece of Western history. This ain't none of those, though. It's a special exhibit. A one-of-a-kind item. Hang for a moment. It'll take me a while to hobble there and back. Amuse yourselves. Like I tell the schoolkids, this should be an educational experience. Come up with a good question and I'll give you a piece of sugar candy.'

Kit's mouth was too swollen to get anything out and his brain was on fire. Holly heard a stream of curse words deep in her mind, where Kit always spoke to her. She was in his head too, taking her share of the pain.

The Tombstone Dime Museum was on the outskirts of town. A light was burning when Kit and Holly chanced along after forty-eight hours on the road in a stolen Cadillac. They hadn't had a feed in three states. Judd was right. They'd taken him for easy prey.

The pit was about twenty feet deep, the walls rough for the bottom ten but smooth above that. No handholds. People had died here. Holly knew from the bad air. Sometimes, when she and Kit were inside each other, things played back like a motion picture on a drive-in screen. A series of death scenes, mostly.

They were vampires, but old Judd was a killer too.

They were made this way. What was his excuse?

She found the worst bites on Kit's arms and suckled them, adapting her fang-teeth to the thin snake-needle holes. She drew out Kit's venom-laced vampire blood. The heady mix hit her between the eyes the way gobbled ice cream had done when she was alive. She spat the poison out like a chaw of tobacco. Kit's face looked less like a big purple bruise.

'Bloody Holly, you sure are beautiful,' said Kit, with difficulty.

'Lambchop, you say the sweetest things,' she said, hearing a hiss in her 's' sounds.

She'd snakeshifted, hair flattened against her neck in a cobra hood, diamondback patterns up and down her bare arms, face a flat-nosed mask, tongue forked. Her eyes, almost on the sides of her head, gave her a wraparound view. Serpents raised in lithe s-shapes, hissing tribute, begging her to be their queen, to lead them out of this dark place.

Kit stroked her scales, adoring her. Whatever she shifted to, he was in love with. He always saw inside. It had been like that before they were reborn into this night-life.

'Missy, you're a nasty one,' said Judd. 'Doin' you a favour, puttin' you out of your butt-ugly bitch misery. And your no-account boyfriend's too.'

The dime museum's curator was sat on a stool by the trap. In his lap was what looked like an outsize toy gun, a Wild West revolver.

'A Buntline Special,' said Judd, hefting the gun, stretching his fingers around the handle, skinny thumb on the cock-lever.

'A real collector's piece. Not many made. This is an eleven-inch barrel. Ned Buntline, the Western writer, had them made special. Only a few proud men earned the right to carry iron like this. Men like Buffalo Bill Cody.'

He twirled the gun in his hand, expertly.

'This wasn't Cody's, though. This exact gun belonged to Wyatt Earp, Marshal of Tombstone.'

'You're ravin', old timer,' said Kit, still in pain, but able to speak again. 'Wyatt Earp weren't real. He was a made-up person.'

'Hugh O'Brian,' said Holly.

'That's right, Bloody Holly. Hugh O'Brian played Wyatt Earp on TV. He was no more a real person than Clarabelle the Cow. The big gun is probably a prop from the show. TV ain't real.'

An explosion, loud as the crack of doom, vaporised a grapefruit-sized chunk out of the wall of the pit. Snakes hissed and rattled and tied themselves in knots. Holly's hearing membranes ached and reverberated.

'Ain't no prop,' said Judd. 'You don't know nothin' about Marshal Earp. Afore there was television, Earp was as real as you or me. An actual historical personage. Cleaned up Dodge and Tombstone. Faced down the Clantons at the O.K. Corral. Left many a badman dead in the dust.'

Holly's hand was webbed, like a lizard's.

Judd opened and emptied the gun.

'Deadfolks have to be treated special. No point wasting lead on you.'

Something gleamed in Judd's hand.

Holly felt that inrush of panic breath, the most intimate thing Kit shared with her. She was the only person who ever knew when he was scared.

She was with him. It didn't matter.

Judd held the shiny bullet between thumb and forefinger.

'This is an antique item, too. Can either of you kids tell me the principal business of Tombstone, Arizona? During the times Earp was lawman here?'

'Cattle,' Kit took a guess. 'Rustlin', ranchin', ropin'. All that cowboy crap.'

Judd laughed. The sound filled the pit.

'That's a no, smartmouth. It was *silver mining*.'

The old man slipped the silver bullet into the gun.

'Notice all the holes in the ground? Like the one you're in. Why do you think folks dug 'em? For their health? They were after *plata*, *compadres*. Bright, shiny metal. Used to be gold was more valuable than silver. Remember that? Then you deadfolks came along, shucking off lead slugs like peas, and silver became the most sought-after stuff on Earth. Not just pretty – practical.'

Judd took other bullets and slipped them into the chambers.

'These rounds were crafted by a man named John Reid. He put on a mask to ride the range, out after your kind. Billy Bonney wasn't the only viper to slither across the Early West. John Reid was the greatest Vampire Slayer of the nineteenth century. I was given these bullets by his nephew, a big newspaperman. Been saving them for a party like this.'

It was time to end this.

Holly had Kit hug her around the neck from behind and pin her sides with his knees, as if she were still twelve giving her younger cousins horsey-back rides. She slapped lizard-hands against the wall, about seven feet off the pit-floor, spreading the finger-webs out to get suction. Her arms, legs and back were extended and flexible.

She zig-zagged up the wall.

Her face was to the rock, but Kit kept his eyes on Judd. Through him, she saw the old man's face gape with shock and surprise. He fumbled one of the bullets, which fell from his fingers and pinged into the pit. His hands were shaking.

Judd saw Kit looking vengeance at him. He tried to close the gun, but they emerged from the snake pit and fell upon him. His pistol skittered away on the floor. Holly and Kit took either side of his scrawny neck. They bit through to the windpipe, kissing in the fountain of blood.

'Bloody Holly,' said Kit.

'Lambchop,' said Holly.

3

The doorbell chimed just after midnight, sounding the first six notes of 'Money (That's What I Want)'. From the first-floor landing Alucard used the universal remote to admit the girl Heidi had sent over. The main doors were California mission relics, hung between Transylvania granite – it had taken some effort to get the hinge-creak, which needed oil and grit every week. He punched in a lighting plan for the reception hall. Artificial moonglobes shone through a blue-and-green stained glass *faux* ceiling, casting bat signals on red-and-white, honeycomb-locked, skull-motif floor tiles.

The girl, pinned in the harsh crossbeams of three movement-sensitive spotlights, had a waist-length fall of raven hair, pale skin surgically taut over model-sharp cheekbones, clunky platinum man-in-the-moon earrings, and a carmine mouth held open in permanent Pepsodent rictus by ivory fangs. A high-collared, floor-length black cape covered her body: she could have been one of those Malay *penanggalan* creatures – a lovely-faced head floating above a sac of bloody innards.

He descended his main staircase, footfalls muffled by thick carpet, eyes on the vampire girl. These nights, Heidi delivered more suitable product than her predecessor, Madame Alex. He'd made the call ten minutes ago and someone fitting his individual requirements was express-delivered to Castle Dracula 90210. He would send Heidi a present, a collectible plate signed by the surviving cast of *Gilligan's Island*.

'I am Alucard,' he said. 'I bid you welcome.'

Acoustics in the hall were perfect for the timbre of his voice. The girl reacted as if his greeting had come at her from all directions at once.

'Come freely and of your own will and leave something of the happiness you bring.'

Red-nailed white hands slid out of the front of her cape and travelled up to her throat. The cloak slithered off slim, bare arms, parting like stage curtains. With a practised twitch, she tossed cape-wings back over broad shoulders and displayed her goods, hands on hips.

She was a big-busted hardbody, a product of aerobics, implants and directed shapeshifting. Her scarlet swimsuit was cut in a V that went below the navel, straps barely covering her nipples. Black leather spike-heeled knee-boots added six inches to her height.

Her knowing smile suggested she expected to make an impression.

'You can call me Vampi,' said the girl.

Oh dear.

The girl – Vampi, doubtless with a little bat over the i – didn't yet realise how special a client John Alucard was, how big a noise he could make in this town and how much he could do for (and to) her. That had been the Father's strength. No one believed the stories about him until it was too late.

The girl strode towards the stairs, puzzled by the follow-spots. She frowned and giggled, eyes blurring red. Her silicone shivered.

To Alucard, Vampi was more dead flesh, a drac package with a date stamp. Admittedly, the wrapping was superior. Hollywood was full of tens. Beauty-contest runners-up and high school athletes had been flooding the town since the 1920s. Most didn't become movie stars but they got together and bred good-looking kids. Los Angeles was brimful with the third or fourth crop of beauties, an infestation of hunks and honeys, ace faces and knockout figures. Excluding character actors and screenwriters, you could go months without running into anyone ugly.

'Leave your cloak and come upstairs,' he said.

She tapped a cameo at her throat and the cape fell away. She turned to catch it, giving him a view of her taut butt: thong-divided buns of steel, untanned skin of velvet. Necrophagous Arabian Nights ghouls and South American plane-crash rugby players always started cannibal cook-outs by eating ass, the choicest meat cut on the human body.

Vampi came up the stairs towards him, swaying with practised ease on her heels.

He stretched out his right hand for her. She was taken with the large ruby on his long forefinger. She bowed her head to consider the ring.

'It was His,' he explained. 'An inheritance from my Father-in-Darkness.'

He pressed a key on the remote. A neon frame illuminated a full-figure portrait, executed by Joseph Sibley to a Royal Commission in 1887. Prince Consort Dracula in uniform as Commander of the Carpathian Guards. His shining steel helm surmounted by a snarling white wolfshead, trailing the entire pelt. His Empire-red tunic heavy with military decorations and orders. The Father's great hand, black-haired, rested on the hilt of a ceremonial sword. The ring was clearly identifiable, a speck of blood bright as a spectral stain.

Vampi was impressed. The ring and painting were very expensive.

'Beyond imagining,' he confirmed, 'but not priceless. Nothing is ever priceless.'

At the touch of a button, the portrait slid soundlessly aside. Lights grew in his den.

'We can be more comfortable in here,' Alucard said.

The girl went into the room and he followed. He offered her blood-threaded Cristal. She accepted, though she just used her flute as a prop. Alucard took a place astride the recliner in the middle of the room, feet on the floor, swivelling to keep track of the girl. Vampi was a walker and a talker. She prowled his lair, examining framed movie posters – his credit growing bigger the more recent the release.

For obvious reasons, he couldn't display that Hollywood den commonplace: photographs of the owner with celebrities from the worlds of politics, business, sports, crime and showbiz. So he kept C.C. Drood on a permanent retainer. When appearing as character witness for Charlie Sheen, Alucard discovered the lightning caricaturist working as a court artist. Now Drood was always on hand when he was out in public or receiving guests at the castle. Sketches captured the moment of Alucard's meetings with the Reagans (he'd been a major campaign contributor in '84), Gordon Gecko,

O.J. Simpson, Arnold Schwarzenegger and Whitney Houston. Vampi found the drawing of Alucard with L. Keith Winton at a launch party for the *Kindred* dodecology.

'I turned my life around through Immortology,' Vampi said. 'Came over to the nightside.'

So she was one of Winton's odd little things. He was polite enough not to laugh.

'When I first turned, I was a mess,' she said. 'In the early days of drac every dhamp in the Valley was out to batten onto a new-born. My seminar guide told us about those sucker-fish, remora. That's what they were like, the dhamps. I had no respect for my pale self. I carried too much baggage from the day-world, screwing up my night-life. A friend, an actress, was killed by a Slayer. Nico was like this luminous flame, flickering. Then, one night, she was snuffed. Stake through the heart. Some mad cheerleader. I got straight, ditched the dhampires and came to the Church. I know myself now. I know what I am.'

She posed against a poster for *Bat-21*, the film he'd made about the US Bat-Soldier School with C. Thomas Howell, Gene Hackman and Kelly McGillis. The top-grossing release of 1988, domestic and foreign. A platinum disc soundtrack and two Number One singles. Shut out of all but the Technical and Original Song Oscars, but the hell with the Academy.

'You should take their tests,' she said. 'The Church has a lot of movie people. Producers and stars. They say the Short Lion's a member. And his mother. There are coded references to Immortologist doctrine in his songs. The *Blood is Not Enough* album is named after the title of the second chapter of L. Keith Winton's *Plasmatics*.'

The Short Lion still hadn't committed to the Concert for Transylvania. The French vampire dandy didn't care about Dracula's old country. But he was out of retirement, following Dylan into a Born-Again period. Right now, he would only sing religious songs. Some of his fans had doused themselves in kerosene and lit matches to protest their idol's abandonment of Satan. In the end, the Short Lion would come round.

'I've learned so much, John,' said Vampi. 'About myself.'

Proselytising was part of the Immortology package. Amusing, really. Alucard had worked with Winton on many of his ideas. The name of the game was Control and Command. The Father understood it was no longer enough to be feared, loved and worshipped. These nights the flock needed to follow a path of self-interest to surrender their individual will, to submerge themselves in something greater.

Whenever Alucard needed wetwork ('spring cleaning'), he called Winton. His people had no police records and would immolate themselves ('go candle') for the Church if caught. He was satisfied with the number they'd done on the financier and petty draclord Roy Radin. Winton's crew ('night deliverers') had taken Radin out to a ravine, made him cough up the required security deposit box numbers, and finished him off execution-style: a single silver bullet to the pineal gland.

'I was taken through past-life regression therapy,' said Vampi, 'to emerge from my warm chrysalis persona and discover my inner nyctlapt imago. L. Keith Winton teaches that we vampires are all old souls, born on a planet where blood flows in rivers and streams, like water on Earth. There, vampirism is not tainted by personal tangles and killing. On the planet, I was the daughter of a king.'

He remembered a saying Gorse had overused: all Americans want to discover that they are really princesses. The Revelation of St Sammy Davis Jr of the Rat Pack was 'and the voice said: "Daddy, there's a million pigeons, waiting to be hooked on new religions."'

Winton, himself only recently turned ('ascended') after twenty years of self-administered training ('night prep'), had helped Alucard understand this country. He'd worked hard to become a citizen of the imaginary America everyone born or accepted here learned to believe in with the fervour of the Faithful who know their place in Heaven is earned and reserved and inalienable. Immortology was spreading outside the States. Winton was on a permanent cruise, living on the *Hope*, a refitted ocean liner which stuck to international waters, outside 'terranean jurisdiction'. Immortology Centres were established around the world, even in former Warsaw Pact countries and the jumble of states and statelets which used to be the Soviet Union. For the first time in a century, vampirism was on the rise in its traditional heartland, Central and Eastern Europe. Winton's Church was there to shape the post-communist wave of new-borns into twenty-first century vampires ('fully integrated nyctlapts').

'When we were reborn on Earth, at the moment of turning, we were open to a raft of bad feelings, impediments to spiritual progress. The I-sems helped me peel them away, like onionskins. Ideally, night prep should start before ascension, but I came half-finished to the Church. I had to catch up on my training.'

She slipped a strap off her shoulder and popped out a cherry-top tit.

'It's a process of true liberation.'

She took her swimsuit off over her boots. Her pubic hair was shaved into a black batwing.

'You can't believe how free I feel.'

He called to her with his mind. She was yanked across the room, boots rucking up the rug, and fell to her hands and knees. He kept tugging. She crawled, ass in the air, face to the floor.

Since coming to Hollywood, he hadn't drunk warm blood. Drac was his invention and he was its master, one of the few who could survive and thrive on a pure diet. Others wound up sucking their own veins dry and burning out their brains. They became zombies or phantoms, scuttling along in the margins, grey faces lit by passing headlamps, ground under cars on the freeways.

Heidi was under orders not to forewarn the girls. Surprise was an essential in the flavour. Whenever the madame bitched about damaged goods, he slipped her novelty crockery and she shut up. Heidi had the largest hoard of sit-com-themed collectible plates in the Greater Los Angeles area. She'd once delivered twelve girls to Max Zorin to get her hands on a rare variant Elizabeth Montgomery/Rosamond Denham with the wrong colour eyes.

Alucard had seen *Bloodwitched* on re-runs. Most vampires found the premise — the suburban housewife who has to pass for warm to support her dim-bulb husband — offensive, though he liked the way Rosamund killed her first husband between seasons and replaced him with another identikit ad-man without anyone in town noticing.

Vampi reached the recliner and wound her fingers around his ankles, then climbed his legs. She laid her face in his lap and, wet-mouthed, began to lick around.

He picked her up and embraced her, looking into her eyes. He got through the fog Winton had whipped up in her mind.

'Princess,' he said, feeding her self-image.

She had thought she was unreachable. She had thought he was just another John.

The Father worked through him, reaching deep into the girl's mind.

Most men in her life wanted her to bite them.

That wasn't going to happen here.

He stuck his tongue into her neck, slitting the silk-soft skin under her jaw and sucked a pulsing stream of her vampire blood. It was more like transfusion than feeding, his mouth-parts perfectly adapted into needles and pumps, his throat a tube into which she gently emptied.

With the blood came everything that she was.

Everything she had been.

The warm girl was of no interest to him, but the vampire she had become, nourished by the blood of Beverly Hills and the illusions of the Immortologists, was a choice creature, a meal and a half.

Even when she realised how far it would go she didn't fight. By then, the greater part of her was within him. Her mind was a broken bird fluttering inside his own skull, wings oiled with thick blood, consciousness shrinking to a black-red pearl and then nothing.

The thing in his lap was a white shell, a scrap of fragile leather between a heavy mane and a pair of kinky boots.

Some life remained. She was a vampire, after all.

He let her go and she tried to stand alone. She fell.

Alucard was full, but not bloated; satisfied, but not glutted. With practice, he'd become able to drain a girl at one feeding, absorbing all her blood without ballooning like the Sta-Puft Marshmallow Man. He considered his livid purple hands, and knew his face must be the same colour.

With each vampire he drained, Alucard became more the King of the Cats. The Father was stronger in him, centuries of memory uncoiling in his brain, swallowing the pearl that had been the call girl. Centuries spent within these walls, these broken battlements foraged from the Old World and thrown up again atop a gentler hill, surveying not the forests and gorges of Borgo Pass but the night-carpet lights of Los Angeles.

If he fed on a warm person like this, he would be overcome by lassitude and drawn to a crypt or catafalque. Vampire blood cubed his energies.

Now, he had a chore to take care of.

Darting swiftly, he picked the wraith-like remains up off the floor. He hadn't spilled a drop. The girl moved too slowly and he broke her arm by rough handling. She wasn't at home to the pain. Her eyes were red blanks. Her hair was white, streaked with unhealthy yellow. Her face was a skull, skin a translucent papyrus. She had no blood in her.

He carried her to the sun room and lay her on a steel table. He pulled off her boots and threw them in the corner, onto a pile of underwear, wigs, leather fripperies and weapons.

Stroking her forehead, he made her smile, showing all her ivory. It would be over soon.

Stepping back into his lair, he pulled the heavy door shut and threw the switch. The whole ceiling of the sun room was a solar lamp, hooked up to panels atop the highest turret. Days and days of California sun stored in special cells poured forth, the full spectrum raining down on the skeleton girl.

A minute or two did the trick. He passed the time watching his bruise-purple hands go pale. When he turned off the sun room and opened the door, Vampi was reduced to a woman-shaped outline of fine red dust, with glinting black truffle highlights.

Alucard took a pinch and snorted it.

It was a purely physical sensation, without the mind-leak or emotion-rush of feeding. But these were purely physical times. Plenty preferred dry drac to the wet stuff.

He took a platinum card and chopped Vampi's skull into three lines, then rolled a hundred dollar bill into a tube and had a private party.

4

The convertible's roof shaded them like a black parasol. The rising sun threw their shadow on the road ahead. It was constantly on the point of being ground under the wheels.

'The brighter the sun,' said Kit, from the driver's seat.

'The blacker the shade,' completed Holly, at his side.

They laughed together, holding hands over the stick-shift.

The car's original owner – a medical supplies salesman they'd run into in a Motel 9 outside Lordsburg – had left a shoebox full of cassette tapes in the car. Holly had hoped for something to sing along with. They turned out to be a self-actualisation therapy course from the Church of Immortology, with titles like 'Step 5: Cultivating the Nyctlapt in You'.

'Funny,' said Holly, 'didn't seem like a viper.'

'He was all over you, Bloody Holly. Lookin' for a change, if you ask me. Beggin' for a slurp of your sweet blood so he could be like us. Just another sad warm wannabe.'

She knew what Kit meant. 'Left me with a good feeling inside, Lambchop. He might have been taking up space, but at least his blood was groovy gravy. His taste is all gone now and I miss it. All I got in my mouth is Judd.'

Kit agreed. 'That Judd was a bitter individual. He had sickness in him, down deep where it didn't show.'

Holly felt the old man's gall in her gut. It would pass soon, but she was queasy. They'd drained him to the point of death, then pitched him into his pit to give his slitherers a chance at vengeance. Disappointingly, the fall broke his neck.

Finding no music in the salesman's box, she tossed tapes out of the window. Kit and Holly didn't need to learn how to be perfect vampires; that blessing was already theirs.

Tombstone was behind them. Judd was inside, fading fast. The movie in the old man's head played itself ragged in theirs. As his killers, his executioners, it was their burden. Mostly, Judd's head had been full of people dying, in the War, in the West or in his pit.

'What d'you reckon his score was, Lambchop?'

In the thirty years since Dr Porthos bit them, Kit had killed 9,682 people, mostly warm but with some vipers tossed in to make a point. Holly had helped a lot, so they shared his score. It was hard sometimes to say they were separate people. For reference purposes, the score was Kit's. Killing was his particular special thing just as shifting was Holly's. Kit was within sniffing distance of his ten thousandth. Holly wanted to make that special, a movie star or a big lawman or a state governor. Someone famous, anyway. Maybe a viper. Special blood for a special man.

'Judd can't count the War,' said Kit. 'Why, if I'd been in a war, say if they'd caught me for Vietnam draft or took me for the Bat-Soldier Program, I'd have racked kills so fast no one could keep count. A score is only real if you do it close, with your eyes on theirs, and their minds open. You have to taste them, at least. You have to take somethin' away.'

'You're right, Lambchop.'

From everyone they killed, they took something: a trophy or a keepsake. Like this car. Or the big gun Judd tried to load with silver. The Buntline wouldn't fit in the glove compartment or even the cache under the seat where the salesman kept a little automatic. It slid about on the back seat. Kit wanted to play with it before selling it on.

In 1959, Holly had been fourteen and Kit eighteen. In a way, they weren't any older now. They'd decided to run off from Fort Dupree together and live on the road. Within nights, they found Dr Porthos. He was from Europe, an elder, but a sorry specimen. A viper hobo. His knees showed through the suit he was buried in. The Good Lord knew how he'd been cast loose in South Dakota. He was in a freight siding, keeping out of the sun in a box-car. He said they should join him on the night-side, become his children-in-darkness, first among his colony of bats. Kit noticed the viper feeling up Holly while lapping her blood and stiffened when Porthos put his mouth on him, but they'd gone through with it. They drank enough elder blood to wake the vampire seeds in their hearts and let themselves bleed empty to drift into the sleep of death. They had woken up together, hand-in-hand, at moonrise. It took a couple of nights to learn what they needed from their maker. Then they'd shown Dr Porthos things wouldn't be the way he'd figured. Holly stuck him in the eyes with a silver hatpin she'd taken from her mother's dresser and Kit put a split length of packing crate through his heart. They left him out on the rail-bed where the sun would fall and huddled in a shack to watch him turn to red dust. Everyone else they tasted stayed with them but Porthos was gone forever. He'd lived too far beyond his time.

Kit and Holly hadn't always got away with it. They'd been in and out of jails, together and apart. Kit had a few heavy convictions. That didn't matter. It meant there was at least some official recognition of his score. Prison walls couldn't hold them long. No law short of the Devil Himself could take them down.

As permanent interstate fugitives, they kept on the road, but the nation was wide enough to offer new places to visit and play. By now, they could go back to their earliest haunts and not be recognised – though they were always remembered. Both, if surprised by a question, were as likely to give the other's name as their own. Both, without quite realising it, spent as much time in the other's skull as in their own. They sometimes really did swap over and become each other.

They had so many names – invented, borrowed, ascribed – it was difficult at times to recall their true ones. Down through the years, they had called themselves or been called Bonnie and Clyde, Bowie and Keechie, Bart and Laurie, Sailor and Lula, Dirty Mary and Crazy Larry, Robin and Marian,

Mickey and Mallory, Butch and Sundance, Sadie and Krug. Really, they weren't even Kit and Holly – names they hadn't chosen – but Lambchop and Bloody Holly.

Many stories and songs – even motion pictures, with stars like Goldie Hawn and Peter Fonda – were versions of their night-lives, moments stolen and changed in the retelling, polished or coloured or clouded, as real or fake as the kaleidoscopes in their minds. Dates, names, facts and rulings existed in the files of the FBI and Sheriffs' departments, but they weren't the whole story.

This was real, the song she was writing as a surprise for Kit's ten thousandth score, 'The Ballad of Holly and Kit'.

> *Holly and Kit in a stolen ride,*
> *Streaking across the sand,*
> *Leaving the scene of a homicide,*
> *Heading for a happier end.*
>
> *Holly and Kit would take 'em*
> *Drinking away the red red thirst*
> *The lawmen swear to stake 'em*
> *But the Devil'll get there first.*

When the police found Judd and searched the Tombstone Dime Museum, another story would be born. Kit and Holly would be bigger and better, killer angels who bested the old man of the mountains. Judd's score would come to light. They'd been down into the pit and come up safe, their faith proven and their love sublime.

'Bloody Holly,' said Kit, 'let's get married.'

She writhed up against him in pleasure.

'Of course I'll marry you, Lambchop.'

Kit whistled in joy and said, 'Only one place to go, then.'

She knew what he meant.

Vegas.

He shifted the attaché case to his left hand and held his right fist up to the door goon, showing the Dracula ring. A rope lifted and he was admitted to the Viper Room. Envious fury poured from a waiting line of gorgeous creatures.

Alucard had a 54 flashback... another coast, another decade, another person. He was not nostalgic about shed snake skins. He was who he was now. Another lesson from the Father: look forward, not back. That set him apart from others who would claim to be King of the Cats. They wanted the old nights back. He wanted the new nights better.

The Viper Room. The name was deliberate provocation, assimilationists like the columnist Harry Martin carped, especially since the club's notional owner was a warm movie star, Johnny Depp. Alucard, who had a piece of the establishment, felt a duty to reclaim for vampirekind the terror squandered over the last century. He avoided fey euphemisms: 'Undead-American', 'pale', 'haemovore', 'type V', 'nightbird'. Alucard preferred fear-striking words: 'vampire', '*nosferatu*', 'leech', 'viper'.

The warm had to learn to be afraid again. So did vampires who pretended they were no different from the living. He thought of some he had climbed past: Katharine Reed, the foolish Irish woman he'd used in the Old Country; Penelope Churchward, Andy's Girl of the Year for 1979; and Geneviève Dieudonné, the elder who ruined Gorse. Alucard remembered their walk-ons in his mental biopic, but other images of them – in old-fashioned clothes, by gaslight or the stars of Europe – crowded in. All three had bad history with Him. Alucard had only made a down-payment on their punishment. The Dieudonné chit had crossed them badly, forestalling a conjuring that would have brought the Father back from beyond the veil. Upon her, Dracula's revenge would be spread over centuries.

He passed through a short corridor hung with string cobwebs and Hallowe'en bats into the small club. A mass of people writhed between the wet bar and the tiny stage. 'Riders on the Storm' pounded, by-passing his eardrums to thrum through his body, thrilling Vampi's blood. Had the management necromanced Jim Morrison back from Père Lachaise? No, it was only Val Kilmer, researching the star part in the expensive film Oliver Stone threatened to make next year or the year after. It would gross forty tops domestic, far short of break-even. A possible rind of future profit from foreign, ancillary and soundtrack.

In this crowd, Alucard couldn't be anonymous. He was given courteous space at the bar. Dancers didn't thrust into the bubble around him.

He made eye contact with Kilmer and let the actor go on with his public audition. Alucard had used him in *Bat-21*.

Alucard did not order a drink. The Viper Room had stuck piglets in harnesses, squealing behind the bar. The spigot-veined warm waitresses all had resumés and 8" x 10" glossies stashed in case some player showed up in search of a new face. Alucard would sooner cast one of the pigs. In back rooms, the occasional live one, hustled through the line and off the streets, could be had if the buyer was willing to pay clean-up costs.

Thanks to underground republication of *The Most Dangerous Game* (Amok Press), a sixty-year-old memoir by the (frankly cracked) White Russian General Zaroff, Hollywood new-borns had a craze for hunting humans. Dusk-till-dawn sports shops up and down the Strip carried equipment for the night-hunter, though purists disdained even Zaroff's Tartar war bow and relied on teeth and claws. Every night, a bat-pack of fresh-risen youths got in touch with their wolf-souls by stalking warm prey as they were told their forefathers-in-darkness had done. It appealed to a more ambitious viper than the lost, dim souls who went for Immortology. Alucard had Adrian Lyne and Kathryn Bigelow independently developing projects about the night-stalker scene – he'd greenlight whichever tweaked his fancy and shitcan the other.

The sharper Zaroff kids might make suitable lieutenants in a reformed Carpathian Guard. Once they learned not to leave prey dazed but walking. Those who shut mouths as they opened throats prospered.

Lately, a string of vamps and dhamps had wound up doing jail time for offences against cocktail waitresses and exotic dancers which wouldn't even be common assault if committed by someone without fangs. Ten years ago, after the conviction of racketeer Salvatore Macelli on a raft of charges which didn't even include felony vampirism, the government reopened Alcatraz Island, refurbished as a maximum security prison for vampires and other 'extranormal' convicts. On the Rock, the Shop's tame mad scientists poked and probed the inmates, building on a century of fruitless scientific study of vampirism.

Dirk Frost, a new-born, approached him.

The short-ish young man had TV credits in docu-dramas about male prostitution and the dhampire problem. Turning vamp, he lost his photographic image and agency representation. So he sought other employment opportunities.

Alucard put the attaché case on the bar.

Inside were a double-dozen vials of pure red dust, a clean drac high with no soul-residue. Money couldn't buy the stuff. These vials were paid for with obedience or favour.

Alucard had gone beyond the need for cash. Aside from rolled hundreds, he rarely carried any. A flash of his ring got him everything he needed, *gratis*. His New York broker kept him abreast of the numbers. He'd learned to read the market runes, appreciating the beauty of greenscreen columns. He had passed beyond mere wealth, and become a man of substance. The fortune was just a way of keeping the score.

Frost didn't open the case, but took it.

The music was too loud for conversation but Alucard had a hook in Frost from an early feeding. He cultivated his tools to keep their self-interest aligned with his own, and disposed of them if they got rusty. After a session in Alucard's private tanning parlour, Frost would fill vials as comfortably as the late, unlamented Vampi.

Tonight Frost had to take care of Spinal Tap, an English metal band from the 'Where Are They Now?' file who didn't yet know they'd be the opening act of A Concert for Transylvania. Frost had laid a taste of drac on them last week, but only the bass player was even a dhampire. Once they'd snorted or shot a couple of hits of red dust, they'd be so into the night-life they'd agree to play the Petaluma Polka Festival for a scratch of California Red. First up at a charity supergig was a poisoned chalice: warm early-comers would be pissed off by the seven-hour wait and weighed down with merchandise they'd had nothing else to do but buy, and vampires would only just be getting into their best frocks to make an entrance later. The Tap could be counted on to deliver a short, explosive set and get out of the way for Bruce Springsteen and the Be-Sharps.

'I'll want the briefcase back,' said Alucard, 'it's raptor skin, from Maple White Land. You can't get it any more.'

Frost kissed the ring and left.

On the stage a shirtless Kilmer was on his knees gasping at a microphone. Alucard decided to tell Carolco to greenlight *The Doors*, to teach Oliver Stone a lesson. He might let Kilmer do 'Light My Fire' in the middle of the concert. A rumour would spread that the real Morrison was returning from the grave to avenge himself on pretenders to the Lizard Crown.

Frost jostled Visser at the door. They didn't know each other – Alucard liked to keep his tools in separate compartments – but Frost's nostrils twitched. He took extra sidesteps to avoid getting close to the warm man.

Like Alucard, Visser could part dance-floor crowds and walk unmolested across the room. Nothing to do with fear and respect, and everything with disgust. Everything the private eye ate contained garlic. The stench radiated from his fleshy face, squeezing out in droplets of alcoholic sweat. The fat old Texan wore a once-white suit and a cowboy hat. His grin was feral enough to pass for a *nosferatu* snarl. He said he'd once tried human meat, to see whether he could stand to turn vampire. According to him, long pig tasted like shit next to the ribs at Dr Hoggly-Woggly.

Alucard indicated an unoccupied back room. Visser's grin broadened and he sauntered in, hitching up a skull-buckled belt under his soft, substantial belly bulge. He moved like an ass-wiggling beauty queen, as if daring the viper crowd to feast on him.

They would not meet here again. Too many would remember seeing John Alucard with such unappetising wormmeat. They'd wonder at his low tastes, though no one would say anything.

Alucard swiftly nipped into the room and closed the door. The small, unlit chamber was soundproofed. The absence of noise was shocking.

A match flared – a magnesium burst to Alucard's night-adapted eyes – and Visser lit a cigarillo, under-lighting his face like a carnival devil. The private eye sat on a leather-upholstered piece of furniture – a cross between a dentist's chair and a tackle-dummy, with manacles, straps and other useful add-ons. Pine-scented air-fresheners hung from the ceiling. The floor was tacky.

'No support for my poor ole back,' drawled Visser, thumping the rape-rack.

'It adjusts,' said Alucard, stepping closer.

Visser seemed to exhale garlic through his pores, halting Alucard in his tracks.

'I'm sure it does, Mr A. I'll just take your word on that.'

Alucard laughed. Visser was terrified of him, which was as it should be. He was a licensed private investigator. Also – a nasty, resourceful little man. He'd come to Alucard's notice when acting for the eleventh husband of vampire socialite Nerissa Simms, managing to take photographs which were evidence of adultery on velvet sheets, though neither the errant wife nor the (female) co-respondent showed up on film. Now on a retainer to one of Alucard's dummy corporations, he followed the private and public lives of persons of interest.

'Our three friends from out of town, Visser? How have they been?'

'All day in coffins in Chateau Marmont,' said the detective. 'Feraru has been at the room service girls and is hitting the parties and the clubs. He was in here last night. Crainic is taking meetings with Undead-American businessmen, third-level government people, journalists. He's got a one-on-one with Harry Martin for *Newsweek*. Most folk he's wooing are Shop in disguise. I have the minutes of a secret conversation he had with Darius Jedburgh out at the Bat-Soldier base in New Mexico. You can guess the gist. "Puh-lease come and help us take over our pissant country, pretty please. We hate commies oh so much even though we licked their red boots for forty years. Gimme foreign aid, Mr President, and we'll be so grateful you'll never want for a blow job in Eastern Europe ever again, no sirree bob."'

Visser was whinier than he was funny, but Alucard recognised good judgment.

'The KGB goon...' he continued.

'*Securitate*,' Alucard corrected.

'Whatever, Streisand... Striescu... He's done it again. Has a powerful red thirst on him, I guess. They'll be calling him the Skid-Row Slasher or Scorpio Junior. Snatched a pimp right off a corner in South Central. Bit his neck through, guzzled down the full eight pints, tossed the empty in a dumpster. The dead guy's name was Momentous Pryde, if you can believe it. Your secret policeman just loves the taste of nigger blood.'

'It's still red. There's no difference.'

'Maybe it's the novelty. So many things you can get here aren't on the menu in the Old Country. Wonder if he'll try Korean while he's in town.'

'There'll be a point to it. Revenge or trouble making.'

'The others don't know about his night stalking. He's careful about that. They don't like each other much, all three of them. The limey is too dumb to notice what the others think of him. He's paying for the whole trip, the hotel tab, everything. You might say he's a real sucker.'

'I've heard all the jokes, Visser.'

The detective chuckled, shaking his chins.

'Suit yourself. Feraru used to be a major dhamp in London, before he turned. Snuffed red all through the boom and the crash. He was drac-head supreme of the Stock Exchange.

Do you know that he still uses the stuff? Isn't that insane? A real goddamned vampire who does drac! What does he get? Fangs on his fangs?'

'It's a habit. Like a lot of things.'

'*Mucho loco* is what it is. He was cruising Hollywood Boulevard last night in a limo. Scored a couple of low-grade vials off some street skag. More cayenne pepper than anything. Feraru spent half the night snorting red, and the other half pouring blood out of his nose.'

Visser finished his cigarillo and lit another one. The night's specific business was done, but Alucard had long-term projects.

'So, Visser, how are my girls?'

'Still goin' strong, Mr A. I got information on 'em all. Recent shit. No major developments.'

Of the three vampire women, only Penelope Churchward was in California. He'd hired her as a technical advisor on *Bat-21*. Another one for reinvention: Penny's latest incarnation was as a Daughter of the American Revolution, an Orange County Republican with the Governor's ear.

'Churchward has re-upped for another dime with the Shop. They don't let her join in all their reindeer games. I pushed a few buttons to find out policy in the event of a sad accident. No one's panties would get in a bunch. She's done for them what they wanted done. Now, she's high-maintenance surplus.'

Alucard shook his head. He saw no particular point in having Penny killed. She couldn't hurt him and had no real reason to want to. She'd quit the New York scene of her own accord, walking out on Andy, making room for Johnny Pop.

'She's definitely made the connection,' said Visser. 'She knows who you are.'

That *was* new material. He wondered whether to spit or swallow. Visser could be stringing him along, creating a need for a high-priced hit.

'She knows who I was once.'

'Same difference.'

'No, it's not.'

The investigator had, of course, dug back and thought

he knew all about John Alucard. It was as well to let Visser play mastermind. He'd learned enough to be respectful, to stay properly scared. A minion should be more afraid of the consequences of breaking faith with his master than eager for rewards others might give him for treachery.

'I have plans for Penny. She's got lines into the music industry which I might need.'

'The Short Lion still holdin' out?'

'Just negotiating.'

'They say the little faggot's lost his voice.'

Alucard snorted. 'Did you ever hear his voice?'

'I like Hank Williams Jr myself.'

The vampire superstars of rock were throwing snits. The Short Lion didn't want to appear on the same stage as Timmy V, but equally couldn't bear to let his rival hog the spotlight. Right now, the eternal child was hotter with key demographics than the exile prince. Only sad urban murgatroyds bought the last Short Lion solo album, *Queen of the Damned*, while every teenage girl in America owned Timmy's *Bat*. The Short Lion was regularly hailed the greatest vampire celebrity of the 1980s, but his dark sun was moving into eclipse. Dating Julia Roberts didn't help. But Alucard still wanted both singers on his bill. And he wanted them together.

'Here are the mick bitch viper's clippings,' said Visser, pulling out a fat folder of pages torn from newspapers and magazines. 'My mailman wonders why I subscribe to *City Limits*, *Searchlight*, *Private Eye*, *Spare Rib* and *International Times*.'

For much of the last decade, Kate Reed had been up to her thick specs in feminist mud at the Women's Peace Camp in Greenham Common, England, popping out of a shallowly buried coffin to chant slogans at the American airbase and file stories about potential (and actual) mishaps with nuclear weapons. After a Romanian jail, a muddy grave in the English countryside was a picnic on the village green. These nights, she was back in a flat on the Holloway Road, sharing rent with a freelance film critic and saving pennies to trade her Amstrad word-processor for an Apple. Her articles appeared in low-paying periodicals whose subscriber base was evenly divided between the radical left and security personnel infiltrating and observing the radical left.

Alucard took the clippings. He would enjoy reading them later. Katie was so far out of the loop she was no real threat. If she ever showed signs of making a move against him, a call to the unlisted number of Caleb Croft in Cheltenham would see her whisked without trial into indefinite detention, preferably in the Little Ease cell of the Tower of London. The silly girl had done enough things in her long life which could be defined as terrorism. Visser had dug up an old story about someone called Eric DeBoys which meant Croft could stick a murder on Kate Reed if he wanted. Furthermore, she was on a stack of shitlists in Thatcher's Britain simply by being, as Visser put it, 'a mick bitch viper'. Thanks to the continuing influence of Lord Ruthven, she could be forgiven for drinking blood, but being Irish, a woman and a loudmouth red-flagged her files in what was left of the British Empire.

'The Frog twist's still with the Mounties,' said Visser. 'Made the news with her testimony at the Lacroix trial. One hundred and twenty-two counts of aggravated vampirism and cold-blooded murder. Fella must have a taste for it, if you ask me. Likes 'em juicy and with a bit of fight in 'em. The Canucks are making a deal to ship him to the Rock for a century or two. He'll make a lot of friends there.'

Alucard had never actually met Geneviève Dieudonné, but had a clear mental image of her. She was living in Toronto, presumably on the grounds that Canadians could at least properly pronounce her name (Zh-NE-v'yev), working as senior forensic technician on attachment to the only North American police department which boasted an equal-opportunity employment policy for vampires. Thanks to do-gooders like Geneviève's cop pal Knight and the romantic novelist Fitzroy, Toronto was known as a hole for Granpa Munsters.

A breed of *nosferatu* suck-up was named after the sickeningly cuddly, non-threatening vampire Al Lewis played on *All in the Family*. Rosamund on *Bloodwitched* was the vixen warm America secretly wanted to be neckraped by; Granpa was the fangless fool who knew his place in the sit-com crypt. Even Carroll O'Connor's diehard ninety-eight-point-sixer Archie Bunker let Granpa cross his threshold, and became best pals with the viper he spent two seasons dreading and plotting to stake.

Geneviève was, Alucard was pleased to learn, a controversial figure even in the Toronto 'pale' community. A growing minority saw her as not merely a Granpa but a diabolical traitress selling out her night-brethren for the meagre approval of the warm. She had worked for the apprehension of a couple of serial killers who turned out to be vampires. Called to justify her actions, she claimed to be following the Zaroff doctrine, but that, for her, the most dangerous game wasn't warm.

'Gorse is on the Rock, too,' said Visser. 'Maybe him and Lacroix will be bunkies. They can pin up a picture of the Frog on their dartboard and jerk each other off as they fantasise about the things they'd like to do to her fine white hide. If they ever get out, she's dust.'

It wasn't worth calling in a Winton favour to have the Dieudonné woman staked. That would be too easy.

'Is Geneviève seeing anyone?'

Visser's grin showed flecks in his gums. 'Jealous, boss? Is she your dream girl too?'

When he conjured up Geneviève's face in his mind, it was through a bloody film, as the Father had seen her from atop a throne at the summit of his red reign. From the summit, there had only been one direction to go. In no small part thanks to Geneviève's intervention, Dracula had lost his position in Great Britain, cut out of power after the death of Queen Victoria and toppled after years of open rebellion. The French elder had been there again, one of the last faces the Father saw as his eyes dimmed, his head stuck on a pole at the Palazzo Otranto in 1959. All three of the women – Penny, Kate, Gené – had been there, at the death. The Father whispered that they had all been involved, had all contributed. Geneviève had undone the conjuring that should have restarted the Anni Draculae. John Alucard's business with that strange trio – they weren't exactly friends, having squabbled over the affections of some warm man years ago – was not over. In the end, he would see dawnlight rise on their ashes.

'I went up to Toronto for her big day,' said Visser, calculation gleaming in his eye. 'Was in the courtroom just for her testimony. She's a honey, all right. Solid nine and a half… a ten, if it weren't for the overbite.'

Alucard's fingers darted out and pinched Visser's greasy dewlap. His nails pressed through slick skin. Blood welled, overripe with garlic stink. The private eye grit his teeth against the pain. His eyes grew as big as saucers. Fear boiled off him like steam, seeping out around his collar and through the damp patches under his arms.

'Give it to me,' Alucard ordered.

He knew what Visser would have got in Toronto.

'Y-yes, Mr A.'

Visser's voice was a squeak, as if Alucard were gripping his testes.

He hissed through fangs. Visser had to submit to him.

'Yes, Master,' he said.

The magic words won the detective's freedom. He held a hand to his ragged neck. He was not seriously hurt. His jugular was safe behind inches of protective flab.

He took a plastic folder from inside his coat.

Alucard snapped his fingers. Visser, hand shaking, lit a match and held up the flame.

Alucard could see perfectly well in this dark, but wanted something close to daylight for this. Inside the folder was a court artist's sketch of a young woman on the witness stand, dressed conservatively, hair loose, fangs perhaps exaggerated, eyes wide, face clear. The anonymous Canadian artist was not up to C.C. Drood standards, but Alucard didn't care.

Visser didn't say anything clever.

Alucard looked at the picture for a long time. He didn't have anyone on the payroll he could trust to take care of Geneviève. Gorse's cheerleader hit-girl had bungled the job. Once, a contract had been put on Geneviève's head with Mr Yee, greatest of all Chinese vampire assassins. She'd wormed her way out of that. The woman had survived notorious Slayers like the Crook, the Crimson Executioner, Anita Blake and Captain Kronos. If he wanted her truly dead, Alucard would have to handle her himself, which he was loath to do these nights, or head-hunt someone special for the sanction. But, he wondered, did he want her dead? So few appreciated what he was up to, it would be a shame to lose such a sharp, appreciative audience.

6

The impersonator turned to her and said, 'Do you, Holly Sargis, take this man, Christopher Carruthers, as your lawful wedded husband, to have and to hold, in death as in life, to share the nights, throughout eternity?'

Holly looked into Kit's eyes, the only mirror she'd ever need, and said, 'I do.'

'Then, by the power vested in me by the State of Nevada, I pronounce you man and wife.'

Kit whooped and swept her off her feet, swinging her around. The little chapel shook. It was done up like a crypt. The short, squat impersonator held on to the prop skull and real chalice which dressed his rickety altar.

'You may now bite the bride,' he said.

She bared her throat and he sank his teeth into her, deep. They didn't do that often enough any more. She nibbled his ear as he tongued away the blood that came from her. The sense tsunami washed over his tongue and drowned his brain, then poured back into her through their mind link. Dry-mouthed, she tasted herself. With the blood came a flow of feeling which wound around them, making them as one. A closed circuit of love.

A blue-haired gnome woman played an electric organ. They'd chosen 'Swan Lake' over 'Toccata and Fugue', but asked her to switch after the ceremony into 'I Got You, Babe' for the biting and kissing. Holly guessed the impersonator disapproved, but he wasn't the one doing the getting married.

It was a tradition every time they passed through Vegas to take their vows. This was their seventh wedding since 1962, when they'd seen Frank and Sammy heckle Dean, then killed some wiseguys and strewn the bones in the desert. Vegas kept getting better with every visit.

This time, they'd selected a late-period impersonator to officiate. He wore a scarlet lamé jump-suit split to the waist to show wolfstooth necklaces and military orders, with a gold-lined batwing-collared half-length black cape, a midnight-black widow's peak wig that melted into flared and trailing eyebrows, and showy artificial fang-points. He had the voice down: the soul-stirring European accent made words into music and impregnated regular phrases with dark meaning.

At any time of night, seventy or eighty impersonators, representing as many different stages in the King's life, milled about the desert city's streets, lounges, bars and casinos. They corralled visitors, told stories to whoever would listen, performed close-up magic, played unusual musical instruments, showed off trained wolves or gila monsters. Morgan Freeman, Dick Shawn and George Hamilton all got their showbiz start working Vegas in capes and fangs. A persistent story was that the King was coming back and would first manifest in the West. She'd heard it too many times, from too many different vipers, to write it off as just sizzle for the tourists.

Still, they didn't need a King of the Cats; they had each other.

The moment of commingling passed. Kit let her go. His mouth and chin were smeared. She licked him clean, mixing in a few kisses.

The impersonator was jealous.

Good. Her neck was for one man and one man alone.

'Let's go have some fun, Bloody Holly,' Kit said.

'Oh, Lambchop, let's,' she breathed.

They paid the impersonator and the organist with bloodied bills and went out into the velvet night.

Holly clung to Kit's arm. For the wedding, she'd chosen a white gown, split up the sides to her armpits and cut low in front, with a string of cultured pearls and matching earrings, and high heels that at least raised her to Kit's shoulder height. The groom wore an orange tux with matching devil's-horns Stetson and a wide tie painted with cartoon characters. They posed under the arch of the chapel. An explosive flashbulb went off, burning their eyes. They kept trying new processes to photograph vampires. Their last wedding photo was an improvement over earlier attempts, with recognisable smoke-shapes rather than empty embracing outfits. For some vipers, photography would never take. It was part of their marriage ritual though. Kit agreed to be back before dawn to pick up the prints. Who knew what this year's picture would show?

All around were points of light, stars fallen to Earth and stuck to hotels. Billions of coloured bulbs. Millions of miles of neon tube. Thousands of folks, attracted to the lights like insects. Coins clinked in polyester pockets like cicada chirrups. Dozens of tunes exploded from street-mounted speakers: 'Here She Is, Miss America' and 'Transylvania Twist' and 'Would You Like to Swing on a Star?' and 'Witch Doctor' and 'Like a Virgin' and 'Me and Bobby McGee' and 'Cold as Ice' and 'Venus' and 'Vampire Junction' and 'Off to See the Wizard' and 'In the Ghetto' and 'Love is Strange'. White stretch limos blocked traffic along the Strip, coffin-cocooning cool celebs and overexcited contest winners. People on the hoof jammed the sidewalks and filled the spaces between cars.

They strolled on, back towards the Voodoo Lounge.

Rival casinos faced each other across the Strip. Two clanking buildings were shaped like Japanese monsters, with room windows in their bellies and arched entrances between their feet. One was a towering dragon, eyes like lighthouse lamps and spiny ridges all over its bulbous avocado-textured walls, plumes of fire projected from its gaping maw; the other was a titanic wing-flapping moth, in white with delicate colour patterns, spewing strawberry fun foam from a spout high on the roof. Crews of employees dressed as the casinos' totemic beasts yelled taunts at each other from their forecourts and bad-mouthed the opposition to the streams of tourists. Sometimes, rivalry exploded into stick fights, swordplay or exchanges of sniper fire. A dozen more bodies and the Nevada Gaming Commission would up the expected bribes to let the *Kaiju Yakuza* stay in business.

Another impersonator, buzzed on drac, stick-thin and ragged-cloaked, was handing out casino flyers. Origami cat-shapes spilled from his hands onto the sidewalk, fanning around his feet, rarely taken by disinterested passersby. A wide-eyed warm man in a tailored Western suit sank slowly to his knees, hands bunched over holes in his shirt. His blood shone bright as neon. He was more surprised than angry or scared. No one was running away. A few stopped to look, giving the gut-stuck fellow room to kneel and bleed. Some licked their teeth. Holly and Kit didn't need any of that action. It wouldn't even count towards the score. They'd only be finishing something someone else started.

They crossed the Strip and went into the Voodoo Lounge.

The door staff were coloured women in skimpy shrouds, white bones painted on their brown skin. The lobby captain was a seven-foot black man in a battered top hat, a brocaded cutaway coat and a loin-cloth of fabric snakes and daggers. Baron Samedi directed customers with a skull-topped quarterstaff. At his side was a sack into which tributes poured as he advised people where in the lounge their particular pleasure could be serviced. Smiling on the newlyweds, he showed ruby blood-drops inset into his pointed front teeth, and a bat tattoo on his long, pink tongue. When he held up his staff to point, one side of his coat lifted to flash an unbuttoned shoulder-holster and a heavy automatic.

The centrepiece of the lobby was a wheezing brass coffin on a gravel bed, hooked up to a complex apparatus. Through an iced-over window, curiosity seekers could see the frost-rimed Howard Hughes, white beard and hair curled around his sunken face. It was considered good luck to rub the faceplate after a wedding. Kit and Holly stepped up and touched their palms to cool glass.

'His eyes moved, Bloody Holly,' said Kit, snatching his fingers away.

'Did not, silly,' she said, scratching his wrist with her nail.

'Had you goin' a second.'

'Wait till I get you upstairs.'

Hughes was no longer warm, not yet a vampire. A thin stream of blood, 'donated' by pure-living Mormons, was circulated through his veins by an impressive arrangement of pumps. The billionaire, owner of the hotels and casinos on this side of the Strip, had definite ideas about when he should rise to continue his work on Earth. A plaque on the cryo-coffin explained that he was to be reactivated when his company filed unspecified aerospace patents which would take the industry to the point where Hughes might deem it interesting again. Until then, his fortune kept him half-alive and hotel profits contributed to his maintenance. A dent in the unbreachable brass showed that someone had tried to put a bullet through his heart. The hotels and casinos on the other side of the Strip were owned by the Five Families and between the two sides existed a permanent state of undeclared war. Last time they passed through, Holly and Kit had picked up a hundred thousand dollars of untraceable Hughes Tool & Die money for adding six goombahs to the score, prompting a change of administration in the Outfit. Since then, they were welcome any time to the Voodoo Lounge.

All around, matrons with zimmer frames and teenagers dressed like hookers popped chips into shiny one-armed bandits modelled on the Hughes cryo-coffin. The crunch of rolling reels and falling metal blended with the noise of a band. Screamin' Jay Hawkins, bone through his nose, sang 'I Put a Spell on You' as if he really meant it. A few people, those not in line for a machine, paid attention.

They had a suite here, but Kit wouldn't gamble in the Voodoo Lounge or any other casino. Whatever game you picked, the odds were in the house's favour. Later, they might try to get into a card game, though no high-roller would sit at a table with a viper couple. It would be like playing with a mind-reader and his assistant. Signals would fly invisibly from the first cut to the last cash-rake.

For them, this adventure was about love, not money.

'What d'you want to do for a wedding night treat, Lambchop?'

Kit gave it some thought. She saw the blood-bursts in his mind and shared his excitement.

'Let's go find one of those lap-dancin' places, suck ourselves fat on long-legged big titty girls or hard-butt gay boys, then score everybody in the place, leavin' but one soul alive to tell the tale of what went down when Kit and Holly came to town.'

He kissed her, sweetly. Over his shoulder, she winked at the Eye in the Sky, which had swivelled their way. They had directional mikes these days.

'Better make it a Mob place, Lambchop. The Hughes folks have been real appreciative. It'd be like doing them a favour, while we were having fun.'

'You're so sweet, Bloody Holly. Viva Las Vegas!'

7

It was unnatural that a warm man should be so enthused at the Hour of the Wolf. Behind heavy-framed glasses, the kid's eyes jittered and shone. He wasn't on drac, so Alucard guessed the auteur-in-waiting had caffeinated himself on a dozen jolts of full-strength Java.

'You are?'

'Adam Simon,' said the kid.

The writer-director wore a too-big check shirt outside khaki pants and hadn't shaved in the twenty-two hours since the last daybreak. He waved his hands constantly, a distraction. If Alucard concentrated, he saw movements beyond the ordinary human optical spectrum. A rarely useful vampire trick. Sometimes he was distracted by artefacting in his vision, almost lulled into fascination by shapes and colours the warm couldn't see.

Simon had made a couple of Roger Corman pictures, *The Howling Man* and *Blood Chemistry 2*. He was looking to pitch something at a major minor or a minor major.

Alucard was an independent with deals all over town. His line of old blood money and new Wall Street finance was the envy of corporate conglomerates who still didn't know what to do with motion picture studios they'd swallowed twenty years earlier. He chose to work out of Miracle Pictures because one of his third-generation companies had controlling interest monopolies and trusts people would never figure. He paid himself rent on office and stage facilities and set it against tax. Most nights, he hit the lot sometime after three and took meetings and calls until dawn. He was at his best and the warm were drowsy or cranked. No one in the business complained about having to stay up or get out of bed to see him. Most would sacrifice more than a few hours' sleep for a face-to-face with John Alucard.

Simon had been haunting his outer office for months, cajoling Beverly for a pitch window. She must have taken pity on the lost soul. He would give her a taste of the cat for that.

The kid sat, without being asked. Visitors' chairs, six inches shorter than Alucard's solid throne, were constructions of chrome and canvas designed to become uncomfortable after a few minutes. This office was his sanctum: it didn't do to encourage people to settle in. Simon sank lower into the chair than he'd expected and found himself craning to see over Alucard's desk, a pair of antique Spanish grandee coffins supported by four bowed hardwood angels. The kid was momentarily distracted by a framed Warhol, a silk-screened red and yellow and black multiple reproduction of an eighteenth century portrait of Carmilla Karnstein.

'I've a project I think you're going to be very excited about, John,' began the writer-director. 'Blockbuster potential, but with integrity. A star vehicle, but with something to say. It's very makeable, within a tight-ish budget. Or on big bucks if that's what it takes. Whatever.'

'Sands are flowing, Adam. Preamble eats into your pitch slot.'

Simon swallowed and began.

'We begin,' he said, hands raised, palms out, opening like theatre curtains. 'A John Alucard Production. An Adam Simon Picture. Big Star Name in... *The Rock.*'

'A boxing picture? Doesn't Stallone own the title?'

'Not *Rocky, The Rock.*'

'I like Stallone, though.'

'So do I, enormously. *Death Race 2000*, great movie. *F.I.S.T.*, very underrated.'

Alucard made a funnelling motion, sand in an hourglass.

'*The Rock*,' said Simon. 'The Big House. Alcatraz Island.'

'A prison picture?'

'Exactly, but with a twist, a new wrinkle, an angle. A prison picture, with vampires.'

Word around town was that John Alucard was a soft touch for vampire pitches. He hadn't green-lighted a viper movie since *The Lost Boys*, but the flurry around the botched conjuring had left a wrong impression with the bottom-feeders. Every night, he nixed vampire pitches. The American public had a limited tolerance for films about the undead. Audiences wanted characters to wake up warm at the sunrise, not go all the way into the night. *The Lost Boys* sailed under the radar because it was a dhampire movie. At the end, bad vampires Kiefer Sutherland and Edward Herrmann were destroyed, and nice kids Jason Patric and Jamie Gertz turned warm again.

'Adam, just because I'm a vampire doesn't mean I'll back a vampire picture. Mayer, Glick and Warner were Jews. How many films did old Hollywood make about Jews?'

'Uh, *The Life of Emile Zola*, *Gentleman's Agreement*.'

'Ancient history. I know all about Alcatraz. You're not the first to come to me with this idea. I've even had your title pitched, by Eszterhas or Shane Black.'

'The title's not important. It could be *From Dusk Till Dawn*. That's classier. Or *Lock-Up*. Or *The Concrete Coffin*.'

'Your Corman background is showing. This is *The Big Doll House* with vampires.'

'"With vampires" isn't the twist. This isn't just another vampire prison movie. They've been done to death with Linda Blair and Sylvie Kristel. I have a new new angle.'

'Sands run low, Adam.'

'Here's our pre-credits sequence. The dock on Frisco Bay. Sunset. An armoured car draws up. It's like a prison cell on wheels, a black iron cage. It's a tank constructed inside-out, not to keep the crew safe from the world but to keep the world safe from the passengers. A boat, also armoured out the wazoo, is waiting to take the new fish out to the Rock. We see the island on the horizon, gulls circling above in the twilight like vultures. A John Ford sky, blood red with grey clouds. Guards with riot-guns, crossbows, burning crosses. We get pro ball players or wrestlers. Huge guys, arms like cantaloupes, slabs of beef. Close-up: silver dum-dums chambered into a pump-action shotgun. The rear door of the armoured transport opens. The grizzled senior guard – Robert Duvall, Gene Hackman – reads off a clipboard, giving us voice-over intro to the cons.'

'The guard is the star part?'

'No. No. Best Supporting Actor Nomination.'

'I like someone younger in the lead. More sex.'

'You'll get it. You'll get a lot of it.'

'Sex in prison? Sounds like a fag art movie. Jean Genet is dead again, you know.'

'The Rock is co-ed. It's for vampires, remember. Some of those *nosferatu* women are hardcore.'

Alucard let that pass. Miriam Blaylock, the most elegant murderess of the '80s, had wound up on the Rock. Ricia 'Rusty' Cadigan, the lonelyhearts killer who'd just lost a final appeal before the Supreme Court, was on the island too, safely welded into her solitary cell.

They were all idiots, to his mind. Like Lacroix and Macelli. Hopped up on what their 'vampire powers' could do, they thought they were beyond the law. Alucard hadn't personally killed anyone warm since 1982.

'We see cons come out of the van,' continued Simon. 'Big, small, mean, sneaky. We get their histories. What they've been convicted of. Horrible, horrible crimes. Mass murder, serial murder, drac-dealing, death cults. One's an elder, nailed with charges that go back centuries. A Transylvania Movement terrorist who led an assault on a Romanian gymnastics team, popping the heads off five fifteen-year-old girls. Call him something like "Baron Monster".'

Alucard smiled. Meinster was too short and prissy to be a movie villain, but Steven Berkoff had already played two *à clef* versions of the TM elder. If Berkoff was busy in the theatre, there was always Julian Sands.

'And there's a woman, America's first home-grown female vampire serial killer.'

'Rusty Cadigan?'

'We change the name, of course. Ratty Cardigan.'

'Good. Cons doing five hundred years have nothing to do but study law and bring nuisance suits.'

Three competing prime time drama-docs about Cadigan were in the works, with Susan Dey, Lauren Hutton and Lynda Carter flashing dental plastic as prettied-up vamps. Hoffman, Rusty's warm lawyer, had a reputation as the most voracious bloodsucker in Los Angeles. He had injuncted transmission of the specials, while co-operating with Nick Broomfield, the British filmmaker, to get his client's bizarre side of the story in a theatrical documentary, *Diamond Skulls*. Rival sets of victims' relatives, standing to benefit financially from their own 'based on a true story' TV movies, were in on the act with their own lawyers, as was the homicide cop who had made the arrest. By the time the legal dust settled, the public would have lost interest and found another monster to care about.

'Anyway, four or five of the worst vampires you ever saw – no offence, John – are on the dock in silver chains. Red eyes, fangs, snarls. Then the last convict, the star part, comes out of the car cage, hands shackled in old-fashioned iron. He looks at the sunset, is dazzled, and shades his eyes. He's a warm man.'

A switch flicked in Alucard's back-brain.

'You have me,' he said. 'What's a warm man doing there?'

'Doesn't matter, really. We contrive circumstances. Say his wife and family were killed by a vampire cult and he took them all down with a flamethrower and stakes. Flashback time, later in the picture. But the cult's leader had connections. A rich kid new-born. His old man a big wheel. Noise has been made in Congress. There are pale anti-defamation groups. Our man has acted just as ruthlessly as a vampire, has done as many dark deeds. So he's the first warm human to be sentenced to the Rock.'

'It couldn't happen.'

'This is the movies. Our man – Clint Eastwood, say, or Scott Glenn – is on the boat to an island full of the blood-sucking undead. The vampires he killed have fathers-in-darkness or get in the population. The whole prison is stuffed with vampires who haven't tasted warm blood since they were slammed up, and who have a collective monster jones for the red red red. And our man is the only warm, pulsing neck in the place. Two thousand nothing-to-lose honest-to-Bram Stoker bloodlusting undead monsters, and one living man in for a hundred years. How can he survive?'

'Does he?'

'Not in the end, that would be ridiculous. They have to tear him apart. He fights and fights, bests the worst of the bad guys, takes down the elder who's the king of the cons, adds to his sentence by killing more vampires. The only ending possible is that he's brutalised so much in stir that he becomes the thing he hates. He turns. We end in solitary, with his red eyes and fangs. He's howling for blood. It'll be a killer finish.'

'I don't like it. Audiences won't go for negative.'

'So he dies a hero. Refuses to turn vampire.'

'That's distasteful. No, he survives, beats the odds, and escapes.'

'No one has ever escaped from Alcatraz.'

'This is the movies. Eastwood already made it once.'

'*Escape From Alcatraz*, Don Siegel, 1980. But that was about the old prison.'

'Scrub Eastwood. I still like Stallone.'

'*Stallone?*'

'He's blue-collar for the sixpack audience, pretty enough to get in women and a few gays, and college kids like to laugh at his mumbling. We get a Frank Stallone song over the end credits. A cover of "The Green, Green Grass of Home". The point is that Stallone survives against the odds. He not only escapes from the prison, but escapes from himself. By breaking out – and he does this with the help of the Ratty character, who redeems herself and dies, but not until after they've had a steamy sex scene which ends with him letting her bite him but refusing to drink her blood and turn vampire – Stallone breaks out of his pattern of hatred for all vampires, which is really the hatred he has for himself because he couldn't save his family. The Supreme Court upholds his appeal, so he's home free and clear for the last scene at his family's graves. We have to say that not all vampires are badasses, because they're an audience too. The Granpas will like the girl who turns good in the end – we could get Brigitte Nielsen practically for free – and the nightriders will read the film as a story about the elder who tells the truth the warm wormmeat won't hear. For the elder part, I like a British voice to sell the dialogue, maybe Anthony Hopkins, Alan Rickman.'

'That's not quite where I was going with it.'

'That's the treatment I've bought.'

'You've bought it?'

'Just now. It happened so fast you didn't notice it. Adam Simon, we're going to make *The Rock.*'

The kid looked as if he'd taken a sledgehammer to the back of the head but discovered that it felt good.

'With Stallone, this picture is a go.'

There were three minutes left of pitch-time. Simon just sat there, scratching his curly hair.

Alucard flipped his intercom and told Beverly to have a contract ready for Adam Simon to sign on the way out.

'I should run it past my agent. And maybe my analyst.'

'Sign while it's hot. Tomorrow night, maybe I take another vampire prison picture pitch. It's in the atmosphere. Steam-engine time.'

'Yeah, you're right. Thanks, John.'

'Thank you.'

He shook the writer-director's hand.

'Have me the treatment tomorrow. I'll get it to Sly.'

'I won't sleep.'

'I wouldn't let you.'

In a cloud of glee and amazement, Simon left the office. Alucard kept the intercom open. He heard a burble of meaningless chatter between the kid and Beverly, then the vital scratching of the pen on the standard contract.

John Alucard now owned *The Rock*.

He ran down short-lists. As policy, he didn't care for writer-directors. He preferred to deal with mutually hostile creatives who'd jostle each other for DGA or SWG credits. None of his films had been written by fewer than twelve people and he used an average of three directors on any project.

For *The Rock*, he liked George Pan Cosmatos to get the master shots, to be replaced in mid-shoot by Russell Mulcahy for the style and the laughs and Peter MacDonald for the action and gore. He would be proud to release a movie with an Allan Smithee credit.

One thing was certain. Simon would end up being grateful for a small-print 'and with thanks to' mention between the location caterers and the licensed music rights in the end credits. Alucard might let him shoot the 'making of' cable documentary.

He listened to the clatter of the kid leaving the outer office, floating off the floor but trying not to bump his head against the lintel.

'Beverly,' he said.

'Yes, Master,' deadpanned his Renfield.

'I'll be expecting an express delivery from Adam Simon tomorrow afternoon. Arrange for him to bike it over.'

'At his expense?'

'How well you know me, my best beloved.'

'It's in the to-do book. I'll have his package by the time you pop out of your coffin at sunset tomorrow.'

'Excellent. Then tell security Adam Simon is never to be allowed on this lot again. Deadly force is authorised if he attempts to violate the ruling. In fact, I want you to buy a big bottle of liquid paper and obliterate his name from all our records except the legally binding contract he just signed. Your primary instruction is never again to speak the name "Adam Simon" in my presence. Am I understood?'

'Yes, Master.'

———————◆———————

Alucard parked his liver-purple Camaro in the handicapped space outside the Video Archives on Sepulveda. He was dead and you couldn't get more handicapped than that. Little people didn't see it that way. Beverly took care of parking fines. He was putting the kids of the Los Angeles Traffic Control Bureau through fancy Eastern colleges. He hoped they got brutally hazed by the Brotherhood of the Bell.

The videos he was returning were in a wino-style brown paper bag on the passenger seat. He checked the titles. Sometimes, what with all the confusion, tapes wound up in the wrong boxes. Video Archives fines added up too. Last week, he'd meant to return *Can I Do It Till I Need Glasses?*, sequel to *If You Don't Stop It You'll Go Blind* and little-known debut of Robin Williams, but the box contained a home-shot video of one of Vampi's predecessors in the act of predeceasing. Quentin, the warm kid behind the counter, made an offer on the rights, saying he had customers who went for viper snuff. A fanged snarl and a hundred dollar bill, pre-rolled and red-dusted, settled the business. He had the *Glasses* tape and his other rental selections of the week, Carol Speed in *Abby*, Dyanne Thorne in *Greta the Torturer* and Bette Midler and Barbara Hershey in *Beaches*. He made a mental note to approach Midler for the Transylvania Concert, though he was also tempted to see if there was a way of having her quietly killed.

Crossing the sidewalk, he saw through the windows, between cardboard standees of Cynthia Rothrock and Jessica Tandy, that a hold-up was in progress. A bald-headed viper in a net-mesh muscle T-shirt and rose-tinted glasses held an unnecessarily large handgun on Quentin, who was reaching for the sky like a cowboy extra. The video kid wore a Hawaiian shirt and sunglasses, and was talking. Thick veins throbbed in his thin arms and wrists, and his Adam's apple bobbed under his scraggle of goatee. Dead customers lay on the floor in pretzel poses, great holes blown out of them. Pooling blood was fast going rancid. A waste. A guy in a tan suit was being bitten – chewed, rather – by an undernourished vampire girl in a Raggedy Ann red wig, spangly halter top, short shorts and cha cha heels. The victim was trying to ward off the vampire with a cassette of *King Kong Lives*. The critics were right – you *should* die before watching that.

Alucard didn't want to put off returning the tapes. He'd driven all the way out here to Hermosa Beach. As he pushed open the front door, an old-fashioned bell tinkled.

'What about that motherfucking *Green Acres*, man,' babbled Quentin, 'that pig Arnold sure was a smarty-pants!'

'You talkin' to me about *sit-coms*, ninety-eight-point-six?' asked the viper.

'Sit-coms, man. Life and death, man. No difference, not really.'

The bell finally registered, catching everyone's attention.

The bloody-mawed girl left off her meal – blood pulsed out of the dying man's neck – and fixed Alucard with violet-red cat eyes.

'Good evening,' said Alucard. 'I'm returning some tapes.'

The hold-up man angled his head up in the air with a 'why me?' eyebrow-lift and swung around to face Alucard, pointing his big gun. He did the thing rappers did on videos, holding the pistol sideways as if it were laid flat in the air. Looks fuck you cool, debatably reduces the likelihood of an automatic jamming and screws up any chance of aiming properly – though this specimen had hit what he was firing at so far. His gun was a revolver, a ridiculous Western relic with a foot-long barrel.

'Who the fuck are you?'

'A man with video tapes.'

'And I'm Kit Carruthers, a viper with four convictions for murder one.'

'How careless. I have no convictions at all.'

'What I'm sayin' is: I go down, I'm for the Rock. Understand, Granpa Munster. That's as bad as it can get. I just friggin' don't care what happens. Me and Holly are going to red dust afore they take us in. We'll drag as many losers to hell with us as possible. Get it?'

'You believe in reincarnation, man?' asked Quentin. 'You all know, in a second life, we all come back sooner or later, as anything from a pussycat to a man-eating alligator…'

On cue, the cat-eyed Holly projected her nose, mouth and chin into a snout. Her skin turned to scaly hide. A thousand wickedly curved teeth gleamed, blooded. From pussycat to man-eating galligator, in a nictitation. If it weren't for her brain-dead b-f, this little viper would have potential.

'What's he talkin' about?' said Kit.

'He's quoting the theme for *My Mother, the Car*.'

'This fuckin' town. Doolally La-La Ville. Got anythin' worth havin'? Or should I stake you straight off.'

'I don't care to be talked to like that.'

Kit snarled, gums receding above inch-long ivories. Tattoos swirled on his shaved head.

'Then eat silver, *Granpa*!'

He fired the gun one-handed, which would have broken a warm man's wrist. The kick flung his arm off to one side. Alucard knew Kit should have held his gun in a proper grip. The silver slug shot past, took off Jessica Tandy's head, and smashed through the window. Alucard got out of the way, swiftly.

Kit's eyes were goggle-open, bigger than the round rose lenses in front of them.

'Where'd he go?'

Alucard was in the porno alcove, an arched-off recess with a hand-lettered 'Pee-Wee's Playhouse' sign. A customer huddled against the far wall, clutching *Lust in the Fast Lane* to his forehead. He recognised the bearded middle-aged man as blacklisted screenwriter Jack Martin.

'I've seen that, Jack,' said Alucard. 'I wouldn't recommend it. Of the Rac Loring oeuvre, I'd suggest *Talk Bloody to Me 3*.'

Martin shut his eyes and held the box over his forehead.

'He's here, Lambchop,' hissed the gator-girl, pointing. 'In with the dirty movies.'

By the time Kit had thrown a shot at a rack of *Buttman*

tapes, Alucard was up on the ceiling, braced in a corner. Kit pointed his gun at Martin's skull but didn't shoot him. The warm writer whimpered. If Martin made it through the next five minutes, Alucard might kick him a dialogue polish on *Untitled Dolly Parton*. He had been out in the cold for a long time. Another of the many lives wrecked by *la belle Geneviève*. They should form a support group.

Alucard skipped across the tops of the racks, arms out like wings, trusting the Father. He stayed light enough not to topple the flimsy units.

'Sister Bertrille, man,' said Quentin. '*The Flying Nun.*'

Alucard descended, settling his feet on the ground.

Kit came charging out of the Playhouse, dry-firing his pistol. Click, click, click.

'All out of buwwets,' said Quentin, doing Elmer Fudd.

Kit tossed the heavy revolver like a knife, aiming for Alucard's head. The gun seemed to take an age to make it across the room, turning over and over and over. Alucard reached up and took it out of the air as if it were a dove. He squeezed and the brittle antique burst into pieces. He pitched a fistful of metal chunks – cylinder, empty cases, butt – which hammered against Kit's slab of chest.

'Who *are* you, Granpa?'

'Death.'

'That your name?'

'No, it's my avocation. My name is Alucard.'

Holly was up on the formica-top counter, more cat than lizard in her claw-tipped paws, but with a red-green iguana frill around her neck and a crest rising under her thick-curled wig.

'Kill him, Lambchop,' she advised.

'I'm tryin' to do that little thing, Bloody Holly. Honest I am. But some nights, it gets real aggravatin'.'

'How did you like *Greta*, Mr Alucard?' asked Quentin, nerving back up to confidence. 'Most of my customers say it doesn't cut it stacked up against the first two *Ilsa* movies, but I'm an *auteurist*. I'll take even the lamest Jess Franco flick over any five Don Edmunds pictures you care to mention. Franco draws Dyanne Thorne out like no other filmmaker. The only other male director who can get anything like the same mileage from actresses across the talent spectrum is George Cukor. *Greta* is Franco's answer to *Heller in Pink Tights*.'

'We tryin' to have a face-off here, little man,' said Kit. 'Me and Granpa. It might improve your chances of long-term survival to keep your fuckin' yap zipped.'

Holly wound herself around Quentin, flicking a forked tongue at his goatee. The video clerk babbled himself silent.

'Better,' said Kit.

Alucard stood his ground. The Father was with him, was *inside* him. His mentacles extended, probing around the store. He latched onto Jack Martin –

Oh god oh man oh god oh man oh god oh man isn't that *John Alucard* oh god oh man I'm gonna *die* oh god oh man wonder if he's read the *American Zombie* treatment oh god maybe if we have to have survivor guilt counselling together I can bring the subject up oh god oh man who am I kidding I'm dead oh god oh man

– and withdrew sharply, then felt around the sub-sentient fudge of the guy on the floor who wasn't dead yet but was on the way out. From the mess of his mind, Alucard gathered he had been an attorney –

No one will goddamn care about this gurgle gurgle like Sarah said when she found out about Linda this country thinks there ought to be a bounty on lawyer pelts gurgle gurgle will I come *back* turned into a pale thing gurgle that might be

– and then he was dead, forever. He got a fix on Quentin, who was coping with the situation by recasting it with '70s exploitation actors –

I'm like a *Slaughter*-era Jim Brown coiled and ready to explode into ass-kicking action… Kit is Andy Robinson in *Dirty Harry* with maybe an overlay of Andrew Prine as the bald psycho in the TV movie *Mind Over Murder*… the girl is maybe Marlene Clark in *Night of the Cobra Woman* or Cheryl 'Rainbeaux' Smith in *The Other Cinderella*… and Mr Alucard stands there like Joe Don Baker playing Buford Pusser in the original *Walking Tall*, packing a baseball bat in his pants…

– and a soul soundtrack, Bobby Womack's 'Across 110th Street'. Alucard kept Quentin in mind, then wound his mentacles around the girl's head, sliding easily into Holly's engorged lizard brain and simply turning her off. He could have mindwiped her with a wink, but she might be worth saving for later. He gave Quentin a nudge and he took Holly's sudden weight, keeping her from falling off the counter. He picked up her floppy arm and laid a paw over his shoulder.

'So, you're Death. Or Alucard. That's what the geek called you, right?'

'It's a name.'

Kit pondered hard.

'There's something about it. A L U C A R D. Like a crossword puzzle or something.'

'Everyone says that, *Lambchop*. "Alucard" is "LaDacru" written inside-out.'

Kit didn't get it.

He had been shifting, replacing his lost weapon. His fangs, as impractical as the eleven-inch barrel Alucard still held, stretched his mouth, giving him Godfather jowls, ripping his lips. Triangular bone-thorns sprouted from his fingertips and knuckles, while scythe-spars slid from his elbows. Kit was a less natural shapeshifter than Holly. Each barb cost him effort and pain. He groaned and sweated blood.

'Die, Death,' growled Kit.

He was across the room with vampire quickness, hands about Alucard's throat, scythes at his sides. But his touch was gentle. Alucard saw puzzlement in Kit's eyes and nodded downward. Kit followed Alucard's eyeline and stood back.

The gun barrel was stuck into Kit's chest like a pipe. An inch or so projected from the front, dribbling blood. Kit twisted his neck and looked down at his back. The length of steel hadn't transfixed him entirely. Alucard heel-jammed the end of the barrel, knocking it flush with Kit's skin, pushing the ragged end through the other side.

Kit's heart poured out.

Alucard licked his palm. Kit's blood was polluted with snakebite. He took only a symbolic taste of the fallen vampire.

Shaking his head to clear it, Alucard let everyone go.

The Father thrilled through his blood.

Quentin, the girl still slumped over his shoulder, tore up a sheet of paper. 'You get free rentals here for all time, Mr Alucard. You're like the Fonz of this Arnold's, the Skipper of this *Minnow*.'

'That's kind of you,' he replied, handing over the paper sack of videos, which he had held all along.

Quentin looked inside. 'There's blood on 'em. Oh well, doesn't matter. What would you like this week?'

Alucard stepped over the shrunken scrawn that had been Kit Carruthers and considered the display of specials. The Video Archives had a name-themed double-bill offer: Stan Brakhage with Stan Laurel, Monty Python with Monte Hellman, Margaret Duras with Margaret O'Brien. None quite tickled his present fancy.

'I'll take Olivia Newton-John and Gene Kelly in *Xanadu*. Madonna and Sean Penn in *Shanghai Surprise*. And Mr Martin's last screen credit, which was, I believe, *Muff-Diving Miss Daisy*.'

Jack Martin was trying to express gratitude. He hoped Alucard would stick around while he fetched a screen treatment from his car. Maybe Ron Bass would be more amenable for the Dolly Parton thing.

'*Xanadu*,' said Quentin. 'That's the third time this year.'

'It's an important film.'

'No argument from me, Mr Alucard. From where I sit, Olivia was gypped out of Best Performance in a Musical or Comedy for *Two of a Kind*. I guarantee she'll be remembered as the Jean Arthur of the '90s.'

The kid lay the girl out on the counter and scouted around for the tapes – he remembered to shut the cash register, which Kit had made him open. The girl shed all her shapeshifts. A ropey mask of reptile skin hung off her face.

'Anything else?' asked Quentin. 'I've got in prime bootlegs of *My Living Doll* episodes which didn't make it to syndication. Julie Newmar is hot.'

'I'll take the girl.'

Quentin was surprised but not upset.

'Sure. You caught her, you keep her.'

Alucard slung the still-limp kitten over his shoulder and collected his rental videos.

'Explain things to the police, Quentin. I'm in something of a hurry. Meetings.'

'Right-a-rootie, Mr Alucard. Just one more thing...'

Quentin was reaching under the counter, for a script.

'I have to go. We'll talk next time.'

Martin was on his feet, still hyped that John Alucard knew who he was, but just starting to be afraid as well. He saw Quentin's script – some viper thing called *Bloody Pulp* – and reacted with instinctive territorial hostility.

'Tell Mr Martin about your project,' Alucard suggested.

Quentin's eyes flashed behind his shades and he turned to the screenwriter, prepared to unload a full-length reading on him.

Alucard carried his rentals and the vampire girl out of the video store, stepping around the broken glass on the sidewalk. He slid Holly into the passenger seat of the Camaro and restrained her with the seatbelt. She murmured. In sleep, Holly had now reverted to her original face, freckled and pretty under skag make-up and shed skin. Using her wig, he wiped dead stuff off her and then threw it in the gutter. Older than a new-born, but fatherless. She'd been wasted on Kit Carruthers. He would have Visser dig up background on the pair of them.

She woke up a few minutes later, as he hit the freeway.

'What's happening?' she asked. 'Who are you? What do you want? Where's Kit?'

'Carruthers is out of the picture, honey. I'm John Alucard.'

'What are you going to do to me?'

'I'm going to make you a star.'

'Cool.' She put her heels up on the dashboard. 'You got a radio here. I like to listen to music.'

He showed her how to turn it on. She spun the dial until she hit Cyndi Lauper. As they drove into the city, she sang along with 'Girls Just Want to Have Fun'. He didn't join in.

When the song was over, she turned off the radio.

'Now you sing, John Alucard.'

He thought a moment, and began 'Hooray for Hollywood'.

9

Her name was Holly Sargis Carruthers. She and her husband were poor white trash from the hills, turned by a wannabe den-master in 1959. They'd destroyed the elder fool and taken off on a spree. Kit and Holly were the vampires Middle America was afraid of. From nothing and with nothing. Childishly destructive and beyond reason. The couple on the run, on the road. Taking cars, cash and lives. In and out of institutions. In and out of each other's skulls. They'd stuck together because they knew no better. They had no get, which was a mercy.

Unlike Alucard, Holly had a reflection, of sorts, shimmering in and out of focus. An interesting effect.

Visser didn't understand why Alucard had taken Holly in.

'She'll turn on you one night,' he said.

Alucard looked across the moon-lounge at the girl curled up on the couch.

'I have no worries.'

'You're the master, Mr A.'

'Yes, Visser, I am.'

The private detective hadn't been to the estate before. His eye kept wandering to some detail. A painting or a bit of statuary. They didn't impress him as pleasing objects, but he had an idea what they must have cost. It was how he judged Holly too. In the long term, Visser thought the girl would be expensive.

'How are things with the parole board? Are we any closer to securing a ticket-of-leave for Mr Manson?'

Visser grinned.

'Three down, which gives us a majority. Two left.'

'It had better be unanimous.'

'The hold-outs won't be bought easy, but there are grey areas. Always are in their position. Either you keep someone innocent locked up or you let out someone horribly guilty. They can't win. One of our hold-outs gave Janos Skorzeny early release – setting him free to tear through that sorority house. He'll be tricky to persuade, but Manson not being a viper counts in our favour. The other hold-out has a daughter in Immortology. She'll switch her vote if we get her the kid back.'

'That can be done.'

'Thought so. Then, Charles Manson, America's most famous vampire hater, will be a free man for a limited window. You can even fix it to get him over to Europe, just so long as he's electronically tagged. All you have to do is persuade him to get up on a stage with a whole horde of vampires. There, I can't help you. We can get him all the smokes he wants, but he knows he's going back inside and not really coming out. Your Pale Anti-Defamation League types will ensure that.'

'I can swing them, too. Chapman has owed me big time since that breakfast food fiasco. It'll be a great occasion. And Manson is, before everything else, a frustrated performer. All he ever really wanted was an audience.'

Visser's eyebrows went up and down.

The duet of the Short Lion and Timmy V was still under negotiation, but Alucard had another team-up coup in mind to top the first half of the show. He envisioned Charles Manson and the pop singer Ralph Rockula standing side by side among columns of light and dark to belt out a catchy hymn to mutual amity between vampires and the warm. It was all very well to use the proven 'Imagine' for the finale, but for this he wanted a hit whose copyright rested with John Alucard Productions. Chained teams of songwriters were working for hire. He intended to add enough to the lyric – 'Pale and Tan, Man to Man… Warm and Cool, Golden Rule' – to personally get a credit and claim performance rights fees forever.

Visser left. His garlic whiff lingered.

'Don't like him,' said Holly.

'Few do,' Alucard confirmed.

'I like *Beverly*.'

'Leave her alone, Kitten. She's much too useful as she is.'

'Spoilsport.'

The girl was posing gauchely, letting her kimono fall open. She had tattoos around her arms and across her belly. Several were snakes winding about the name 'Kit'.

'Do we need those? Really?'

Holly was thoughtful. He projected himself into her mind again, feeding her his image of her future self, her final snakeskin, the girl in the spotlight.

'Guess not,' she said.

Her little face screwed up in concentration. Her tattoos dwindled and vanished.

'There now, that's better.'

She looked as if she was about to hiccough. She indicated that she needed a vessel. He gave her a seashell ashtray. She squirted a thin stream of blended inks into it. Holly's body control was remarkable. Alucard had noticed that straight off, when she changed. Kit used to call her his bendy toy. She was plastic fantastic – she could squeeze through a drainpipe or elongate across a room.

He took a handkerchief and wiped her chin.

'Nice Kitten.'

He'd decided to call her that for the moment. Kitten.

'Miaow,' she said, stretching. Her midriff thinned and her backbone popped up a few extra vertebrae. 'Thirsty.'

He was weaning her off warm blood.

She crawled against his chest and fussed with his shirt-buttons.

'Very well,' he said.

With a thumbnail, he drew a bloody line on his breast. Kitten lapped at his welling wound. He gave her just a taste.

When Kit died, he'd torn a part of her mind away. Over the years, they'd dribbled into each other, becoming halves of a single entity. It happened with evenly matched vampires, as opposed to the master-slave relationships elders cultivated with new-born get.

It was good that there was so much missing. Kitten was easier to teach.

Kitten liked Beverly because Alucard had his Renfield fetch a whole new wardrobe for her. The clothes she'd arrived in were impossible and the call-girl leftovers strewn around the mansion only a little more suitable. Beverly went up and down Rodeo Drive with his Platinum card, picking nice things from Maxfield and Madeleine Gallay, as if dressing a doll. Kitten now had outfits for every occasion, in various lengths to suit the shapes she could choose.

He put Kitten down on the couch. She dabbed her lips dry. After tasting him, she was quicker, smarter, more open. He was almost skull-walking her. He saw himself as she saw him, filling her world. Sharing the suppleness of her body, he experimentally doubled the length of his fingers, adding extra knuckles. It was just a trick. She had done the same thing, his thought sparking in her body.

'Teach me to fly, John.'

He was amused.

'Not yet, Kitten.'

'Pretty please.'

'You will fly. I promise.'

She mewed with pleasure.

10

Sometimes, it was as if Kitten had always lived at the castle. She knew she'd once gone by other names, but when she went back into her memory and found herself in a passenger seat, she'd turn to the driver and see only a blank face. Something had happened to her head. Stuff had been spilled. She didn't exactly miss what was gone, but was eager to fill the hole with something. When John let her taste his blood, she had all the answers. They rarely stuck in her mind, popping like bubbles after moments, but she was the better for her glimpses of truth.

This evening, they were receiving. Beverly helped her select a gown for the occasion, something elegant in black from

Versace. A golden mesh studded with pearls fitted over her crown like a hairnet, a single teardrop pearl dangling dead centre of her high forehead, matching her Spanish earrings.

Her hair was purged of the dyes and treatments that used to mar its silkiness. Her default colouring had gone from straw to gold. Even among vampires, chameleon hair was an unusual talent. It took concentration to wake the roots and force the new hue through all the tiny channels. But this kitten could change her spots. Under her pearl net, she wished for tiger stripes, streaks of velvet black and reddish blonde.

'Good girl,' said Beverly, surprised. 'If you could teach that, you'd make a million dollars.'

John's personal assistant was a warm, light-skinned black woman. She earned more than the last four generations of her family put together, but was still on the LA equivalent of starvation wages. Kitten was under orders not to touch, but knew Beverly was interested. The woman wondered what it would be like to give blood, to John or to Kitten. She'd stayed in the job longer than others because of that barely admitted fascination, but she was too handy a Renfield to waste.

Kitten stood, steady on four-inch heels. In the dressing-room mirror her Versace hung elegantly under the skull-shaped veil of pearls. Her face was there, too, from some angles. A watery transparent mask.

Beverly nodded approval.

'You'll kill 'em, Kitten. You really will.'

Kitten laughed the laugh John had taught her. It didn't mess up her face. Laughter should be like making music not breaking wind. A controlled flow, not an unconfined explosion.

'Kitten,' John's voice came from a speaker, 'you may join us now in the reception hall. Our guests await your pleasure.'

'Go on,' Beverly said, 'make an entrance.'

Kitten rid herself of nervousness. She knew John's friends were important, but she had a sense of her own importance to him. Nothing could threaten that.

Leaving Beverly in the dressing room, Kitten walked down a short corridor to the first-floor gallery and stepped into a spotlight. She looked down at a crowd. Conversation and sipping stopped as they saw her. Waiters and waitresses circulated with trays, bearing thimble-beakers filled with their own blood. The caterers John used guaranteed golden quality.

Kitten smiled.

John was near the main doorway with a woman in a man's evening suit – black tie and tailored tux, very tight black pants with a violet stripe down the side, glittering black pumps. John, in Astaire white tie and tails, transmitted encouragement to Kitten, his blood singing in her brain.

She drifted along the gallery, hand trailing the balustrade, and paused at the top of the steps, then descended, without a wobble, heels spiking red carpet, head high, shoulders back, chest out. Beverly had taught her that clothes were all about posture. A circle of men and women waited at the bottom of the stairs. John made his way through them.

'Kitten, how kind of you to appear,' said John.

She smiled and said nothing. He took her hand and she stepped off the bottom step as if alighting from a heavenly chariot to join the mortals on Earth.

'You must meet everybody,' said John, guiding her across the hall. 'Mr Feraru, of the Transylvania Movement, with his associates Mr Crainic and Mr Striescu. They have the confidence of Baron Meinster and stand high in the Romanian provisional government. Hamish Bond, of the British Secret Service. Allegedly retired. Be on your guard with him. He has a reputation with the ladies. Griffin Mill, from the studio. Griffin has just come in on *The Rock*, the project I was telling you about. We're very excited about the Eddy Poe rewrite. Mr William Gates, the entrepreneur who does clever things with computers. Captain Gardner, of the American Bat-Soldier Program. Warren Beatty and *la bella signorina* Ciccone. *Dick Tracy*, I have to say, kids, I think you can be very proud of the picture, though I also have to say we made the right decision to let it go to Disney. Mr Chapman, of the Pale Anti-Defamation League, who has done so much to gain acceptance for our kind. Thanks to his lobbying, General Mills were forced to withdraw their disgusting "Count Chocula" cereal from the warm market. Mr Edward

Exley, our estimable chief of police. If you've got a concealed cam-corder, don't mention it to him. Just kidding, Ed. Fine job on the post-King verdict clamp-down. Jack Nicholson, of course, devouring something from the live buffet. Crispian, who runs the Viper Room and other clubs too cutting-edge for us to have heard of yet. Sebastian Newcastle, a big wheel at CAA. He's agenting L. Keith Winton's twelve-volume *Kindred* saga. He used to be a nuclear physicist, but he's found a field where he can let off the really big bombs.'

Kitten kept track of them. John had briefed her on the guests. Almost all vampires. All important people in Los Angeles, and therefore the world. She knew who was in favour, who was here to be wooed, who was on the way out, who could be safely ignored. Of the movie folk, she knew the grosses on their last, second-to-last and, in almost certainty, next pictures. Of the political and business folk, she knew what they wanted and the likelihood of them getting it.

Oddly, the only person she hadn't been briefed on was the dark-haired woman in the tux. She squeezed a waiter's forearm, squirting blood-drops through a spigot into a shot-glass. John steered Kitten through the crowd towards her. She let the waiter go and reddened her mouth with a sip. She had a summer smile on her face but winter in her eyes.

'This is someone who'll be very close to you,' said John. 'Penelope Churchward, Lady Godalming. I've asked her to do me a kindness and become, well, I suppose we should say your mentor, but I hope most of all she will be your friend.'

The woman took a frosty look at Kitten.

Cleaned-up guttersnipe, but with possibilities. Very faint, but there all the same –

Kitten shut the woman's thought out, batting it back.

You can hear me, how divine! And you can touch me in here, too. You are a Project.

She shook her cold hand.

'Call me Penny,' said the woman. 'Ignore the rest of these *nouveaux*. They'll only talk about themselves and their money. You should be more interested in yourself. After all, they're finished and done and turned into what they wanted to be or need to pretend to be. You're still on the way. Never become a waxwork, my dear. That's my first lesson. Keep changing with the times.'

Penny was in her mind, just like John.

Like someone else had been. Someone she couldn't picture.

Forget that. We'll deal with it later.

'How do you like her? Will she do?'

Penny saluted John and said, 'She certainly will.'

Winter was still in the woman's eyes, shot through her heart and soul. But Kitten didn't take against her.

'Look around,' Penny whispered in her mind. 'Ignore the lightweights. The one-off murderers and the dream merchants. Who's dangerous?'

Everyone in the room had thought about fucking or killing – or fucking and killing – everyone else. Some were constructing elaborate fantasies of conquests, but she discarded most of them – they were the least likely to act out. Who were the real killers?

'Striescu, Bond, Gardner... Villanueva?'

'Newcastle, yes. Well done. You've missed only two.'

'Three. John, me, you.'

'You're flattering me.'

'No I'm not.'

Penny almost showed a real smile. Hamish Bond and Captain Gardner, ferocious but controlled, were fixed on her from across the room. Kitten could see the hooks she had in these trained killers.

'Maybe you aren't, at that,' Penny admitted.

Hamish Bond, supposedly squiring a tall black woman with snarly eyes, was now hungrily eyeing Penny *and* Kitten. He raised his glass. A lemon-curl floated in his bloody martini. Kitten saw a tumble of limbs and lips in his mind. Women in segments, dead eyes open, drifting by accompanied by guitar music, overlaid on one another, with guns and cars. Kitten didn't want to be in that movie. She blinked the kaleidoscope out of her head.

'Penelope will be the making of you,' said John.

'You'll make yourself. I'll just clean away the mess we don't need. The first thing to go will be that awful name. I bet a man gave it to you. Am I right or am I right?'

'You're not wrong,' said John.

Penny looked reproach at John Alucard, then had a moment of doubt before sticking to her guns. She was on probation, but could see, do and say things John could not. There was no point sucking up to him when he'd brought her in to complement his skills.

'What was your warm name, dear?'

Kitten concentrated, working around the gaps. 'Hazel?'

John shook his head. It came to her, through the fog.

'Holly,' she admitted.

John nodded.

'Couldn't be bettered,' said Penny. 'Beautiful, romantic, thorny, homey, bitter, cute. Not a saint's name. Pagan. Holly will do nicely for all concerned. No last name, I think. That was a good idea, John. Holly. Just Holly.'

Kitten was gone. She was Holly.

Fine. Holly was fine.

11

Alucard had called in favours from Chief Exley – whose fantasy was that if *Dragnet* were back on the air, the Rodney King burning would vanish from public consciousness – to have Griffith Park sealed off until after dawn. The Wild Hunt was not the real Zaroff deal, but a fund-raising excuse for a mock stalk and semi-orgiastic bleedings.

Many industry figures – not all of them vampires – were willing to cough up the ten-thousand-dollar entry fee to be let loose after a mixed band of warm starlets and overconfident stuntmen. The foxes were well-paid to lead the hounds in a satisfying chase with an innocuous finale. Eisner was out there with nightscope glasses and a crossbow, wondering if he could get away with sticking a sucker-tip arrow on Katzenberg 'by mistake'. Lajos Czuczron, Meinster's 'military attaché', intended to get away with murder and claim diplomatic immunity. Jean-Claude Van Damme was flying on drac-wings among the quarry, a three-picture deal depending on his 'surviving' the night. If any vagrants had slipped through the LAPD's park clearance operation, they were fair game.

From Bronson Canyon, one of his favourite spots in the city, Alucard commanded the park. In this powerful psycho-cultural nexus, John Wayne lifted Natalie Wood at the end of *The Searchers* and Kevin McCarthy kissed Dana Wynter in *Invasion of the Body Snatchers*. The space-helmeted gorilla of *Robot Monster* and the Venusian fanged turnip of *It Conquered the World* had lurked in the tunnel that was usually shot to look like a cave. The Batmobile roared out of it in that '60s comedy show which pretended Batman was a warm millionaire in a mask. Los Angeles was haunted by the movies shot here.

Media presence was concentrated around the Observatory from *Rebel Without a Cause*, where *Entertainment Tonight* were doing 'info-tainment' interviews with familiar faces. Alucard had lined up David Mamet to deliver a soundbite lecture on the noble kinship of hunter and prey, claiming one was never more alive than during a potentially fatal stalking even if you were technically dead. Mamet could dress it up more credibly than Robert Bly, and had enough screen credits for it not to seem like a joke. He might come in for a dialogue polish on Rafkin's rewrite of Rifkin's rewrite of *The Rock*.

Holly and Penny were in the undergrowth somewhere, operating independently. Penny said her pupil learned more refinement every night. She could be trusted to cover her tracks. The girl needed to feed often, having never tried to resist her red thirst, but was becoming more discriminating. From different ends, Exley and Visser had erased her from law enforcement databases. Records of the crime spree of the late Christopher Carruthers now listed Holly Sargis as hostage rather than accomplice. Of all people, Quentin from the Video Archives was putting together a script about the killer couple, spinning his survivor status into a first-look deal with Miramax. Jack Martin, slower off the mark to register a treatment, was shut out again. He'd be lucky to get a last-look deal with Troma. Alucard would not figure in any Kit Carruthers films; a fictional cop – Scott Glenn, Fred Ward, Alec Baldwin – would get credit for bringing down the killer and saving the girl.

Alucard knew the Romanians were coming long before he could see them. The Father cloaked his head and shoulders as if flowing from the cavern behind him. Dracula entered the tracery of nerves and veins in his face, sinking into his brain, pulsing through his entire body, penetrating and overlaying, informing and insinuating. Beyond the limits of his sharp night vision, Alucard tracked the movements of minds, as if he were simultaneously himself standing in a canyon and a great bat hovering above the park. By psychic echo-location, he knew the precise courses of dozens of creatures. Feraru and Crainic were slowly following the instructions they had been given. Their thought-tangles were beacons, blazing that blue light the Father associated with lost treasure.

If Alucard let Dracula grow within him, their shared mind would extend beyond the park, spreading throughout Los Angeles, in a sense becoming the city. They would build Transylvania in the desert by the sea, mentacles laid under boulevards like television cables.

Feraru was wondering whether Winona Ryder was old enough to be seeing anyone and what she'd look like with pearly little fangs. The new-born had been disappointed to learn that Jennifer Beals was spoken for. Crainic, more cautious, worried that they were being lured into a trap. Without Striescu, Crainic felt degrees less safe in this far foreign land – though the thug was ready to kill him at a nod from Meinster. It's just that Striescu wouldn't let anybody else ice the senior academician.

Someone screamed as a sucker dart stuck to them. Someone else whooped in victory. Crainic had been certain he was about to be destroyed, but it was just part of the game.

Striescu was back in Romania on urgent state business. On June 14th, Bucharest had been invaded by a mixed band of miners from the Jiu Valley and vampires from Bistritz. They came not to stage a coup but in support of the provisional government, who were taking criticism over the slow pace of reform and the way that odiously familiar faces from the Ceauşescu days kept popping up in their old positions. The mob, hardly unruly since it was effectively NCOd by ex-*Securitate* hardmen, destroyed the offices of the two main opposition factions, the Liberals and the Peasants' Party. On the streets, they collared and roughed up, or simply 'disappeared', many 'trouble-makers' – mostly students and journalists, with a few vampire-hating priests mixed in. President Iliescu appealed for calm and tried to distract his 'followers' with the progress of the national side in the soccer World Cup, but Baron Meinster had authorised a few tactical murders only a wet-worker of Striescu's skills could be trusted with. When the dust settled, the United *Nosferatu* Party would be in a stronger position to make territorial claims. Alucard's concert was a distant half-year away. In six months, the situation could change again and again and again.

The world paid little attention to Romania, distracted by the Gulf. Iraq had invaded and occupied oil-rich Kuwait and the tiny principality of Lugash. Saddam Hussein claimed to be acting under direct orders from Allah to depose the decadent vampire sheikhs who'd been bleeding the region dry for centuries. Whether Allah also told him to steal everything of value in both countries for himself was a question Saddam would not be drawn on. President Bush was rallying NATO and the UN in favour of counterattack. There was talk of US Bat-Soldiers being deployed for 'surgical strikes' against Baghdad. The whole sordid mess suited Alucard.

Feraru appeared first, Crainic huffing after him.

'Good evening,' Alucard spoke out of the darkness, surprising even the nyctlapts. He stepped from the shadow of the cavern mouth.

Feraru smiled, eager.

'My London people have got a commit from Cliff Richard to headline at Stonehenge. He's going to sing the Lord's Prayer backwards to the tune of "Mack the Knife". It'll be the Christmas Number One in the UK. And he'll make it a

TM charity record.'

Alucard now knew who Cliff Richard was. An eternally youthful vampire pop singer whose fame had never crossed running water.

Crainic said nothing. The elder was worried about the Old Country, troubled by methods used in the cause to which he was committed. Too many brutes who'd opposed the counter-revolution were transformed into its servants. Yet again, tyranny shapeshifted, absorbing those who stood against it. Crainic's thoughts of his homeland were overlaid by stamping boots, tearing teeth and thumping fists.

'We can't rely on others to give,' said Alucard, in Romanian. 'We have to take. This is the lesson.'

Crainic realised he was being addressed in his own language.

The Father was an armour around Alucard, the old wise mind shot through his get's brain. It was as if the conjuring had not been thwarted. At this moment, Alucard was the ghost and Dracula the physical presence. They were aspects of the same being.

'Who are you, John Alucard?' Crainic asked, in Romanian. 'Who are you really?'

The Father spoke. 'King of the Cats.'

Alucard felt Crainic's mind changing. Until now, embarrassed by Meinster's love of titles, he'd not understood the Baron's need to claim this particular meaningless distinction. Count Dracula had been the undisputed ruler of pale-kind, but the title expired with him and it was futile for the Baron or this Hollywood player to lay claim to it. To declare oneself King of the Cats was not to accede to Napoleon's throne but to claim to *be* Napoleon, a cartoon lunatic with a sideways hat and paw stuck in his institutional shirt. Now, Crainic knew better. Everything that had been Dracula's, physically and spiritually, was Alucard's by right. If *nosferatu* were to have Transylvania, this man – their father and furtherer – must be recognised.

Crainic went down on one knee and bowed his head, pulling off his student's cap.

'I acknowledge you, master,' he said. 'In death and life,

Count Dracula.'

The Father withdrew. Alucard was alone in his mind again, shocked clean. A point had been made.

Feraru, whose Romanian was basic, wasn't following this.

He had only seconds to think, anyway. Holly came out of the night and fell upon him. Two strokes of her nails and a mouth over the wound. No blood fell.

Crainic noticed his comrade being taken. He accepted what was happening.

Penny was with them, approving Holly's strike.

Feraru's money was committed, which was what mattered. He was just a walking wallet, for Meinster and the Movement, even for his own family. His consciousness, his body, was surplus.

As Holly sucked purposefully, Feraru's face shrivelled. His eyes opened wider, irises paling to transparency, thread-thin vessels emptying of red. The girl took more than blood from him. His hair bleached white. He was in shock.

'Crainic, you must trust me,' said Alucard. 'There is no Transylvania Movement, there is no Baron Meinster. It's all a sham. It's all so hideously small. But what we are – what we are doing – is important. It will win us not a province, but a world. I need to know you're with me.'

Alucard extended his hand. In the night, to the others' eyes, the ruby ring was black, but Alucard saw the bloody spark in its heart. He made Crainic see it too.

Crainic kissed the ring.

Holly stood, gore-smear on her face, eyes wide red. As the last of Feraru's blood rattled in her throat, her face shifted like a dissolve. Alucard looked at Holly, at the new face she was wearing.

INTERLUDE

MISS BALTIMORE CRABS

ANNO DRACULA 1990

1

———————◆———————

Two homicide detectives stood over a body. Number One Male, late teens/early twenties, five-nine. Black cloak with red trim, jeans, serious running shoes. Face down on the street. Scarlet spider-web radiating along cracks in the asphalt. The rank tang of dead blood at dawn. Cause of death: multiple GSW.

Murder? Yes – obviously. Yet, not her bailiwick… except technically.

At first lookover, Geneviève diagnosed a characteristic East Baltimore disagreement-over-the-sale-of-illicit-substances slaying. The crime scene: a come-down-in-the-world neighbourhood. Boarded-up row-houses. Sturdy Victorian homes for the well off, sub-divided a few Depressions back for the struggling poor. Now, shells for skells. Gang graffiti. Junked cars. A violently orange couch upended next to a dumpster. Thin crowd of kept-back-beyond-the-yellow-tape citizens. They'd have seen nothing.

Her blue windbreaker had OCME on the back in oversized yellow letters, in imitation of those FBI jackets worn to help limit the number of times when federal agents got accidentally shot by fellow law enforcement professionals. She went through a pair of Nike knock-off trainers a month. This gig regularly took her into alleys carpeted with bottle shrapnel and across floors sticky with undrinkable body fluids. She toted her forensic kit in a Gladstone bag she'd had since Gladstone was alive.

She had parked her cherry-red Plymouth Fury just behind the white van from the morgue. The car had been with her longer than most men in her life, and given her less grief. Blake and Grimes, her morgue attendants, were on the scene already, breakfasting on Pop-Tarts.

Walking from her car, she passed a lounger who eyeballed her from under a cowboy hat. Big white guy, out of state. Creepy. Then again, this was Creep Town.

Docs and cops were like aliens here. Real vamps were scarce on the drac corners. Plenty of dhamps hereabouts, though. That's what rattled her cobweb. Folks thinking hard about what she had in her veins, what it could do for them.

She bet Dracula hadn't seen that coming when he made his damn Declaration.

The cops looked up from the body.

'Gené Dee, Gené Dee, what have you got to say to me,' sung-chanted the light-skinned African-American detective who always wore a hat.

'*Ou se trouve l'assassin diabolique?*' asked the underfed Jewish detective who always attempted French *avec l'accent diabolique* when talking with her. He lowered his hipster shades to show her soulful comedy eyes.

There had to be something she'd not been told.

'What troubles the mighty murder police?' she asked.

She'd moved from Toronto to Baltimore at the specific request of the Office of the Chief Medical Examiner for Maryland. For some reason Crab Town got more than its share of gimmick killings. Rare moth cocoons in the gullets of preserved severed heads. Mad poets walling themselves up in tribute to Edgar Allan Poe. Giant crustacean attacks. Lately, there'd been a rash of vampire-related freak crimes. A hundred years after the Dracula Declaration, there were still few specialists in vampire medicine, let alone vampire forensics. Despite what had gone down in Los Angeles, she'd been headhunted back to the USA.

...but not to work routine drug shootings.

'True you busted Jack the Ripper?' asked the black detective.

'There was no Jack the Ripper,' said his partner. 'It was a Masonic conspiracy...'

'You don't know the half of it,' she said.

Sometimes – like now – she felt it was still 1888 and she was stuck in Whitechapel. This was another old, bad district. More open to the skies, less crowded – block after block of empty or seemingly empty houses – but the same stink. City jungle, predators and prey.

Then, she'd lived in the middle of the slum. This time, she was snug across town in a Federal Hill apartment, an easy walk from the morgue on Penn Street. Rents near the harbour were high, so she roomed with two other professional women. Lorie Bryer, an editorial contributor to the *Baltimore Sun*, was intelligent, reasonable and empathetic, which was probably why she got more hate mail than anyone else on the paper. Emma Zoole, an architectural model-maker, specialised in crime scene reconstructions used in court to walk juries through murders. Neither was a vampire, though Emma was a weekend dhamp. Geneviève was gently trying to persuade Lorie, whom she liked a lot, to ease Emma, a flake with a colourful love life, out of the flat. Geneviève spent enough on-the-job time at crime scenes without coming home to find a doll's house replica of the Tri-State Hooker Hacker's latest killing room on the kitchen table.

Mr Deceased had six holes in the back of his cloak. An unusual garment, but surely not why Geneviève was here. Dressing like a vampire – rather, like vampires were supposed to dress – didn't make you undead. It was arrant stereotyping, anyway. Unlike Emma Zoole, she didn't sleep in a white coffin and have a wardrobe full of shrouds.

'Meet Alonzo Fortunato,' said the black cop. 'Honour student. High school athlete. Once a.k.a. "Track" Fortunato. Gave up on gold and started peddling red. Got hisself a new street name. "Drak"…'

'Hence the *un*-fortunate Mr Fortunato's distinctive choice of attire,' put in the other detective. 'He was a walking billboard for his putrid product. The finest powdered *sang de vampire* in the city, *probablement*.'

Geneviève shuddered. The drac craze had followed her from Los Angeles to Toronto to here. It was still spreading.

KIM NEWMAN

According to DEA reports, the business of selling vampire blood in liquid or powdered form, in various degrees of purity or adulteration, started in New York in the late 1970s, a country away from where she'd been at the time. She still took it personally. Nico, someone she hadn't saved, was one of her personal ghosts. The vampire waif was an early casualty of the drac scene; not of the bleeding process – plenty of vampires bled to nothing to make red powder – but the whole bloody business.

She gave Alonzo Fortunato, today's victim, due consideration.

'Cause of death was a handgun, discharged repeatedly,' she said. 'You find owner of said gun, you solve case. Drak goes up on the board in black. Commendations all round. Now can I get back to my morgue? I have pressing whodunits…'

'Ah ah ah, not so fast, Dr Dee,' said the black detective. 'Come into the parlour…'

When shot, Fortunato had been running from a particular house. She back-tracked his likely trail up some steps to an open door. A uniform was stationed on the stoop.

The detectives ushered her inside. The stench was worse here.

Though the windows were boarded, the house was in use. Power was hooked up. Coats on a rack. She was directed into a reception room off the hallway.

Seven more dead people. Four males, two females, one whose sex would have to be determined at autopsy. Predominantly black. Comprehensively shot. Weirdly stretched, as if sculpted from warm wax. A still life with weapons, shell casings, drugs paraphernalia, blood spatter, death. Feathers from murdered cushions still floated like zephyrs on the summer breeze. A free-standing lamp had been felled, casting harsh film noir shadows.

Too many bodies for Blake and Grimes to get into the van for a single run. They'd need back-up. Admin had been on at her about the expense of additional journeys in city vehicles. If they got their way, corpses would be stacked like firewood and moved like furniture.

'Welcome to the war zone,' said the Jewish detective.

'Savour one of the city's happiest traditions: the yo-on-yo firefight and general massacre… Time to sort out who shot who in what order.'

'I don't think so,' said Geneviève, gingerly moving around the room, trying not to step in or brush against anything that might be mentioned in court. 'The limp on-the-couches positions of the bodies indicate a leisurely moment of communal relaxation interrupted by an armed visitor or visitors who unloaded before this krewe could respond. See: all the bullet holes are on that side of the room, away from the hall door. Note firearms still in waistbands, pockets or on side tables. At a guess, Fortunato was upstairs sleeping or in the can at the time of the surprise visit. He made a vain attempt to use his track skills to get away. Unless they bumped a head on a lintel, your doer or doers probably got in and out without sustaining a scratch. This was a murder raid.'

The black detective thumped his partner's arm with a told-you-so grin.

'I still don't understand why you asked for me,' Geneviève said.

'Coupla things… the teeth, the claws, the eyes.'

She had noticed what the detectives meant. She'd need them naked on a table under a good light to be sure, but the corpses all looked dhamp. Sharpened teeth and nails. Bleeding gums and cuticles which weren't yet accustomed to popping fangs or talons. One had an elongated neck, which could have been congenital. Again, this wasn't too surprising. Drac was the drug flavour of the new decade. Cocaine cartels and poppy growers were hurting.

'No, no, no,' she said. 'A drac angle doesn't make this vampire related. I'll have Scheiner briefed when these bodies come in…'

'These bodies?' said the Jewish detective. 'You thought we'd called you to look at *these* bodies? Oh, no no no… wrong end of the stick, meet Geneviève Dieudonné. If you'll kindly step this way, through the beaded curtain charmingly redolent of the summer of love, you shall find the reason you and only you are the ME for this…'

He held the curtain aside.

Geneviève passed through and into the next room – a kitchen.

Only one dead person was here, a very fat man in very tight scarlet underwear. Most of the back of his head missing.

GSW, again. Nothing unusual.

Light was low, but something glittered on the linoleum. An antique carved box lay upside-down, lid open. Small white objects scattered.

'Are them what we think them is?' asked the black detective.

Geneviève opened her bag and found the proper implement. She crouched and picked up one of the objects with a large pair of tweezers.

It was a fang. A vampire tooth.

2

There were thirty-eight fangs, presumably not all from one victim – though, since vampire teeth grew back if pulled or broken, it was just conceivable they'd sprouted from the same jaw. Incisors, canines, biters. No molars. A couple were grossly oversized specimens – three-inch tusks. One had a black diamond set in it.

'Another Poe killing?' she asked.

Staging murders in imitation of the tales of Edgar Allan Poe was an odd fad which had caught on lately, especially in Baltimore. In 1849, Poe had died here during a ballot-stuffing bender and been buried (by a nasty irony, prematurely) in a churchyard on West Fayette Street. A headstone still stood and someone's bones lay under it. The poet was supposedly exhumed and reburied in 1875 and Walt Whitman (who attended the ceremony) claimed he recognised Eddy by the distinctive forehead of his skull. Whitman was mistaken. Another unknown egghead lay in the grave. Poe was still around as a vampire, squirming on *Oprah* or *The Jerry Langford*

Show whenever another ardent fan sicced an orang-outang on his girlfriend's mother or rigged up a basement pendulum to bisect a vacuum-cleaner salesman.

The black detective looked blank.

'"Berenice",' said his partner. 'In that *conte cruel*, first published in the *Southern Literary Messenger* in 1835, the perverted perp Egaeus keeps his cataleptic cousin Berenice's gnashers in a box, much like the one these spilled out of.'

'And the body outside,' said Geneviève. 'His name was Fortunato…'

'Just like the victim in "The Cask of Amontillado". Probable coincidence. Poe killers usually go the whole hop-frog. Wall up their Fortunatos and Madelines… hearts under the floorboards… plague bacillus spread through the prom. They all have pet ravens or one-eyed cats. I can't recall a Tale of Mystery and Imagination in which a melancholy protagonist muses on the loss of a pale young woman and opens up with an Uzi to ventilate a roomful of sleazoid drac-heads. Of course, I've not kept up with the latterday *oeuvre*.'

'None of the Poe killers count the recent books,' she said.

'I like Ed McBain,' said the black cop. 'No hump ever kills another hump because he read an 87th Precinct paperback.'

Geneviève stood. She had an urge to collect the fangs and put them back in the box. The crime scene needed to be undisturbed a while longer.

'Edgar Allan Poe is a special case,' she said. 'A vampire writer.'

She'd seen Poe from across the room a couple of times, when they both had an Italian period. He'd been there in 1959, the night Dracula was killed. They'd not actually met, but she had followed his career.

A few years ago, Alexandra Forrest, a New York editor, sunk her claws into the author and struck a deal for a series of saga-length sequels to his most famous works. *The Usher Syndrome, The Dupin Tapes, The Valdemar Validation, The Pym Particles.* Poe blew the advance on 'golden' – high-quality human blood Geneviève could seldom afford on her salary – and a tabloid sensation marriage to a warm groupie who

---

turned out to be thirteen years old, then failed to deliver. Forrest, it was rumoured, did something terrible to Poe's cat. The books eventually came out with Poe's notorious name huge across the covers and tiny footnotes about less-regarded co-authors. Jack Martin, her one-time Hollywood source, was the actual writer of *The Mentzengerstein Factor*. He was also the 'as told to' on the title page of freshly annulled Lydia Deetz Poe's tell-all memoir *Eddy Dearest*, which Geneviève, guiltily, had relished. Now, there was a film out, with a starved-to-a-skeleton Dennis Quaid and black lace-wreathed Winona Ryder.

Poe was in Hollywood too, working for John Alucard. All monsters together. She had a pang at that, reminded of her exile. It had been ten years. She could probably go back. She was, after all, a government employee now. Still, what was there in Los Angeles for her?

'Who's the tooth-collector?' she asked. 'He isn't called anything like Benny Egaeus, is he?'

'No, worse luck,' said the well-read detective. 'Though his name is a literary reference, intentional or not. The rotund, scatter-brained gent is Wilkie Collins, rising captain in the Barksdale organisation. Risen as far as he can, now. Fallen, too.'

'This is a Barksdale house?' she asked.

'Yes, indeed. The Avis of Baltimore drug-dealing concerns. They try harder, because they're number two…'

'Which means your prime suspect is Number One…'

'…with a bullet,' said the black detective. 'Luther Mahoney.'

'Charm City's own Kingpin of Krime-with-a-K,' said his partner. 'The Napoleon of Narcotics… the Diocletian of Drac… There never was a cat of such deceitfulness and suavity…'

'Not that he pulled the trigger. Too busy shooting hoops with the Mayor at a rally for underprivileged youth. This bloodbath is absogoddamnlutely Mahoney, but we ain't gonna put it on Luther. He be the Untouchable Man.'

Geneviève understood from Dan Hanson – Lorie's on-off boyfriend, a crime reporter – that the Mahoney organisation was Baltimore's outstanding supplier of drac, crack and smack. Dan said they probably also dealt in horse, whores and s'mores. If Mahoney let competition stay in business, it was because scrabbling for small change was beneath him. Recently, Barksdale, another family concern, had made aggressive moves into the market, absorbing a succession of Mom and Pop drug dealerships into a loose affiliation. This sort of shift in the city's criminal geopolitics entailed bodies getting dropped. Mahoney was big on endowing community centres, free clinics, playgrounds and cultural events with some of his cash backwash, but he really ought to bestow an additional wing to the city morgue.

Mahoney wasn't a vampire. But he had vampires on his krewe.

If anyone pulled their fangs, he'd be pissed.

Rumour had it that Luther Mahoney was seven feet tall, an African-American albino, an avatar of Baron Samedi. Dan said he was just a smarter-than-average, smugger-than-hell regular gangster. Besides an office building and a palace on the harbour, Mahoney owned a bank on Grand Cayman, a fleet of limousines, a private jet, some major Modiglianis, the bones of Mighty Joe Young and a great deal of Fells Point real estate.

A uniform, Turner, came into the kitchen. She was tall, trim, short haired – the sort of look seen more often on the cover of work-out videos than at squad room roll-call. Both detectives straightened up when Turner was around, but she was all work.

'You'll want to see the basement,' she announced.

The detectives looked at each other. Turner wasn't saying any more.

While Geneviève had been yakking with homicide, uniforms and CSI had been going through the house. Burke and Grimes were still waiting to get the meat in the wagon and back to the morgue.

'Any more bodies?' she asked.

'Not exactly…' said Turner.

'Bodes ill.'

There was a classic door-under-the-stairs basement entrance. A set of rickety wooden steps led into the darkness.

She trusted they weren't going to find a mummified Moms Barksdale down there.

Geneviève let the detectives go first. They had to do their job before she could start hers. If she even had a job here.

For some reason she didn't want to think about, her fangs had inched out and were sharp in her mouth.

Of course it smelled bad in the cellar.

Flashlight beams played across coils of rusty wire, old bicycles, bundles of the *Sun*, a shopping trolley full of looted copper pipes. A headless torso provided a momentary scare. It was a wasp-waisted dressmaker's dummy.

Turner showed them a path through the treacherous piles of oddments.

The rear of the basement was where Poe killers liked to put up their new walls. Here, there was a separate room.

'Hello,' she said. 'Serious security.'

The door was open, but it had several locks, some shiny and new.

'A stash?' she ventured.

Turner shrugged.

'Let me guess,' ventured the black detective, 'the goods is gone…'

'So this was more than a murder raid,' said Geneviève. 'A heist?'

'Look inside and draw conclusions…'

The windowless room was lit by fluorescent tubes in wire-mesh cages. Scatter-cushions on the concrete floor, stained with newish and oldish blood. A sink, half full of rusty water.

She knew from the smell that someone had been living here.

A chain ran from bolts in the wall to a shiny shackle. It had been sheared through. Still-slick blood glistened on the links.

Someone had been *kept* here.

'That silver?' asked the black detective.

'Looks like…' said Geneviève.

She touched the metal as lightly as possible with the pad of her little finger, and pulled back as if she'd pressed against a hot stove.

'…and is, *ouch*. Silver.'

A vampire had been imprisoned here.

Silver was too soft and pricey to chain the warm, but handy for anyone who wanted to add a vampire to their collection. Sporting goods stores sold silver fishnets, barbed wire, man-traps and bullets for 'home protection'. Such transactions were protected under the second amendment. God bless America. Many more wooden pickets were sold than there were picket fences, too.

'Whoever the Barksdales' unwilling anchorite was, they're in the wind now…' said the Jewish detective.

'Or someone else has them in another basement,' she said.

She looked about the small room for traces of the occupant. Above the sink was a lighter patch of plaster where a mirror had been bolted. A corner still attached showed that it had been smashed. Thumbtacked up were magazine photographs of nude black women with huge afros and defiant stares. A psychedelic astrological chart included unfamiliar houses like Dentalium, Hirudo and Ophiuchus. Hirudo (the leech) was a recent zodiac adoption, the star sign of the vampire.

A Dansette gramophone was plugged in. On the turntable was 'Supernatural Voodoo Woman (Does Her Thing at Night)' by The Originals. A selection of super 70s soul singles was stored in a toast rack.

The detectives found a pile of fifteen-year-old *Playboy* magazines and went straight to the centrefolds. The nudes' necks had been scribbled and scratched…

'Perhaps *not* purchased for the enlightening interview with Kurt Vonnegut or the darkly witty cartoons of Gahan Wilson,' commented the Jewish detective.

The decor, magazines and music suggested the Barksdales wanted to at least try to keep their captive entertained. The pin-ups implied he was a he. The bloodstains indicated he'd been fed or bled. Probably both.

Geneviève took latex gloves out of her bag. She would have preferred a spacesuit to examine this crime scene.

It wasn't just the filth; it was the concept. This room was a cell, not a lair. She felt the prisoner's rage and despair…

...presumably alleviated by the rescue or escape, but lingering still.

In the unlikely event of this ever coming to trial, Emma Zoole might have to make a model of this basement, with miniature chain and toy furniture. The space shrank around her, walls closing in like Poe's pit, ceiling lowering. She wanted out of the cell, the basement, the house, but there was more to see.

'Here,' said Turner, nudging a cushion aside with a boot.

A pudgy rag-doll – brown with scarlet trunks – lay face down, with a rusty nail stuck through the back of its head.

'Remind you of anyone?' Geneviève asked.

3

She didn't get out of the row-house until afternoon.

This was a case where she was required as a vampire rather than for forensic insight. Blake and Grimes had made a start on removing the bodies. At the morgue, others could probe them for usable-in-court bullets. Geneviève had to hang around and give the cops the undead angle.

At interview, OCME had specified this would be part of her remit. She'd been too bemused by the notion of characterising herself as an expert to quibble. She'd lost count of the agencies and institutions – FBI, ATF, CTU, NSA, BPRD, Johns Hopkins, the Baltimore State Hospital for the Criminally Insane – she was theoretically on call for, though only BPRD made regular use of her supposed specialist knowledge. She wondered if the Diogenes Club was still in business. They had used her in a similar fashion, not always happily. Last she'd heard, Mrs Thatcher was trying to sell off the building in Pall Mall and shift the Club's functions to paper shufflers in Cardiff. Where once Mycroft Holmes stood in for the British government, there might soon be yuppie flats.

On the whole, vampire crime in the USA was much the same as ordinary crime – just with fangs. Bank robbery, with fangs. Car theft, with fangs. Jaywalking, with fangs. Aside from the specific felony of criminal assault with the intent to consume human blood, which was rarer than the tabloids said, American vampires were statistically less likely to commit most crimes – including murder – than the warm. Courts were handing down 500-year sentences to penalise the long lived, which threw up new problems for penitentiaries. Lethal injection of a solution of silver sulphate, a ghastly way to go, was the preferred method of vampire execution in death penalty states.

The factor which threw everything out was drac.

The drug itself was only marginally illegal – how could you legislate against a substance derived from organic matter freely flowing in the veins of law-abiding *nosferatu*? Statutes against organ snatching and private sale of body parts were extended to cover the sale of vampire blood to the warm, though they were seldom invoked if the transaction was the other way around. A tax-paying, Congress-lobbying catering industry, dependent on supplying vampires, wanted no part of this mess.

It was impossible to stay in the drac trade without breaking a dozen state and federal laws a day, but cases against drac lords were even trickier to bring than cases against regular drug cartels. There were task forces all over the place, but few big successes in the War on Drac. Nancy Reagan's 'Just Say Yuck' campaign was the punchline of too many red-eyed dhamp stand-up routines.

Geneviève almost missed the innocent days of pale poets quaffing absinthe or hippies tripping on Bowles-Ottery ergot.

It also creeped her out – and she was well aware of the irony – that drac-heads wanted to get into her veins. This wasn't just in the 'hoods, but everywhere. They didn't want to turn, but they wanted to try…

She had to worry about what Emma Zoole might do if her dealer didn't come through while Geneviève was helpless in her monthly state of lassitude. If a little cut healed by the time she woke up, would she even know?

A swelling minority argument wanted to legalise, regulate and tax drac.

She couldn't tell the detectives much they hadn't worked out for themselves. But she stood on the stoop, looking down at the body-tape outline that showed where Fortunato had fallen, and ran it through for them, anyway…

'Besides whatever kick it is dhamps get out of being vampires for a few hours, the appeal of drac to your traditional drug dealer is ease of supply. It doesn't have to be muled in from Burma or Colombia. You just need a vampire. Either a willing, paid donor or, as the shackle suggests was the case here, a patsy snatched off the street and milked. Drac production isn't quite as simple as squeezing a vein into a baggie. The powdered form common on the street is vampire blood, usually cut with human or animal matter, exposed to sunlight until it granulates. You can leave it out all day to congeal and dry, at the risk of losing a lot of red to evaporation, or you can repurpose the grow lamps you bought when you were raising marijuana to hurry things along.'

In a room with polythene sheeting on the walls and floor, trays of drac were processed this way. Here, Barksdale red was measured into foil triangles. That location turned up more dead soldiers – two middle-aged Hispanic women and a pre-*quinceañera* girl, huddled together. For work, they were stripped to bra and panties accessorised with surgeon's masks, shower-caps and disposable gloves. They'd been unsentimentally plugged, execution-style. More haulage for Blake and Grimes.

On the street, Barksdale drac was sold as 'Fright Night'; the foil wraps had little bat stickers to identify the brand. Mahoney's double-star baggies were known as 'Near Dark' in the projects or 'Once Bitten' in uptown night-spots. Other common North-Eastern drac varieties were 'Vamp', 'Monster Squad' and 'Lifeforce'. Out of New York came 'Innocent Blood', 'Habit', 'Addiction' and 'Nadja'. Along the Tex-Mex border, a strain called 'Cronos' was popular. An especially lethal drac known as 'Black Lodge' or 'Killer Bob' was spreading from Canada down into Washington State.

California had 'Hellmouth', 'Embraced' and 'Lost Boy'.
Back in Toronto, dhamp-scene murgatroyds snorted or shot
'Forever', 'Night Inside' and 'Amarantha'. A lot of crap was
talked about bloodlines and purity of sources; it was all the
same poison.

Geneviève would never know what a drac hit felt like –
it didn't work on vampires. Then again, it didn't need to.
Vampires had their own, exclusive high. Every night of the
week. The thickness of skin away.

'With demand ever on the increase, drac outfits need
multiple vampires in chains or on staff. They get used up
rapidly, unless handled with great care. If you want me to
take a wild guess at what happened here, I'd say one drac
concern had hit on a prime source of red, and another has
moved swiftly to acquire the asset. This wasn't a rescue, this
was a snatch and grab. The murders were incidental. Or just
to leave the trademark. This many dead drac dealers is like a
double star on the bag. You know who…'

The detectives did.

'What about the voodoo hoodoo?' asked the black cop.

Geneviève had been thinking about the makeshift doll.

'Chalk that up to an uncanny coincidence. You don't really
believe shoving a rusty nail through the back of the head of a
doll in the likeness of Wilkie Collins could actually cause his
brains to burst through a gunshot-like hole in his skull?'

'I believe you can turn into *un chauve-souris enorme*,' said the
Jewish detective.

'Well, more fool you because I can't.'

She tried flapping her arms.

'Any ideas as to the identity of our formerly cooped-up
fount of all things *rouge* and rotten? Connoisseur of soul and
smut?' he asked.

She shook her head.

'Take a look through the missing persons files and flag the
vampires. Though we're a cagey, elusive lot. We disappear
frequently and our vanishing acts can easily go unreported.
It's as if no one misses us, officers. How can that be?'

The cops shrugged, as one.

Her beeper went off.

'That's me,' she said. 'Another call on the Medical Examiner signal. So I'm into the ME-mobile and away to fight more dastardly crime. Tell me how this works out, if it works out.'

She left them and found her car. The Plymouth still had its hubcaps and was free of gang tags, scratches, bullet holes and piles of human ordure. There was a fresh blood pool in the gutter, though. She unhooked a recently severed human finger from the radiator grille and left it on the sidewalk. If reclaimed, it could probably be reattached.

Like voodoo, her car's self-protection system was something she didn't think about too much.

4

If this evening was a fair representation of what was on offer through the dating section of the *Sun*'s personal columns, Geneviève would look for another way of meeting eligible men who weren't dead on a table.

Her date was a reasonable-looking, divorced guide-book writer who spoke in a monotone about his ex-wife, his ex-girlfriend and his ex-dog. He dissected his crabs the way she autopsied corpses. She started on golden and moved to pig's blood, remembering they'd agreed to split the bill. Towards the end of the meal, he began fiddling with the button under his tie-knot. A 'bite me bite me' tell.

She tuned out when he left off his former dependents to deliver a lecture about 'travel-size packets'. Normally, when her shift was over, she could forget what she saw on the job... today, she kept flashing back to the Barksdale basement. She knew her priorities were wrong – by any objective standards, the needless murder of the women in the processing room was the worst horror of the house – but that silver chain and the tiny, strip-lit space haunted her.

Her date didn't notice she'd drifted away.

His top button was undone now. His pulses were strong, but she had a notion that his blood would be milky. The *aperitif* hits of golden had given her a warm glow, which the pig's blood cocktail turned into a savage, needy burn of desire. Not for this man, though.

She'd rather bite his dog.

At that thought, she giggled – inappropriate to his point about favouring shaving gel over foam – and he was offended.

His Adam's apple showed.

She looked at the neatly cracked, sliced and prised-apart crab exoskeleton on his plate.

In her reverie, she found herself in the Ten Bells in Whitechapel in 1888, at a table with Charles. They were talking about the murders.

'It's been nearly a month, Charles,' she ventured, 'since the "double event". Perhaps it's over?'

'No,' he said. 'Good things come to an end, bad things have to be stopped.'

Damn, he was right. Always.

And he was gone, not even a ghost…

The present faded back up and her date was talking at her. Like most Americans, he called her Genevieve.

Every time he used her name, which he did unnaturally often, it sounded odder to her, more grating…

At nine-thirty, Lorie – who was responsible for directing Geneviève to the *Sun*'s personals in the first place – would call her beeper. They had agreed on a cut-off point. If the evening was worth pursuing, Geneviève could tell her date it was a wrong number and carry on. If not, she could claim to be summoned to a bloodbath on the other side of town. Door number two was the current favourite.

Her big wrist watch was for work, so she wasn't wearing it. She couldn't see the restaurant clock from where she was sitting.

He was talking about shampoo and conditioner. Time stood still.

Prison was boring. As mind numbing as this. She'd been

imprisoned in her time. In dungeons, convents, an eighteenth-century zoo. In well-appointed apartments and shacks. She had mostly shut down and tried to stay calm, secure that she could outlive confinement, waiting for the walls to fall down or her captors to age and die. She had been forgotten in *oubliettes*. Before the Dracula Declaration, that was easier than it would be now. Then, few had believed what she was.

She didn't know what she'd do if she were captured and held nowadays.

If what went on in the Barksdale basement was now a thing, she must at least work out contingency plans. It could happen to any vampire.

Cut-off time must have come and gone. McCormick & Schmick's Steak and Seafood was emptying out.

Lorie must have got distracted by a deadline, an argument with Dan or one of Emma's loser guy crises. Geneviève would make her pay for that.

At last, *beep beep beep*.

She didn't even bother with an excuse, just collected her coat and left. She threw down her half of the bill – worked out to the cent in her mind, as an exercise – to avoid any obligation. There would not be a second date.

'I have your number,' she said.

When, for convention's sake, she checked her beeper, she didn't recognise the number. Odd. Lorie should have been calling from the apartment. As part of the escape routine, she made a beeline for the restaurant's bank of payphones. She had planned to call Lorie and vent.

A large, rumpled man hogged one of the phones. He was in the habit of eating too much garlic. She took the kiosk furthest from him.

She fished a quarter out of her purse and dialled the number. It rang for a long time. Then was picked up.

Silence. Except for breathing. Not Lorie's.

'Doctor Dee,' she identified herself.

'Listen to me, Doctor Dee,' responded a voice she didn't know – male, loud. 'I got your gal pal here. A clean snatch. She ain't been punctured, so far. But things can change, baby. In a flash. You come see me, sister, and we can rap. You don't come, consequences there be, you dig?'

A frightened squeal, curtailed.

'Picture in focus, doll?'

'Yes.'

'There's a diner on Reistertown and Rogers. It's open late… we be waitin'. I strongly recommend you make good time…'

5

She had walked to the restaurant from her apartment and her car was parked at the morgue anyway. So Geneviève took a cab to Northwest Baltimore.

The intersection of Reistertown Road and Rogers Avenue was in Woodmere. Once predominantly Jewish, now middle-class black. Few bodies dropped suspiciously in this neighbourhood, so she hadn't been here often.

The diner was easy to find. It was an Americana postcard, an aluminium-sided '50s relic. The boxcar-shaped building supported a huge orange neon sign which just said 'Diner'.

The windows were steamed up, but she could see people-like shapes inside.

She had the cab cruise by and drop her three blocks up.

For her date, she was wearing her good black dress, heels and one of Lorie's puffy-shouldered jackets.

She took off her shoes and put them in her bag, then put her purse and ID in an inside jacket pocket.

She owned a gun, a habit from her private detective nights. It was locked safely in her desk at the morgue.

Walking the three blocks, cold sidewalk under her soles, she felt her hackles rise. She salivated as her fangs slid from gumsheaths. Her nails elongated and curved.

No one could mistake what she was.

People – not that there were many around – got out of her way.

She hid her bag behind a potted shrub in the diner's parking lot. The only vehicles here were a Cadillac pimpmobile, a beat-up Ford truck and a rusty black van with 'Mondo Trasho' written on it in lipstick pink. A late-in-the-day punk band? Some freak subculture she'd not come across yet?

She half-expected to be shot with silver as soon as she barged through the diner door. Instead, she got a slow handclap.

Sat at a table waiting for her was a smiling African-American vampire with a helmet of conked hair like James Brown's, and fur on his cheeks and the backs of his hands. He wore tartan flares over yellow stack-heeled boots, a wide-lapelled jacket with a zigzag pattern in mauve and electric green and matching coat-hanger-shaped tie, plus wraparound mirror shades. His clock had stopped in 1973, which – at a guess – was when he turned. If they didn't go the murgatroyd route with black capes or gauze shrouds, twentieth-century vampires tended to dress the way they had when they died.

She remembered the toast rack of soul records and knew who this was. He seemed to be enjoying his freedom.

The other people in the diner were dhamps, not vamps. A gaggle of flaming creatures: a 400-pound man with a cockatoo mohawk, squeezed into a frilly scarlet ball gown; a mad-eyed old woman, toothless but for temporary fangs, in a ragged nightie; a cadaverous, long-haired white dude with purple moustaches and bullet holes in his sports jacket; a beehive-do blonde sweater girl with a sardonicus smile; an emaciated punker, trussed up in bondage trousers and a ripped Ramones T-shirt. This must be the Mondo Trasho gang.

They were mostly crammed into a booth, surrounding a terrified Emma Zoole.

Geneviève was tempted to say 'wrong roommate' and leave… But she couldn't let Emma take the heat for her and, worse, she had this nagging itch to find out what the hell this was all about.

She could blame Charles for inculcating in her a need to know.

Emma wasn't dhamped. She kept her head down.

'Doctor Dee, Doctor Dee,' said the soul vampire.

'You have a name too?'

'Willis, baby. Willis Daniels.'

He left a pause for it to sink in.

She had never heard of him, so she couldn't give him the 'we meet at last' response he clearly craved.

'Mamuwalde's get,' he elucidated.

Prince Mamuwalde was an African vampire. Not a cat to be invoked carelessly. Geneviève had met him and been impressed.

She suspected this son-in-darkness was not a credit to the Prince.

'*Salaam Alaikum*,' she said.

Willis tittered, showing a long right fang and a short left one.

'Peace on you too, sister,' he said. 'Now set your bootie down and let's get to talkin' business...'

She slid onto the red-upholstered chair opposite him.

Everything in the diner was cherry-red or silver-chrome, and bolted to the floor. A giant jukebox bore the smiling, faded face of Corny Collins, whose 1960s music show still played late at night or early in the morning on local television. Corny promised 'All the teen beat hits to set your toes tappin' and your fingers snappin'!'

The juke played Gene Pitney's 'Town Without Pity'. A tragic wail of a song.

A blood splatter arced on the wall behind the counter. This krewe had taken out the staff. One of the Mondo Trasho dhampires – a disco punk with roller-skates and an orange crinkly headband – had an unconscious waitress in his lap and was nuzzling her neck with teeth not sharp enough to puncture a vein.

She had no reflection in Willis's shades, but saw the purple-moustache guy moving to block the door she'd come through. He put up the closed sign. A tall, warm, black woman with angry eyes and a leopard-print outfit sat on a stool at the far end of the diner. She was straight, not flying on drac-wings, and had a Glock 9mm on the counter. Geneviève took the Leopard Lady for the most dangerous person in the room...

No, she told herself, *second* most dangerous person in the room. She hadn't lasted since 1416 by being a pussycat.

Emma, the connoisseur of terror, was not enjoying this. She was morbid, but no masochist.

Geneviève tried not to show her fangs.

Willis dipped a long forefinger in a spill of sugar from the table dispenser and drew a smiley face. He licked sugar off his finger.

'I have your missing tooth,' she said. 'At the morgue.'

He shrugged. 'It's growin' out, sweet cheeks.'

'Don't you want the diamond?'

'Easy to come by.'

'For some.'

'You an' me, girl. We don't have to try so hard, do we? What do they call it — power of fascination? The oogada-boogada? The Charm.'

He made hypnotic gestures.

'Slap the Charm on a person, make 'em do what you want. A trip and a half, Doc. Open up the cash register... open up a wrist. Hah, bein' unborn is the best thing ever happened to Mrs Daniels' boy, and that's the truth.'

'What *are* you talking about, Willis?' she asked.

He was flustered for a moment, suspicious, prickly. He liked to be taken seriously. He was fundamentally insecure.

In street terms, he was just Blacula's bitch.

Which did not make him any less dangerous.

If it came down to *Die Hard in a Diner*, she could take Willis. She could even deal with the dhamps. But Emma would be killed. The waitress, too. If the Leopard Lady was packing silver bullets, and she had no reason to think she wasn't, Geneviève wouldn't make it either. At her age, she'd go to dust — some dhamps snorted *that*! — which would spare Blake and Grimes the embarrassment of hauling their boss to the morgue.

Emma whimpered. The big Mondo Trasho transvestite stuck a long tongue in her ear. The hag cackled.

'Emma,' Geneviève said, 'don't worry. They can't hurt you.'

'Oh I think they most surely purely can,' said Willis.

'Not if you want to keep talking with me.'

He held up his be-ringed, hairy hands and made a Stepin Fetchit I's-so-scared face, then chuckled.

'The Charm, you know,' he continued. 'It come natural to me. Not from bein' a vampire and shit, but from birth. Mrs Daniels was mama-loi from the islands. She never turned, but she had the Charm. S'what voodoo's all about. Makin' puppets of people...'

'Puppets of people,' Geneviève echoed.

Willis let his grin widen. She intuited he'd practised that so his diamond would glisten. It was wasted now.

'In that basement, someone put you on strings, Willis.'

'Mr Wilkie Collins,' he said. 'Look at him now.'

He made a puff gesture at the back of his head. A fraction of an expression crossed the Leopard Lady's face. So Geneviève knew who'd raided the Barksdale house. Looking at her, it seemed possible she'd gone in alone.

'Are you really off the string? Or on another one?'

She indicated the woman with the Glock.

Willis laughed but his cheek-fur bristled. An unusual tell.

'You are misunderstandin' the situation, Doctor Dee. Me an' Georgia Rae's tight.'

Georgia Rae Drumgo. Not a name you were likely to forget. Dan Hanson had mentioned her while running through the players in Baltimore's crime organisations. Luther Mahoney's sister. Married to an ex-*Tonton Macoute* Haitian who was currently missing presumed dismembered. Reputed avatar of the avenging, red-eyed spirit Erzulie Ge-Rouge. Executioner and enforcer.

Willis's favourite song came to mind, 'Supernatural Voodoo Woman'.

'Me an' you could be tight too,' said Willis. 'What you might call a business opportunity is openin' up...'

She knew what was coming but let him continue.

'This drac thing, man, it's huge already. Gonna get bigger. You and me – vampires – we have to be on top of it, or else it be on top of us, you dig?'

He slid his shades down his nose and flashed his eyes at her.

Did he really think his Charm would work on an elder?

'The krewe I was with thought small. Too small.'

'Grab a cow, pen a cow, milk a cow?'

He didn't like to be reminded. He would have slice marks on his arms. Drac was the only drug where the dealers got the tracks.

'No longer a feasible business model, Doc.'

Eventually, your abducted vampire got used up and went to dust. No more cash flow.

She thought about all those teeth in Wilkie Collins's box. If he only pulled one keepsake from each of his drac-cows that meant Barksdale had been through thirty-eight vampires.

'You don't need a cow, you need a flock…'

'Cows come in herds, Willis.'

'Whatever… do I look like Pa Kettle to you? We're speakin' metaphorically and you started the cow talk.'

'Am I to understand that your plan is to turn selected people vampire? The homeless, the lost, stolen children? Then reap the blood harvest…?'

'See, you *do* dig, mama.'

That was why there'd been no epidemic of vampire disappearances anyone could notice. Barksdale had Willis make vampires out of people who'd already fallen off the map. It was also why they got used up so fast. The stock would be poor in the first place. Then, there was Mamuwalde bloodline. The story went that the Prince was personally turned by Dracula, and so inherited the Dracula rot… his get were feeble, and the bloodline thinned with each turning…

'You'd *be* the mama.'

She felt Georgia Rae Drumgo's eyes on her.

Willis was moving his lips and making a noise, but Georgia Rae was doing the talking. He was still the puppet. She assumed Georgia Rae had a Willis doll somewhere.

If the Mamuwalde bloodline failed to take, Mahoney needed something stronger. Like hers.

So far, Geneviève had refrained from bestowing the Dark Kiss. She'd begged Charles to accept it, but he had refused 'til the end. That was as close as she had come to having get. She wasn't about to break the habit of centuries to keep Luther Mahoney's drac corners hopping with dhamps.

She said nothing.

She could still see Willis's eyes… a spark died in them. He had made promises she would not keep.

'Won't come willing; can't be broke,' said Georgia Rae, raising her Glock. 'Drain her for drac and kill the other bitch.'

Geneviève ducked under the table as Georgia Rae fired.

Shots ploughed into the Formica and chrome. Willis yelped as a silver slug punched through his sleeve and the meat of his arm.

'Hey, man, mind my threads!'

The dhamps were on Emma or up and about, bumping into one another, too blitzed to pay attention.

Geneviève lizard-slithered across the tile floor as fast as she could manage.

So much for her good black dress. Lorie's jacket ripped under the arms.

Georgia Rae fired again. Purple-moustache guy got in the way of a bullet and fell.

'Willis, she'll kill you too,' Geneviève shouted.

No use. Blacula's bitch wasn't growing any balls tonight.

'You gotta be *reasonable*, girl!' he whined. He was up from the table, hopping in frustration and excitement, like a kid who needs the bathroom.

He must see another basement in his immediate future. Mahoney would keep him going longer than Barksdale, but he'd still be used up…

Geneviève back slid into a booth, using the table as a shield, but there was nowhere else to go.

On the whole, she wished she'd stayed with her date.

No… she didn't. She wasn't like that. Georgia Rae, of all people, had seen it straight away. Won't come willing; can't be broke…

She saw Georgia Rae's legs – she had leopard-pattern high heels, too – as she marched across the diner. She rapped on the table with the gun.

'Come out,' she said.

Geneviève eased herself up from the floor and sat in the booth, fixed table between her and the Leopard Lady. Erzulie Ge-Rouge ascendant. Just now, eyes ablaze, gun smoking, Georgia Rae Drumgo was gunpowder, gelatine, dynamite with a laser beam...

There was no use trying to talk with her.

'Blast the bitch, why don't you?' shrieked Willis.

'She ain't goin' nowhere.'

Geneviève sensed a moment. Georgia Rae didn't want to draw this out. She'd used her full clip and needed to reload.

The diner door opened and someone wide and whiffy walked in.

'Hey, honkie, can't you see we're closed?' said Willis. 'What kind of a jive-ass, mutha-gropin', toad-lickin'...'

A very loud noise sounded.

The front of Willis's zigzag eyesore exploded red. His eyes were frozen in surprise.

As Geneviève's ears rang, Willis slowly buckled – threads of scarlet and gristle seeming to float in the smoke around him – and he fell on the floor.

The drac-heads pushed Emma – who was going to need serious therapy if she lived much longer – away and pounced, crawled and leaped across the room, shoving their faces into Willis's wound, snorting and licking, feet turning clawed inside confining shoes, teeth so big they cracked jaws and split cheeks.

The newcomer was a gross warm man with a Stetson and a sawn-off double-barrel shotgun.

Geneviève recognised him. He'd been at the restaurant. And around before then. Outside the Barksdale house this morning. She even remembered him showing up in Canada, sitting in court as she gave evidence against Lucien Lacroix.

Georgia Rae had her gun on the fat cowboy. Stand-off. Except... he had one more shell under the hammer and she was empty.

Geneviève slipped out of the booth, quickened by the golden she'd had earlier, and took away Georgia Rae's gun.

She put her teeth against the Leopard Lady's jugular and pressed enough to leave dimples, then stepped back.

Georgia Rae looked angry enough to kill with her bare hands.

'Uh uh, honey,' said the gunman, finger tight on the other trigger. 'Message from on high. Don't mess with the mademoiselle. Nod your head to show you understand.'

After a long moment, the Leopard Lady deliberately nodded.

Geneviève spat at Georgia Rae's shoes. A display of French contempt.

'Best take your posse and ride off into the sunrise, I reckon,' said the gunman. He had a grating Texan accent.

With a sweet smile, Geneviève gave Georgia Rae back her empty Glock. The Leopard Lady put the gun in a shoulder black and snapped her fingers. The Mondo Trasho dhampires left Willis alone, and came to heel.

Glaring, Georgia Rae moved towards the door.

'On high means *West Coast*, Miz Drumgo,' said the man. 'Tell Luther… tell everyone you know. Change is coming. Get it?'

'Got it.'

'Good.'

Georgia Rae and the dhampires left. Some of the pack were howling and laughing. They didn't know this was real.

Geneviève checked the waitress. Unconscious, but alive. Behind the counter was a cook with his throat cut. Dead.

Emma Zoole was in shock.

'Where's Lorie?' Geneviève asked.

'At the *Sun*. She left a note to call.'

So the roommate she liked was safe. Sweet.

'I'm thinking of moving out,' Emma said.

'We can talk about that later.'

Geneviève turned to the man with the gun, the man from the West Coast. He was gone. The jukebox whirred, though. He must have dropped a coin in one of the table-top selection machines.

Roy Rogers sang 'Happy Trails'.

'How about that?' she said, to no one in particular.

She heard sirens from outside. Someone had called the cops. Uniforms came through the door. And a familiar detective.

'*Sacre bleu, mon brave. C'est un tableau de* splatter *avec jolies filles.*'

PART FIVE

A CONCERT FOR TRANSYLVANIA

ANNO DRACULA 1990

1

Francis had changed. So had Alucard.

He could tell Francis dimly recognised something in him and was troubled, but he made no connection between John Alucard and the boy who had slipped out of Romania under his company's wing. They had inevitably run into each other around town. He'd decided against green-lighting *Tucker: The Man and His Dream*.

The director lived too much in his Silver Fish trailer, commanding sets from inside a chromed cocoon with video-camera eyes, multiple editing benches and womb-like wall-padding. Francis thought of the master of the Miracle lot in terms of his own movies: Pacino's dead face in the dark at the end of the first *Godfather*, Hackman's attentive eyes in *The Conversation*, Anjelica Huston's fingernails in *Captain Eo*, Brando's snarl as *Dracula*. An interesting collage: Alucard wondered whether he was not Francis's get as much as Dracula's, or Kate's or Andy's or Welles's. When Coppola came to Transylvania, he had given shape to a dream, encouraged an unformed vampire boy along a path which led inevitably to this office, to this crown. The Father had turned him, but the movies *made* him. Like all vampires, all predators, all parasites, Alucard needed, loved and despised his prey.

Transylvania and Hollywood had marked the face of Francis (no longer Ford) Coppola, as had family tragedies and the collapse of his San Francisco-based Zoetrope set-up. Francis had regained all the weight he'd lost in the Carpathians; but where he'd once been a confident, well-fed Hercules, he now sagged and slumped inside his safari jacket and chinos. There was more grey than black in the still-thick beard that all but covered his cheeks, and some of the grey was grizzling to white. Behind professorial glasses, his eyes were evasive, unable to fix on anything that wasn't a screen or a monitor.

Francis wasn't shooting anything at the moment.

Yesterday, in the screening room at the house, Alucard had run *The Godfather*, *One from the Heart*, *Peggy Sue Got Married* and *Gardens of Stone*. Pauline Kael wasn't the only person to say that *Dracula* had sucked Francis Coppola dry. The earlier pictures, even the insane choices, were the work of a filmmaker. The later ones could have been made by anyone with a range-finder. Holly, an innocent eye, liked *One from the Heart* best of all. It touched parts of her life locked away inside her. She had walked out on the film about cemeteries, upset and bored.

Was there anything left?

Just now, Francis sat in the uncomfy chair that had made Adam Simon squirm. The kid had been eager to pitch and too overjoyed at the reception to ask the hard questions. Francis – who'd been an Adam Simon once, grinding out quickies for Corman – was uncharacteristically meek and restrained. He had been summoned for this audience, not had to plead his case for months with Beverly. His gun-for-hire movies were commercially as hit-or-miss as his auteur work. He'd gone to Oklahoma and shot a couple of teenage movies back-to-back on tiny budgets to prove he didn't need to bankrupt a Third World country to bring in a film. Alucard had cast C. Thomas Howell in *Bat-21* after seeing him in *The Outsiders*.

Francis still gave off the scent of death, of being lost. Once he had been the far-sighted look-out at the prow, the only man who knew where the ship was going.

They talked about people they knew.

Alucard told Francis how happy he was with *The Rock*, now Steven E. DeSouza's punch-up of Robert Towne's rewrite of Ron Bass's draft was in. He had firm commitments from

Stallone for the con, Connery for the guard and Jeremy Irons for the villain. He had come close to nailing Brigitte Nielsen for the 'Ratty Cardigan' character, but an early screening of *Total Recall* inclined him to take a chance on Sharon Stone, who was overdue to break and desperate enough to eat cockroaches on camera. Now Eli Cross was off the project, John McTiernan could be trusted to tidy up after the second-unit directors and the effects and opticals units. Adam Simon was wasting his time pleading with the Writers' and Directors' Guilds, but his signature was on the contract and he was legally out in the cold. *The Rock* was shaping up as *the* big release for summer '91.

Francis ventured no opinion, except to comment that Towne was a better writer than director. Alucard gently tortured Francis by asking whether he might put in a word with his nephew, Nicolas Cage, whom he liked for the small but vital flashback role of the degenerate viper who killed the hero's family. He was ready to forgive Cage for his bizarre performance as the drac-head literary agent in *Dhampire's Kiss*, though some had said the actor used Alucard as a model for the semi-vampire character.

'That's next year locked down,' said Alucard. 'Now I have to think about 1992.'

Francis shifted in the chair. Like a lot of directors who were addicted to cutting, he had a bad back.

'Do you know what my biggest disappointment was?'

The director shrugged, not knowing where this was going.

'*Dracula*,' said Alucard. 'No, not the one you made. I just stood back and admired on that. The other one, the one nobody got to see.'

'Orson's?'

'If only... if only...'

Three people in the world had known why Orson Welles walked off the set of his potential masterpiece. Welles was dead, leaving just Alucard and Geneviève Dieudonné.

'I was on set that day,' said Francis.

'I know.'

'When I heard Welles was making *Dracula*, I don't know

what I felt. No, that's not true. I was angry and afraid. You can't know what my *Dracula* cost me. Cost us all. None of us came back from Transylvania unchanged. Talk to Marty or Dennis. For a moment, I thought it'd all be for beans. My picture was going to end up a footnote, like the 1931 version of *Maltese Falcon* with Ricardo Cortez, or that Martin Ritt gangster film everybody said was a bad precedent when I was prepping *Godfather*. Why couldn't Orson have done *Don Quixote* or *Heart of Darkness*? If he'd signed for *Godfather, Part III*, I'd have given him my blessing and a case of wine. But *Dracula* was too much a part of me. I didn't want to let it go, let *him* go.'

Alucard shrugged. 'Then, for you, it was a happy ending.'

'No,' Francis insisted. 'When Orson shut down, I was devastated. I'd been torn up by the idea of an Orson Welles *Dracula*, but when it went away I realised I didn't care what *Cahiers du Cinema* said about "Francis Ford Coppola's *Dracula*" in some 1999 century-of-film retrospective. What I wanted was to see the picture that wasn't made. You understand? Somewhere there's a magic theatre, in a valley at the edge of the world, where they show movies that are only dreams. The complete *Greed*, the Laughton/von Sternberg *I, Claudius*, Hitchcock's *Mary Rose*. If that theatre was showing Orson Welles's *Dracula*, I'd leave everything – the movies, the vineyard, the studio – and wander the world until I found the place.'

Alucard's fangs were sharp in his mouth. It happened in this office sometimes, independent of feeding. There was so much need and desire in the air.

'I'm glad you feel so strongly, Francis. I want you to make a film for me, for 1992.'

Francis was jarred from his fantasy. He was cautious and cunning again, survivor of Hollywood jungles, the cultured San Franciscan among LA barbarians.

'Medium-high budget. Star names. Commercial subject. I can pre-sell this to the whole world. You will direct but not produce, not write. You'll forgive me for bringing it up, but I'll insist on a tight schedule and personally oversee the shoot. I'll have Peter Hyams on speed dial in case you fall behind.

It'll be shot here on the lot, in the studio. I've got writers on staff who can take care of the script. The effects work we can farm out. I know you enjoy tinkering, but you'll only get a few months to play this game.'

Francis was waiting for the trap to snap shut.

'What's the title, John?'

'John Alucard presents A Francis Coppola Film, *Dracula Part II*.'

'Dracula died at the end of my film.'

'Vito died in *The Godfather*. Impersonating Dracula, incidentally. You still made *Part II*.'

'There was Michael.'

'There's always a Michael. And Dracula only died because Stoker wanted him to. In the real world, he lived on, until 1959, remember? Who knows, perhaps longer than that.'

Francis was conflicted. He needed a summer picture to raise his stock for the films he wanted to make. He didn't want anyone else doing a sequel to his *Dracula*. He was keen to work with studio resources again. But he knew he couldn't match the first film under John Alucard conditions.

'I won't do a sequel whose most notable feature is that it's easy to get financed. It'd be like grabbing some crusading lawyer best-seller off the racks and shooting it with this year's Tab Hunter. Everything I've done so far has meant something.'

'*Tonight for Sure*? *Dementia 13*?'

'They meant something to me at the time. They opened things up.'

'And *Dracula II* means something to me.'

The sentence sank into Francis's brain.

'It won't be a masterpiece, Francis.'

The director's eyes widened.

'It doesn't have to be. It will, however, change minds. About the first film. About you. About me. About Him.'

'Dracula?'

'Yes, the Father and Furtherer.'

Alucard looked into Francis's glasses and saw the spark in the director's mind. He was remembering that John Alucard bit into human necks and drank blood.

'Brando is too difficult, too fat, too expensive. He wouldn't come back for *Godfather II*.'

'I don't want Brando. I see Dracula younger. This is the love story.'

'There's a *love story*?'

'Dracula came to England to get married. He made the Queen young again.'

'I've been trying to find something for Sofia,' said Coppola.

'Your daughter?' Alucard remembered the little girl on the set in Transylvania. He tried to see her as a princess. 'Excellent. Fine casting as the young Queen Victoria. We'll get her the Academy Award for her birthday if you like. Can't fix it for Meryl every year. Feel free to use your nephew and sister in the cast too your father for the score. This is a story about family.'

'A royal family.'

'You're like him, you know. You were a father to me once, when I gave you a staff and found shelter in your crew. And He was a father to me first, when he turned me.'

Francis didn't follow.

'A staff?'

'Do you still have it?'

Alucard allowed his face to shift a little. Recognition sparked in Francis's mind. He dredged for a name.

'Ion?'

Alucard nodded.

'I owe three debts, Francis. One of my benefactors is beyond repayment, though he is with me still.' He nodded towards the Warhol Carmilla. 'With this project, I hope to go some way to settling the other two, to you and to Him.'

Francis was astonished.

Overwhelmed, for one of the few times in his life, he wound up signing a contract.

Holly and Penny sat in the back of the pink Rolls, shaded from the high sun by a tinted plexiglass bubble, as one of John's warm security people drove them out to Mojave Wells. Penny leafed through *The Lady* while Holly looked at sand and rocks. She'd seen a million miles of landscape through fly-specked windshields – much of it like this, Mars with cactuses. Alien worlds weren't really like California desert, John had told her; *Planet of the Apes* and a few *Star Trek* episodes were shot here and that made people think far-off planets seemed like a stretch of barren Earth a few hours' drive away from LA. The artefacts left behind by these expeditions were forgotten lens caps, faded strips of marker tape on rocks and expired call-sheets with waitresses' phone numbers scrawled in the margins.

'There it is,' Holly said. 'Manderley Castle.'

Penny folded away an article about what to wear at Crufts and cocked an eyebrow at the turrets rising from the desert.

'So it is,' she said. 'Should have been left where it was, if you ask me. There'll be a gaping hole in Kent, thanks to some megalomaniac millionaire. Yanks think they can buy anything and transplant it. As it happens, they usually can. But not all English roses flourish in this foreign soil.'

John didn't own this castle, but had connections to the people who did. It was a retreat for the Church of Immortology. Some of the *nosferatu* celebs and demi-celebs who hung about John's parties swore Immortology was the one true vampire faith. Penny, sniffy about tax write-off religions, told Holly not to pay attention to talk like that.

The chauffeur parked the Rolls in the courtyard and released the DeLorean-style door-hatches. The one-of-a-kind custom vehicle had been put at Penny's disposal.

For over a month, since the night of the Wild Hunt, Holly had been wheedling and nagging at both Penny and John to be allowed to take the next step. Penny, usually hard to convince, had turned round and become her supporter.

Holly wished John were here, but he had business in town. There was a crisis on *The Rock*. A new writer, Martin Amis, had been brought in to explain Sean Connery's accent. John had to smooth things over.

Feraru's blood had changed her.

She had never bled another vampire to nothing before. She'd drunk Porthos's blood to be turned and exchanged blood with Kit, whom she was remembering more. She'd been turned inside out by John Alucard's blood and Penny had let her take drops of her own rich red in water. But it was different with Feraru. As the vampire emptied his last into her, she'd swallowed a soulseed, something that expanded inside her.

Penny had been shocked when Holly turned into the English Romanian. Until now, Holly had only been able to shapeshift into human-animal forms. With Feraru, the shift was perfect, good enough to fool anyone. Standing over a brown mummy no longer recognisable as Feraru, she was the real man, the original. The feeble cast-off on the ground seemed fake. John had Holly spend time with Crainic, who corrected her few errors. When she became Feraru, she could call up his mind, his self, and live inside it, knowing everything he'd known, remembering his short, silly life and death as a man and a vampire. With Penny and Crainic, she'd spent a night as Feraru, going from club to club and to a meeting of TM sympathisers in Malibu. She could pilot her shifted body and call to mind the names of those Feraru knew, to give all the right answers and ask the right questions. She'd bled Feraru's warm mistress and the girl hadn't known the difference.

John was pleased with her. That made her pleased with herself.

Penny was a little frightened, but she needn't be.

Holly would never hurt Penny.

And if she did, it wouldn't be killing. Penny would live on, inside. Just as Feraru lived on. He was like a boxed videotape on a shelf, taken down and played from time to time.

Holly had other videotapes now. Vampires John had

had her drain. A rock singer named Josie Hart, who would appear at the Concert for Transylvania, and whose music was now the soundtrack running in the back of Holly's mind. A businessman named Frene, a spoiler of the stock market, whose interests she kept up at long distance, doing his voice over the phone, signing his papers. It was important she have her own money, and keeping up Frene's life and accounts was useful for that. A precocious eternal child named Rudolph, whose inoffensiveness made him a handy back-up shape if escape were ever called for. These selves had been picked carefully. Penny thought there might be a limit to the number of vampires Holly could store, but Holly was certain she had room for more.

On the dull trip to Mojave Wells, she experimented with her four secondary selves, shuffling between them. Her clothes became tight or loose as her shape changed completely. She wore a backless ballet leotard, Nikes and a padded hunter's vest. The ensemble did well for everything but Frene's big feet, which were cramped in the puffy shoes, and Rudolph's little legs, which made the leotard comically baggy.

In the shadow of Manderley Castle, Holly was her default self. She looked up at the battlements and saw a man. His white face surmounted a tall, cloaked body. Then the cloak unfolded of its own accord and spread out into a bat-wing silhouette.

'Don't mind him,' said Penny. 'He likes to show off.'

The vampire leaped up onto the battlements and stepped off, into the air.

Holly had never seen anything so beautiful.

Tonight, she would learn to fly.

The vampire landed casually, folded away his wings, and shifted into more human form. He was a GI Joe-handsome young man in a black jump-suit, slit to bare-skin under the sleeves, down the sides and at the back. The garment was fixed only at wrists and ankles and belt.

'Meet Banshee, an old friend,' said Penny.

The grinning youth kissed the Englishwoman, but his eyes were on Holly.

'This is your fledgling?'

'Don't judge by appearances,' said Penny.

At Penny's nod, Holly took off her vest and shifted. Banshee's wings were transformed arms, veined membranes stretched between his wrists and ankles. Her black-feathered spread grew out of her back like a classic angel's, leaving her arms free. New muscle ropes wormed around under her skin, settling in her chest and shoulders.

'For show,' said Banshee. 'She can't get in the air with those.'

'You'll be surprised,' said Penny.

Other people were present.

'This is General Count Iorga,' said Penny, indicating a paunchy elder in a black polyester leisure suit, 'late of the Carpathian Guard and the Imperial German army, now of the Church of Immortology and the State of California.'

Holly thought Iorga a sad relic. He clicked his heels and nodded, as if meeting a junior officer about to be promoted above him. From the number of titles and footnotes Penny used, Holly gathered Iorga needed to compensate by inflating his letterhead.

'And this is, uh, Mrs Meinster,' said Penny, gesturing at an ordinary-looking vampire woman.

'*Baroness* Meinster,' corrected the creature, radiating hostility.

'She's taking care of the interests of her husband, Baron Meinster of the Transylvania Movement.'

Holly shifted inside her mind, channelling Feraru, who remembered this woman. The Baroness, an Englishwoman who had in life been named Patricia Rice, was the most fanatical of her husband's followers. A former art student, she'd already designed the flags, uniforms and postage stamps of the new country her husband intended to rule. She was working on a National Anthem too, but unable to get 'Don't Cry for Me, Argentina' out of her head. Baroness Meinster longed to sing the lead in *Evita* at the opera house her husband promised to build in Timişoara.

Penny didn't think much of her countrywoman. She recognised that once, long ago, she'd been rather too much like Patricia Rice.

It was keen, knowing what everyone was thinking. She'd picked up the knack. Holly had to remember to be herself but had an advantage over everyone in mindshot.

Except John. His skull was shut, even though she'd tasted his blood.

A shadow rose and terror clutched Holly's heart.

'This is Graf von Orlok,' said Penny.

She hadn't sensed *his* mind either. The elder was barely human, a yellow-domed skull with flared rat-ears and greening fang front-teeth. His nails curled in on themselves, his long coat had seen centuries of wear and his smell was a miasma which made even undead eyes water. Banshee, stereotypically fearless, held himself stiff and alert at Orlok's approach.

The elder said nothing but looked at Holly and knew everything. His lips twitched.

'Let's get this over with,' said the Baroness.

The plan agreed with the Transylvanians was the sacrifice of Banshee, a veteran of the US Bat-Soldier Program. With his fresh young blood in her, Holly could soar above the canyons like an eagle.

She fixed Banshee with Josie's eyes and sang a wordless tune – inaudible to warm human ears – which resonated with all the vampires save the plodding Patricia.

Wheeling around, non-functional wings spreading like a black swan's, she fell upon the Baroness, knocking her onto the sandy concrete. Holly's mouth projected, lips and teeth fusing together into a razor-billed beak. With a *snip*, she scissored Patricia's throat to the bone.

Penny held Banshee back, whispering to him. Orlok laid a sharp hand on Iorga's shoulder.

Holly beaked into Patricia Rice's heart and drank her dry.

When she stood up, she was Baroness Meinster.

For a moment, she wasn't even Holly. She felt the rage of betrayal.

'My husband will have you tortured for this,' she spat, meaning it. 'This outrage will be the end of you all!'

Orlok's mouth fell open, displaying scarred gums and rows of crusty teeth. He was laughing, silently.

Holly shifted, swallowing the Baroness.

'I take it back,' said Banshee. 'She can fly.'

Holly spread her wings and rose towards the bright stars.

3

Alucard let the minions mill around the conference room before the meeting. He moved among them, lightly tapping their thoughts in passing, getting a sense of their moods. They were relaxed, even Penny. He pressed flesh and offloaded conventional greetings, brushing off questions with assurances.

The Rock was proceeding as smoothly as a sixty-million-dollar picture with an action star who liked to remind people of his writer/director credits ever could. Alucard had been right about Sharon Stone. Her dailies were dynamite, especially in the soon-to-be-notorious shower scene. She'd definitely make it onto the poster, her body at a contractual seventy-five per cent the size of Stallone's face. Stallone and Connery, working from different scripts with different directors, were each convinced the other only had a cameo in the picture. It would cut together. Once the gross points came in, no one would complain.

With the Hallowe'en and Thanksgiving weekends gone, the industry had a clear run 'til Christmas – with only the Longest Night in the way. It was up to Alucard to make this year's solstice bigger than Christmas. The Concert for Transylvania, which *Variety* called 'Bloodstock', was coming together, an initial trickle of sign-ups turning to a cataract. Already, some early committals – comeback kids, wannabes, the overly charitable – had got bumped in favour of harder-to-hook names. Reluctantly, he had abandoned his plans for Charles Manson, who insisted on performing only his own material and an unacceptable slice of the merchandising.

Visser, the only warm man in the room, loitered by the awards cabinet with Penny and Holly. Alucard joined them.

'Lot of trinkets, Mr A,' said Visser. 'But I don't see the baldie with the sword. Why ain't there no Oscars?'

Alucard took out the golden bust. It represented a long-faced young man.

'This is an Academy Award,' he said. 'The Irving G. Thalberg Memorial Award. It goes to "the producer with the most consistent high quality of production". It was presented to me in 1986.'

'That's no Oscar,' said Visser. He took a pull from a flask. Jack Daniel's.

'It is an accredited Academy Award. Alfred Hitchcock won one, and Steven Spielberg.'

'Is that right?'

'The Thalberg began as a backslap for moguls and toadies,' explained Penny. 'In the 1920s, Irving Thalberg invented the job of producer by firing Erich von Stroheim and locking him out of the cutting room on *Greed*. He was responsible for clawing control of any given film away from the director and towards the producer, and ultimately the studio. He died young in 1936 and the Academy of Motion Picture Arts and Sciences, then as now essentially a company union, named their award for best-behaved company man after him. Lately, it's become an apology, chucked at producer-directors like Hitchcock and Spielberg who've not been given Best Picture or Best Director Oscars they deserved. John is a rare actual producer to have won the award in the last decade.'

'That's more than I wanted to know,' said Visser.

Alucard looked sideways at Penny. He hadn't thought her that well up on Hollywood lore, then remembered she'd turned before the Lumière Brothers showed their first motion picture. She'd lived through the entire history of the movies, and had simply been paying attention. Still, he wasn't sure about her tone.

Sometimes, Penelope Churchward presumed. Alone in this room, she wasn't remotely afraid of John Alucard. She didn't underestimate how dangerous he was, but had grown out of really caring what happened to her. She accepted that she deserved any punishment or fate that came her way. It was hard to frighten someone like that. If Penny had been like this even with Dracula, Alucard understood why the Father came to rely on her.

'We should get started,' said Alucard. 'My friends, if you would all take your places.'

They settled into the chairs at the long table. Before withdrawing to guard the outer sanctum, Beverly had laid out neat folders as place mats. Glass jugs of iced *sanguinello* – a mixture of red orange juice and virgin blood smuggled up from Mexico, where it was mixed in convent schools Alucard endowed – were placed at intervals. Plastic cups, early designs for the McDonald's tie-in with *The Rock*, were within reach of every chair but Visser's. Finger-bowls of beef cubes, red blocks like blood-oozing dice, were provided for anyone with the munchies. Alucard didn't choose to partake, but indicated that everyone else should.

Holly poured out a measure of *sanguinello* and wet her cupid lips, taking the curse off for everybody else. Alucard was pleased with the way she was turning out. Already, she'd shown talents he hadn't expected when he took her out of the video rental store. Others reached for jugs and cups or popped meat-cubes into their mouths. Discreet spittoons were provided for chewed-dry lumps of muscle and fat.

From his elevated position at the head of the table, Alucard considered this inner circle: Holly, Penny, Visser, Crainic, Dirk Frost (a degree or two too wasted, as if he were high on his own supply), General Iorga (with a titload of unearned medals and a carpet remnant toupee), Sebastian Newcastle (representing L. Keith Winton) and Mr Kurt Barlow (from the Shop).

Newcastle, survivor of centuries, had worked out six ways to escape from this room. He had dozens of fall-back positions and underground routes prepared in the event he was required to flee the city, the state or the country. If South America ever got too hot for him, the artist formerly known as Don Sebastian de Villanueva had probably bribed techs at Cape Canaveral for a berth on the space shuttle.

The grim-faced Barlow, a low-profile elder indentured

to the Shop as a way of wriggling free of atrocity charges after misconduct in New England, was deputed to speak for Jedburgh, though he seldom said anything. Barlow had ambitions to be a Cat King in his own right. Alucard assumed it would only be a matter of decades before he found himself killing the old man.

Graf von Orlok stood in the corner, leaning into a shadow, so straight-backed Alucard wondered if he could sit down without breaking vital bones. At a nod, Holly took the discomforting ancient a cupful of *sanguinello*, which he lapped with a long tongue that poked out of a leer of gratitude. Even the Father had been cautious of Orlok, the creature Dracula would have been if appetite overruled ambition.

There was another new face at the table.

'Before we start,' said Alucard, 'I'd like to introduce you to a valued associate. Ernest Gorse. He has been, ah, underground for a while. At the disposal of the United States government. I used a little of our pull in Sacramento to have him turned over to us, ostensibly as a technical advisor on *The Rock*. He's up to speed on the Transylvania project and will be overseeing – though not *overlooking* – our security. We need to control the flow of information, to maintain several levels of understanding. Mr Gorse is an expert.'

'Evening, everyone,' said Gorse. He still affected librarian glasses and wore English tweeds. 'I can't say how delighted I am to be back in dear old Los Angeles. I'd like to thank Mr Alucard for arranging my liberty to work with you all. I don't care for getting so peremptorily down to business, but I'm afraid I'll have to schedule individual chin-wags with each of you, to go over what you've been doing so far, fixing it so all of our systems are in harmony. No need to worry. That's all.'

Gorse fitted in as Alucard had known he would. None of the others took him seriously yet, except Penny. She'd heard of Ernest Ralph Gorse before. The pair made wonderful British book-ends. Alucard expected them to hate each other at first, but form a working liaison.

'On a personal matter,' said Alucard, 'before we discuss the Transylvania situation, our warm comrade Mr Visser has news of an old friend. This will interest you, Ernest. And the General, and you too Penny.'

Visser smiled, enjoying his moment, and opened his file. His fear-sweat stung in Alucard's nostrils – the warm man could put on a show of confidence in a roomful of vampires, but body chemistry gave him away.

'The frog viper,' he said. 'Sorry, Mr A, I still can't pronounce her name. Jenny-vev?'

'Geneviève Dieudonné,' said Alucard.

Gorse hissed hatred, resentment on his face like a jail tattoo. Penny was surprised, edging round a black pit in her mind, touching on the secret she kept wrapped up. So Geneviève was part of that story too.

'Yes, her,' said Visser. 'The pest.'

'For those of you unfamiliar with the story so far, this vampire has never been a friend to our cause. Often, she has thwarted the will of the King of the Cats. I think it's best if we keep an eye on her.'

Frost glanced sideways at Alucard. The new-born, youngest viper in the room, had run through his meat-cubes and *sanguinello* like a junkie through methadone and was jonesing for stronger stuff. His jug was empty but for rinds of red slush.

'The *Mademoiselle* From Hell was up in Canuckland for a couple of years,' said Visser. 'Working with the Toronto cops, taking on-the-job training as a, whatchumacallit, "forensic technician". Well, our gal's all trained and qualified. She's "Doctor Dee" and she's taken a job in the States, as a medical examiner in Baltimore.

'Your favourite viper chick is on call for bizarro cases. I went out there myself on Mr A's dime and spied her at work. I was tempted to go in disguise as a corpse, but I can't pull that act off as well as some round this table, haw-haw. She's got a knack for the sleuthing. Takes one look at a stiff and can rattle off stats about cause of death, probably pin the killer in a blink. The Feds use her for their thornier whodunits. That makes her an Honorary G-Girl. She has a decoder ring and everything.'

Gorse was intent and Penny surprised. Most of the rest were

puzzled by the weight Alucard gave this stray elder. General Iorga was embarrassed, calling to mind two occasions – outside Buckingham Palace in 1888, then again ninety years later at the castle in the desert – when killing the upstart out of hand would have forestalled later trouble. Alucard thought that if Iorga had tried, he'd probably not be in this room now.

'I popped in on her, found her in the middle of a bad situation, and got her out of it. As instructed, I saw no harm came to her. She owes us, now.'

Penny was intent. She had mixed feelings about Geneviève.

'Why did you not just let her be killed?' asked the General.

'It would have been easy,' said Visser.

'Messages needed to be sent,' said Alucard. 'Not just to Geneviève. I want the warm to think more of vampires, to be wary of killing them. But I want her safe. No one touches her, but me… We're sparing with our assassinations here.'

Someone thought 'you could have fooled me' and Alucard's mind-touch flickered around the room searching for the culprit. Newcastle. Fair enough. He knew about Feraru. So did Meinster, which was to be expected. Alucard poked a bit deeper and found Newcastle had no other names in mind. Iorga and Orlok – who was impenetrable, mind a focused mouth – could have dredged up at least one.

'Mr Visser, thank you. We shall list Geneviève as "pending business"…'

'Too right, old son,' muttered Gorse.

'…and proceed. Holly, will you fetch our other guest, then take Visser's report to Beverly.'

Holly stood up, took the folder, and left the room.

Moments later, Patricia Rice stepped in. She wore a long white PVC coat and an oversized peaked cloth cap over Holly's blouse and skirt. She had buckles – eye-catching touch – velcroed to her shoes.

Crainic and Newcastle, who knew Rice but didn't know what had happened to her, glanced her way. Simultaneously, the vampires bit down on spurts of irritation and put on approximate smiles. Newcastle did a better job of it than the blank senior academician. The Spaniard got up to kiss

Patricia's hand and help her take the seat she had, as Holly, just vacated.

'So delightful that you could join us, Baroness.'

The Transylvanian oozed sincerity.

'How are you finding California?'

'Too sunny,' snipped Patricia. 'Fifty-two channels of telly and no *Coronation Street*.'

Crainic thought the game had shifted again, and he had been duped into standing in the wrong corner. Newcastle shrugged.

'And the roads are bloody impossible,' continued the Baroness. 'This is not how things will be run in the coming vampire state, mark my words.'

Even Orlok's talons curled in irritation.

'Now, if Holly would come back,' said Alucard.

The Baroness Meinster shut her eyes and Holly Sargis opened them. The shift was instant, over in a ripple. James Cameron couldn't have done better.

Newcastle pantomimed thigh-slapping astonishment and delight.

'An astoundingly successful disguise.'

'A poor word, Don Sebastian. Holly does not *disguise*, she *becomes*. As far as is possible, we were in the presence of the genuine Baroness Meinster. Or Feraru.'

In the Baroness's dress and hat, Feraru sat there.

Then the famous rock singer.

The child.

Kit Carruthers.

The businessman.

Holly took off the coat. Black angel wings extended through vents in her blouse.

Alucard's protégé had an unexpected face in her repertoire. He understood how close Holly and Kit had been, how much they'd lived in each other's skins. Kit was not a welcome revenant, but it was as well to know he was there.

Most of the company applauded. Frost flapped his hands like seal-flippers and thought of feeding. Newcastle wanted to find out if Holly had representation. Iorga was sadly amazed at the things young people could do these days.

'I trust you are all convinced we can get close to Baron Meinster.'

A chorus of yeses and appreciative grunts. Alucard made eye-contact with the unforthcoming heavy-hitters, Orlok and Barlow. They understood.

Another demonstration was needed, though.

Dracula rose in him again, a black cloud inside his eyes, commanding. Alucard became a passenger in his own brain.

The Father surveyed the company, saw the weaknesses, the fears, the potential and actual betrayals. He remembered the slice of silver through his neck and took Penny's secret from her: she'd been there at Dracula's last death, sharing responsibility. He saw the envy that curled around the loyal Iorga's heart, the dreadful need to be a man he was not. He accepted Holly as his get. He drew on the fealty of the other vampires, elders all. It was as in the old days, when his lieutenants followed him without asking themselves whether they did so out of love, fear, ambition, nobleness or need. They recognised him as the dark star of their world and pledged their swords to his dragon standard.

Dracula was a memory again.

Alucard stood and looked at the quieted group. They had seen his true face, the face behind his eyes. Barlow, the most reticent, all but whistled. Any ties he had to the Shop were torn. Newcastle saw him as the ultimate escape route, the one that led to mastery of his destiny, an end to running and hiding. All those in this room made before 1888 were his entirely. Frost would stick with whoever kept him bloated with blood, cash and drac. Penny and Holly, who could never truly accept Alucard as the King of the Cats Incarnate, were vital to the plan. Their flickers of independence and initiative were strengths that the blindly loyal or devoutly selfish could never have.

'One more thing,' said Alucard, lifting the bust of Irving Thalberg as he had on the night he had accepted it from Richard Zanuck, cradling it by the base. 'This *is* an Academy Award.'

Frost laughed at the incongruity, but the chuckle died.

Alucard stalked around the table.

'It is an honour bestowed by peers,' he said.

Visser was drenched with sweat, a tangy stench all around him. Newcastle and Iorga, either side of the warm man, edged away from him, shifting their chairs.

'It recognises "the most consistent high quality of production".'

Alucard stood behind Visser, looking down at his bald pate. Piggy eyes turned up at him, black raisins in a dripping mask of dough.

'Sometimes, my friends,' Alucard said, to the vampires in the room, fangs sharp and exposed, 'we *nosferatu* forget what we are. We have worked hard for acceptance, to find a place in this world without Dracula. Now we should remember everything, we should not be ashamed. We should exult.'

Visser hawked up a nervous laugh, then a grin grew. He began a shrug.

Alucard brought the Thalberg down on Visser's head, scraping skin from skull. A blurt of blood splattered across the polished tabletop. Shocked and instantly high, Frost licked his lips and restrained himself from lunging. Alucard picked the twitching private eye up one-handed and hefted his considerable bulk onto the table, dragging him feet-first along its length. Others stood up, knocked over chairs, and got out of his way. Visser's kicking cowboy boot smashed a jug of *sanguinello*, which slicked the table under him. Alucard let go of Visser's damp shirt-front and smashed his face with the now-messy award, raining three precise blows to obliterate nose and eyes.

Alucard bent over and chewed a hole in Visser's wattles. He drank the blood of the dying man and stood aside, nose and chin red. The others stood, red in their hungry eyes and sharp white in their humourless smiles. He was proud of his monsters.

'Be vampires again,' he ordered.

They fell on the warm man, and drained him.

'Come to me, my Patty-Pat,' said the apparently youthful fellow on the heart-shaped bed, extending a lacquer-nailed hand. 'My babies have missed you ever so lots. We were ready to curl up and diedy-die, were we not, preciouses? Yes, we were.'

Baron Meinster was propped up on a dozen red satin pillows. They looked like cherry chocolates from *Land of the Giants*. The vampire poodles were attached to his quilted violet bed-jacket, one as an epaulette nuzzling his ear with a fat worm of crimson tongue, the other a brooch hung on his chest with paw-hooks. The Baron's elaborate hair was set with papers and pins. On his forehead, giving him a four-eyed look, was a pink velvet sleep-mask with Audrey Hepburn eyelashes.

Patricia Rice, the tiniest guiding spark of Holly inside her mind, kicked off court shoes and padded across the deep pile pink carpet. The Baron always insisted on hotel rooms reserved for visiting royalty, but the Chateau Marmont had palmed off their 'Honeymoon Princess' suite on him. If the gesture was supposed to be an insult, it sailed right under his radar. He adored the riot of pink and gilt, the red and white flower arrangements, the heart-shaped Charles and Diana portrait. The would-be King of the Cats was besotted with the Princess of Wales and read every magazine that put a picture of her on the cover. Patricia would cheerfully have chewed through Di's windpipe.

She slipped onto the bed and close to the Baron, who kissed her cheek and nipped her neck. A poodle got in the way and squealed.

'Did-ums hurt ums-self?' he cooed, kissing the rat-sized dog and petting it gently, licking through its soft fur with a long tongue and gazing with love into its huge, watery eyes. The dogs were fed only on golden, a damfool expense.

If it came to it, Penny advised Holly to lie back and think of Transylvania, but it wouldn't. The Meinster marriage was traditional European politics, more an alliance than a passion. Each time she wore the Baroness's self-shell, Holly was surprised by how much of Meinster's business he entrusted the woman with. The Baron's talent was persuading other people, usually women, to do things he found tedious.

It was a mistake to think of Meinster as dumb. Foolish, perhaps, but not dumb. He'd lived for decades underground, surviving Puritans, Nazis and commies. He had come through a cluster-massacre of vampire elders in 1923 and not been put off his political ambitions. He'd been raked over by the scandal sheets for men's room arrests. He'd shrugged off the waspish witticisms of his ex-lover, Herbert von Krolock, who had a Vegas nightclub act built on gossip about him. Not so long ago, American news media had called Meinster a terrorist – he'd occupied an embassy and taken hostages. Only a concerted press campaign had reformed him into a freedom fighter.

When Dracula died, the Poodle Prince was best prepared to step up and become King of the Cats. Even now, Meinster knew he was in an undeclared contest with John Alucard for the title, and that moves were being made against him. Patricia was supposed to have been his eyes and ears in the enemy camp.

'Have they got Crainic, Patty-Pat?'

'Yes,' she allowed.

'I knew it. When they had Feraru killed, it was obvious. The Englishman was the only one who'd have stayed loyal to the Cause. We can buy back Striescu if we want to. But Crainic will have to be convinced. Be careful around him, *liebling*.'

'I'm not afraid. Not with you to protect me.'

'So you shouldn't be. But be cautious. I am inside these people, all of them. I know what they're like. Waverers in the wind. Out for themselves above all. No sense of the worth of the Cause. To them, Transylvania is just a place name on a map. The soil isn't in their veins. They'll serve us, but only if we are strongest.'

The poodle at his chest chewed his jacket. He stroked its ears flat.

'And who's King of the Cats?' he asked the dog.

The poodle yelped a sound that might have been 'You are!'

'Yes I are, aren't I? Isn't that clever, Patty-Pat. I've been training my babies to speak. When I am King, I shall declare them first ministers just to see the looks on the sour faces of Crainic and his cronies. And you shall be my Queen.'

Patricia was excited by the prospect.

Once, long ago, she'd been dead set against queens and kings. Now she was on the point of becoming royalty. It was an inevitability of history. She'd been wrestling with that even in her Marxist days. This was just a logical outcome of her thinking.

Her coronation robe would be a stunner. She would make Meinster forget Princess Di.

'This John Alucard? What is he like?'

The name cut through Patricia like a code-word and woke up Holly. She looked at the big vampire baby in the bed with her and picked her words carefully.

'Powerful,' she said. 'Not old, like Orlok or Iorga, but of good bloodline. He reminds me of you. Some say he is Dracula's get. Like you.'

Baron Meinster's face was a paper mask. He claimed he'd been personally turned by the Count, but details changed with each telling.

'But he is an American? Dracula never set foot here.'

'He seems American. Perhaps in the War?'

'Ah yes, the War. So much goes back to that.'

'You should meet him.'

Meinster wasn't hot for it. Holly had known he wouldn't be. The Baron was torn between dealing with Alucard through unreliable tools and risking a face-to-face which might end up with him forced to back down.

'He likes you, though, Patty-Pat. And you'll never go the way of Crainic. I made you, and I alone care for you. We are equal partners in our future.'

She stroked a poodle's head.

The thing bit her, leaving two red marks in her hand. It had pinprick fangs. The bite stung.

She almost shifted, almost showed Holly's face.

'Naughty beast,' chided Meinster, indulgently, wiping the dog's bloodied mouth. 'Mustn't snack off Patty-Pat. She's ours to play with, not yours.'

She laughed, Patricia's high-pitched (annoying) laugh.

'What is it, my darling?'

'Nothing,' she said. 'The bite tickled.'

The poodle, alone of all creatures, saw through Patricia to the Holly beneath.

5

The Rock cell-block set filled the Monroe Stahr Stage, largest soundstage on the Miracle lot, like a black cathedral: slab after slab of fibreglass granite, tier after tier of plastic silver-barred doors, a steady glisten of wet-look gel. Batteries of coloured lights came on, casting atmos shadows throughout the vaulted space. Massed smoke machines choked out dragon-breath clouds of oily grit.

Alucard and Gorse stood on the studio floor.

Christopher Neville, this week's career limbo director, was up on the camera crane arguing with his operator. Lucky Cameron, Sylvester Stallone's 'unbreakable' stunt double, walked through a fight rehearsal with Brion James, Brian Thompson and Jenette Goldstein. The villain actors were hampered in action by the futurist Nazi body-armour the wardrobe department decided looked better on prison screws than the bland blues Alcatraz guards actually wore. Caine, the combat advisor, showed the players how to make quarterstaff- and sword-moves with lengths of pipe or electrified night-sticks.

Stallone, in his *Rocky* robe, sat to one side in a canvas chair with his name stencilled on the back, paying attention. After Cameron took a few hours of solid beating in long-shot, the star would be needed to step in for bloodied, determined facial close-ups. Cross-legged on the concrete beside Stallone was a writer on a dog-leash, scribbling on a note-pad and passing torn-off pages up to his master. The 'additional dialogue' merchant had been ordered to come up with five possible laugh-lines for Sly to snarl after killing the corrupt chief guard. So far, none of his zingers had zung.

'Does this take you back?' asked Alucard.

'My cell was a white room,' said Gorse. 'Not very gothic. Not like this at all. The real punishment is the boredom.'

The Father had spent centuries in his castle, doing nothing. And that was how he had ended up.

'This is the movies,' said Alucard. 'We make it better than it is.'

'Less boring, I hope.'

The rough-cut had previewed in Sherman Oaks. The test audience got fidgety in the third act. Stallone had insisted on a scene where the hero tells Sharon Stone about his dead family. The kids in the valley shouted 'fast forward fast forward' as Sly sobbed through a speech he'd written himself. He read dialogue as if chewing raw hamburger. They'd rather see bad guys buying it than listen to an Oscar clip, so Brion James was getting a more elaborate death scene.

'In Alcatraz, the convicts are separated and doped,' said Gorse. 'Buried in their coffins and fed hygienic rat-blood dosed with god-knows-what. It's depressing, more than anything else. Not many punch-ups or escape attempts. In ten years, I didn't see any of the women prisoners. And nobody ever, *ever* calls the place "the Rock".'

'Quibbles, Ernest. They won't show this movie in prisons, so we have latitude about the details.'

'Whatever you say, Johnny.'

'That's right. Whatever I say.'

Gorse coughed and lowered his voice as if someone was listening.

'Holly called in last night from a secure payphone. The Baron's on his way back to bat-land, happy as a sandboy. She arranged for him to meet Josie Hart, a trick I'd love to have seen. Our *soi-disant* King of the Cats was star-struck and delirious to learn that Josie and her girls would be reforming for "his" concert. He's requested that they cover "He's a Rebel", apparently a favoured pop pick in his circles. I like ska, myself. Our Girl Friday has a few more Patty Rice meetings to take, then she'll be back in her own self. The coup is shaping up nicely. All the right people here and in Romania have been oiled with *baksheesh*. I say, Johnny, are you really going to let that little *pouffe* take over a country?'

'Why not? I don't live there.'

'Good point.'

'It's just dirt, Ernest. Not even real estate. You could exchange a square mile of Beverly Hills for all of Transylvania, have Moldavia thrown in as a freebie, and still feel cheated.'

'I'm sure you know what you're doing.'

'So am I.'

An assistant director looked at Alucard for approval, received the nod, and called quiet on the set. Neville called action and Brion James whanged his cattle-prod down on Cameron's pipe. The electrical effect didn't work properly first time, so they tried it again. There was a satisfying shower of sparks. After four more takes for luck, they went on to the next set-up. A make-up crew came in and fixed short ends of pipe to James's forehead and the back of his skull, for the pay-off shot of the guard's death.

'"You need that like a hole in the head",' read Stallone. After a pause, everybody laughed. 'There's something familiar about that.'

Alucard knew what it was.

'That was in Adam Simon's script,' he said. 'Cut it out. Say "I told you there was one thing you'd have to get through your thick skull!"'

Stallone laughed and wrote it down.

'Why don't you ever have ideas like that?' he said to the writer, kicking him.

'I hesitate to bring up the subject,' began Gorse, 'but...'

'She'll be seen to, Ernest. Don't worry. For the moment, I want her alive and around. So few people will appreciate what it is we're going to do. Your friend Geneviève is one of them. This is show business, my friend. Above all else, we need an audience.'

6

Through Kurt Barlow, Alucard sub-contracted travel arrangements to the Shop. As a precaution, he had Newcastle set up a Church of Immortology fall-back for every leg of the long journey from Beverly Hills to Castle Dracula. Commodore Winton maintained a private fleet of ships and planes, crewed by 'fully-ascended nyctlapts' in uniforms copied from 1950s kink erotica and Disneyland, Bettie Page short shorts and Donald Duck sailor hats.

On December 20th, the day before the concert, Alucard flew in an unmarked private jet – with Gorse, Iorga and Crainic – from Los Angeles to a government proving facility in Florida. There, the party transferred to an 'experimental' naval transport rocket-plane and made a sub-orbital swoop across the Atlantic, touching down on the USS *Philip Francis Queeg*, a carrier with the US Sixth Fleet, at sea off Cyprus. Alucard, as a personal quirk, preferred his pilots to be warm professionals who didn't think they were immortal.

The *Queeg* was a Shop cover, the only ship in the Mediterranean paying more attention to Central Europe than the developing situation in the Persian Gulf. Alucard's deal with the Shop was that his venture should be over before George Bush's deadline for Saddam's withdrawal from Kuwait came at the end of the year. It ought to be a nice little work-out before the allies took on Iraq.

He was able to run a spot-inspection of the Bat-Soldier Corps. As producer of *Bat-21*, he was an honorary member of the elite cadre. He found the flyboys (and girls) below-decks in an oak-lined cabin the size of a ballroom, playing ping-pong faster than the human eye could track or composing letters home to families who couldn't know how much their kids had changed in the service.

Captain Gardner, an old World War II hand who'd personally bested the last of the *Bat-Staffel* mutants Hitler inherited from Dracula, was quietly prepared for action. Alucard said it was unlikely to come to much. The idea was that the Bat-Soldiers were a contingency in case coup and counter-coup got out of hand. Banshee, Penny's sometime 'friend', was gung-ho for US intervention and a rematch with 'Meinster's Monsters'. Czuczron, an old Carpathian Guard blade, had assumed command of the Transylvania Movement Bat-Soldiers – he was Meinster's paid-for poodle and needed to be watched. Banshee asked after Penny and Alucard told the flyboy she was already at Castle Dracula, working behind the scenes to keep the performers out of each other's throats. Actually, he had Penny in Romania to keep Holly grounded. The shapeshifter was juggling the identities of Patricia Rice and Josie Hart, both of whom had a lot to do during the concert.

The President, intent on Saddam Hussein, still hadn't signed off on any military action that might be necessary, but Jedburgh was primed to invoke the Shop's secret protocols and go right ahead with World War III – or, at least, World War II, Part II – anyway. The man from the Shop was swanning around the deck in rumpled naval whites and a cowboy hat, scanning the horizon.

'Fool Georgie Bush thinks he's runnin' the country, Johnny-Boy,' Jedburgh told Alucard. 'This Iraq situation is his chance to be Gary Cooper. He ain't lettin' that slip, not after four years of sidekickin' Ronnie like some preppy Gabby Hayes. He ain't gonna let no pore little innocent Kuwaiti squillionaires suffer under any invader's yoke, even if they are neo-mediaeval tyrants in Gucci robes who'd sell their own grandmammies for a buck-fifty and all the camel-dung they can smoke. Georgie is watchin' out for Saddamite patrols, Johnny-Boy, and hearin' Tex Ritter sing "Do Not Forsake Me, Oh My Darlin'" through his deaf aid. He's Company from way back, so he ought to know goddamn better. They all forget, once they get in that oval office, what their job really is. Think they got a mandate from the American people to go their own way and the hell with the big picture. Except for darlin' Ronnie. He stood up and read his lines like he was supposed to, even when the script said he had to take a bullet. I purely do miss Ronnie the Ray-Gun, Johnny-Boy. After the nightmares we had keepin' Lyndon Blow-Job and Slippery Dick in line, not to mention Jimmy-Earl Moron, Ronnie was the Prez who knew his goddamn place.'

At midnight, Alucard's Huey, a CH-46 Sea Knight, took off, circled the *Queeg*, and set a course for Romania. Within sight of the *Queeg*, the helicopter was brushed by two large bat-shapes, wavered a little in the air, and blew up.

Jedburgh covered his eyes with his hat.

Alucard stared straight at the explosion, seeing the flame-blossom as a pixillated series of still-images, each lingering seconds in his eyes, overlaying the next. Fire and metal rained into the sea. The sun-bright white burst of exploding fuel highlighted the bat-men who hovered like kites at a safe distance.

'Carpathians,' said Jedburgh, as if swearing. 'Usin' goddamn limpet mines. We taught 'em how to do it, too. It's Lesson Two of Elementary Airborne Personnel Strategies, all the way back to Eisenhower's Rocket-Man Program.'

Alucard signalled Gardner and Banshee to scramble after the enemy fliers. They popped wings and took to the air, rising high in seconds, then swooping down. Two more Bat-Soldiers, Iceman and Nikita, stepped into place and spread wings, ready to be deployed at a nod.

'That took bare face,' said Gorse.

Alucard agreed.

'Meinster may be a candy-ass little bastard,' said Jedburgh, 'but he's got some moves on him. I guess you don't become a vampire elder without learnin' a little sneaky. You heard what Kissinger said when Baron Meinster went up against Ceauşescu?'

'"It's a pity they can't both lose."'

'You did hear? Well, Henry Hawk was wrong, Johnny-Boy. In some wars, everybody loses. That's the point.'

Gardner and Banshee, flying in formation, went after the Carpathians. The limpet-miners had flapped a lot of miles from their roost – Meinster must have had them on Crete or one of the smaller islands – and were in no shape to outpace a pair of fresh fliers. Jedburgh ordered a flare popped so personnel on deck without *nosferatu* night-eyes could catch the show.

It was swift and brief.

The Americans let one Carpathian go free 'to tell the tale' and brought the other – whom Banshee introduced as 'a loser named Al Ziska' – back to the *Queeg*, wings ripped and useless.

'It was Czuczron, sir,' said Gardner.

Alucard remembered the hearty elder at the Wild Hunt, thumbnail tearing into a girl's femoral artery as if opening a shrink-wrapped CD. Dracula remembered Czuczron as a useful blade in a melée, but only when the gold was clinking his way. Meinster's man. Bought and paid for, at least for tonight.

'Give pursuit,' Alucard told Iceman and Nikita. 'Make it good, but let him lose you. Show proper frustration.'

'Yeah,' put in Jedburgh. 'That little bastard just offed Johnny Alucard!'

The fliers were gone in a second, zooming across the sea like darts.

Attention turned to the prisoner.

'The pretender is dead,' declared Ziska, an old Carpathian hand, looking from Gorse to Jedburgh. 'What you do to me means nothing.'

'The pretender?' asked Alucard, amused.

Ziska looked at him and saw the Father.

Alucard shifted, mostly inside his skull. Each time it happened, it was faster and easier and more complete.

'Alexis, you have made a mistake,' said Dracula. 'You know what you must do.'

Ziska, shocked into terror, shrugged free of Banshee and Gardner. He couldn't fly away. He knew better than to beg forgiveness. He raised an arm in salute and levered loose a long bone-spur that projected from his elbow, ripping away the last of the wing-membrane. Blood pattered on the deck.

Dracula looked at the sheared end of the bone.

'It is well,' he said.

Ziska took a step forward, bone-dagger raised, then fell to his knees, leaning forward onto the spike, slipping it under his ribs like a *seppuku* samurai, forcing it through his heart.

The fire in the elder's eyes went out. He crumpled into a coherent statue of cinder, ash and dirt. Even his baggy flight suit blackened and flaked.

Dracula filled his lungs and exhaled, a concentrated blast of cold.

Ziska fell apart.

'Get someone to clean this up,' said Jedburgh. 'We're supposed to be a ship-shape ship.'

The Father folded inside Alucard.

'That was an attack on American forces,' said Alucard.

'Indeed it was, Johnny-Boy. Shop protocols apply. If we want, we can make this a shootin' war and Georgie can't bleat about it. So long as the other feller draws first, no court in Dodge is gonna throw us a neck-tie party for pluggin' him.'

How long would it take for Czuczron to report back to Meinster?

General Iorga came up from below-decks and reported that the real helicopter was ready. He was well aware that Alucard must have weighed up the advantages of putting him on the first Huey, to add conviction.

'Then, my friends,' said Alucard, 'let's go to the castle.'

7

———————◆———————

Dry-ice fog banks dissipated on late afternoon breezes, revealing a life-size cutaway diagram of an Aztec step pyramid. A place of perfect sacrifice. Stage centre, tilted as if in an undertakers' showroom, were three black coffins, emblazoned with scarlet inverted crosses. A heavy, simple drumbeat started. An electric piano laid down jangled, ominous chords. Observing from the battlements of Castle Dracula, Holly felt the thrum in the roots of her fang-teeth.

With three explosions, two coffins burst open. Out jumped the lead and rhythm guitarists of Spinal Tap, all straining spandex and hair extensions, dhamped to the eyeballs.

Striking pelvis-out, guitar-heiling poses, they shouted 'Hell-o-o-o-o-o, Transylvania!' The amplified greeting resounded from treetop and mountainside. The band should have remembered the traditional Carpathian peasant saying 'they only come out at night'. In the distance beyond the under-populated amphitheatre, mountain goats bleated. The guitarists held their pose, fangy snarls stuck on their faces. A few roadies and merchandise-hawkers gave a charity clap. All seven members of the local chapter of the fan club — three *babushkas*, two sociologists, a seriously out-of-style vampire elder, some poor slob in full leather-chains-and-wig gear and a sullen nine-year-old girl — whirled bull-roarers and waved placards with Romanian slogans.

The third coffin, still clamped shut, leaked fire and screams. Minions scurried in with extinguishers and axes, and set about rescuing the trapped bass guitarist. Ignoring this frenzied activity, the currently uncoffined band members launched into a messy cover of Meat Loaf's 'Bat Out of Hell'. Just as the song finished and the others returned to their coffins, the bassist was freed. A stage-hand gave him an extinguisher blast, whiting his blacked face and putting out the flames incubating in his piratical nest of hair. The fans cheered wildly, which might have been a consolation.

After nights as Patricia, trotting after Baron Meinster like a third poodle, and Josie, rehearsing with her all-girl band, Holly enjoyed this moment as herself. She liked being up high, with a panoramic view, finally seeing how all the pieces John put on the board fitted together.

The Baron was under the castle in the 'communications centre', hooked into the TV and audio set-up, leeching time from the broadcast team to keep abreast of the movements of his people, who were in place all over the province. Giant screens were erected in the squares of Timişoara and Cluj, the principal cities of Transylvania. Every village and town hall had its own television set on a wall-bracket. The show was a line of communication for the coup. Carpathian community leaders were prepared to cut in as the concert reached its climax at dawn. It was Crainic's responsibility to recruit these spokespeople. Meinster had Patricia go over the list to weed out those more loyal to the Cause than the Baron. That useful chore meant she could sideline vampires John suspected of counting on Meinster for advancement in the new Transylvania.

Penny, custom-fitted earplugs in place, looked out over Borgo Pass. She summoned Holly to watch the sunset. 'Saliva of the Fittest', Spinal Tap's second number, could safely be ignored.

Stands of trees had been felled for the lumber used to erect benches and bleachers around the open-air stage. A mountain crag was levelled to make a performance space, with the castle itself dramatically off to one side. From the tower-top, Holly and Penny had a skewed view of the arena. They could see into the wings, where dozens of people swarmed and fussed to keep the show moving.

Castle Dracula, uninhabited for over a century, was now head-quarters for the talent, the techs and their hangers-on. Crypts were now dressing rooms. Torture chambers were rehearsal spaces. John had contracted Swan, the innovative record producer, to stage-manage the concert. The apparently youthful mastermind, in command of a crew which would shame NASA Mission Control, had outfitted the East Tower as a state-of-the-art broadcast facility. A giant RKO logo aerial on a nearby peak transmitted to the one-man T5 space station, which John was sub-leasing for one night only from an international disaster relief organisation. The signal was relayed to sub-stations around the world by a ring of satellites.

As Patricia, Holly had averted daily thermonuclear conflicts between Swan and Meinster. Both bighead boys needed to see themselves as ultimate puppet-master of this event, though that position was, of course, already taken.

The courtyard helipad was in constant use, over a dozen choppers in the air at any time. As the concert began, many headliners weren't even in Europe. Their global positions were marked on an electronic big board in Swan's turret. Even now, the Short Lion wasn't one hundred per cent confirmed, though his people were talking with the control room. Swan cooed promises into a throat-mike, constantly upping the offer. The Short Lion was in the air, either over Mexico or India. Timmy V's people were dawdling en route from Thailand, intent their superstar shouldn't arrive first. It was easier to arrange the overthrow of a European government than to get the leading vampires of rock onto the same stage at the same time. If it fell through, Swan would shove Jagger and Bowie out there, get a backing band to play 'Give Me the Moonlight, Give Me the Music' and hope for the best. But Alucard would still take revenge on the recalcitrant superstars. Even literal immortals could be hustled prematurely into Rock n' Roll Heaven. If there really was such a place, they must have a hell of a drug problem.

The opening band wound up a short set and jeered 'Goodbye, Transylvania'. In the wings, exultant after his frenzied performance, the band's red-faced, drac-bloated drummer tried to sprout Satanic metal horns and his head exploded. Shame he hadn't managed that onstage. *Then*, Spinal Tap would have been a hard act to follow. As it was, he left a mess that had to be stepped over or cleared up.

Holly slipped into Penny's mind and asked about John. Czuczron had showed up early this morning and reported to Meinster that 'the pretender' was no longer a problem. John's position was not on the big board.

'Part of the plan, dear,' mouthed Penny.

Holly thought that if Alucard were truly dead, she'd know. It would be as if a part of her were ripped away. As it had been when Kit died.

She remembered Kit now. She remembered who she had been.

It didn't seem quite real. Thirty years on the road, with only speed and blood.

The sun was down now. Artificial moons illuminated the stage. Crowds poured along torch-lined paths from villages where ten-lei-a-night hostel accommodation was going for five hundred American dollars. The stands filled. On stage, Paul Simon and a Szgany band played a selection of newly composed traditional tunes from his *Land Beyond the Forests* album. Some warm Romanians chanted anti-gypsy slogans and were quieted by vampire bouncers. Decades after Dracula's passing, the Szganys, his traditional servants, remained under his protection. Simon welcomed a 'very special guest', the English rock star Fang. They played duelling throats on 'They Bleed Alone', Fang's protest dirge about the mass impalement of hopping *jiangshi* in Communist China. In a pause not filled by applause, Fang produced a yellow scroll and read a lengthy message of support from someone or for someone. Simon whipped his gypsies into line and belted out something Romanian that locals enthusiastically joined in with, drowning the speech.

'That sounds just like "My Old Man Said Follow the Van",' commented Penny. 'Marie Lloyd. Now, there was a *star*. Not like these clods.'

Fang slunk off. Gloom squirted out of his ears and nose like octopus ink.

Josie's band, the Pussycats, weren't on for hours.

Of her back-up selves, Holly liked the singer best – but when she shifted into her she had the least control. Josie Hart was certain of who she was and Holly needed a code-word (they had picked 'Shazam') from Penny to trigger a reverse shift. It'd be easy to slip into Josie's life and not come back. She was performing all the time, but never pretended she wasn't. Her sense of taste was extraordinarily well developed, distinguishing amongst the thousands of flavours of choice blood. Before she became a star herself, Josie had battened on many gods and goddesses of rock – some now truly dead, others on the bill tonight – and taken something of each, leeching and learning. When she stepped on a stage, the taste of Janis Joplin was in her mouth, sharpening her fangs.

Holly looked at Penny's programme.

Next up was a goth gore girlie with red skin and horns. She used special effects magic in an act which had as much goat-sacrifice as music in it. Not all the goats were goats. Performers hated going on after her because the stage was tacky with discharges. The short straw went to Jackson Browne. Though warm himself, he wanted to show support for '*nosferatu* self-determination' with a reprise of 'Before the

Deluge'. He was surprised on the final chorus to be joined by a red-eyed Fang, who fought his way through roadies to come out, warble harmonies, and cut into Browne's encore by reading the rest of his statement. In the wings, a stage manager made vivid throat-cutting gestures.

Still to come, here at the epicentre or in hook-ups from key sites around the world: the Eurythmics, the Deep Fix, the Pet Shop Boys, Herb Alpert and the Tijuana Brass, Cher (ordered not to sing 'Gypsies, Tramps and Thieves'), Screaming Lord Sutch ("Til the Following Night'), Frozen Gold, Judas Priest, Loud Stuff (the band who used to record as Loud Shit), Tony Bennett and Bob Dylan ('Blue Moon'), Strange Fruit, Huey Lewis and the News, Whip Hand, The Railtown Bottlers, Automatic Dlamini, Crucial Taunt, Bob Geldof and Midge Ure ('Don't They Know It's Hallowe'en?'), Iggy Pop and Deborah Harry ('Swell Party'), the Jake Hammer Band, Nik Kershaw, Debbie and the Dayglos, Black Roses, Alice Cooper ('I Love the Dead'), Phoenix ('Old Souls'), Coil, the Johnny Favorite Big Band, Rick Springfield, Bobby 'Boris' Pickett, Ivor Cutler, the Dangerous Brothers ('Grab Yourself a Sheep'), Steven Shorter ('I've Been a Bad, Bad Boy'), Talking Heads, Barbara Cartland ('A Nightingale Sang in Ba-a-a-rk-eley Square'), the Impossibles, the Ramones, Satanico Pandemonium (with her snake act), Dire Straits, Kylie Minogue, Aled Jones...

Pale or warm, hot or cold, group or solo or bizarre once-in-their-careers combo (Stephen King, Warren Zevon and Dick Contino?), they all had reasons to show up here. Some were Immortology believers, others had a commitment to the Transylvania Movement, some needed a charity gig on the resumé to demonstrate social worth to a disapproving judge, a few saw an opportunity for a chart comeback or to unveil a new personality, a couple were addicted to the lights and the buzz, maybe a dozen had traded sexual favours with Swan, two or three had been blackmailed, one had literally committed murder, and Phil Collins just turned up unannounced at Stonehenge and was given a slot by a minion too embarrassed to say he wasn't wanted.

Dawn was a long way off. When it came, the world would be changed.

And so would Holly.

8

'Would you like the concert fed through, sir?' asked the pilot.

'Not really,' said Alucard.

Now it was happening, he wasn't that interested. Putting it together had been the challenge. The show must take care of itself. He could rely on Swan to make the best of it, to exploit disasters as well as triumphs. There was a healthy market for a *Most Embarrassing Concert for Transylvania Flops, Bloopers and Out-Takes* video.

As they took off from the *Queeg*, for real this time, news came in off the wire that the Short Lion's jet was down in the Bermuda Triangle and all hands lost. The crooner Petya Tcherkassoff went on stage in a flood of crocodile tears and announced a tribute to the fallen rock prince. He was struggling to impress a shocked-silent audience with a dreadful cover of the Short Lion's bad-enough whinge single 'Louis Louis' when word came through that the Short Lion hadn't been on his jet. He was un-destroyed, aboard the Istanbul Express and nearing the concert. It was a master-coup, even if it did entail sacrificing a backing band. The response from the Timmy V camp – issuing formal denial of responsibility for any rocket attack – was weak. If the duo did make it on stage at the same time, Alucard didn't know whether they would sing together or bite through each other's throats. Either way was fine with him.

Alucard's entourage flew in a Super Jolly CH-53, larger than the Sea Knight Czuczron had blown up, with manned door-guns and a belly full of Bat-Soldiers. He hadn't had a backing band to throw away, but the stratagem had meant writing off a Huey as collateral damage. For show, *someone* had to be on board – Dirk Frost. He'd been told he was making an urgent drac delivery to the dressing rooms.

Meinster had too much self-belief to double-check the good news. By now he'd be as distracted as a boy on Christmas morning, opening all his presents at once. Street-fighting had started in Timişoara, expected flashpoint of the Transylvania coup. Key elders had taken positions around the province and were practising their speeches. Behind them, quiet vampires held hardwood daggers and Kalashnikovs. In Bucharest, President Iliescu would soon discover phone-lines into Transylvania were down. The concert's enormous broadcast bandwidth blotted out military and civilian radio communications. With the T5 under Alucard's command, even an international distress call would go unanswered. Iliescu would have to watch the revolution on television like everyone else. On CNN, it would appear in a tiny iris in a corner of the screen as the pop concert dominated the image.

'We are now entering Romanian air-space, sir.'

They had flown across Turkey and Bulgaria. Alucard looked out of the armoured glass window of a nearby gunport.

'Is this a homeland, Iorga?' he asked.

The elder scowled, uncomfortable. Some people around here had long memories.

The dark landscape was nondescript. The few towns were like signal fires in a black plain. Fir trees rose like a forest of stakes. Below was Wallachia, homeland of Vlad the Impaler. In warm life, Dracula ruled not Transylvania but its neighbouring province. If that history, which the Father remembered in flashes, was indeed his own. Holly could steal whole lives at a feeding. Some argued that the Dracula who came to London in 1885 was not the Dracula who had been Vlad Tepes. It didn't matter who the Father had been; the question was who he was now.

'Bogeys, sir.'

Bat-shapes rose from the trees.

The Delta Force door-gunner locked and loaded. Silver slugs shone like ball-bearings in his ammunition belt. He angled around, getting a fix on the flitting wings.

Alucard indicated they should hold fire.

The bat-creatures fell into a holding pattern, keeping pace with the Jolly.

'Our escort has arrived, gentlemen,' Alucard announced.

The door-gunner stood down.

Ahead rose the jagged peaks of the Carpathians. The pilot took the helicopter up, out of shadow and into clear night sky. The escort kept pace, even up here where the air was thinner and colder. They crested the mountains and were over Transylvania.

Some part of him felt home.

Another part remembered why he had left.

Alucard folded back inside himself and the Father took over. Gorse noticed the shift and removed the earpiece he had tuned to the BBC World Service. He gave a curt nod of respect. It passed around the helicopter. Everybody knew they were in the Presence.

'Now,' said Dracula. 'The music.'

The radio operator flicked switches. Ralph Rockula and Lesley Gore were duetting with 'Judy's Turn to Cry'. The song filled the interior of the helicopter.

Dracula smiled.

9

———◆———

'Shazam,' said Penny, sending Josie Hart to the Phantom Zone.

Holly came back, ears ringing from music and applause, cat-suit stretched onto her taller shape. They were backstage, in a red room. The green room, full of flowers and live snacks, was for acts about to go on; the red room, a bare space which didn't encourage anyone to stick around, was for those who had just come off. Over the p.a. system, Elton John and Kiki Dee introduced each other, then segued into a duet, 'Bleedings (Woe-Woe-Woe, Blee-eedings)'.

Josie had gone down a storm. Holly still felt the buzz in her mind and the thrill in her insides. A mental loop of 'Calling Occupants of Interplanetary Craft' stuck in her skull. Sweat cooled on her face and back. But the singer was packed up and back in her box.

'Good show, Holly,' said Penny, producing a plastic-shrouded suit on a hanger. 'You slew them where they stood. Want to do the Snooty Bitch now?'

A Josie-esque pout, unbidden, plumped Holly's lower lip.

'If I have to.'

'I'm afraid you do. It's no pleasure for me either. I have to look at her.'

'I have to look out from *inside* her, Penny.'

'Oh yuck.'

She let herself change slowly, putting Patricia Rice on like a disguise. She shucked out of Josie's rainbow-patterned leotard (with cat tail) and silver wig (with cat ears). Penny helped her into Patricia's Evita-in-waiting trouser suit.

'How do I look?'

'Like her. But you're you in the eyes.'

Patricia was struggling. She took over sometimes, if Holly's guard was down. That wouldn't happen tonight. This was Patricia's last public outing. When concert and coup were done, Holly intended to purge herself of her troublesome tenant. Penny was sure that could be done, like having a tooth out.

A backstage minder barged in, clipboard in hand.

'Where's Josie gone?' he asked.

Holly and Penny shrugged.

'They're all like this,' said the roadie. 'Hell, she's done her turn, so who needs her any more? She can go bleed this god-rotten country white. Just so long as she signed the release.'

The roadie left. Holly and Penny giggled.

'We must go to the castle,' said Holly. 'I should be at my husband's side at daybreak, when all he deserves will be his.'

'That's good,' said Penny. 'It's Patty-Pat to the tee.'

Outside, concert chaos continued. The stands were full to overflowing. Big acts jostled to milk their minutes in the spotlight. Swan was throwing superstars onto the stage in fours and sixes, to cram in as many as possible. Ringo Starr hurried past in starry Merlin robes and a pointed wizard hat, grateful for the opportunity to clank a triangle five times during a multi-celeb singalong of 'Midnight at the Oasis'. As Sade hit her highest note, shattering watch-faces and spectacles across the valley, the public address system cut in.

'This is a health warning. Vampires, do not drink the brown rats' blood. Do not drink the brown rats' blood. It carries a virulent strain of...'

The announcement shut off and Sade shrilled back.

Penny and Holly looked at each other. Who knew what kind of plague was raging through the audience?

The Short Lion, allegedly back from the dead again, still wasn't here. Reports had his train steaming through darkest Transylvania towards the special station at Bistritz. Timmy V, body guarded by six Thai boxing priests, had twitched first and shown up, but threatened to leave unless his demands were met. Timmy wanted two dozen white mice, now.

Mobs of torch-bearing concert-crashers, ink still wet on their forged tickets, clashed with the security squads. They were for the most part European Hells Angels and *Securitate* vampires, desperate to get in before the show turned to dust and discarded food wrappers at dawn.

The path from the stage to the castle was busy, but Holly and Penny had no trouble walking against the tide towards the ancestral seat of European vampirism. Unsurprisingly, given her efforts as an anthemist, Patricia was tone-deaf. The music was just noise in her skull. That cut out a distraction.

'Let us pass,' Patricia snapped at anyone in the way.

They entered the Great Hall, then made their way down to the crypt where Meinster's command centre was set up. The neglect Jonathan Harker had observed was long since repaired, all the dust and cobwebs cleaned away. Thick electrical cables snaked along the flagstone floors like Ariadne's thread. Patricia inspected uniformed staff, and grimly enjoyed handing out criticisms of overlooked flaps and buttons. The Baron's men were impassive but respectful.

Wobbly sliding doors opened to admit them to Baron Meinster's lair. It was modelled on the bridge in the original *Star Trek* series.

Raised on a dais to give him commanding height, the Baron lounged in a black Captain Kirk swivel chair, issuing orders to the faithful, poodles unruly in his lap. He wore a claret-coloured frock coat, tight around the torso but generously flared below the belt, with pleats in the sleeves and neon-lime frogging on the wide lapels. Crainic stood in the Spock position, phone clamped to one ear and finger in the other, face discoloured by anxiety and illness. Czuczron, a *Next Generation* fan, loitered like an out-of-time Riker, wondering how to usurp action hero honours (and girl guest stars) from the Captain. His dashing Carpathian Guardsman's uniform was complete with non-ceremonial sword. Three vipers manned the Uhura, Sulu and Chekhov positions – relaying messages, fiddling with dials and switches on mixing boards.

'We have the town hall in Timişoara,' said 'Sulu', Rose Murasaki, a delicate blood flower in traditional Japanese dress. Foot-long needles held her hairstyle together. 'The militia have come round. Striescu is in control.'

Meinster clapped and worked the jaws of his poodles.

'Come in, Patty-Pat. Everything is going to plan. Nothing can possibly go wrong.'

A poodle began to pee ammonia, like a vampire bat. The Baron skilfully directed the stream away from his velvet trouser-cuffs and towards Crainic's corner. Crainic's eyes flicked to Holly and Penny.

'Unscheduled vehicle over the helipad,' said 'Chekhov', a fright-faced, malodorous elder named Czakyr. 'With a swarm of attendant fliers.'

'Who is it?'

'I'm just getting that information, Baron. They are identifying themselves. It's the Short Lion.'

'Isn't he on a train?'

'Apparently not,' said Crainic.

'That explains the fliers,' put in Holly. 'Probably his fan club.'

'I suppose we should clear the minstrel to land,' mused the

Baron, 'or that Swan fellow will throw another of his hissy fits. Though, after his last LP, it's tempting to bring the Lion down with a photon torpedo. However, one can't stop de carnival, no matter how pressing other matters might be. Let them land, but insist the Short Lion come directly to me. Get a sketch artist in here. We must preserve the moment of our meeting. After all, I'm about to become more famous than he is. We should get some piccies of him paying homage, kissing bottom and so forth. Agreed?'

The last word was addressed to Patricia.

Holly nodded. Czakyr passed on the instructions.

'Resistance in Cluj,' said Rose Murasaki.

'It must be crushed,' said Meinster, holding up a fistful of poodle. 'Crushed utterly.'

The Baron was enjoying himself. Between orders, he hummed along to the concert, which was relayed in on audio and playing on CNN. At Stonehenge, the London Company of the musical *Bats* were prancing with paper wings and singing 'Count Boris Bolescu and the Black Pudding'.

'The warm used to be afraid of us,' said Penny, looking at the monitor.

'They will be again,' promised the Baron.

'You never said a truer word,' said Holly.

The Baron chortled, and whispered to his poodles.

'Striescu is dead,' said Rose and Crainic at the same time. They looked at each other and at their phones, wondering if they were speaking to the same person.

Meinster frowned. This was not on his schedule.

'His lieutenants must extract reprisals,' he decreed. 'Instant, bloody, disproportionate.'

'His lieutenants killed him,' said Rose.

Meinster was shocked and annoyed. A photographer, darting out of an alcove, took a shot with the blinding flash necessary to fix the Baron on film. The lightblast lingered in everyone's eyes. So did the Baron's pout of acute discomfort.

'I want that film,' he said.

The photographer bleated that he had been summoned to take pictures.

'An announcement is being made,' said Crainic, interrupting the interruption. 'Look.'

CNN had a feed from Timişoara. Outside the city hall, a mob were kicking apart a crumbling corpse. Someone read out an admirably thorough list of Striescu's crimes. On the balcony the unmistakable scarecrow shadow of Orlok was cast against the building, arms and talons outspread. The Graf himself could not be caught by electronic devices like television cameras.

Meinster's face went grey under powder. Graf von Orlok was the one vampire everyone remembered to be afraid of.

'He's on his way down,' said Czakyr.

'Who?'

The elder shrugged. 'The Short Lion?'

'Not a good time. Patty, deal with it.'

Holly nodded but did nothing.

'It's not just Striescu,' said Rose Murasaki. 'In Cluj, five elders are down. All over the place, it's happening. A coup within a coup. Our ringleaders are being staked from behind, and minions are taking their places.'

'Such treachery will be punished,' screamed Meinster. His poodles picked up his mood and yapped ferociously. 'Who are the culprits? Who must I kill?'

Crainic and Czuczron looked at each other.

'How close are my enemies?' asked Meinster.

'In Cluj, they say *he* has returned. And in Oradea, and Lugos, and Sibiu. Responsibility is being claimed by… the Order of the Dragon.'

'Impossible. *I* command the Order of the Dragon. I revived it personally. Executing the will of my father-in-darkness. He speaks through me. To defy me is to resist His will.'

Patricia remembered banners unfurling on the face of an embassy, just as they were flapping from the hall in Timişoara. Orlok had been there too.

'We've lost,' said Czakyr, downing headphones.

'Nonsense,' said the Baron, chest puffed with indignation, strands coming loose from his pompadour. 'These flags, they are in support of us. That must be it. We've not lost. We've won.'

The doors opened.

10

He was known at once. This was his castle. He was its master by right of conquest and possession.

Vassals paid attention, then prostrated themselves at his feet. An oriental woman knelt before him, forehead against stone floor, neck exposed for the blade. Czuczron, a captain of the Carpathian Guard, offered his sheathed sword. Elders hung their heads and opened their hands, awaiting punishment.

His women lowered their eyes and stood at his side.

His lieutenants, having trotted at his heels as he made his way through these familiar halls, filtered into the command room. They took over stations the usurper's people had been manning, picking up telephonic apparatus, glancing over charts and maps, checking audio and visual input.

The Romanian, Crainic, and the Englishman, Gorse, took up phones and gave code-words. The American, Captain Gardner, posted his soldiers throughout the castle, relieving the few who still pledged allegiance to the usurping Meinster. Any disputes were swiftly resolved, with his Bat-Soldiers kicking the red dirt that had been their enemies. Word came down from the battlements that General Iorga, finally doing something useful, had relieved the commandant of the guards of his duties. The elder vampires who had flown in with the helicopter took up their positions, and ran up flags.

In moments, he was again master of this land.

The usurper stuttered in the middle of the room, a popinjay clutching two absurd dogs. He was a girlish boy, caught wearing his mother's ball gown. Red tears flowed from pale eyes, rouged mouth opened and closed like a fish.

He fixed Baron Meinster with his eyes.

The usurper knew everything at once. Knew him for who he was and who he had been.

Puzzled, the Baron groped deep in his mind for a name.

'The boy,' he said, 'at Dinu Pass. What was your name? Did you even have a name?'

Ion Popescu, they thought, together.

'No,' said Meinster. 'Not the boy.'

The Baron understood at last what had happened in the Keep, what had been done to set them on the course that inevitably led to this place, to this moment.

He extended his hand to Meinster. The blood ruby glowed on his forefinger. The Baron, sobbing silently, stepped forwards, over his abject people, and made his way to him. He looked up with fear and love and could say nothing.

Meinster pressed his face to the ring and clutched. His dogs fell free.

'Master,' he said, acknowledging a truth.

He looked down at the usurper's shaking back.

'I didn't turn you,' he said.

Meinster squeezed his hand and wet it with tears.

'My punishment,' the Baron got out. 'What is my punishment to be?'

'You are not worth punishing. You are no martial man, to be sent to honourable death. You are a dog, like your pets. And so it shall be.'

He withdrew his hand. Meinster fell to the floor.

He called the tiny minds of the dogs. Quietly, with no yapping, they came to attention, fixed on white throat, and attacked. Their fangs tore through ruffles and sank into skin and vein.

Spoiled blood spilled.

His women were at his shoulder, watching the usurper suffer.

The Baron's mind bled out through the rips under his chin, gushing and dissipating. He wondered where the century had gone.

The usurper's mouth pursed.

'P-Pat...'

Meinster looked to the woman he had called bride, seeing her face blur and shift. His eyes burned bright for a moment and were dull. He murmured through the hole in his throat and lay still, meat in the shape of a man.

With his passing, the last memory of a warm boy who had met the King of the Cats in a granite keep vanished from the world. Now no one remembered him, it was as if he had never been.

'Let them know that I have returned.'

'Yes, Count,' said Crainic.

He turned to the woman who had shaped herself to get close to the usurper.

In her place, in her clothes, stood a boy with a gun, aimed at his face.

'Re-ma-ma-re-muh-me-member me, Granpa?' said Kit Carruthers.

11

Granpa Munster was going to take a silver slug between the eyes, then his long-dead brains were going to splat out of the flap in the back of his head and redecorate these walls. Kit had seen it before. It always struck him as funny. All that a person was could become grey and red mush at a single trigger pull.

'Been bidin' my time 'til now,' he said. 'Makes it more special.'

'Holly,' said the Englishwoman. 'Come back.'

'Holly ain't home, sweet thing. Just me. The Big Bad Wolf with a Big Bad .44 Magnum, all loaded up for bat. Steel-jacketed silver rounds. One of these pops inside your viper ass and it's *sayonara senorita*.'

'Shazam.'

'That's for the songbird. Don't work on Killer Kit.'

Granpa was a picture of rage. He stood tall, just like in the video store. Dressed all in black for his own funeral. His face stretched into a fearsome mask, white as milk with lines of scarlet around his eyes and mouth.

A fancy-pants viper in some kind of uniform made a move, trying to untangle his side-arm from a webbing of braid and sash. Kit swivelled, put a silver starburst in the elder's heart, and, ignoring the recoil that hammered his wrist and elbow, drew a bead again on Granpa. In the flash of distraction, the old man had taken a step towards Kit, hands raised like the boogedy man, nails thorny diamond barbs.

'You'd purely like to get your hands on me, wouldn't ya? Your hands *into* me?'

The dead elder was on his knees, coming apart inside his tunic, black flakes falling away from his bones. His chest cavity was exploded from the inside, as if his heart had hatched into a hand grenade.

Holly was inside him somewhere, his woman like always, back on the team. She had wavered, been tempted away by this mad old man, left Kit for dead. But he had always been with her, small and quiet and healing. They had known they would always be together. Now they were as together as people could be, sharing one skeleton.

Granpa dropped his hands, straightened up.

His backbone was iron. He didn't know he was broken yet. Kit had met too many like him over the years, starting before Doc Porthos turned him and Holly. All had looked down at him and learned – if not lived – to regret it.

Kit gestured with his smoking Magnum.

'Granpa, I guess this makes me Master of the Universe.'

Kit decided to get it over with and pulled the trigger.

12

———————◆———————

He was still faster than a speeding bullet, even one fired so close to his face.

He saw the silver point emerge from the barrel of Kit's typically overgrown gun. He fixed on the killing streak as it inched across the space between them. He put his head to one side, and watched the bullet drill lazily past him, spinning as it travelled.

His hand fastened on Kit's gun hand, squeezing.

The boy's eyes were wide in a 'not again' expression. Kit's flesh and bone was crushed, the gun began to buckle. Inside his fist, something cracked.

He reached into the boy's head and flicked a switch.

Holly looked at him, appalled.

'He's gone now,' he told her. 'Forever.'

He let her go. The useless gun fell from her hand. She shifted the mangled ruin, fixing everything.

Penny took Holly away. The Englishwoman was shocked, and feared reprisals. When she looked at him, she could peel away the faceskins of John Alucard and Johnny Pop to see Dracula. He remembered Penelope Churchward from the old nights, saw himself in her mind as he had been when weak, exiled, despairing, desiring true death. That Dracula was deleted, wiped off the slate. Now the times were right and he was what he had been. All who had beset him were shrugged off. Here, in this castle where it had all begun, he was again King of the Cats.

Music filled the room. Two voices, joined.

'Imagine…'

Yes, he had imagined. And he had made the whole world imagine along with him. He was master of this land, and of so much more.

'They need you on stage, Count,' said Gorse. 'Now.'

'Of course.'

13

John wasn't himself any more, or he was more himself than Holly had ever seen. She was changed too. Kit no longer coiled in her depths. She was at last free of him, even of the sense of who he had been, what part of her he had fulfilled. He'd gone to another kind of true death.

Captain Gardner had people taking away the bodies. Nikita and the Angel carried the slack Baron Meinster between them, his fat poodles loping at their heels. Czakyr, a sheepish elder, had been given a broom and pan and told to deal with what was left of Lajos Czuczron and several other Meinster supporters who were in the same condition.

At their stations, Ernest Gorse and Crainic were talking with a dozen people all at once, liaising with the world's media and the coup's ringleaders. On stage, the Short Lion and Timmy V sung John Lennon's song. The whole world was watching.

An attendant scurried up to the vampire who had been John Alucard and settled a black, floor-length cloak on his shoulders.

Penny gripped Holly's arm. She was terrified and struck with wonder.

'It's Him,' she said. 'He's come back.'

Holly stroked Penny's face with her nails.

'Yes,' she agreed. 'He has.'

14

The two singers, a youth and a child, stood in their respective circles of light winding pure, cold voices around each other. Out on the hillside, a hundred thousand points of light burned, fires against the coming of dawn.

The vampires sang of what was to come. Of the world without heaven or hell, without property or theft. Of the world with peace and order, with love and obedience. As they finished, there was a moment of silence, like the long seconds between lightning and thunder, pregnant with applause and acclaim.

The silence lengthened.

The singers were both astonished, robbed of their power, wondrous at what could turn off such an inevitable hurricane of noise.

He stepped out through the door in the backdrop. Alone.

The singers knew him at once. Even they were humbled.

He flung open the wings of his scarlet-lined black cloak, displaying the red dragon on his black silk tunic, and walked across the stage.

He needed no microphone.

'I bid you welcome to my house,' he announced to the multitudes on the mountainside, and to the billions watching around the world. 'Come freely. Go safely, and leave some of the happiness you bring.'

Like a divine wind, it rushed at the stage. The sound of the people, of *his* people. More than applause and cheering, it was a massed cry of triumph and sacrifice and homage and love. It was his right.

There was only one more announcement to make. It needed to be said aloud.

'I… am… Dracula.'

INTERLUDE

DR PRETORIUS AND MR HYDE

ANNO DRACULA 1991

No wonder the old Count picked London as the capital of his vampire empire. Grey cloud rendered the sky sunless at two in the afternoon, as if the day had given up early. Streetlamps stubbornly refused to shine, but everyone drove with headlights on. The well-lit cheer of January sales shops just reminded Kate Reed of the prevailing misery. It was as cold and wet as it could be without actual rain. At least there was no fog. The Clean Air Acts of the 1950s had dispelled the city's 'pea-soupers' forever.

She was in a quiet square, one of many corners removed from the flow and bustle of the metropolis. Even a hundred years ago most of these Georgian mansions had been sub-divided into flats, carved up in the first of many calamitous property gold rushes. Buildings bristled with satellite dishes and estate agents' signs.

Crazy prices. Boom and bust.

Her landlord kept offering to buy her out of the tenancy agreement she'd signed with his father ('They call *me* a bloodsucker, ha-ha!') in 1955. The son still believed he could make a packet by getting rid of his sitting tenants and the ground-floor launderette and converting the building into a yuppie hive. Holloway Road was bound to gentrify. The first espresso machine had already been sighted north of Highbury and Islington Tube Station. But the long-lived clung to their few legal rights, an inconvenience for anyone who wanted to cash out and retire to Spain. Kate would give in eventually and accept her cut of the silly money floating about London even after the last stock market quake. She thought the landlord might be on the point of switching from carrot to stick.

An instinct sharpened over a century suggested she was often – indeed, now – shadowed by someone stealthy enough to stay out of her eyeline whenever she turned. To whit: someone more dangerous than her.

Once, when she had semi-official status with the Diogenes Club, she'd have had Nezumi, her former neighbour, watching her back. A thousand-year-old schoolgirl who could do as much damage with a hockey stick as a samurai sword was always welcome on any dangerous jaunt. The last Kate had heard, the Japanese vampire was working in the public sector, as *yojimbo* for the Nakatomi Corporation.

The address she sought was marked by a blue plaque. Henry Jekyll 'chemist and natural scientist' lived here from 1868 to 1902. He was honoured for scientific researches into the vampire condition, but Kate remembered the name from a run of minor scandals. The good doctor was known for keeping bad company: vivisectionists, bully boys, resurrection men, low people of all sorts. A string of murders was laid at the back door of this house, attributed to a monkeyish lout named Edward Hyde, bosom pal (and more?) of Dr Jekyll. Hyde, infamous after skewering a vampire Member of Parliament, eluded the long arm of the law and apparently escaped to the Continent or the Americas.

In the 1880s and '90s, when Dracula ruled England, ordinary villains often got away with crimes that in more reasonable times would have been punished. Last Sunday's *Independent* had run a piece on the papers of Sir Rodger Baskerville, unsealed fifty years after his peaceful death in bed surrounded by doting grandchildren. It seemed the West Country baronet had acceded to his title in 1889 by contriving the deaths in improbable circumstances of relatives who stood between him and the family fortune. No one had been around to stop him. The most notable criminal investigators of the period tended to be labelled enemies of the crown they had once served, and got packed off to the Tower or the internment camp at Devil's Dyke. Only a lifelong tendency to mouse-like unnoticeability had preserved Kate from such a fate.

She was more and more reminded of those times.

Last year, on the eve of April Fool's Day, she'd taken part in a peaceful protest against Mrs Thatcher's Poll Tax and found herself – for the second time – caught in Trafalgar Square between rioters and the police. Memories of the Bloody Sunday of 1887, when radicals were left dead after the melée, came back in a rush as a young vampire plod battered her with a plexiglass shield and dragged her off to be charged with breach of the peace.

Mrs Thatcher was gone now. But Dracula was back.

It had to be true. She'd seen it on television.

There was no point in dawdling on the pavement. She felt in her blood that someone was in the square, out of sight, intent upon her. It was beyond her skills to lure her stalker into the open. He, she or it was just a distraction. She had a call to make.

The names by the buzzers were mostly typed or dymo-taped, but the one she was looking for was scrawled in a spidery hand on a yellowed strip of card.

Just the surname: Pretorius.

Or Pretorious or Praetorius, no one seemed quite sure how it was spelled. From the card, it was impossible to tell.

She pressed the entry-phone button and waited.

She tried to suppress unease. Whoever was tracking her shouldn't have the satisfaction of knowing she was spooked. She was, after all, a blood-sucking fiend. She ought to be beyond fearing the reaper.

The door clicked open with an insect buzz and she stepped into a dreary hallway. The tile floor was dusty and scuffed. Two expensive-looking bicycles were chained to a clunky old radiator. A junk-shop table was piled with circulars, letters and rolled magazines.

Most of the mansion was carved into flats, but Pretorius

leased a separate building accessible across a courtyard. She understood it had once been Jekyll's laboratory.

The man appeared at the end of the passage. Ancient but spry, with cracked papery skin and an arrangement of fine, white, flyaway hair, he wore a white medical smock which flowed down past his ankles. He was not a vampire but she recognised in him the symptoms of a long, long life.

She'd run into other shady characters who persisted in clinging to warmth, preserving themselves like living Egyptian mummies. The Daughter of the Dragon ran an investment bank from a glass tower in Docklands, built where the Lord of Strange Deaths once operated opium dens and smuggling rackets.

'Reed, I presume,' Pretorius snipped. 'Come in, come in. No need to stand on ceremony. My time is too valuable to waste on faffing about.'

'Quite,' she replied.

He turned and scuttled through a door. Following him, she found herself in the courtyard. Little light filtered down into the stone well.

'Cheerless, is it not? Your Victorian friends loved their Sunday gloom like a scourge.'

'Hardly *my* Victorian friends.'

He stopped short and turned to her.

'But you are *that* Katharine Reed, are you not? The Irish insurrectionist and scribbler?'

'That's me all right. I just don't think of myself as a typical Victorian.'

He barked. It took seconds to register as a laugh.

'Nonsense. Look at you. Buttoned up to the neck and down to the ankle. Hair up under your hat, with just one long red strand out of place. And those wire-framed spectacles. You dress like a governess.'

'I narrowly escaped that fate, I admit. By taking on a career.'

'And becoming a monster?'

'A vampire.'

'Quibbles, quibbles. Monsters, vampires, men, women. All the same. Blood and bone and meat and that vital spark. Enter my lair, Ms Reed.'

He pulled open a door in the wall.

The laboratory was a barn-like space, musty with trapped air and stale chemicals. Alcoves were curtained off with sacking. Against the walls stood benches piled with complex arrangements of tubes and retorts. Dozens of specimens were displayed in sealed test tubes, marked with runes she couldn't interpret. A patched-together computer grew out of a roll-top desk bored through with cable-holes, a walnut-veneer '50s television cabinet housing the monitor, an old Remington portable typewriter hooked up with a thousand copper wires as a keyboard.

Pretorius took a stoppered bottle of clear liquid and a couple of beakers down from a shelf.

'Would you like some gin? It's my only weakness.'

He unstoppered the bottle. At five paces, her nose and eyes stung. He must distil the juniper himself, refining spirits that could legally be classed as a poison.

She waved a polite turn down.

'Don't mind if I tipple? I promise not to topple.'

He giggled at his wordplay, decanted a calculated measure, showed her his teeth, and took a sip. Perhaps it wasn't just gin. Maybe it was his *elixir vitae*. She had no idea how old he was. Geneviève had said he looked this age in 1959. The only picture in his *Guardian* cuttings file was from 1935; it showed exactly this face lurking at the back of a society wedding. Something about the Pretorius countenance was mediaeval. He might be a heretical monk or a cynical inquisitor.

'Do sit down. Clear off that chair.'

She lifted a pile of petit-point magazines, labelled with the address of a nearby dentist, and settled in a battered old armchair. The furniture was her vintage. She remembered Uncle Diarmid, who'd gently tugged her into journalism, spending his last, gout-ridden years in just such a chair, railing against the injustices of the world and the poor prose of those who now wrote for the journals he'd kept alive during the Terror.

Pretorius preferred to stand. Not a tall man, he liked a dramatic backdrop. It struck her that this scientific clutter might not actually work. The apparatus was put together like a live-in sculpture, to give the impression of a mad scientist's lair.

'So, the famous Kate Reed comes a-calling? She must be on the trail of a story. What story, pray, could interest such a distinguished lady scribbler? Only one springs to mind this cold, cold January.'

'Dracula.'

The scientist looked up at the corners of his space, mobile eyebrows vibrating like antennae. He arranged his wrinkles into a wry smile.

'That name. So familiar, yet so strange. Three syllables. Dra. Cu. La.' He threw in a Transylvanian flourish, fluttering his dry-stick fingers, gesturing with an imaginary cape. 'Count Dracula. Prince Dracula. King of the Cats. *Vampirus Rex Redivivus*. He who was dead and walks once more.'

'You watch television, then?'

'Avidly. Though the medium has not recovered from the cancellation of *Crossroads*.'

'You've seen the Concert for Transylvania?'

'Who hasn't?'

The finale had been repeated more often than the *Monty Python* Dead Parrot sketch. Whole talk shows and quickie paperbacks were devoted to picking over what had actually happened barely a month ago, after the Short Lion and Timmy V finished squawking through 'Imagine'.

'"I... am... Dracula,"' quoted Pretorius. 'Easy to say, of course.'

She remembered Marlon Brando repeating the line for a whole night's shoot. In Transylvania.

'But hard to mean,' she said.

'Oh yes. Very hard to mean.'

'I saw Dracula dead. In Rome, in 1959. I saw his head struck off. I was covered with his blood. Later, on a beach, I saw his body burned. Ashes scattered.'

Pretorius nodded.

'You performed the autopsy, Doctor. My friend Geneviève Dieudonné identified the body in the morgue where you were working.'

'I remember. Pretty girl. Blonde. Nice smile, if you like smiles.'

'Was there anything unusual about the corpse? Something that didn't get into the reports?'

'My dear Ms Reed, there was *everything* unusual about the corpse. It was *Count Dracula*. Don't you understand? He was not – as you are not – a *natural* being. We are all law-breakers now, violating a dozen of God's ordinances every day. Just by wearing spectacles, you refuse to accept the heavenly verdict of myopia. And by turning vampire, you venture into regions where science can be of only limited help. The Count journeyed far further. You have turned and stopped. He kept turning, turning, turning.'

The gin gave Pretorius strange inner fire. She wondered if she should have accepted his drink offer.

'I know it was Dracula who died,' she said. 'But, thinking back, I don't know if it was him we burned.'

The doctor barked again and his skinny body shook with mirth. He raised fingernails to his mouth, like a baroness covering a belch.

'You think I sewed his head back on? Hooked him up to a car battery with jump-leads? Did I bring him back to life? Not just a vampire, but a zombie of science, a revivified corpse?'

Kate knew she was blushing.

'Your assistant in Rome was…'

'Herbert West. Little American pipsqueak.'

'He once published a paper…'

'…on reanimation of dead tissue through a glowing reagent. Tomfoolery, piffle, flimflammery, nonsense and bullshit. He could never get it to work. His results were more pathetic than those of… well, a name best forgotten. Let us say the American never equalled the achievements of the Swiss, and the Swiss was merely a pupil who trotted along in my tracks. A C-grade student.'

'So West couldn't have brought him back?'

'A beheaded vampire? No.'

'Could you?'

He saw the trap she had manoeuvred him into.

'If I'd put my mind to it, I daresay I could have. I enjoy a challenge. But it seemed at the time a fruitless avenue of research. Still does. If I put my mind to it, I could develop an otherwise harmless retrovirus that would turn the whole human race a nice shade of eggshell blue. Even a scientist as pure as I, needs some sense of practical application.'

'A blue world might exist without racism.'

'Touché, Ms Reed. As it happens, Dracula seems to have returned without my genius.'

Kate thought of the face on television.

She'd only ever seen Dracula dead. Truly dead. When he was in England a hundred years ago, she'd gone to great lengths *not* to meet him. In exile, he had kept out of the way. Geneviève and Charles had seen him in London, at his zenith. Penelope Churchward saw him in Rome, when he was a fading presence. Penny was with the Count at the moment of death. The true death that now seemed to have been revoked.

Was this moving, living face the Count?

Dracula had lacked a reflection, but the man at the concert cast an image that could be transmitted. A strange image, like a photo-realistic Max Headroom. Fixed and perfect, while other, human, images had a slight flicker as signal lines were misread by the eye as a coherent picture.

Was she right about the face?

She wouldn't have recognised Dracula, but she did see in this face someone she knew, or had known. He was changed, but still there.

It didn't mean he *wasn't* Dracula.

'For what it's worth, Ms Reed. I think it *is* him. It may be that somebody has to be Dracula. His bloodline is by far the most powerful, the most widespread in the world. More vampires claim descent from him than any other father-in-darkness.'

That was true. She was herself of the Dracula line, three or four times removed. Most new-borns of the 1880s were, not all to their advantage.

'I took some of his blood in Rome,' said Pretorius, reaching for a test tube of scarlet fluid. 'I've puzzled over it ever since. Still fresh, you know. Still alive in this tube, as in the veins of his children-in-darkness. It has transformative qualities, beyond those you might know about.'

She wasn't a shapeshifter.

No, she *chose* not to be a shapeshifter. She could do fangs and claws. She was too timid or sensible to go further, remembering what that led to. Others had gone far beyond human shape, becoming beings even she thought of as monsters. During World War I, when Dracula was in Germany, scientists experimenting with the shapeshifting ability of his bloodline created a strain of bat-warriors. Since then, others had pursued the project. Kate stuck close to who she had been, wary of launching into unknown darknesses which might end with the loss of her self.

'Dracula spread his bloodline,' said Pretorius. 'It may be there was a purpose to that we didn't perceive. He turned his get like all vampires, by giving blood as well as taking. The gift may have concealed a surprise. A passenger, like a parasite egg. I think his unique blood trails invisible kite-strings. He has followed one of these strands to batten onto one of his get, slipped into a skull and taken up residence, to redecorate and restore.'

Kate watched and listened.

The blood in the tube moved as Pretorius gestured. She'd woken once with that stuff all over her and a murder charge in the offing. But it wasn't to that memory Dracula's blood called, but to the vampire strain in her veins, the blood the Count had passed to a Carpathian, who had passed it to her father-in-darkness, who had passed it to her.

What would happen if anyone drank that blood? What if, here in Jekyll's old laboratory, she or Pretorius were to unstopper the tube and drain it down? She had already turned once. Into a vampire. If, as a vampire, she turned again, what would she become?

'He was tired, though,' she said. 'His death in '59 was as much suicide as murder.'

'He was tired in 1959, but what about 1945 or 1888 or 1720? He used himself up many times over. It seems he has come back not as he was at the end, but as he was in his prime.'

Kate remembered to be scared.

It was dark in here, even to her vampire eyes. Pretorius stood in a shaft of light, face etched with expressive shadows. Dracula's blood had a dark neon shine.

'I've missed him, you know,' he said. 'Dracula makes things interesting. And these times. How he will love them, how he will fit in with them.'

She knew he was right.

Not, she hoped, about everything. But he was right about the times.

Last week she'd visited Richard Jeperson at the Diogenes Club to talk about the Dracula situation. He was the last caretaker of an abandoned building, keeping everything in his head because all the files were compromised. The club, sponsor to Charles Beauregard and Edwin Winthrop, had been levered out of its position in British Intelligence, which was now run from Cheltenham by Caleb Croft. Only Jeperson, a faded dandy, remained at his post. His Lovelies were scattered. Sergeant Dravot was assigned to a retirement colony for spies in North Wales. Hamish Bond was back on the active list, working behind the scenes in the Persian Gulf.

With Thatcher ousted by a typical Tory free-for-all backstabbing, Lord Ruthven, that great political survivor, was again Prime Minister. Jeperson said Ruthven wasn't sorry to see Baron Meinster dead and was all too ready to do business with this new Dracula. Transylvania was now the vampire homeland Meinster had agitated for, but Dracula announced he would maintain residences in Los Angeles, London (he still owned property in Piccadilly) and New York, leaving to others the governance of a country he could call a private fiefdom.

This time, the Count was a global presence, head of a corporation registered in a land where he could write his own laws. His power was in information technology, entertainment and finance, not the petty businesses of martial conquest and political office. Under the guise of putting together the

Concert for Transylvania, Dracula had assembled a fair-sized media empire. He had already scooped up enough magazine and newspaper ownerships to drive Kate out of the business if he could be bothered with her.

She was afraid the times were changing back.

'Now Ms Reed, I have to shuffle you off. I am in the middle of a course of experiments. The previous tenant left behind interesting notes about rejuvenation and shapeshifting. I scent lucrative patents. Do you know what fools we were? My Swiss pupil, the good Dr Jekyll, the cat-torturing Moreau, life-chasing Nikola, skin-grafting Orloff, the clod West? We toiled amid bones and stinks in cramped laboratories and crypts, violating the laws of God and man. For what? To say we had done it. For the thrill of power over nature. We never, *ever*, thought about what profits there were to be had. Dracula saw clearly. In that confection of truth and fancy Stoker put together, do you recall what the Count is doing when we first meet him? Looking for *treasure*. He saw that blood, that *life*, was not enough. Always, he fed on gold. Cash. Pounds sterling. The almighty greenback dollar. When he was stabbed, he bled money. This time, I intend to license my findings. To the Body Shop or Glaxo or whoever will pay the healthiest royalty.'

She left the scientist to his money dreams.

It was full dark in the square. The presence she'd sensed earlier wasn't gone.

Fed up, depressed and frightened by what she had learned or imagined, she decided to have it out with the landlord's agent. She stood on the pavement and spread out her empty hands.

'Come on, then,' she said, letting the Irish into her voice. 'If you think you're hard enough...'

Her words came back to her, an echo.

For a moment, she thought she was being silly. No one was after her. No one would come out of the dark.

Then, they did.

PART SIX

CHARLES'S ANGELS

ANNO DRACULA 1991

1

———————◆———————

Earthquake, brushfire, riot and the opening weekend figures
of *Hudson Hawk* changed nothing. It was as if she'd never
been away.

Geneviève drove along Sunset, at sunset. Ahead, the blood-
red daystar sank swiftly into shimmering haze. Windows
flashed green-gold in pastel stucco facades, reflecting distant
fires. Titanic billboards for the new Stallone loomed above
the cityscape, visible from low Earth orbit. Everything was
new, but already faded.

Ever since her flight entered California airspace, she'd
expected the evil angels would come out of the sky and tear
her apart. She knew better than to think twenty years away
meant forgiveness and forgetting. The powers she'd upset held
grudges like champions. They had the patience to carry out a
plan of revenge over decades. Kate Reed, of all people, knew
this... but the Irish woman was right – Los Angeles was where
they both needed to be right now. If they were really marked,
punishment could reach them anywhere in the world.

She passed the Church of Immortology Celebrity Drop-In
Centre. People queued outside as if it were a trendy club.
Scrubbed, enthusiastic vampire youths chattered non-stop to
keep the half-hearted from growing bored and dropping out
of the line before they passed the velvet rope to exchange
donations for enlightenment. L. Keith Winton was missing
on the high seas. The rumour was that he'd not long survived

his own turning – a major embarrassment, since he'd had years to prepare a perfect 'ascension'. The Immortologists were now run by her old desert acquaintances, General Iorga and Diane LeFanu. The scam might collapse. With Dracula back, lesser undead gurus were superfluous.

Like the rest of the world, Geneviève had caught the Big Comeback on television. The Dracula story had stayed at the top of the bulletins for barely two months before George Bush and Lord Ruthven went into Kuwait and the Bat-Soldiers started unloosing smart bombs over Baghdad. Now that unsatisfying little war was over, Dracula was back in the news again. His resurrection was blindly accepted in the media and his spell in True Death was vanishing from official biographies. She guessed John Alucard had tried another conjuring, one that played more like usurpation than transformation. The vampire who'd driven her out of town in 1981, whoever he had been, was obliterated. Now there was only Dracula.

The Hertz rental was a hard-top with a tinnitus of air conditioning she didn't know how to switch off. Her bare arms and face were blasted with ice molecules. She turned on the car radio.

'That's the same engine under the hood,' sang Wynonna Judd, 'carried young Elvis to Hollywood…'

The song, '(Look At It Now) It's Just Like New', gave her a bone chill beyond the prickle of the in-car blower. America always had a soundtrack. Pop music was everywhere, like weather. The pathetic fallacy was false no longer. The whole world really reflected your emotions, sticking a pin through your heart and freezing you in place. She was the fifteenth century fox – the first songs she had heard or sung were labelled 'early music' in the record stores which carried that sort of thing – but she was exactly as the country singer advertised, 'just like new'.

For a year she'd lived in something like her European idea of a city – crowded, intense, directed, noisy. A city without a centre is not necessarily a city without a heart, but the pulse of Los Angeles was harder to find than the beat of Baltimore.

California was eerily quiet, diffuse as sunset through smog, a desert mirage which would evaporate when the oasis ran dry. The gumshoe once told her LA was called the City of the Angels because it was an afterlife community. As retirees flocked to Florida or young pioneers headed for Oregon, the just-dead came here. He hadn't only meant vampires. She wasn't much for graves, but would try to find out where the old man was buried. He'd given her a gentle push at a moment when it would have been easy for her to drift away from humanity.

People filtered onto the street, coming awake. A rag-like human shadow tugged at her attention, but was gone when she looked.

She kept glancing at a blizzard of signage, determined not to miss her turn-off. Even street-names had to compete with ads and announcements. Any available space – bus stops, benches, car-bumpers and doors, loose clothes, bare flesh – bore a commercial, public message or hey-look-at-me proclamation. A vampire woman, an unreflecting Amazon called Illyana, appeared on vast painted billboards not to advertise anything, but to become and remain famous.

Geneviève's four years in Los Angeles were more vivid to her than whole decades in other places. In modern times, only the years with Charles burned more intensely in her crowded memory. She was here because of a man dead for over thirty years. Charles Beauregard tied her to the world Dracula made far more than the ancient accident of turning vampire. He'd found her in the margins of a changing society and taken her on an uncomfortable journey through it, a path which led inevitably to the Count. Charles had died in 1959, just before Dracula – still fighting the man and the monster. Then again: Dracula was back, and Charles was still dead.

When she left LA, under orders, Geneviève had broken with the memory of Charles. He would have stayed, no matter the cost.

In Toronto and then Baltimore, she'd tried to live as her warm lover would have wished. In Los Angeles, influenced by the gumshoe, she'd worked by herself, for herself, doing good by stealth. Away from this city, she'd rejoined society, taken the courses, got the qualifications, drawn salary, tried to make the system better. As an ME, she didn't have a badge but she was a police. Sometimes it was frustrating – just as Charles had been politely infuriated by the deviousness and bureaucracy of the Diogenes Club – but the hard-won victories were mostly permanent. If she'd gone after Ernest Ralph Gorse as she had after murderers in Canada and Baltimore, assembling evidence and trusting law enforcement professionals to carry the case on, then perhaps the Overlooker would still be in Alcatraz.

She turned onto Cynthia Street and drove two blocks south, towards Santa Monica Boulevard. She had a 'unit' reserved in the name of the Baltimore Medical Examiners' Office at the Le Reve Hotel, which was actually a motel as opposed to a 'motor inn' or a 'hotel'. '77 Units. Rooms & 1-bedroom units with living room; most with gas fireplace. Refrigerator, A/C, C/CATV, movies, radios, phones; 16 efficiencies. Coin laundry, whirlpool, rooftop pool. Pay garage. No pets. Monthly rates avail. AE, CB, DI, MC, VI. Room service avail.'

After parking in the pay garage, an off-street cavern that made her uneasy, she checked in, presenting her Visa (VI) card at reception. She thought of telling someone there might be something in the garage, keeping to the shadows, waiting for a moment to pounce. But the feeling was vague and had been with her even on the plane. It didn't do to cry wolf; not when there were always wolves.

The girl on reception was a blonde vampire, turned early in her teens. Her tag read 'Crosby'. No indication whether it was a first- or surname. She wore a green blazer and matching skirt. Her fluffy crimson scarf-cum-choker was another sign, an indication of dhampire-sexual availability or unavailability depending on the side of her throat the knot was tied. Crosby was, quite properly, not in the bleeding business while on duty. She stood on a wooden block to give her the height to see over the desk, but her reach wasn't quite enough to hand across the key without stretching.

Geneviève's unit turned out to be a divided space that wanted to be a suite when it grew up. Bedroom, living room and bathroom fitted together as neatly as compartments in a recreational vehicle. She stacked her cases in the living room, filling the gap between couch and television. The TV was on when she stepped into the room. She turned it off. The place was quiet, except for the whirr of A/C and distant city noises. She could live with it.

She didn't need to sleep but checked the bedroom anyway. It was mostly bed. A wardrobe could be angled down, base sliding up in a cunning levered arrangement like a Murphy bed, and made into a coffin. If she were in town long enough to have a spell of lassitude, she'd use the bed.

On the pillow was a cream envelope with her name written on it in a copperplate hand. Not Kate's writing – that was an illegible scrawl or, if she needed to communicate, a childish arrangement of unjoined letters. Kate probably had to type love letters and shopping lists.

Geneviève picked up the envelope and slid a thumbnail through the flap.

A red-edged card came loose.

MIRACLE PICTURES

invites

Geneviève Dieudonné

to a very special screening of

"THE ROCK"

in the presence of

COUNT DRACULA

June 16th, 1991. 10.30 reception for midnight start.
At the Directors' Guild of America Theatre,
7920 Sunset Blvd., #230, Los Angeles, CA 90046

Black tie. Refreshments. Beverages.

He knew she was here. That was the first message. But she still couldn't tell who He was. Anyone could call themselves Count Dracula. It wasn't as if 'John Alucard' ever had the ring of being a real name. Whoever he was, he knew they would meet, and wished it to be on his terms.

She considered the bland invitation.

Twice before, she'd been summoned into the Royal Presence. All the world knew how those parties had turned out: with a spark that lit the fire of revolution, and a death that seemed to end the reign of the King of the Cats. This was Hollywood. Dracula was in the movies now. If he wanted to direct yet another remake, he could come up with an ending to suit him this time.

What would Charles have advised? Or the gumshoe?

'Snap,' said a voice she knew. 'I've got one too.'

Geneviève turned swiftly. Kate stood in the bedroom doorway. She must be growing stealthy in vampire mid-life, for she'd entered without making a sound. Kate held up her own invitation to *The Rock*.

'Kate,' said Geneviève, delighted at not being alone.

'Gené,' said the Irish vampire, weakly, holding back.

Geneviève advanced to embrace, then saw the change in her friend. Kate's hair was arranged unusually, blossoming over her forehead and half her face. She swept the hair-mask away, and brought her face into the light for examination. Under her glasses a patch covered her right eye. Red nail-rakes began at her hairline and scraped under the patch and down across her cheek, cutting into her upper lip, drawing her mouth into a half-snarl, and terminating in gouges along her jaw-line.

'Don't I look a fright now?' said Kate.

Geneviève leaked sympathy.

'You don't want to know how it happened,' said Kate, dropping her hair.

Geneviève felt the pain pouring out of Kate's heart and was dismayed at deeper changes. The mark went beyond the skin, biting into the person Katharine Reed had been. No wonder she had cultivated stealth.

'Was it Him?'

Geneviève held up the card.

'Dracula? No. One of his creatures. There are more and more of them. A woman thing. Horrible Holly. She's always nearby, I think. In the shadows, stalking. A huntress and a shifter.'

'But he had it done?'

'That he did. And don't think I escaped – I was left alive. It's not enough that we be killed. We have to join his parade. Go to his party. Once before, we had a choice. We could have prospered by declaring ourselves for him. Now, we have that choice again. I don't know about you, my darling, but I don't think I can go through it all again. I won't step willingly into the dark.' The woman sagged, clinging to the door-frame for support.

Geneviève put her arms around her – Kate had always been tiny, but now she was frail, without weight – and hugged her. Kate began to cry silently, her whole body shaking. Tears of blood welled from her remaining eye and smeared her cheek. Geneviève cradled Kate's head and held it to her chest, feeling the trickle of her own tears.

She saw the oblong invitations, both dropped to the floor. It would not end here.

2

Only half of Kate was in the Le Reve Hotel with Geneviève. The rest was outside, looking from a dark place at a tiny arena of light. Ever since the attack in London, she had been split into pieces. Part of her was torn away and beyond her control, mind flapping in the wind.

She had been gutted, her person stolen by the girl-thing who had raked her face and bitten her neck. Nearer death than at any time since her turning, she was tempted to let go and surrender to the siren lure of not-being. Truly dead girls don't have to worry about the landlord's complaints or the resurrection of the Prince of Darkness. They just play the harp on a cloud, sleep away the ages or go into the light.

When Dracula's Bitch sank fingertips up to the knuckles into her skull, Kate dwindled to human stickwood. For a while, she'd been folded up in a travel container, imported to the United States as airmail. She wasn't a person with a passport, but 'experimental vegetative matter'. Then, for untold weeks, she'd been stacked in an Alucard-owned facility outside the city, the Alcore Institute.

Now, in this tiny room, Kate looked out of one eye and heard herself telling her friend to give up. Dracula had won, again. In the long run, his will was too strong. If they stood against him, they'd always be on the outside, wounded and weak. The whole world *wanted* Dracula. He was an absolutist tyrant, but if he ran for election he'd get in on a landslide. Transylvanians rejoiced under his rule. Pledges poured into his coffers. He was *Time* Man of the Year.

Next to him, they were two old women.

But she couldn't really believe it. She couldn't let go yet. Even on ice, with a drip-feed doling diluted blood into her, she'd known she must fight. She thought of Charles, keeping at the battle 'til the end. As keenly as he fought the obvious enemy, he'd struggled to keep his cause from becoming a dark mirror of the standard he rode against. Kate had eluded Caleb Croft's Secret Police in 1893, been buried under the treads of a clanking war machine in 1918, woken up covered with Dracula's blood in 1959, had survived the Black Monk BOP trip of 1968 and dug herself out of a Romanian jail with her fingernails in 1977. A bed of ice cubes in a steel coffin wouldn't be her final resting place.

Other human-vampire remnants in the institute were maintained at the lowest level of life. More than trophies, they were templates in cold storage. In arctic dark, they whispered their former names: Feraru, Josie, Patricia, Rudolph, Frank. Their persons – everything that made them who they were – had been stolen with their blood. While they survived as intermittent blips on the monitors, their shapes were available to the shifter, Holly. Kate shuddered to realise the dormant Patricia was

Patricia Rice, whom she had met (and not liked) at the Embassy siege, reduced to a weathered mummy, a skin-clad stick-figure.

Physically she was in as bad shape as the others. But something independent had remained in her, worm-like. Perhaps because she was fresher than the rest; perhaps because she had a longer, harder history. She'd escaped, disguised as the 'medical waste' Alcore dumped in the storm drains. Then, she'd found her way across town, slipping from shadow to shadow like a ghost fleeing the exorcist, following a golden mind-thread that led her, as she'd hoped and feared, to her friend Geneviève. They must know now that she was free. Even if the corpsicle containers weren't regularly checked, the shapeshifter would know Kate was loose. Holly maintained intimate contact with those she fed off.

Her hand crept up Geneviève's back. She felt her friend's heart, her paradoxical *warmth*. She concentrated, cutting through alien fog in her mind, calling the missing half of herself. A curved barb sprouted from her thumb.

The embrace loosened. Kate's sharp nail slipped against Geneviève's throat.

Kate struggled with herself.

She would not be a part of this.

Geneviève would see it soon. The French girl had always been a mind-reader, mostly through instinct and long experience.

She clamped her hand on Kate's wrist, forcing the thumbnail away from her pulse.

Red points sparked in her clear eyes. Understanding.

'*What have you done to my friend?*'

Geneviève gripped the throat of the woman in her room and slammed her back against the wardrobe. Her pretty, mediaeval face shifted into a furious mask. She was enormously fanged, nostrils and eyebrows flared, chin pointed, cheekbones sharp, eyes flames.

'*Where is she?*'

Kate tried to say, but Holly was too strong. Kate was outside, tapping unnoticed at the bedroom window; not inside, summoning strength for a fight to the end. The thread between her mind and the shifter's — which had allowed her to be Kate inside Holly inside Kate for a moment — whipped around, tearing at her skull.

'What have we here?' asked a man, his hand taking hold of Kate's neck. 'Some fools will insist on leaving their bloody rubbish lying around all.'

His accent was English and cruel, like the Black and Tans she'd dodged in 1920. Kate was picked up. Her legs and arms dangled, nerveless.

Inside the room, Geneviève and the Kate-faced Holly turned, attracted by the commotion. Kate saw genuine recognition in her friend's expression. She looked far less like herself than the woman Geneviève was throttling, but her friend knew the difference.

'Let's join the ladies, shall we?' said the Britisher.

Kate couldn't see the man's face. Like her, he had no ghost of reflection in the glass. From the strength of his grip, she knew he was a vampire.

A bad one.

He smashed her head against the window. The glass wobbled in its frame but did not break.

Geneviève was distracted.

The other Kate, Holly-as-Kate, opened her mouth and craned her neck, going for Geneviève's throat.

The British vampire hammered Kate's face against the window.

Glass broke.

Blood spilled. Everything went red.

3

Geneviève lost her grip on the shifting thing that wore Kate's face. The creature was cut under the chin where Geneviève, fending off her dangerous mouth, had caught her with sharp nails. She pressed a red-lined frill of skin against her neck, smoothing away a messy wound. Her power of recuperation was enviable.

'Hello again, old thing,' said Ernest Ralph Gorse through the shattered window, holding what appeared to be a human dishrag. 'Is this yours?'

She spat mediaeval French at him. During the Hundred Years' War many insulting colloquial expressions were coined to describe the English. As long as she and Gorse were both still alive, they wouldn't fall into disuse.

'Because of my classical education, I know what that means,' he drawled. 'Rather, I would if I'd applied myself more. I found it fearfully hard to summon up the *enthusiasm* for cramming. There are always short cuts to favour. I suppose you were a good little girl when you were in school. If they had schools when you were a child. Weren't you expected to get married at nine or something? Squirt out a tribe of sprogs, then drop down dead from the plague. All very "knights of old".'

Gorse kicked away the remains of the window and stepped over the low sill into the room. Gripped in one hand hung a creature who might have lived a thousand years the hard way – without turning vampire. The real Kate Reed was more ruined than the shapeshifter's impersonation. Gorse held a shoulder skinfold in a bunch, pulling discoloured hide tight across Kate's fleshless body. Her withered face was one-eyed, marked by scratches like those the shifter had faked. This was what Geneviève had glimpsed on Sunset and sensed in the garage. Not a threat, but a friend.

She should have known the truth at once. She wasn't supposed to go by appearances. She had intuitions.

She swore at Gorse again.

'Funnily enough, I get your gist,' he said, arching an eyebrow. 'Yes, you are quite correct, I'm a complete and utter sod. Unmitigated rotter to boot. With a side order of absolute bastardy. Always was, always will be. Not that you or this potato-peeler are in any state to do anything about it while my changeable chum-ette is around.'

The woman who wasn't Kate was shifting.

'How do you like our handy Holly, by the way? Isn't she a step up from my former protégé, the much-missed Barbara Winters? This one bends a bit more. Thinks for herself. Can be trusted to get the job done. She doesn't just slay vampires, she vampirises them. In a most interesting way, as you've found out.'

It was more than disguise. Holly really had been Kate. It was how she had got in under Geneviève's radar. When she shifted, Holly assumed an internal shape, rearranging her mind, summoning the original memories and habits. Plainly a risky game: Kate had almost been able to force her hand, take over entirely.

'They're digging a Channel Tunnel, you know,' said Gorse. 'It's been one of Ruthven's pet projects ever since he was warm. He first pitched it to Napoleon. My homeland and yours will be linked by railway. No more risky sea voyages or aeroplanes. Symbolic of something, wouldn't you say?'

He shook Kate as if wagging a gift dolly to get a child's attention.

'Not much left in this old rag and bone, eh?'

Only now did Geneviève realise her shrunken friend was naked, the skin of a great-great grandmother wrapped around the skeleton of a six-year-old.

She was careful not to be too distracted by Gorse. Holly was still here. Her neck-gouge was smoothed now, just like new.

Geneviève looked at the vampire who had tricked her.

Holly took off Kate's glasses and eyepatch. She was a lightly freckled, straw-haired nondescript *nosferatu*. Fine lashes and pale eyes. Kate's clothes were tight on her.

Who had this girl been?

Holly gathered herself and writhed, as if trying to work an ache out of her back. Her hair changed colour, her face filled out.

She was another woman, then a young man, then an older man, yet another woman, a little boy. It was a fluid shuffle through selves. Geneviève recognised one of the faces, a singer who had been on the bill at Dracula's concert. The others were strangers.

'She's a proper little Mike Yarwood,' said Gorse.

Geneviève was puzzled.

'Weren't in England in the '70s, were you? The Yank equivalent would be Rich Little. The impressionist. Still not funny, though? I tell you, it's wasted over here. They don't do irony. You used to be sharper, didn't you? Until America got into your blood and made you thick.'

'How was prison?'

An irritated pause.

'Delightful. After an English public school, Alcatraz is a holiday island paradise.'

'How's the minion business going?'

'Can't get me there, dearie. I've no shame. I know a big fish when I see one, and I'm a minnow. Content to swim along in the wake.'

'A remora, you mean.'

'Now, now, now. Come, come, come. No need to be nasty.'

Holly was still changing. Geneviève couldn't see a point to it. Her other selves were second-raters. It must have been easy to overwhelm and drain them. Only Kate had been a challenge and she had escaped.

Reptile roughness spread across Holly's face.

'Oh no you don't,' said Geneviève. She took hold of the vampire and threw her against the wardrobe. Wood cracked.

Snaketeeth sprouted and eyes yellowed.

'This one you'll like,' said Gorse.

Holly sprang up, slamming Geneviève against the flimsy partition wall. Lath and plaster gave way. She was shoved into the living room, tumbling backwards over piled cases.

'Not a lot, but you'll like it.'

Holly was on top, pinning Geneviève's ribs with her knees. Her hands were stubby cat's paws, flicking out yellow garden-fork claws. Her face shifted somewhere between cobra and panther, black and yellow, with a flaring, furry, muscular hood, and a diamond-pattern forehead like multiple widow's peaks. Her bare arms were sinuous with muscle.

'This has been in the repertoire for a long time,' said Gorse. 'Well before the Count came along. She's self-taught. Very adaptable.'

Geneviève held Holly's wrists and tried to keep the claws

away from her face. The points came nearer. Her own wrists bent the wrong way.

'It didn't matter so much with carrot-top, but you won't be pretty any more, old thing. Does that bother you? Without mirrors, do you have vanity? Or are all men mirrors? You know what you look like by the way we look at you. Is that deep or what?'

In Holly's slit pupils, Geneviève saw no remaining humanity. Just cunning and malice.

Resolved, she braced her elbows and locked her wrists. There was an agonising grinding and snapping, but the descent of claws was halted. Holly had good animal senses and understood her hands were out of play for the moment. Geneviève tried to block the screaming pain in her arms from her mind.

Holly still had teeth. And an anglepoise neck.

Her head rose from her shoulders like a snake from a charmer's basket. Her spine popped more vertebrae, her throat showed more reptile rings.

Holly stretched her long neck. She opened her fang-crowded mouth and gave a tuneless mew. Then she dipped down elegantly and nestled her head on Geneviève's chest, nuzzling her mouth against throat and chin. A scrape of tongue slithered across Geneviève's face, leaving behind a stinging secretion.

'You have to admit she's extreme.'

Gorse sat on the bed, holding Kate in his lap like a ventriloquist's dummy.

Holly's mouth fixed against Geneviève's jugular.

'Now this is a turn-up,' commented Gorse. 'How many necks have you nipped in your night? Tens of thousands. Is this the first time it's been someone else's teeth in you? It's all the rage now. Bleeding vampires. It was Him, you know. His idea. Giving blood back, selling it. Without Dracula, there'd be no dhampires, no drac trade. None of this lovely mess. He's modest and likes to keep it to himself, but he had the idea. Back in New York in the '70s.'

Holly's mouth stayed over Geneviève's pulse. Sharp teeth pressed against skin. If Geneviève moved, she would be slashed. Holly would drink.

JOHNNY ALUCARD

Then, Geneviève would be like Kate. Someone else would use her face, her person. She wouldn't even have to yield to this new Dracula. Holly could do it for her. Would that satisfy the Count?

She saw Gorse fanning Kate with a white card. One of the invitations.

Click.

'You're doing this on your own,' Geneviève said.

The card stopped moving. Geneviève took a breath.

'Dracula wants me alive, to surrender, to kiss his ring. I know that. Someone from the West Coast said as much to me, last year. If anything, I'm under his protection. So's Kate – she was hurt, but not killed. You're the one itching for me to die this minute. You're still a schoolboy, Ernest. You must have your treat now, not later. The Count understands a pleasure stretched across centuries. You don't. Will he be pleased when he finds out?'

She was talking to Holly as much as Gorse.

The shifted creature couldn't cope with ideas but had instincts. The wet mouth withdrew a touch, breaking the contact between lips and skin. A breath escaped.

'And who's going to tell him?' asked Gorse, petulantly.

Geneviève was quite relaxed. The weight was off her.

'You really think he'll need to be told?'

A doubt passed over Gorse's face. He was justifiably afraid of Dracula. In the past lieutenants who betrayed the Count, or even failed to carry out any trivial task, suffered undignified and uncomfortable deaths.

'You'll look like an ice lolly on a stick,' she said.

Holly rolled off Geneviève and gathered herself in, shedding her snake-self, becoming the real girl again. Gorse had let her believe she was acting on their master's wishes. A mistake. Playing with girls' minds was a habit with Ernest Ralph Gorse. Second nature.

Gorse flung Kate away, letting her fall like an old blanket.

'I was saving this for later.'

He took a linen-wrapped parcel from inside his tweed jacket. He shook the wrappings loose and held up a scalpel. It shone, silver.

483

'Recognise it? You should. It has a lot of history.'

Gorse stood and stepped through the enlarged door.

'It killed a Queen once. And a King of the Cats.'

She remembered the blade from Whitechapel, from Buckingham Palace, from the Palazzo Otranto. It was an instrument, not a weapon. She used a post-mortem scalpel exactly like it most days of the week. Yet it had become bloody, over and over.

'I knew you'd like to see this again. I borrowed it from the Count's souvenir drawer. You have to admit it's a neat twist. You came into the story because of the silver knife, and now you're going to make an inglorious exit with it stuck in your tit.'

She stood up. Her wrists hurt. A lot of little bones were cracked or snapped. She wasn't as swift a healer as Holly. It would take minutes before she was right again.

Gorse crouched, shoulders swelling, jacket-seams parting.

'Our Holly's not the only shifter in the room.'

His face expanded, filled out with fur.

Geneviève backed against the unit front door. The wall behind her was more substantial than the partition. A fair-sized animal charging at her would crush her against it rather than shove her through into the courtyard and the swimming pool. She tried to work the door handle, but her smashed wrists rendered her fingers useless clumps. She was bleeding from her sides, where barbs from the Holly thing's knees had sunk in.

'Say goodnight, Geneviève,' growled Gorse.

4

Kate opened her dry mouth and bit into the British vampire's ankle, blunt fangs sinking through wool to scrape the skin. She didn't have the strength to close her jaws. She was choking on an argyle sock.

Gorse looked down at her, surprised and annoyed. A nasty smile played around his fur-fringed lips. He had comical Big Bad Wolf eyebrows.

'I'd better cut out the bog-trotter's heart first,' he said.

He bent down, angling the silver-coated scalpel.

But Kate wasn't just in her own mind. The golden thread still ran.

Holly's mind, where Kate nestled as a passenger, was crowded, but there was a serene patch of self, where the real Holly lived, the girl she had been before Dracula found her, before she had even turned.

There was a switch. Kate threw it.

'Let me go,' said Kate, through Holly.

Gorse was distracted. He looked across the room at Holly and saw Kate.

The barest pulse of Kate remained in her own form.

'*Now*,' insisted Holly-Kate.

Gorse moved fast for such a bulked-out vampire, blade arcing ahead of him. But Kate had Holly sidestep. On the pass, she tore at his ribs with six-inch finger-daggers, shredding through his heavy jacket and raking meat to the skin.

The silver scalpel bit into the wall.

5

Someone in the next unit shouted for them to keep the noise down.

Geneviève could hardly see Holly for Gorse's huge shape. But the shifter was Kate again, completely this time, with two eyes and the fighting Irish in her. Geneviève held her elbows close to her sides and tucked her injured forearms out of the way. Then she launched a series of kicks at Gorse's rump, back and head, stabbing higher and higher with her shoe-tip. She was wearing the comfortable sneakers she liked to travel in, but put enough force into the kicks to make them seem like steel-tipped combat boots. There was a crack. Thick red gruel seeped through the mat of fur on the back of Gorse's skull.

He turned around and stared hate at her.

'The French they are a funny race,' he chanted, 'they fight with their feet…'

Geneviève flew at him, mouth open, fangs extended.

'…and they fuck with their face.'

He put a meaty palm in front of her chin and braced himself to snap her head off. She slipped round it, incisors sinking into his hand just below the root of the little finger, then scraping over his wrist, clamping tighter, scoring two red lines through his sleeve and arm.

She was inside his guard and could have torn his throat and face if her hands were any use.

Holly-Kate's hands weren't injured. She had claws in the soft part of Gorse's neck, wriggling in deeper past tendon, bone and vein.

Geneviève got her shoulder under Gorse's chest and heaved him up off the floor, shifting his balance. He pressed down on her, bearing on her spine as Holly had borne on her wrists. New agonies clamoured in the small of her back and up along her spinal cord. If she cracked again, she would be out of the game for good.

Gorse had his scalpel back and his arm raised.

She saw him thinking, deciding which woman was the bigger threat. Holly-Kate won, and the scalpel descended towards the back of her neck. Her hands were deep in Gorse's throat, occupied.

Geneviève reached up and put her hand in the way.

One advantage was that she hurt so much already that it could hardly feel any worse. No, that wasn't true.

The silver knife stuck through her palm, and its point slid out between her knuckles. The weapon's descent was, for a moment, hardly slowed. Geneviève's useless hand was carried with the thrust, to be pinned against Holly-Kate's jugular.

Gorse snarled.

The pain in her hand, and the poison shock of silver, was

enough to evict her from her own body. She hurtled away, looking down from above into the cramped space where, shoved into a corner, four living dead folk were locked in blood and pain. Then, pulled back, she found herself screaming.

There was serious hammering on the door.

Holly-Kate took one red hand out of Gorse's neck and held Geneviève's swollen wrist, gripping to realign snapped bones. Geneviève's skewered hand was almost black. Holly-Kate put a thumb to the handle of the scalpel and pressed, shoving the entire blade and an inch of handle out through the back of Geneviève's hand.

Geneviève understood.

Gorse's jacket hung open. Geneviève roughly angled her hand so the point of the scalpel was over the top pocket of his tweed waistcoat, above the heart. It took all the strength of three women to force the blade through the material, between the ribs. But the silver point sank in.

'The Devil take all vampire bitches,' said Gorse.

His mouth opened, drooling red. His fur vanished. He was just a once-handsome middle-aged Englishman, a roguish uncle with cold, cold eyes.

He was a deadweight.

Geneviève's hand was an inflated horror. She tugged, feeling the handle – unsilvered, so less of an agony than the thin blade – pass between the bones. She pulled away and was free, then collapsed into a chair. Holly-Kate held up the dead vampire, whose face was flaking away.

The door opened. Crosby was there, ahead of a towering warm fellow in a dressing gown. The complaining neighbour.

Crosby gravely assessed the damage to the unit. She smelled all the vampire blood. She saw the stranger holding up a truly dead corpse, the naked human remnant strewn across the floor, and the guest holding a venom-bloated right hand.

'Is everything all right?' she asked.

'I could do with some clean blood,' said Geneviève. 'To fend off silver-rot. I've hurt myself a bit.'

'I'll have some "golden" sent over.'

'Thank you.'

'It's no problem.'

Crosby led the warm guest away.

Geneviève breathed again, her mind fuzzy with exhaustion but periodically cleared by waves of pain.

Gorse was dropped.

Holly was completely Kate now. Kate in a new body. She stood over the straggle of flesh where she used to live. Then, a shiver came. A flash of Holly's eyes, but only a flash.

'I may have to say goodbye now, Gené.'

Geneviève's vision blurred. She formed an adieu in her mouth, but a pulse of pain stopped her.

'No,' she said. 'Not yet.'

6

She drank half the jug of 'golden' Crosby sent over, and used the rest to wash out her wound in the tiny bathroom sink. The hole closed over, but the veins were black. Geneviève's wrists were better now, but silver-poisoning was serious. She wouldn't play the piano again soon. She'd taken it up two centuries ago, becoming a virtuoso in thirty years of intense, obsessive work before the craze passed and she more or less abandoned it, save for a brief fling with ragtime in the 'teens. She didn't think she'd lose the hand, but she'd have arthritic twinges for a long while.

The blood – real 'golden', not the commercial stuff sold in cartons – was on the house. Geneviève realised she had a protector. Someone must have put the invitation on her bed. Someone apart from the management of the Le Reve was paying Crosby, who'd also arranged for a 'cleaner' – a dapper fellow with a trimmed moustache – to have what was left of Ernest Ralph Gorse quietly gathered up and spirited away, presumably to the nearest drac factory. She was not comfortable to be in debt to an anonymous, if guessable worthy, but the blood was a godsend. Without it, she'd be shopping on Rodeo Drive for a claw prosthesis.

So they'd worked for Dracula after all – disposing of the inconvenient, used-up Gorse. Had John Alucard known that when he had her protected in Baltimore? This was what it was like having a King of the Cats again. Being stuck in a giant web.

She stepped back into the bedroom-living room. The unit was one big space now, with mess on the floor. Holly and Kate lay on the bed in a tangle. They seemed more like Young Kate and Old Kate. The old woman, the original, was comatose, but the copy was alert, active. Kate was struggling to stay in control. Holly was asleep, but stirring.

'I can't hang on much longer,' Kate said.

'You're going to have to let go. I think you have to be in your own head for this to work.'

Kate's face showed distaste. Then it was slack, a Kate mask on Holly's face.

'You have something of my friend's,' said Geneviève, to Holly. 'Something she needs back.'

Swiftly, she sat on the bed, her uninjured hand against Holly's neck. Her pale eyes looked out from Kate's fading face. She would not be Kate much longer.

Geneviève could kill the woman relatively easily. She had the blessed silver scalpel. But murder would do nobody any good.

Instead, she tore open Holly's neck with her nails, in the place where she had been ripped earlier.

'Kate,' she said, 'you have to take back from her. Do you understand?'

Kate, single eye bright in the brown-grey of her face, made a nodding motion. Blood fell on her skin, like cream. With heroic effort, she sat up and reached for the throat of the woman who had stolen her form and so much more. She made a fang-mouth and fixed herself to the vampire girl's wound, sucking, sucking…

Geneviève held Holly down and stroked Kate's hair as it grew back, transforming from wispy white to healthy red. As she drank, Kate regained substance, face and form. She had the angry wounds the shapeshifter had imitated, still fresh and ugly.

KIM NEWMAN

'Thank you, Gené,' she said, mouth scarlet.

'Take more,' Geneviève encouraged.

'Don't mind if I do.'

Kate made a new hole, on the other side of the shifter's neck, and suckled delicately, more like her old self than the industrial-vacuum-cleaner-cum-giant-leech she'd needed to be to get her strength back. She drank and the scores in her face narrowed to red lines. Her missing eye emerged blinking from a vanishing ball of scar tissue.

'Am I spoiled?' she asked.

Faint trace-marks were across her face. Kate had no reflection, so she would never see them for herself.

'Good as new,' Geneviève said. 'No scars at all.'

Kate smiled weakly, her old smile.

'I'm blind without my specs.'

Geneviève found the glasses, which Holly had worn. One arm was bent, and the lenses were smeared. She did her best to straighten and clean them and handed them over.

With her glasses on, Kate was herself.

'I'm also naked.'

'I hadn't noticed. I'll get you a robe.'

She opened her suitcase and handed over a green silk kimono. Kate wrapped it around herself and Geneviève showed her how to tie the belt.

'Holly helped,' said Kate. 'With Gorse. It wasn't just me.'

'I know.'

'I found a lot of strange things in her. About people we know.'

Holly was not in as bad a state as Kate had been, but was out of action. She was still trying to change. She ran through other faces but couldn't manage any with any conviction.

'I've a lot of her in my head,' said Kate, thumping herself above the ear with the heel of her hand. 'Too much.'

'It passes.'

'I should bloody hope so.'

She wondered if Holly-as-Kate would have convinced her to support the Count. That was what her job had been, no matter what else Gorse tricked her into. Geneviève tended to go along with things, to follow the principled examples of her friends rather than take on her own. She had been led by Charles, by the gumshoe, by Kate. With a persuasive argument, would she have settled in for an eternity as a minion or a court ornament?

She hoped not. But she would never know.

'Good grief,' said Kate. 'Holly knows Penny!'

Geneviève had lost track of Penelope Churchward, though she knew she lived in the States these nights.

'It's "Bad Penny Blues" all over again,' said Kate. 'That girl has made more trouble than anyone else of her generation. She was a horror as a child, you know. Next time I run into her, I'll give her such a bollocking! And I don't care if her family did have more servants than mine in 1885.'

Sometimes Geneviève felt she'd come into the story too late to understand it. She had met Charles through John Seward, after the deaths of Pamela, Charles's wife, and Lucy, Dracula's first English get. The two women, one dead in childbirth in India, the other the first step in the Count's rise to power, were vivid memories for Penny (Pamela's cousin) and Kate, but shadow-ghosts to Geneviève. She'd only known Dr Seward and Mina Harker after they'd been changed by Dracula, and she had barely met Lord Godalming, Seward's rival with Lucy and Penny's father-in-darkness. These people had grown up together, in an intricate tangle of warm relationships and rivalries. The only Jonathan Harker, Quincey Morris or Abraham Van Helsing she could imagine were fictionalised characters from Bram Stoker's book, though she had a sketchy idea where Stoker and his wife, Florence, fitted into the jigsaw too. Charles had been more than half of her world while alive, but she could never follow his part in this extended true-life soap. That gave her something in common with Dracula: he had sliced his dragon's sword through the Gordian knot and let the ends fray.

Kate, invigorated by fresh blood – in fact on a little drac high – sorted through Holly's bag.

'This is mine,' she said, opening it. 'She even has my passport. And my rent-book. Damn, but I'll have lost the flat.

It's months since I paid rent. What is it, June? July? It was January when she did for me. Ah-hah. Traveller's cheques. American money. Credit cards in several names. Prickly little Holly owes me some clothes, I think. And a selection of Los Angeles luxuries. I've never been here before, you know.'

'I have,' said Geneviève.

She had human connections too, to the living – Jack Martin, the Dude, the Lieutenant, Kenneth Anger, Iorga – and the dead – the gumshoe, Moondoggie, Orson Welles, Nico, even Gorse. Here, Kate would have to pick up the threads as she went along. It was a mistake to think, as Dracula had done for a while, it possible to live outside the world, imagining master-slave as the only possible relationship. Just by walking into a bar, you initiated a dozen stories, in which you were a star or a walk-on.

Kate found the invitations for the screening of *The Rock*.

'I think we should go to this,' she said. 'To show him we're still here. That we can't be touched.'

Geneviève wasn't sure.

'I don't mean "can't be touched" like that. Of course we can, Gené. We'll have to be on our guard. But we've warred against him before and survived. Just because the world has forgotten what he's like, there's no reason that we should go along with it. What would Charles have said?'

'"Never surrender."'

'Indeed he would. And indeed we won't.'

7

The Rock wasn't the worst vampire movie ever made. It wasn't even as bad as that '80s atrocity *Bat-21*, much less *The Vampire Happening*, *The Lost Boys* or – from what Geneviève had seen of it – *Debbie Does Dracula*. However, it was, in her view, dreadful. Reel after reel of straining, oiled muscles – with 'funny' lines after each spectacular killing. If not for a ridiculous shower sex scene with a new blonde actress, it could be mistaken for an amazingly well-budgeted gay porn movie intercut with butcher's training film clips. After screening buzz was that *The Rock* would blockbust Labor Day opening weekend records and stay on 'legs' well into the fall. It was the tentpole of the summer release schedule.

Outside the DGA cinema, a hyperactive, dark warm man was discreetly restrained by wrestler-shaped vampire bouncers in custom tuxedos. He begged departing audience members, all dressed up for the post-movie bash, to tell him if his credit was on the film. He said his name was Adam Simon. Geneviève couldn't recall if he was listed, but she'd ducked out of the endless credits crawl to avoid the Frank Stallone song 'Blood is Thicker Than Water'.

A tide of industry invitees was directed towards a cavernous ballroom where smiling, mostly fanged staff in prison uniforms – abbreviated convict denims for girls, fetishist guard leathers for boys – offered trays of canapés. Beverages for all tastes were served in battered tin cups, suitable for scraping across the cell bars to start a riot. Geneviève and Kate both took 'hot shots', measures of blood and vodka produced not by déclassé mixing in a vat, but in a human shaker. The donor downed dangerous levels of spirits and was bled as soon as the alcohol hit his or her circulatory system. Another high life variant involved injections of a Holmesian seven per cent solution of cocaine or, in clubs like the Viper Room, heroin or Bowles-Ottery ergot. It was smooth and expensive, usually reserved for the 'upstairs' stock of the wealthiest Hollywood vampires. Here, gallons flowed as if from the base of the throne. People who should have known better were lapping it up. Kate pointed out a couple of grimacing warm party-goers sampling vampire fare just because it was otherwise prohibitively costly.

On a dais a swing combo in arrow-patterned tuxes played prison-themed tunes in fashionable-again arrangements: 'Riot in Cell Block No. 9', 'Jailhouse Rock', 'Rubber Bullets', 'Folsom Prison Blues', 'Working on the Chain Gang'. The Johnny Favorite Big Band, surprise hit of the Concert for

Transylvania, was popular again, especially among American new-borns for whom the 1940s were the farthest reach of living memory. Fair enough, Geneviève supposed. She single-handedly kept in business a company which released French mediaeval *chansons* on CD.

Another glittering event. Everyone in sight was famous or beautiful or both. Movie stars, political figures, vampires. Popes and popsies. That put her on her guard. Some of the guests had been at Buckingham Palace in 1888 and/or Palazzo Otranto in 1959. Dracula balls tended to begin with lavish hospitality and dancing, then go on to heads stuck on spikes and the secret police pursuing early leavers.

Holly was in the crowd, wearing her own face for a change, sporting a secret-agent earpiece and a tailcoat cut to conceal a shoulder-holster. The shapeshifter had Gorse's old job, head of security for Alucard Industries. She had profited from the Overlooker's true death.

Kate, given height by heels, was accosted by a greying bear Geneviève recognised as Francis Coppola. The director, bludgeoned by *The Rock*, forgot to be surprised that Kate was in Los Angeles.

'Do you remember that boy?' he asked.

Kate nodded.

'I'm making *Part 2*,' he admitted, glumly. 'Then I'll do one from the heart.'

'God, Francis, please, don't,' said an industry figure, a sinewy woman in a red sheath dress and a dye-job buzzcut. 'Not again.'

'I liked *One From the Heart*,' Kate said, quietly.

Coppola sweetly kissed Kate on the cheek, and was dragged away by the bloodsucking producer. Back bent and weary, he allowed himself to be shown off, to own up that he had signed on for the next Alucard production. There were more ways of feeding off the warm than the obvious.

Two producers, an American named Dragon and a European named Drakoulias, tried to tell Geneviève and Kate they would be good for a picture they wanted to produce in Prague. Kate, a bit tipsy, strung them along, playing up her accent (as she always did when flirting) and refusing to say whether or not she was an actress or had an agent, before admitting neither of them showed up at all well on film.

'There's always video,' said Dragon. 'New media will be big. Have you heard of the Internet?'

'Digital imaging,' said Drakoulias, sagely.

Racquel Ohlrig, a stunning and practised creature, swanned across the room in a silver dress that defied several physical laws. Since her 'rescue' from the Immortologists, Racquel had done vampire porno (as 'Rac Loring'), made a John Waters movie, cut a few records, rustled up mainstream actress credits, appeared on calendars, and become a club diva. She'd be around forever. Geneviève thought that if she and the gumshoe had left the girl with Winton's hucksters, she'd be running the Church by now.

By the wet bar, Penelope Churchward was talking urgently with a waiter. She was back in Dracula's orbit, which wasn't exactly a surprise.

Kate and Geneviève stuck together, watching each other's backs. It was likely this new Count still thought they were worth murdering. Crosby, the girl from the Le Reve, was with Holly's security team, a killer-in-training. Now the Gorse business was done, who knew what orders she'd have? Again, Dracula was gathering his people. General Iorga and Diane LeFanu were here, and, representing Lord Ruthven, Caleb Croft. Among the movie stars and studio execs were Carpathian officers in blinding white uniforms.

Flanked by squat African-Americans with silver-plated guns was the Leopard Lady of Baltimore herself, Georgia Rae Drumgo. Drac Witch of the East, even without Willis Daniels or Geneviève on tap. She had turned vampire. Spotting Geneviève, she showed that her new fangs matched her tiger-striped sheath dress. The bodyguards were just for show – Georgia Rae was the fiercest predator in her pride.

This time, the Kingdom of the Cats went beyond politics, beyond crime, extending into the media, finance, manufacture, information – everything. Dracula wanted to own the culture.

'When he comes on stage, will he be a head on a stick again?' asked Kate.

That was too much to hope for.

There he was, suddenly. In the crowd. He didn't seem to have made an entrance, just appeared. Buzz spread through the guests. Heads turned.

It was Dracula. Young again. Full of plans.

She had no doubts about that.

The Count wore black Armani. Not a speck of colour about the ensemble. His perfect hair and trimmed goatee were as black and smooth as the expensive fabrics of his superbly cut shirt and jacket. His face was white as polished bone. He was no taller, no more beautiful, than the people who stepped aside for him, but he had Presence.

In London, he'd been a monster. In Italy, he was a relic. The *idea* of Dracula, too huge to contain in a human shape, had exploded out through his eyes and mouth. He'd drunk so deeply that drops of blood welled up through his pores. There'd been a terrible untidiness about that Dracula, a barbarian stench, a wrecker's blundering. Here, the King of the Cats had it together, locked down tight. He was compact, controlled, concentrated. His resurrection had not just been about coming back, but coming back in a shape that made sense for the turn of this century and, horrible thought, the foreseeable future. This Dracula had a Project.

He was with the blonde from the film. Sunburst flashbulbs went off. The blonde would register. He would be a black outline, an absence.

Dracula looked at her. At them.

He smiled. He knew he was in complete command, that he was unstoppable. Yet he'd been stopped before. He knew they still stood against him and respected that. He valued his enemies above his friends. He believed in hatred, trusted it more than love. Enemies couldn't fail or betray him. They kept him sharp.

'He's a monster,' Kate breathed.

Geneviève nodded.

'And we're the only two left. He owns everyone else.'

Geneviève didn't want to agree. But was worried that she would have to.

Then, slipping like a fish through the crowd, Adam Simon ran at Dracula. The hefty bouncers barrelled over guests as they tried to catch him. Simon held a bowie knife, an improbably hefty instrument. That long fat blade suggested the late Jim Bowie was compensating for something.

'You stole my movie,' he shouted.

Dracula's face was benign, puzzled. Among so many victims, he couldn't remember this one.

'Who *is* Adam Simon?' Geneviève asked.

Kate shrugged.

Simon shouldered aside Sylvester Stallone and made a leap at Dracula. His bowie slashed in an arc across Dracula's single-button black jacket and ruffled black shirtfront.

Everyone took in a breath.

Geneviève's heart leaped. Surely, after so long, it couldn't end like this? A lone grudge-holder with no plan, just running up to the King of the Cats with a silver sticker, bringing down the reborn empire. After the long road back from death and the rapid rise to power, would this renewed Count be cut off by a random assassin?

Simon was on the floor, yelping. The bouncers were on top of him, bearing down with all their weight. The bowie knife skittered away into Holly's hand.

'Plain steel,' she reported.

Simon could have done no harm with it except to Dracula's suit.

Kate took Geneviève's arm.

'Look,' she said, 'he's bleeding gold.'

Dracula's shirt parted around the cut, exposing dead white skin. Coins dripped out, pattering onto the floor, spilling around his shoes. He must be wearing a money-vest. Shining gold rolled away from him. The Count laughed, sprung finger-claws, and slashed at his sides, his hips, his loins, opening silky rents in his clothes, transforming himself from Oscar night elegant to shredded vampire punk. From every gape in his suit, gold spurted, coins in an almost liquid flow. More than ought to have been possible.

He extended his hands and stood, a fountain of money.

It took a moment. No one would know who was first but someone snatched a coin from the floor. Then someone else took a fistful. Five or six others dived and scrabbled. Even the richest of the crowd struggled through to pick up the spilled cash. Minimum wage catering staff and million-a-year execs jostled each other to get the gold.

Dracula let them claw and fight. He *was* money; he didn't care. He loved what money made of men, just as he loved what the vampire red thirst did to them. There was blood spilled too, inevitably. This spectacle, unedifying yet elegant, was what he wanted. A beautiful woman on her knees stuffed gold into an arm-length evening glove; another, with no other receptacle handy, filled her mouth with coins; men fought seriously and in play; some snatched with humour, without shame, while others filched sneakily and hoped no one would notice.

Independent of the melée, coins rolled at their feet.

Kate picked one up and showed it to Geneviève. It was old gold but new-minted, with the profile of Dracula.

'Don't bite it,' Geneviève told her friend.

Her hand, discreetly black-bandaged, throbbed. It wouldn't be better for a long time. The poison of silver had struck her; but it was nothing to the poison of gold.

Kate flicked away the coin. Francis Coppola snatched it out of the air and sadly closed his fingers around it.

Geneviève looked at Dracula.

He stood above it all, laughing through a fanged grin, clothes in tatters, face shining red and gold, eyes midnight black. There was a terrifying joy and purity to him. She understood the fear and love he could inspire, and why people would follow him into the fire. She knew how much easier life was for those who signed up with the Order of the Dragon or Alucard Industries or whatever he was calling his invisible, world-spanning kingdom. And she knew that she could never be a part of it.

Never.

With the memory of Charles, the example of Kate,

and her own burning blood, she could not become one of Dracula's acolytes.

She shook her head. He knew.

The next time would be worse. Always, the next time.

'Come on, Kate,' she said. 'This isn't our party.'

'Too true, Gené.'

Leaving, they passed Penny. For a moment, the three vampire women looked at each other. At this party, they'd not even talked.

For Charles's sake, Geneviève let Penelope be. This time.

Outside the black-glass building, on Sunset, nightbirds passed by on foot and in shining automobiles. A billboard for *The Rock* dominated a dozen blocks.

'You have to admit it's bloody impressive,' said Kate.

'It won't be there forever. This is Los Angeles. Nothing is permanent. That'll be gone next week. It's what he's forgotten. Again. He wants to stand for all time, a statue of gold. He's a man of blood and iron and gold. Centuries will wear him down, break him in the end.'

'Us too?'

Geneviève shook her head.

'We can change. He can't. When I first came here, someone told me I was good and that I could do good. I needed to hear it. Just as you need to hear it now, Kate. We're good. We are. Sometimes, it doesn't seem that way, but it's true. Independent witnesses verify it. There won't be any money in it, but we're going into business together. The world is drowning in Dracula's gold, so we have to work on a case by case basis. We've done it before, remember? We have skills. We can figure things out. You can write and report. I can open doors. We can catch the killers and save the girls.'

Kate thought about it.

'He'd like that,' she said. 'Charles.'

Geneviève didn't have to say anything.

Arm in arm, they walked along Sunset. They weren't warm, but they were alive.

APPENDIX ONE

'DESTROYING DRELLA'
BY KATHLEEN CONKLIN

Paper delivered at 'Warhol's Worlds', inaugural conference of The Andy Warhol Museum (April 21–23, 1995); revised for publication as 'Warhola the Vampyre' in *Who is Andy Warhol?* edited by Colin MacCabe with Mark Francis and Peter Wollen (The British Film Institute and The Andy Warhol Museum, 1997).

They were calling him a vampire long before he turned.

At the Silver Dream Factory, the Mole People, amphetamine-swift dusk-til-dawners eternally out for blood, nicknamed him 'Drella'. The coven often talked of Andy's 'victims': first, cast-offs whose lives were appropriated for Art, rarely given money to go with their limited fame (a great number of them now truly dead); later, wealthy portrait subjects or *Inter/VIEW* advertisers, courted as assiduously as any Renaissance art patron (a great number of them ought to be truly dead). Andy leeched off them all, left them drained or transformed, using them without letting them touch him, never distinguishing between the commodities he could only coax from other people: money, love, blood, inspiration, devotion, death. Those who rated him a genius and those who ranked him a fraud reached eagerly, too eagerly, for the metaphor. It was so persistent, it must eventually become truth.

In *Swimming Underground: My Years in the Warhol Factory* (1995), supervamp Mary Woronov (*Hedy/The Shoplifter*, 1965; *The Chelsea Girls*, 1966) writes: 'People were calling us the undead, vampires, me and my little brothers of the night, with our lips pressed against the neck of the city, sucking the energy out of scene after scene. We left each party behind like a wasted corpse, raped and carelessly tossed aside… Andy was the worst, taking on five or six parties a night. He even looked like a vampire: white, empty, waiting to be filled, incapable of satisfaction. He was the white worm – always hungry, always cold, never still, always twisting.' When told that the artist had turned vampire, Lou Reed arched a ragged eyebrow and quizzed, 'Andy was *alive*?' In the multitude of memoirs and word or song portraits that try to define Andy Warhol, there is no instance of anyone ever using the adjective 'warm' about him.

Valerie Solanas took superstitious care to shoot him with homemade silver bullets. She tried wrapping .32 ammunition in foil, which clogged the chambers, before resorting to spray-paint in the style of Billy Name (Linich), the silver-happy decorator of the Factory who coffined himself in a tiny back room for two years, coming out only at dead of night to forage. The names are just consonants short of anagrams: Andy Warhola, Wlad Draculya; Valerie Solanas, Van Helsing. Valerie's statement, the slogan of a fearless vampire killer: 'He had too much control over my life.'

On the operating table – 4.51 pm, Monday, June 3, 1968 – Andy Warhol's heart stopped. He was declared clinically dead but came back and lived on, his vision of death and disaster fulfilled and survived. The stringmeat ghost of the latter years was sometimes a parody of his living self, a walking Diane Arbus exhibit, belly scars like zippers, Ray-Ban eyes and dead skin.

Warhola the Vampyre sloped *nosferatu*-taloned through the seventies, a fashion-setter as always, as – after nearly a century in the open in Europe – vampirism (of a sort) at last established itself in America. He had no get, but was the fountainhead of a bloodline. You can still see them, in galleries or *People*, on the streets after dark, in the clubs and cellars. Andy's kids: cloned creatures, like the endless replications of his silkscreen celebrity portraits, faces repeated until they become meaningless patterns of coloured dots.

When alive, Andy had said he wanted to become a machine and that everybody should be alike. How did he feel when his wishes were coming true? How did he feel about anything? Did he feel? Ever? If you spend any amount of time trying to understand the man and his work, you can't help but worry that he's reaching from beyond the grave and forcing you to become Valerie.

Consider the signs, the symptoms, the symbols: that pale, almost-albino face, simultaneously babyish and ancient, shrinking like a bucket of salted slugs when exposed to the sun; the sharp or battered black clothes, stiff from the grave; the goggle-like dark glasses, hypnotic black holes where eyes should be; the Slavic monotone of the whispery voice and the pared-down, kindergarten vocabulary; the covert religiosity, the prizing of sacred or silver objects; the squirrelling away of money and possessions in a centuried lair; even the artificial shocks of grey-white-silver hair. Are these not the attributes of a classical vampire, Dracula himself? Look at photographs taken before or after June 1968, and you can't tell whether he is or isn't. Like the murgatroyds of the 1890s, Andy was a disciple before he became a vampire. For him, turning was dropping the seventh veil, the last chitinous scrap of chrysalis, a final stage in becoming what he had always meant to be, an admittal that this was indeed what was inside him.

His whole life had revolved around the dead.

Andrew Warhola was an American – born in Pittsburgh on August 6, 1928 – but his family were not. In *The Life and Death of Andy Warhol* (1989), Victor Bockris quotes his statement 'I am from nowhere,' but gives it the lie: 'The Warholas were Rusyns who had emigrated to America from the Ruthenian village of Mikova in the Carpathian Mountains near the borders of Russia and Poland in territory that was, at the turn of the century, part of the Austro-Hungarian Empire.' Introducing early the theme that comes to dominate his biography, Bockris takes care to note, 'The Carpathian Mountains are popularly known as the home of Dracula, and the peasants in Jonathan Harker's description kneeling before roadside shrines, crossing themselves at the mention of Dracula's name, resemble Andy Warhol's distant relatives.'

The third son of Ondrej and Julia Warhola grew up in Soho, an ethnic enclave that was almost a ghetto. From an early age, he seemed a changeling, paler and slighter than his family, laughably unfit for a future in the steel mills, displaying talent as soon as his hand could properly hold a pencil. Others in his situation might fantasise that they were orphaned princes, raised by peasant wood-cutters, but the Warholas had emigrated – escaped? – from the land of the vampires. Not fifty years before, Count Dracula had come out of Carpathia and established his short-lived empire in London. Dracula was still a powerful figure then, the most famous vampire in the world, and his name was spoken often in the Warhola household. Years later, in a film, Andy had an actress playing his mother claim to have been a victim, in childhood, of the Count, that Dracula's bloodline remained in her veins, passing in the womb to her last son. Like much else in Andy's evolving autobiography, there is no literal truth in this story but its hero spent years trying to wish it into reality and may even, at the last, have managed to pull off the trick. Before settling on 'Andy Warhol' as his eventual professional name, he experimented with the signature 'Andrew Alucard'.

Julia was horrified by her little Andrew's inclinations. For her, vampires were objects not of fascination but dread. A devout Byzantine Catholic, she would drag her children six miles to the wooden church of St John Chrystostom on Saline Street and subject them to endless rituals of purification. Yet, among Andy's first drawings are bats and coffins.

In the 1930s, the American illustrated press were as obsessed with vampires as movie stars. There were several successful periodicals – *Weird Tales*, *Spicy Vampire Stories* – devoted almost entirely to their social activities. To look through these magazines, as the child Andy did, is to understand what it is to learn that a party is going on after your bedtime, to which you cannot possibly secure an invitation. Literally, you had to die to get in. In Vienna, Budapest, Constantinople, Monte Carlo and private estates and castles scattered in a crescent across Europe, vampire kings and queens held court.

Young Andrew clipped photographs and portraits from the magazines and hoarded them for the rest of his life. He preferred photographs, especially the blurred or distorted traces of those who barely registered on cameras or in mirrors. He understood at once that creatures denied the sight of their own faces must prize portrait painters. He wrote what might be called 'fan letters' to the leaders of vampire fashion: the Short Lion of Paris, Herbert von Krolock, the White Russian Rozokov. His especial favourites among the undead, understandably, were the child-vampires, those frozen infant immortals Noel Coward sings about in 'Poor Little Dead Girl'. His prize possession as a boy was an autographed portrait of the martyred Claudia, ward of the stylish Short Lion, considered a paragon and an archetype among her kind. He would later use this image – a subscription gift sent out by *Night Life* – in his silkscreen, *Vampire Doll* (1963).

In his fascination with the undead, Andy was in the avant-garde. There were still very few vampires in America, and those American-born or -made tended to flee to a more congenial Europe. There was a vampire panic in the wake of the First World War, as returning veterans brought back the tainted bloodline that burned out in the epidemic of 1919. The lost generation new-borns, who all incubated within their bodies a burning disease that ate them up from the inside within months, were ghastly proof that vampires would never 'take' in the New World. Congress passed acts against the spread of vampirism save under impossibly regulated circumstances. J. Edgar Hoover ranked vampires just below communists and well above organised crime as a threat to the American way of life. In the 1930s, New York District Attorney Thomas Dewey led a crusade against an influx of Italian vampires, successfully deporting coven-leader Niccolo Cavalanti and his acolytes. In the South, a resurgence of the Ku Klux Klan viciously curbed a potential renaissance of interlocked vampire *hounforts* in New Orleans and throughout the bayou country.

America, like Julia Warhola, considered all vampires loathsome monsters. Yet, as Andy understood, there was a dreadful glamour. During the Depression, glimpses of the high life lived in another continent and by another species, seemed enticing. The Hungarian Paul Lukas was the first Hollywood actor to specialise in undead roles, from *Scarface* (1932) to *The House of Ruthven* (1937). A few real vampires, even, made it in the movies: Garbo, Malakai, Chevalier Futaine.

With the rise of fascism and the Second World War came a trickle of vampire refugees from the Old World. Laws were revised and certain practices tolerated 'for the duration', while Hoover's FBI – constantly nagged by America's witch-hunters Cardinal Spellman and Father Coughlin – compiled foot-thick dossiers on elders and new-borns alike. As Nazi eugenicists strived to cleanse his bloodline from the Reich, Dracula himself aligned with the Allies, and a vampire underground in occupied Europe co-operated with the liberating forces.

When the War was over, the climate changed again and a round of blacklistings, arrests and show-trials – notably the prosecution for treason of American-born and -made vampire Benjamin Lathem by Robert F. Kennedy – drove all but those who could 'pass for warm' back to Europe. That was the era of the scare movies, with homburg-hatted government men taking crucifix and stake to swarthy, foreign infiltrators: *I Married a Vampire* (1950), *I Was a Vampire for the FBI* (1951), *Blood of Dracula* (1958). Warhol was in New York by now, sketching shoes for ad lay-outs or arranging window displays for Bonwit Teller & Co, making a hundred thousand dollars a year but fretting that he wasn't taken seriously. Money wasn't enough for him; he needed to be famous too, as if under the curse described by Fritz Leiber in his short story 'The Casket Demon' (1963) – unless known of and talked about, he would fade to nothingness. Like America, he had not outgrown his vampire craze, just learned to keep quiet about it.

In 1956, the year *Around the World in 80 Days* took the Best Picture Oscar, Andy took an extended trip with the frustratingly unforthcoming Charles Lisanby – Hawaii, Japan, India, Egypt, Rome, Paris, London. Throughout that itinerary, he saw vampires living openly, mingling with the warm, as adored as they were feared. Is it too much to suppose that, in a maharajah's palace or on a Nile paddle-wheeler, spurned by Charles and driven to abase himself before some exotic personage, he was bitten?

Vampires show up in the 1950s fashion drawings, if only through coded symbols: ragged-edged batwing cloaks draped over angular figures; red lipstick mouths on sharp-cheeked black and white faces; tiny, almost unnoticeable, fangs peeping from stretched smiles. These in-jokes are self-criticism, a nervous admission of what had to happen next. To become 'Andy Warhol', the illustrator and window-dresser must die and be reborn as an Artist. Those who accuse him of being concerned only with his earnings – which, to be fair, is what he told anyone who would listen – forget that he abandoned a considerable income to devote all his energies to work which initially lost a lot of money.

Shortly before the Coca-Cola Bottle and Campbell's Soup Can series made him famous, and in a period when he feared he had recovered from one 'nervous breakdown' only to be slipping into another, Warhol did a painting – synthetic polymer and crayon on canvas – of '*Batman*' (1960), the only vampire ever really to be embraced by America. Though justifiably eclipsed by Lichtenstein's appropriations from comic strip panels, '*Batman*' is an important work in its own right, an idea seized but abandoned half-finished, the first flash of what would soon come to be called Pop Art. Like much from the period before Warhol hit upon repetition and manufacture as modes of expression, it seems incomplete, childish crayon scribbles across the cowled Bob Kane outline of the classic vampire vigilante. Exhibited at the Castelli Gallery, the work was the first Warhol piece to command a serious price from a private collector – an anonymous buyer on behalf of the Wayne Foundation – which may have encouraged the artist to continue with his personal work.

During an explosion of creativity that began in 1962 and lasted at least until he was shot, Warhol took a lease on a former hat works at 231 East 47th Street and turned the loft space into the Factory, with the intention of producing art on a production line. At the suggestion of assistant Nathan Gluck, Warhol seized upon the silkscreen process and ('like a forger') turned out series of dollar bills, soup cans and Marilyn Monroes. It seemed that he didn't care what his subjects were, so long as they were famous.

When Henry Geldzahler, assistant curator for 20th Century American Art at the Metropolitan Museum, told him he should apply himself to more 'serious' subjects, Warhol began his 'death and disaster' series: images of car crashes, suicides and the electric chair. Straddling the trivial and the serious are his vampire portraits: *Carmilla Karnstein* (1962), *Vampire Doll* (1963), *Lucy Westenra* (1963). Red-eyed and jagged-mouthed undead faces, reproduced in sheets like unperforated stamps, vivid greens and oranges for skin-tones, the series reinvents the nineteenth century genre of vampire portraiture. The vampire subjects Andy chose shared one thing: all had been famously destroyed. He produced parallel silkscreens of their true deaths: impalements, decapitations, disintegrations. These are perhaps the first great works, ruined corpses swimming in scarlet blood, untenanted bodies torn apart by grim puritans.

In 1964, Andy delivered a twenty-by-twenty black and white mural called 'Thirteen Vampires' to the American pavilion at the New York World's Fair, where it was to be exhibited beside work by Robert Rauschenberg and Roy Lichtenstein. Among the thirteen, naturally, was Warhol's first Dracula portrait, though all the other undead notables represented were women. The architect Philip Johnson, who had commissioned the piece, informed Warhol that word had come from the Governor that it was to be removed because there was concern that it was offensive to the God-fearing.

When Warhol's suggestion that the portraits all be defaced with burning crosses to symbolise the triumph of the Godly was vetoed, he went out to the fair with Geldzahler and another of his assistants, Gerard Malanga, and painted the mural over with a thick layer of undead-banishing silver paint, declaring, 'And that'll be my art.' We can only speculate about that lost Dracula portrait, which none of the few who saw it can describe in detail. Which of the many, many images of the King of the Vampires – then, truly dead for only five years – did Warhol reproduce? The most tantalising suggestion, based on Malanga's later-retracted version, is that for the only time in his entire career as an artist, Warhol drew on his own imagination rather than copied or reproduced from life. Andy lied constantly, but this is the only occasion when anyone has ever accused him of *making something up*.

Warhol's first experiments with film, conducted in real-time with the co-opted collaboration of whoever happened to be hanging about in the Factory, are steeped in the atmosphere of vampirism. The camera hovers over the exposed throat of John Giorno in *Sleep* (1963) as if ready to pounce. The projection of film shot at twenty-four frames per second at the silent speed of sixteen frames per second gives Giorno's six-hour night a suggestion of vampire lassitude. The flashes of white leader that mark the change of shots turn dirty sheets into white coffin plush, and the death rattle of the projector is the only soundtrack (aside from the comical yawns and angry ticket-money-back demands of any audience members happening upon the film in a real theatre).

That same year, Warhol shot more explicit studies of vampirism: in *Kiss*, a succession of couples osculate like insects unable to uncouple their complex mouth-parts; in *Eat*, Robert Indiana crams his mouth with unidentifiable meats; and *Suck Job* is an extended (thirty minutes) close-up of the face of a young man who is being nibbled by beings who never intrude into the frame or register on film. For *Suck Job*, Warhol had arranged with Stefan Grlsc, a real vampire, to 'appear' but Grlsc didn't take him seriously and failed to show up at the Factory for the shoot, forcing the artist to substitute pasty-faced but warm hustlers dragged off the street.

When Warhol turned his camera on the Empire State Building in *Empire* (1964), it saw the edifice first as the largest coffin in the world, jutting out of the ground as if dislodged by seismic activity. As night slowly falls and the floodlights come on, the building becomes a cloaked predator standing colossal over New York City, shoulders sloped by the years, head sprouting a dirigible-mast horn. After that, Warhol had fellow underground filmmaker Jack Smith swish a cape over Baby Jane Hudson in the now-lost *Batman Dracula* (1964). Only tantalising stills of Smith with a mouthful of plastic teeth and staring Lon Chaney eyes, remain of this film, which – as with the silver-coated 'Thirteen Vampires' – is perhaps as Andy wanted it. As with *Sleep* and *Empire*, the idea is more important than the artefact. It is enough that the films exist; they are not meant actually to be seen all the way through. When Jonas Mekas scheduled *Empire* at the Filmmakers' Co-Op in 1965, he lured Warhol into the screening room and tied him securely to one of the seats with stout rope, intent on forcing the creator to sit through his creation. When he came back two hours later to check up on him, he found Warhol had chewed through his bonds – briefly, an incarnation of Batman Dracula – and escaped into the night. In the early sixties, Warhol had begun to file his teeth, sharpening them to piranha-like needle-points.

From 1964 to 1968, Andy abandoned painting – if silkscreen can be called that – in favour of film. Some have suggested that works like *Couch* (1964) or *The Thirteen Most Beautiful Boys* (1965) are just portraits that move; certainly, more people caught them as an ambient backdrop to the Exploding Plastic Inevitable than endured them reverentially at the Co-Op. *Movies*, not films, they were supposed to play to audiences too busy dancing or speeding or covering their bleeding ears to pay the sort of attention demanded by Hollywood narrative.

By now, 'Andy's vampire movies' had gone beyond a standing joke – *Eight hours of the Empire State Building!!* – and were taken seriously by genuine underground filmmakers like Stan Brakhage (who considered silent speed the stroke of genius). The Filmmakers' Co-Op regularly scheduled 'Warhol Festivals' and word got out that the films were, well, *dirty*, which – of course – pulled in audiences. *Suck Job* was about as close to vampirism as even the most extreme New York audiences had seen, even if it was silent, black-and-white and slightly out of focus. Isabelle Dufresne, later the supervamp Ultra Violet, saw *Suck Job* projected on a sheet at the Factory, and understood at once the strategy of incompletion, whereby the meat of the matter was beyond the frame. In *Dead for Fifteen Minutes: My Years With Andy Warhol* (1988), Ultra Violet writes: 'Although my eyes remain focused on the face of the young man receiving the suck job, my attention is constantly drawn to the empty space on the sheet below the screen. I am being visually assaulted and insulted at the same time. It is unnerving: I want to get up and seize the camera and focus it downward to capture the action. But I can't, and that's where the frustration comes in.'

Ultra Violet also reports that during that screening some Factory hangers-on present relieved the frustration by nibbling each other, drawing squeals of pain and streaks of quick-drying blood. Such tentative pretend-vampirism was common among the Mole People, the night-time characters Andy gathered to help make 'his' movies and turned into his private coven in the back room of Max's Kansas City nightclub.

With no genuine undead available, Andy made do with self-made supervamps, who showed up on film if not at rehearsals: Pope Ondine (who drew real blood), Brigid (Berlin) Polk, Baby Jane Hudson (who had once been a real-live movie star), Gerald Malanga's muse Mary Woronov, Carmillo Karnstein, Ingrid Supervamp. Brian Stableford would later coin the term 'lifestyle fantasists' for these people and their modern avatars, the goth murgatroyds. Like Andy, the Mole People already lived like vampires: shunning daylight, speeding all night, filing their teeth, developing pasty complexions, sampling each other's drug-laced blood.

The butcher's bill came in early. The dancer Freddie Herko, who appears in *Kiss* (1963) and *Dance Movie/Roller Skates* (1963), read in Montague Summers' *The Vampire: His Kith and Kin* (1928) that those who committed suicide spectacularly enough 'without fear' were reborn as 'powerful vampires'. Just before Hallowe'en 1964, Herko danced across a friend's Greenwich Village apartment, trailing a ten-foot Batman/Dracula cloak, and sailed elegantly out of a fifth-floor window. Having skim-read the Summers and not bothered to form a Pact with the Devil, an essential part of the immortality-through-self-slaughter gambit, Herko did not rise from the dead.

When he heard of Herko's defenestration, Warhol was almost irritated. 'Gee,' he sighed, 'why didn't he tell me he was going to do it? We could have gone down there and filmed it.' Herko was just the first of the Warhol death cluster, his personal disaster series: Edie Sedgwick (1971), Tiger Morse (1972), Andrea Feldman (1972), Candy Darling (1974), Eric Emerson (1975), Gregory Battcock (1980), Tom Baker (1982), Jackie Curtis (1985), Valerie Solanas (1989), Ondine (1989). And Warhol himself (1968?). Only Andy made it back, of course. He had to be the vampire they all would have been, even Valerie.

In 1965, the term 'vampire movies' took on another layer of meaning at the Factory, with the arrivals of Ronald Tavel, a playwright hired to contribute situations (if not scripts) for the

films, and Edie Sedgwick, a blueblood blonde who was, in many
ways, Andy's ultimate supervamp. Movies like *The Death of Radu
the Handsome* (1965), with Ondine as Vlad the Impaler's gay
brother, and *Poor Little Dead Girl* (1965), with Edie as the vampire
Claudia, run to seventy minutes (two uninterrupted thirty-five
minute takes, the length of a film magazine, stuck together),
have intermittently audible soundtracks and mimic Hollywood
to the extent of having something approaching narrative. Were
it not for the incandescent personalities of the supervamps,
the beautiful and the damned, these efforts would be more like
'zombie movies', shambling gestures of mimesis, constantly
tripping up as the immobile image (Andy had the most stoned
Mole Person handle the camera) goes in and out of focus or the
walk-on 'victims' run out of things to do and say.

Ondine, Edie and a few others understand that the films are
their own shot at vampire immortality. With dime store plastic
fangs and shrouds from the dress-up chest, these living beings
cavort, preserved on film while their bodies are long in the
grave, flickering in undeath. For Andy, the film camera, like the
silkscreen or the polaroid, was a vampire machine, a process for
turning life into frozen death, perfect and reproducible. Hurting
people was always so interesting, and left the most fabulous
Rorschach stain patterns on the sheets.

Edie cut her hair to match Andy's wigs and took to wearing
imitations of his outfits, especially for photographs and
openings. They looked like asexual twins or clones, but were
really trying to model themselves on that most terrifying
denizen of the world of darkness, the old vampire couple.
R.D. Laing's study *Helga and Heinrich* (1970) suggests that, after
centuries together, vampire couples mingle identities, sharing
a consciousness between two frail-seeming bodies, finishing
each other's sentences as the mind flickers between two skulls,
moving in on their victims in an instinctive pincer movement. If
one partner is destroyed, the other rots in sympathy. Edie would
probably have gone that far – she did eventually commit suicide
– but Andy was too self-contained to commit anything or

commit to anything. He saw her as the mirror he didn't like to look in – his reflection reminded him that he was alive, after all – and would often play the mimic game, patterned after Harpo Marx, with her, triumphantly squirting milk from his mouth or producing a walnut from a fist to show he was the original and she the copy. When he said he wanted everyone to be alike, he was expressing a solipsist not an egalitarian ideal: everyone was to be like him, but he was still to be the mould.

Warhol and Ronnie Tavel made *Veneer* (1965), arguably the first film version of Bram Stoker's *Dracula* (1897). In *Stargazer: Andy Warhol's World and His Films* (1973), Stephen Koch reports: 'Warhol handed Tavel a copy of the novel with the remark that it might be easier to compose a scenario based on fiction than one spun out of pure fantasy. He had acquired the rights to the Stoker book for $3,000, he said; it ought to make a good movie. And so it did. It's not hard to guess why Warhol was impressed by *Dracula*. (I should mention in passing that, contrary to the myth he propagates, Warhol is quite widely read.) The book is filled with the sexuality of violence; it features a tough, erotic vampire dandy joyously dominating a gang of freaks; its theme is humiliation within a world that is simultaneously sordid and unreal; it is a history which at once did and did not happen, a purposeful lie. Finally, there is the question of class… I think Warhol participates very deeply in America's best-kept secret – the painful, deeply denied intensity with which we experience our class structure. We should not forget that we are speaking of the son of semiliterate immigrants, whose father was a steelworker in Pittsburgh. Within the terms of his own intensely specialised mentality, Warhol has lived through American class humiliation and American poverty. And *Dracula*, although British, is very much about the sexuality of social class as it merges with spiritual domination.'

Casting Edie as an ephebic silver-haired Dracula (Drella, indeed), Gerard Malanga as a whip-wielding but humiliated Harker and Ondine as a sly Van Helsing, Warhol populated the Factory's Transylvania and Carfax Abbey (the same 'set', black sheets hung with silver cobwebs) with lost souls. Well before Francis Ford Coppola, Warhol saw that the problems in filming the novel could be sidestepped by force of will. Indeed, he approached the enterprise with a deliberate diffidence that all but ensured this would not be a 'proper' film. Ronnie Tavel at least read half the book before getting bored and typing out a script in his usual three days.

Since shooting consisted of a complete run-through of the script as a performance, with breaks only when the magazine ran out, Tavel considered that there ought to be actual rehearsals and that the actors should stoop to learning their lines. Too fearful of confrontation to disagree, Warhol simply sabotaged the rehearsals Tavel organised and even the shooting of the film by inviting the press and various parasites to the Factory to observe and interfere, and sending Malanga off on trivial errands or keeping him up until dawn at parties to prevent him from even reading the script (as in the book, Harker has the most to say). Koch, again: 'The sense that making a film was work – that it should involve the concentrated attention of work – was utterly banished, and on shooting day the Factory merely played host to another "Scene", another party.'

Stoker's intricate plot is reduced to situations. Harker, in black leather pants and Victorian deerstalker, visits Castle Dracula carrying a cross loaned to the production by Andy's mother, and is entertained, seduced and assaulted by the Count (Edie's enormous fangs keep slipping out of her mouth) and his three gesticulating vampire brides (Marie Mencken, Carmillo Karnstein, International Velvet). Later, in Carfax Abbey, Harker – roped to the Factory couch – watches as Dracula fascinates and vampirises Mina (Mary Woronov) in a tango that climaxes with Mina drinking Campbell's Tomato Soup from a can Dracula has opened. with a thumb-talon and which he declares is his vampire blood. Van Helsing appears, with his fearless vampire hunters – Lord Godalming (Chuck Wein),

Quincey Morris (Joe Dallesandro), Dr Seward (Paul America) – dragged by Renfield (a young, ravaged Lou Reed), who is leashed like a bloodhound.

Crucifixes, stakes, whips and communion wafers are tossed back and forth in a bit of knockabout that makes some of the cast giggle uncontrollably and drives others – notably, the still-tethered Malanga – to furious distraction. In Tavel's script, as in Stoker's novel, Van Helsing's band corner and destroy Dracula, who was to be spray-painted silver and suffocate, but Ondine is distracted when a girl who happens to be on the couch for no real reason – she seems to be a set-visitor straying into frame – calls him a 'phony', and Ondine ignores the King Vampire to lash out at this impertinent chit, going for her face with his false fingernails. Ondine's methedrine rant rises in a crescendo, peaks and fades: 'May God forgive you, you're a phony, Little Miss Phony, you're a disgusting phony, get off this set, you're a disgrace to humanity, you're a disgrace to yourself, you're a loathsome fool, your husband's a loathsome fool… I'm sorry, I just can't go on, this is just too much, I don't want to go on.' The camera, handled this time by Bud Wirtschafter, tries to follow the unexpected action, and for a few brief frames catches the ghost-white face of Andy himself hanging shocked in the gloom; the removal of this slip is perhaps the only proper edit in any Warhol film made before the arrival of Paul Morrissey. Van Helsing, inconsolable, stands alone and the film runs on and on, as he reassembles himself.

Edie, fangs spat out but still regally and perfectly Dracula, gets Wirtschafter's attention by tossing the soup can at him, spattering the lens, and commands the frame, hands on hips, for a few seconds before the film runs out. 'I am Dracula,' she insists, the only line of dialogue taken directly (if unintentionally) from the book. 'I *am* Dracula,' she repeats, sure of herself for the last time in her life. Stoker had intended to inflict upon Dracula the defeat he eluded in reality, but Edie has dragged Warhol's Dracula movie back to the truth. In the Factory, Drella bests the squabbling Vampire Slayers and reigns forever.

It is easy to overstate the importance of Nico to Warhol's late '60s work. She was, after all, his first 'real' vampire. Croaking, German and blonde, she was the dead image of Edie, and thus of Andy. Nico Otzak, turned some time in the '50s, arrived in New York in 1965, with her doll-like get Ari, and presented her card at the Factory. She trailed the very faintest of associations with Dracula himself, having been a fringe member of that last party, in Rome 1959, which climaxed in the true death of the Vampire King. 'She was mysterious and European,' Andy said, abstaining from any mention of the v word, 'a real moon goddess type.' Like Dracula, she gave the impression of having used up the Old World and moved on, searching for 'a young country, full of blood'.

In *Edie: An American Biography* (1982), Jean Stein definitively refutes the popular version, in which the naive, warm American is supplanted by the cold, dead European. Edie Sedgwick was on the point of turning from vampire to victim before Nico's arrival: she had made the cardinal error of thinking herself indispensable, a real star, and Andy was silently irked by her increasing need for publicity as herself rather than as his mirror. She had already strayed from the Factory and towards Bob Dylan's circle, tempted by more serious drug habits and heterosexuality. Edie was justifiably miffed that the limited financial success of the films benefited only Andy. His position was that she was rich anyway – 'an heiress', one of his favourite words – and didn't need the money, though far less well-off folk did as much or more work on the films and silkscreens for similarly derisory pay. Edie's self-destruction cannot be laid entirely on Andy and Nico – the Dylan crowd hardly helped, moving her up from amphetamines to heroin – but it is undeniably true that without Warhol, Edie would never have become, in the British expression, 'dead famous'.

With Nico, Andy finally had his vampire. At the back of their association must have been the possibility – the promise? – that she would turn him, but for the moment, Andy held back. To

become someone's get would have displaced him from the
centre of his life, and that was insupportable. When he turned,
a circumstance that remains mysterious, he would do so through
anonymous blood donation, making himself – as usual – his
own get, his own creature. Besides, no one could seriously
want Nico for a mother-in-darkness: for the rest of her nights,
she drew blood from Ari, her own get, and this vampire incest
contributed to the rot that would destroy them both.

Andy was especially fascinated by Nico's relationship with
mirrors and film. She was one of those vampires who have no
reflection, though he did his best to turn her into a creature
who was all reflection with no self. He had her sing 'I'll Be Your
Mirror', for instance. 'High Ashbury', the oddest segment of
****/*Twenty Four Hour Movie* (1966), places Ondine and Ultra
Violet either side of an absence, engaged in conversation with
what seems to be a disembodied voice. There are signs of
Nico's physical presence during the shoot: the displacement of
cushions, a cigarette that darts like a hovering dragonfly, a puff
of smoke outlining an oesophagus. But the vampire woman just
isn't there. That may be the point. Andy took photographs of
silver-foiled walls and untenanted chairs and passed them off as
portraits of Nico. He even silkscreened an empty coffin for an
album cover.

Having found his vampire muse, Andy had to do *something* with
her, so he stuck her together with the Velvet Underground – a
band who certainly weren't that interested in having a girl singer
who drank human blood – as part of the Exploding Plastic
Inevitable, the club events he staged at the Dom on St Mark's
Place in 1966. Amid so much black leather, he dressed Nico
in bone-white and put an angelic spotlight on her, especially
when she wasn't singing. Lou Reed bought a crucifix and started
looking for a way out. The success of the EPI may well have been
partially down to the wide cross-section of New Yorkers who
were intrigued by Nico; most Americans in 1966 had never been
in a room with a vampire, a real vampire. Andy knew that and
made sure that, no matter how conveniently dark the rest of the

packed club was, Nico was always visible, always the red-eyed wraith murmuring her way through 'Femme Fatale' without taking a breath. That song, of course, is a promise and a threat: 'Think of her at nights, feel the way she bites…'

As the Velvets performed, Warhol hid in the rafters like the Phantom of the Opera, working the lights and the projectors, cranking up the sound. Like Ulysses, he filled his ears with wax to get through the night. Behind the band, he screened his films. Often, as his real vampire paraded herself, he would show *Veneer*, trying to project Edie onto Nico as he projected himself upon them both.

Everybody agrees: between 1966 and 1968, Andy Warhol was a monster.

Valerie Solanas was the founder and sole member of the Society for Killing All Vampires, authoress of the self-published *SKAV Manifesto*. In bite-sized quotes, the *Manifesto* is quite amusing – 'Enlightened vampires who wish to demonstrate solidarity with the Movement may do so by killing themselves.' – but it remains a wearisome read, not least because Solanas never quite sorted out what she meant by the term 'vampire'. Of course, as an academic, I understand entirely the impatience she must have felt with what she considered irrelevances like agenda-setting and precise definitions of abstruse language. In the end, Solanas was a paranoid sociopath, and the vampires were her enemies, all whom were out to get her. At first, she didn't even mean *nosferatu* when she referred to vampires, but a certain type of patriarchal oppressor. At the end, she meant everyone else in the world.

She is in one of the little-known films, *I, Vampire* (1967) – mingling briefly with Tom Baker as the vampire Lord Andrew Bennett, and Ultra Violet, the wonderfully named Bettina Coffin and a Nico-shaped patch of empty screen. She had various grudges against Andy Warhol – he had lost a playscript she sent him, he wouldn't publish her book, he didn't make her famous – but no more than any one of a dozen other Mole People. Billy Name has said that he was never sure whether he should kill himself or Andy, and kept putting off the decision. Oliver Stone's *Who Shot Andy Warhol?* is merely the culmination of thirty years of myth and fantasy. It bears repeating that the conspiracy theories Stone and others espouse have little or no basis in fact: Valerie Solanas acted entirely on her own, conspiring or colluding with no one. Stone's point, which is well-taken, is that in June 1968, *someone* had to shoot Andy Warhol; if Valerie hadn't stepped up to the firing line, any one of a dozen others could as easily have melted down the family silver for bullets.

But it was Valerie.

By 1968, the Factory had changed. It was at a new location, and Warhol had new associates – Fred Hughes, Paul Morrissey, Bob Colacello – who tried to impose a more businesslike atmosphere. The Mole People were discouraged from hanging about, and poured out their bile on Andy's intermediaries, unable to accept that they had been banished on the passive dictate of Warhol himself. Valerie turned up while Andy was in a meeting with art critic Mario Amaya and on the phone with yet another supervamp Viva, and put two bullets into him, and one incidentally in Amaya. Fred Hughes, born negotiator, apparently talked her out of killing him and she left by the freight elevator.

It was a big story for fifteen minutes, but just as Andy was declared clinically dead at Columbus Hospital news came in from Chicago that Robert Kennedy had been assassinated. Every newspaper in America remade their front pages, bumping the artist to 'and in other news…'

Kennedy stayed dead. Andy didn't.

Now Andy was really a vampire, we would all see finally, doubters and admirers, what he had meant all along.

It has been a tenet of Western culture that a vampire cannot be an artist. For a hundred years, there has been fierce debate on the question. The general consensus is that many a poet or a painter was never the same man after death, that posthumous work was always derivative self-parody, never a true reaction to the wondrous new nightlife opened up by the turning. It is even suggested that this symptom is not a drawback of vampirism but proof of its superiority over warm life: vampires are too busy *being* to pass comment, too concerned with their interior voyages to bother issuing travel reports for the rest of the world to pore over.

The tragedies are too well known to recap in detail. Poe reborn, struggling with verses that refuse to soar; Dalí, growing ever richer by forging his own work (or paying others to do so); Garbo, beautiful forever in the body but showing up on film as a rotting corpse; Dylan, born-again and boring as hell; the Short Lion, embarrassing all *nosferatu* with his MOR goth rocker act. But Andy was the Ultimate Vampire before turning. Surely, for him, things would be different.

Alas, no.

Between his deaths, Andy worked continuously. Portraits of Queens and inverted Tijuana crucifixes. Numberless commissioned silkscreens of anyone rich enough to hire him at $25,000 a throw. Portraits of world-famous boxers (Muhammad Ali, Apollo Creed) and football players (O.J. Simpson, Roy Race) he had never heard of. Those embarrassingly flattering likenesses, impossible to read as irony, of the Shah, Ferdinand and Imelda, Countess Elisabeth Bathory, Ronnie and Nancy. And he went to a *lot* of parties, at the White House or in the darkest dhampire clubs.

There's nothing there.

Believe me, I've looked. As an academic, I understand exactly Andy's dilemma. I too was considered a vampire long before I turned. My entire discipline is reputed to be nothing more than a canny way of feeding off the dead, prolonging a useless existence from one grant application to the next. And no one has ever criticised elder vampires for their lack of *learning*. To pass the centuries, one has to pick up dozens of languages and, in all probability, read every book in your national library. We may rarely have been artists, but we have always been patrons of the arts.

Among ourselves, the search has always been on for a real vampire artist, preferably a creature turned in infancy, before any warm sensibility could be formed. I was tempted in my reassessment of Andy's lifelong dance with Dracula to put forward a thesis that he was such a discovery, that he turned not in 1968 but, say, 1938, and exposed himself by degrees to sunlight, to let him age. That would explain the skin problems. And no one has ever stepped forth to say that they turned Andy. He went into hospital a living man and came out a vampire, having been declared dead. Most commentators have suggested he was transfused with vampire blood, deliberately or by accident, but the hospital authorities strenuously insist this is not so. Sadly, it won't wash. We have to admit it; Andy's best work was done when he was alive; the rest is just the black blood of the dead.

He had written his own epitaph, of course. 'In the future, everyone will live forever, for fifteen minutes.'

Goodbye, Drella. At the end, he gave up Dracula and was left with only Cinderella, the girl of ashes.

The rest, his legacy, is up to us.

APPENDIX TWO

———————◆———————

'WELLES'S LOST DRACULAS'
BY JONATHAN GATES

First published in Video Watchdog No 23, May–July 1994

Orson Welles arrived in Hollywood in 1939 having negotiated a two-picture deal as producer-director-writer-actor with George Schaefer of RKO Pictures. Drawing on an entourage of colleagues from New York theatre and radio, he established Mercury Productions as a filmmaking entity. Before embarking on *Citizen Kane* (1941) and *The Magnificent Ambersons* (1942), Welles developed other properties: Nicholas Blake's just-published anti-fascist thriller *The Smiler With a Knife* (1939), Conrad's *Heart of Darkness* (1902) and Stoker's *Dracula* (1897). Like the Conrad, *Dracula* was a novel Welles had already done for the *Mercury Theatre on the Air* radio series (July 11, 1938). A script was prepared (by Welles, Herman Mankiewicz and, uncredited, John Houseman), sets were designed, the film cast, and 'tests' – the extent of which have never been revealed – shot, but the project was dropped.

The reasons for the abandonment of *Count Dracula* remain obscure. It has been speculated that RKO were nervous about Welles's stated intention to film most of the story with a first-person camera, adopting the viewpoints of the various characters as Stoker does in his might-have-been fictional history. Houseman, in his memoir *Run-Through* (1972), alleges that Welles's enthusiasm for this device was at least partly due to the fact that it would keep the fearless vampire slayers – Harker, Van Helsing, Quincey, Holmwood – mostly off screen, while Dracula, the object of their attention, would always be in view. Houseman, long estranged from Welles at the time of writing, needlessly adds that Welles would have played Dracula. He toyed with the idea of playing Harker as well, before deciding William Alland could do it if kept to the shadows and occasionally dubbed by Welles. The rapidly changing political situation in Europe, already forcing the Roosevelt administration to reassess its policies about vampirism and the very real Count Dracula, may have prompted certain factions to bring pressure to bear on RKO that such a film was 'inadvisable' for 1940.

In an interview with Peter Bogdanovich, published in *This is Orson Welles* (1992) but held well before Francis Ford Coppola's controversial *Dracula* (1979), Welles said: '*Dracula* would make a marvellous movie. In fact, nobody has ever made it; they've never paid any attention to the book, which is the most hair-raising, marvellous book in the world. It's told by four people, and must be done with four narrations, as we did on the radio. There's one scene in London where he throws a heavy bag into the corner of a cellar and it's full of screaming babies! They can go that far out now.'

Throughout Welles's career, *Dracula* remained an *idée fixe*. The Welles-Mankiewicz script was RKO property and the studio resisted Welles's offer to buy it back. They set their asking price at the notional but substantial sum accountants reckoned had been lost on the double debacle of *Ambersons* and the unfinished South American project, *It's All True*.

When Schaefer, Welles's patron, was removed from his position as Vice-President in Charge of Production and replaced by Charles Koerner, there was serious talk of putting the script into production through producer Val Lewton's unit, which had established a reputation for low-budget supernatural dramas with *Cat People* (1942). Lewton got as far as having DeWitt Bodeen and then Curt Siodmak take runs at further drafts, scaling the script down to fit a strait-jacket budget. Jacques Tourneur was attached to direct, though editor Mark Robson was considered when Tourneur was promoted to A Pictures. Stock players were assigned supporting roles: Tom Conway (Dr Seward), Kent Smith (Jonathan Harker), Henry Daniell (Van Helsing), Jean Brooks (Lucy), Alan Napier (Arthur Holmwood), Skelton Knaggs (Renfield), Elizabeth Russell (Countess Marya Dolingen), Sir Lancelot (a calypso-singing coachman). Simone Simon, star of *Cat People*, was set for Mina, very much the focus of Lewton's take on the story, but the project fell through because RKO were unable to secure their first and only choice of star, Boris Karloff, who was committed to *Arsenic and Old Lace* on Broadway.

In 1944, RKO sold the Welles-Mankiewicz script, along with a parcel of set designs, to 20th Century Fox. Studio head Darryl F. Zanuck offered Welles the *role* of Dracula, promising Joan Fontaine and Olivia de Havilland for Mina and Lucy, suggesting Tyrone Power (Jonathan), George Sanders (Arthur), John Carradine (Quincey) and Laird Cregar (Van Helsing). This *Dracula* would have been a follow-up to Fox's successful Welles-Fontaine *Jane Eyre* (1943) and Welles might have committed if Zanuck had again assigned weak-willed Robert Stevenson, allowing Welles to direct in everything but credit. However, on a project this 'important', Zanuck would consider only two directors; John Ford had no interest – sparing us John Wayne, Victor McLaglen, Ward Bond and John Agar as brawling, boozing fearless vampire slayers – so it inevitably fell to Henry King, a specialist in molasses-slow historical subjects like *Lloyd's of London* (1936) and *Brigham Young* (1940). King, a plodder who had a brief flash of genius in a few later films with Gregory Peck, had his own, highly developed, chocolate-box style and gravitas, and was not a congenial director for Welles, whose mercurial temperament was unsuited to methods he considered conservative and dreary. The film still might have been made, since Welles was as ever in need of money, but Zanuck went cold on Dracula at the end of the War when the Count was moving into his Italian exile.

Fox wound up backing *Prince of Foxes* (1949), directed by King, with Power and Welles topping the cast, shot on location in Europe. A lavish bore, enlivened briefly by Welles's committed Cesare Borgia, this suggests what the Zanuck *Dracula* might have been like. Welles used much of his earnings from the long shoot to pour into film projects made in bits and pieces over several years: the completed *Othello* (1952), the unfinished *Don Quixote* (begun 1955) and, rarely mentioned until now, yet another *Dracula*. *El conde Dràcula*, a French-Italian-Mexican-American-Irish-Liechtensteinian-British-Yugoslav-Moroccan-Iranian co-production, was shot in snippets, the earliest dating from 1949, the latest from 1972.

Each major part was taken by several actors, or single actors over a span of years. In the controversial edit supervised by the Spaniard Jesús Franco – a second-unit director on Welles's *Chimes at Midnight* (1966) – and premiered at Cannes in 1997, the cast is as follows: Akim Tamiroff (Van Helsing), Micheál MacLiammóir (Jonathan), Paola Mori (Mina), Michael Redgrave (Arthur), Patty McCormick (Lucy), Hilton Edwards (Dr Seward), Mischa Auer (Renfield). The vampire brides are played by Jeanne Moreau, Suzanne Cloutier and Katina Paxinou, shot in different years on different continents. There is no sight of Francisco Reiguera, Welles's Quixote, cast as a skeletal Dracula, and the Count is present only as a substantial shadow voiced (as are several other characters) by Welles himself. Much of the film runs silent, and a crucial framing story, explaining the multi-narrator device, was either never filmed or shot and lost. Jonathan's panicky exploration of his castle prison, filled with steam like the Turkish bath in *Othello*, is the most remarkable, purely Expressionist scene Welles ever shot. But the final ascent to Castle Dracula, with Tamiroff dodging patently *papier-mâché* falling boulders and wobbly zooms into and out of stray details hardly seems the work of anyone other than a fumbling amateur.

In no sense 'a real film', *El conde Dràcula* is a scrapbook of images from the novel and Welles's imagination. He told Henry Jaglom that he considered the project a private exercise, to keep the subject in his mind, a series of sketches for a painting he would execute later. As Francis Coppola would in 1977, while his multi-million-dollar *Dracula* was bogged down in production problems in Romania, Welles often made comparisons with the Sistine Chapel.

In 1973, Welles assembled some *El conde Dràcula* footage, along with documentary material about the real Count Dracula and the scandals that followed his true death in 1959: the alleged, much-disputed will that deeded much of his vast fortune to English housewife Vivian Nicholson, who claimed she had encountered Dracula while on a school holiday in the early '50s; the autobiography Clifford Irving sold for a record-breaking advance in 1971, only to have the book exposed as an arrant fake written by Irving in collaboration with Fred Saberhagen; the squabbles among sundry vampire elders, notably Baron Meinster and Princess Asa Vajda, as to who should claim the Count's unofficial title as ruler of their kind, King of the Cats. Welles called this playful, essay-like film – constructed around the skeleton of footage shot by Calvin Floyd for his own documentary, *In Search of Dracula* (1971) – *When Are You Going to Finish el conde Dràcula?*, though it was exhibited in most territories as *D is for Dracula*. On the evening Premier Ceauşescu withdrew the Romanian Cavalry needed for Coppola's assault on Castle Dracula in order to pursue the vampire banditti of the Transylvania Movement in the next valley, Francis Ford Coppola held a private screening of *D is for Dracula* and cabled Welles that there was a curse on anyone who dared invoke the dread name.

Welles's final Dracula project came together in 1981, just as the movies were gripped by a big vampire craze. Controversial and slow-building, and shut out of all but technical Oscars, Coppola's *Dracula* proved there was a substantial audience for vampire subjects. The next half-decade would see Werner Herzog's *Renfield, Jeder fur Sich und die Vampir Gegen Alle*, a retelling of the story from the point of the fly-eating lunatic (Klaus Kinski); of Tony Scott's *The Hunger*, with Catherine Deneuve and David Bowie as New York art patrons Miriam and John Blaylock at the centre of a famous murder case defended by Alan Dershowitz (Ron Silver); of John Landis's *Scream, Blacula, Scream*, with Eddie Murphy as Dracula's African get Prince Mamuwalde, searching for his lost bride (Vanity) in New York – best remembered for a plagiarism lawsuit by screenwriter Pat Hobby that forced Paramount to open its books to the auditors; of Richard Attenborough's bloated, mammoth, Oscar-scooping *Varney*, with Anthony Hopkins as Sir Francis Varney, the vampire Viceroy overthrown by the Second Indian Mutiny; of Brian DePalma's remake of *Scarface*, an explicit attack on the Transylvania Movement, with Al Pacino as Tony Sylvana, a Ceausescu cast-out rising in the booming drac trade and finally taken down by a Vatican army led by James Woods.

Slightly ahead of all this activity, Welles began shooting quietly, without publicity, working at his own pace, underwritten by the last of his many mysterious benefactors. His final script combined elements from Stoker's fiction with historical fact made public by the researches of Raymond McNally and Radu Florescu – associates as far back as *D is for Dracula* – and concentrated on the last days of the Count, abandoned in his castle, awaiting his executioners, remembering the betrayals and crimes of his lengthy, weighty life. This was the project Welles called *The Other Side of Midnight*. From sequences filmed as early as 1972, the director culled footage of Peter Bogdanovich as Renfield, while he opted to play not the stick insect vampire but the corpulent slayer, finally gifting the world with his definitive Professor Van Helsing. If asked by the trade press, he made great play of having offered the role of Dracula to Warren Beatty,

Steve McQueen or Robert De Niro, but this was a conjurer's distraction, for he had been fixed on his Count for some years and was now finally able to fit him for his cape and fangs. Welles's final Dracula was to be John Huston.

Welles began filming *The Other Side of Midnight* on the old Miracle Pictures lot, his first studio-shot – though independently-financed – picture since *Touch of Evil* in 1958, and his first 'right of final cut' contract since *Citizen Kane*. The ins and outs of the deal have been assessed in entire books by Peter Bart and David J. Skal, but it seems that Welles, after a career of searching, had found a genuine 'angel', a backer with not only the financial muscle to give him the budget and crew he needed to make a film that was truly his vision, but also the self-effacing trust to let him have total artistic control of the result.

There were nay-saying voices and the industry was already beginning to wonder whether still in-progress runaway budget auteur movies like Michael Cimino's *The Lincoln County Wars* or Coppola's *Dracula*

follow-up *One From the Heart* were such a great idea, but Welles himself denounced those runaways as examples of fuzzy thinking. As with his very first *Dracula* movie script and *Kane*, *The Other Side of Midnight* was meticulously pre-planned and pre-costed. Forty years on from *Kane*, Welles must have known this would be his last serious chance. A Boy Wonder no longer, the pressure was on him to produce a 'mature masterpiece', a career book-end to the work that had topped so many Best of All Time lists and eclipsed all his other achievements. He must certainly have been aware of the legion of cineastes whose expectations of a film that would eclipse the flashy brilliance of the Coppola version were sky-rocketing. It may be that so many of Welles's other projects were left unfinished deliberately, because their creator knew they could never compete with the imagined masterpieces that were expected of him. With *Midnight*, he had to show all his cards and take the consequences.

The Other Side of Midnight

occupied an unprecedented three adjacent sound-stages where Ken Adam's sets for Bistritz and Borgo Pass and the exteriors and interiors of Castle Dracula were constructed. John Huston shaved his beard and let his moustache sprout, preparing for the acting role of his career, cast apparently because Welles admired him as the Los Angeles predator-patriarch Noah Cross (*Chinatown*, 1974). It has been rumoured that the seventy-four-year-old Huston went so far as to have transfusions of vampire blood and took to hunting the Hollywood night with packs of new-born vampire brats, piqued because he couldn't display trophies of his 'kills'. Other casting was announced, a canny mix of A-list stars who would have worked for scale just to be in a Welles film, long-time associates who couldn't bear to be left out of the adventure and fresh talent.

There were other vampire movies in pre-production, other *Dracula* movies, but Hollywood was really only interested in the Welles version.

Finally, it would happen.

After a single day's shooting, Orson Welles abandoned *The Other Side of Midnight*. Between 1981 and his death in 1985, he made no further films and did no more work on such protracted projects as *Don Quixote*. He made no public statement about the reasons for his walking away from the film, which was abandoned after John Huston, Steven Spielberg and Brian DePalma in succession refused to take over the direction.

Most biographers have interpreted this wilful scuppering of what seemed to be an ideal, indeed impossibly perfect, set-up as a final symptom of the insecure, self-destructive streak that had always co-existed with genius in the heart of Orson Welles. Those closest to him, notably Oja Kodar, have argued vehemently against this interpretation and maintained that there were pressing reasons for Welles's actions, albeit reasons which have yet to come to light or even be tentatively suggested.

As for the exposed film, two full reels of one extended shot, it has never been developed and, due to a financing quirk, remains sealed up, inaccessible, in the vaults of a bank in Timişoara, Romania. More than one cineaste has expressed a willingness to part happily with his immortal soul for a single screening of those reels. Like Rosebud itself, until those reels can be discovered and understood, the mystery of Orson Welles's last, lost *Dracula* will remain.

AUTHOR'S NOTE AND ACKNOWLEDGEMENTS

Sections of this novel have appeared, in slightly different form, disguised as novellas. Thanks are due to editors Stephen Jones ('Coppola's Dracula'), Pete Crowther ('Andy Warhol's Dracula'), Marvin Kaye ('The Other Side of Midnight'), Ellen Datlow ('Castle in the Desert') and Paula Guran ('You Are the Wind Beneath My Wings'). Others who rate a credit include Pete and Dana Atkins, Nicolas Barbano, Anne Billson, Sebastian Born, Randy and Sara Broecker, Kat Brown, Eugene Byrne, Susan Byrne, Pat Cadigan, Sophie Calder, Loretta Culbert, Les Daniels, Fay Davies, Alex Dunn, all at *Empire*, Dennis (aka Jack Martin) and Kris Etchison, Martin Feeney, Leslie Felperin, Larry Fessenden, Jo Fletcher, Martin Fletcher, Barry Forshaw, Neil Gaiman, Lisa Gaye, the late Charlie Grant, Jon Courtenay Grimwood, Antony Harwood, Jennifer Handorf, Georgina Hawtrey-Woore, Sean Hogan, Alan Jones, Yung Kha, Jonathan Kinnersley, Nick and Vivian Landau, James Macdonald Lockhart, Donna and Tim Lucas, Paul McAuley, Maitland McDonagh, Maura McHugh, Glenn McQuaid, Helen Mullane, the NECON 99 crew, Julia and Bryan Newman, Sasha and Jerome Newman, Marcelle Perks, Sarah Pinborough, David Pirie, David Pringle, Robert Rimmer, Silja Semple, Adam Simon (the real one, not the character in *The Player*), Helen Simpson, Russell Schechter, David Schow (who took us to Bronson Canyon), all at *Sight & Sound*, David J. Skal, Brian Smedley, Mike and Paula Smith,

Somtow Sucharitkul (as S.P. Somtow, author of *Vampire Junction*), Cath Trechman, Doug Winter and Jack Womack.

The library of books consulted includes, but is not limited to: Anna Abrahams, *Warhol Films*; Patricia Altner, *Vampire Readings: An Annotated Bibliography*; Rafael Alvarez, *The Wire: Truth Be Told*; William Amos, *The Originals: Who's Really Who in Fiction*; Nina Auerbach, *Our Vampires, Ourselves*; Steven Bach, *Final Cut: Dreams and Disaster in the Making of Heaven's Gate*; Nicolas Barbano, *Verdens 25 hotteste pronostjerner*; Barbara Belford, *Bram Stoker: A Biography of the Author of Dracula*; Peter Biskind, *Easy Riders, Raging Bulls*; Victor Bockris, *The Life & Death of Andy Warhol, NYC Babylon: From Beat to Punk*; Marlon Brando, with Robert Lindsey, *Brando: Songs My Mother Taught Me*; Matthew Bunson, *Vampire: The Encyclopedia*; Glennis Byron (ed), *Dracula: Contemporary Critical Essays*; Simon Callow, *Orson Welles: The Road to Xanadu*; Robert L. Carringer, *The Making of Citizen Kane*; Raymond Chandler, *The Long Good-Bye*; Wensley Clarkson, *Quentin Tarantino: Shooting From the Hip*; Steven Cohan, Ina Rae Hark (ed), *The Road Movie Book*; Terry Comito (ed), *Orson Welles, Touch of Evil*; Eleanor Coppola, *Notes on the Making of Apocalypse Now*; Francis Ford Coppola, James V. Hart, *Bram Stoker's Dracula: The Film and the Legend*; Peter Cowie, *Coppola, The Godfather Book*; Mike Davis, *City of Quartz: Excavating the Future in Los Angeles*; Mark Dawidziak, *The Columbo Phile: A Casebook*; John Gregory Dunne, *Monster: Living Off the Big Screen*; James Ellroy, *My Dark Places*; Dennis Etchison, *The Dark Country*; Robert Evans, *The Kid Stays in the Picture: A Hollywood Life*; Charles Fleming, *High Concept: Don Simpson and the Hollywood Culture of Excess*; David Flint, *Babylon Blue: An Illustrated History of Adult Cinema*; Karl French, *Bloomsbury Film Guide: Apocalypse Now*; Otto Friedrich, *City of Nets: A Portrait of Hollywood in the 1940s*; George Galloway, Bob Wylie, *Downfall: The Ceausescus and the Romanian Revolution*; Joan Gordon, Veronica Hollinger (ed), *Blood Read: The Vampire as Metaphor in Contemporary Culture*; Christopher Golden, Nancy Holder, *Buffy the Vampire Slayer: The Watcher's Guide*; Ronald Gottesman, *Focus on Citizen Kane*; Phil Hardy, Dave Laing, *The Faber Companion to 20th-Century Popular Music*; Leonard G. Heldred, Mary Pharr (ed), *The Blood* is the Life: Vampires in Literature; Tod Hoffman, *Homicide: Life on the Screen*; James Craig Holte, *Dracula in the Dark: The Dracula Film Adaptations*; Stephen Jones, *The Essential Monster Movie Guide*; Lyndon W. Joslin, *Count Dracula Goes to the Movies: Stoker's Novel Adapted, 1922-1995*; Pauline Kael, Herman J. Mankiewicz, Orson Welles, *The Citizen Kane Book*; David P. Kalat, *Homicide Life on the Street: The Unofficial Companion*; Stephen Koch, *Stargazer: Andy Warhol's World and His Films*; Robert Phillip Kolker, *A Cinema of Loneliness*; Andy Lane & Paul Simpson, *The Bond Files*; Barbara Leaming, *Orson Welles: A Biography*; Clive Leatherdale, *Bram Stoker's Dracula Unearthed*; Jon Lewis, *Whom the Gods Wish to Destroy... Francis Coppola and the New Hollywood*; Colin MacCabe, with Mark Francis, Peter Wollen (ed), *Who Is Andy Warhol?*; Joseph McBride, *Orson Welles*; David McClintick, *Indecent Exposure: A True Story of Hollywood and Wall Street*; Frank McShane, *The Life of Raymond Chandler*; Paula Mitchell James, *And Die in the West*; Greil Marcus, *Lipstick Traces: A Secret History of the Twentieth Century*; J. Gordon Melton, *The Vampire Book: The Encyclopedia of the Undead, The Vampire Gallery: A Who's Who of the Undead, VideoHound's Vampires on Video*; Russell Miller, *Bare-Faced Messiah: The Story of L. Ron Hubbard*; Peter Occhiogrosso, *Inside Spinal Tap*; Laurence O'Toole, *Pornocopia: Porn, Sex, Technology and Desire*; Anthony Petkovich, *The X Factory: Inside the American Hardcore Film Industry*; Julia Phillips, *You'll Never Eat Lunch in This Town Again*; Michael Pye, Lynda Miles, *The Movie Brats*; James Riordan, *Stone: The Controversies, Excesses, and Exploits of a Radical Filmmaker*; Ed Robertson, *"This is Jim Rockford...": The Rockford Files*; Robin, Liza, Linda and Tiffany, *You'll Never Make Love in This Town Again*; Julie Salamon, *The Devil's Candy: The Bonfire of the Vanities Goes to Hollywood*; Jon Savage, *England's Dreaming: Sex Pistols and Punk Rock*; Jack Sergeant, *Born Bad*; David Simon, *Homicide: A Year on the Killing Streets, The Corner*; David J. Skal, *V is for Vampire: The A-Z Guide to Everything Undead*; Robert Sklar, *Movie-Made America: A Cultural History of American Movies*; Kent Smith, Darrell W. Moore, Merl Reagle, *Adult Movies*; Amy Taubin, *BFI Classic: Taxi Driver*; David Thomson, *A Biographical Dictionary of the Cinema, Overexposures: The Crisis in American Filmmaking, Suspects, Rosebud: The Story of Orson Welles*; Keith

KIM NEWMAN

Topping, *Slayer: The Totally Cool Unofficial Guide to Buffy*; Parker Tyler, *Magic and Myth of the Movies*; Ultra Violet, *Famous for 15 Minutes: My Years With Andy Warhol*; Andy Warhol, *Warhol's America* (esp p. 25); Orson Welles, Peter Bogdanovich, *This Is Orson Welles*; Linda Williams, *Hard Core*; Mary Woronov, *Swimming Underground: My Years in the Warhol Factory*; Maurice Yacowar, *The Films of Paul Morrissey*. The bulk of the work on this novel was done before I came – along with the rest of the world – to rely on the internet as a research tool, but subsequent drafts have been shored up by resorting to the IMDb and Wikipedia; at one point, I had to look up one of my fictional characters online to check something I'd forgotten.

A note which can stand for the whole *Anno Dracula* series is that though many of the characters bear the names of real people or made-up people from other works of fiction, they exist only within this alternate time-line, at least two removes away from actual history or their primary fictional stamping grounds. I should like sincerely to thank all the hard-working authors, actors, directors, screenwriters, artists and even musicians – sadly, a legion too vast to be name-checked here – who have established the many people who populate the *Anno Dracula* universe, and hope that they will recognise that any co-opting has been done in the spirit of homage rather than assault. The same goes for any real people, public figures and private, represented here in a fictional context. My apologies to people whose work in the real world has had to be wiped out to make room for the alternate history of *Johnny Alucard*, especially the directors F.W. Murnau, Tod Browning, Terence Fisher, Paul Morrissey and John Badham and the actors Max Schreck, Bela Lugosi, Christopher Lee, Frank Langella, Gary Oldman and Udo Kier.

ABOUT THE AUTHOR

Kim Newman is a novelist, critic and broadcaster. His fiction includes *The Night Mayor*, *Bad Dreams*, *Jago*, the *Anno Dracula* novels and stories, *The Quorum* and *Life's Lottery*, all currently being reissued by Titan Books, *Professor Moriarty: The Hound of the D'Urbervilles*, *An English Ghost Story* and *The Secrets of Drearcliffe Grange School* published by Titan Books and *The Vampire Genevieve* and *Orgy of the Blood Parasites* as Jack Yeovil. His non-fiction books include the seminal *Nightmare Movies* (recently reissued by Bloomsbury in an updated edition), *Ghastly Beyond Belief* (with Neil Gaiman), *Horror: 100 Best Books* (with Stephen Jones), *Wild West Movies*, *The BFI Companion to Horror*, *Millennium Movies* and BFI Classics studies of *Cat People* and *Doctor Who*.

He is a contributing editor to *Sight & Sound* and *Empire* magazines (writing *Empire*'s popular Video Dungeon column), has written and broadcast widely on a range of topics, and scripted radio and television documentaries. His stories 'Week Woman' and 'Ubermensch' have been adapted into an episode of the TV series *The Hunger* and an Australian short film; he has directed and written a tiny film, *Missing Girl*. Following his Radio 4 play 'Cry Babies', he wrote an episode ('Phish Phood') for Radio 7's series *The Man in Black*.

His official website can be found at

www.johnnyalucard.com

An English Ghost Story

KIM NEWMAN

A dysfunctional British nuclear family seeks to solve their problems and start a new life away from the city in the sleepy Somerset countryside. At first their perfect new home creates a rare peace and harmony, and the four grow steadily closer. But when the house begins to turn on them, it seems to know just how to hurt them the most – threatening to destroy the family from the inside out.

A standalone novel from the acclaimed author of *Anno Dracula*.

"That oh-so-unassuming title does not equip you for the journey you're about to undertake. Immersive, claustrophobic and utterly wonderful." M.R. Carey, bestselling author of *The Girl With All the Gifts*

For more fantastic fiction, author events, exclusive
excerpts, competitions, limited editions and more

VISIT OUR WEBSITE
titanbooks.com

LIKE US ON FACEBOOK
facebook.com/titanbooks

FOLLOW US ON TWITTER
@TitanBooks

EMAIL US
readerfeedback@titanemail.com